The Poacher's Daughter

Margaret Dickinson, a *Sunday Times* top ten best-seller, was born and brought up in Lincolnshire and, until recently, lived in Skegness where she raised her family. Her ambition to be a writer began early and *The Poacher's Daughter* is Margaret's thirtieth novel – most of which have been set in her home county but also in Nottinghamshire, Derbyshire and South Yorkshire.

Margaret Dickinson

The Poacher's Daughter

PAN BOOKS

First published 2023 by Macmillan

This paperback edition first published 2023 by Pan Books
an imprint of Pan Macmillan
The Smithson, 6 Briset Street, London EC1M 5NR
EU representative: Macmillan Publishers Ireland Ltd, 1st Floor,
The Liffey Trust Centre, 117–126 Sheriff Street Upper,
Dublin 1, D01 YC43
Associated companies throughout the world
www.panmacmillan.com

ISBN 978-1-5290-7796-4

Copyright © Margaret Dickinson 2023

1 3 5 7 9 8 6 4 2

A CIP catalogue record for this book is available from the British Library.

Typeset in Sabon by Palimpsest Book Production Ltd, Falkirk, Stirlingshire
Printed and bound by CPI Group (UK) Ltd, Croydon, CR0 4YY

Visit www.panmacmillan.com to read more about all our books
and to buy them. You will also find features, author interviews and
news of any author events, and you can sign up for e-newsletters
so that you're always first to hear about our new releases.

For all my family and friends for their love, encouragement and help throughout the years

ACKNOWLEDGEMENTS

My love and grateful thanks to Helen Lawton and Pauline Griggs for reading and advising on the first draft. Your comments are always spot on and so very helpful.

My special thanks to my fantastic agent, Darley Anderson, who is always at the end of the phone for advice and encouragement. I wouldn't be where I am today (thirty books and counting) without the wonderful support and help of you and your team.

And then, of course, there is the marvellous team at Pan Macmillan, headed by my lovely editor, Trisha Jackson. You all know who you are and I thank each and every one of you for the work you do to help bring my books to my readers.

And last, but never least, are my loyal readers. I hope you will all enjoy *The Poacher's Daughter* as much as I have loved writing it.

One

'Hello. I hope you're not poaching my father's fish.'

Rosie looked up from her crouched position on the bank of the stream near the stepping stones. Standing above her was a handsome young man with black hair and the bluest eyes she could ever remember seeing. He was tall and athletic, with a strong, square chin that might have been cut from granite. She hadn't heard him ride up on his black stallion, whose sleek coat matched its rider's hair. She rose slowly to her feet and stood facing the young man squarely. She knew exactly who he was; Byron, the only son of William Ramsey, who owned the Thornsby estate and most of the dwellings in the village. She had often seen Byron riding around the estate although she had never been this close to him before. But she was not afraid of him; Rosie Waterhouse was not afraid of anyone. With her wild red curls and her quick wit, she was a match for most folk. And now, as she smiled up at him, her green eyes sparkled with mischief. 'I didn't know your dad owned the stream, an' all.'

Byron threw back his head and laughed, the sound carrying on the breeze. 'Just the bit that runs through

1

his lands. If you want to fish here, you need to get a licence.'

Rosie cocked her head on one side and regarded him saucily. 'I don't reckon they'd let me have one, d'you?'

'Probably not. How old are you?'

'Fourteen. How old are you?'

Byron blinked at her boldness, but answered her anyway. 'Twenty.'

He dropped the horse's reins, allowing it to graze contentedly. He moved towards her. 'But I, of course, am allowed to fish here whenever I want to. So, let's see if we can catch a trout for your tea, shall we? I see you've got some string and a hook, but what we really need is something to use as a rod.'

He glanced around and saw a fallen branch, from which he broke off a length of about four feet.

'This should do it,' he said, coming back to stand beside her.

For the next hour they sat side by side on the bank, hardly speaking but concentrating hard on the end of the gnarled branch for any sign of movement. At last, the end of the makeshift rod twitched and Byron hauled it out of the water.

Rosie gasped to see a huge fish on the end of the string. Byron despatched it expertly as it lay twitching on the grass between them.

'There,' he said, smiling. 'That should feed you and your family for a couple of days.'

'There's only me an' my dad. Mam died when I was two, having another baby. A little boy. He died an' all.'

'I'm sorry to hear that. It must be hard for you, not having a mother.'

Rosie shrugged. 'I don't know owt different. I can't really remember her.'

'Where do you live?'

Now Rosie knew to be careful exactly what she said. 'On the edge of the village. Me dad works for you sometimes. Your farm bailiff sets him on at busy times like harvest and 'tatie picking.' She grinned. 'I come and help then.'

'Oh yes. Jack Pickering. He's a good man. He sees to the day-to-day running of the estate and keeps an eye on our two tenant farmers. And our own farm too, of course, though nothing much escapes my father's eagle eye.' He paused and regarded her. 'You'll have been busy recently, then, with the harvest. It's mostly gathered now though. So, what does your father do in the winter?'

'Hedgin' an ditchin' mostly,' she answered promptly. 'Your tenant farmers use him too if they're too busy to do it themselves.'

Byron laughed. 'Or too idle. It's quite a hard job.'

'And he's the local rat and mole catcher, too. Everyone fetches him in to do that.'

Byron paused. He was beginning to realize who she was. Softly, he asked, 'So, what's your name? I can't go on calling you "little girl", can I?'

She ran her tongue around her lips. 'Rosie.'

'Rosie – what?'

She hesitated a second, but there was no way she could not answer his question. 'Waterhouse.'

Byron stared at her. 'You must be Sam Waterhouse's daughter.'

Rosie nodded.

'Ah, that explains it then,' he said softly, almost more to himself than to her. She was the daughter of the local poacher. For a few moments he seemed lost in thought. Then he cleared his throat. 'I'll meet you here again this time next week and I'll bring you a pole with a hook on the end and teach you how to fish with that.'

Rosie said nothing. Her father already had such an implement – a gaff, he called it – but it wouldn't do to tell Byron Ramsey that. She merely nodded, shocked by what he had just said. She could hardly believe it. The son of the estate owner, who virtually ruled the lives of almost everyone in the village, was offering to teach her how to poach fish from the stream that ran into the huge lake in front of the manor house, then out again, twisting and turning on its way towards the coast.

'My father keeps the lake well stocked with fish – trout mostly – but some escape down the stream.' Byron gathered up the reins and mounted his horse. 'I'll see you next week. Same time, same place.' With a salute and a grin, he turned and spurred the animal into a gallop.

Rosie's gaze followed him until he was out of sight and her young heart felt as if it was doing somersaults in her chest.

It was a strange coincidence that on the same evening when Byron had caught Rosie trying to poach fish, her father should decide that it was time she learned the tricks of his trade.

'I'm not a church-going man, Rosie, as you well know,' Sam began. 'In Mr Ramsey's eyes, I'm a rogue he'd love to slam in gaol before throwing away the key, but I do have my own principles. I never kill for sport, only to feed oursens and others in need. And I kill as humanely as possible. I try never to let an animal suffer if I can help it.'

Rosie regarded him with her piercing green eyes. 'But the master kills for sport, doesn't he? He allows the local hunt to come across his land chasing a poor, defenceless fox until their hounds catch it and tear it to pieces. And he holds shooting parties every autumn that kill hundreds of birds they've raised 'specially just to be shot at. And at those times,' she added, with a tinge of accusation in her tone, 'you go as a beater to frighten the birds into flight for him and his gentry cronies to shoot down.'

Sam sighed. 'Yes, I do, and I can't pretend I like doing it, but needs must. I need to earn a bit of money for things we can't provide for oursens. We live well off the land, Rosie . . .' Like everyone in the village, Sam had a patch of ground behind his cottage where he grew vegetables and rhubarb. He also kept hens, ducks and a few geese. 'We're even lucky enough to have our own apple and plum trees. Not everyone has. And then there's fruit from the hedgerows and mushrooms in the woods and – I go poaching.'

'On the master's land,' Rosie said softly, her gaze never leaving his face.

'Aye, I do, and it's illegal – you've got to understand that – but, to my mind, wild animals don't belong to Mr Ramsey.'

5

'But they're on his land and you're trespassing.'

To this Sam had no answer, except to say, a little sadly, 'So, do I understand that you'd rather not learn my ways?'

Rosie smiled now and her whole face lit up. 'Oh no, Dad, I want you to teach me everything you know.'

Sam and his daughter lived in the tiny cottage where he had been born, half a mile to the south of the village of Thornsby, set on the edge of the Lincolnshire Wolds and close to woodland; all of it belonging to the Ramseys' estate. Houses and cottages clustered around a small village green with the road in and out of the village running from north to south. The church with its small cemetery stood on a hill top at the northern end. The only time Sam ever went near the church was to visit his wife's grave three times a year, to lay flowers on her birthday, their wedding anniversary and Christmas Day. The village had one shop, run by Ben Plant and his wife, which sold everything one could think of – and more besides – from milk and meat to candles and soap. The carrier called twice a week to replenish the stock of items that Ben couldn't source from the local farms. The village had one pub, the Thornsby Arms, and a wheelwright-cum-carpenter, who was also the local undertaker. The only 'upholder of the law' in the village, other than William Ramsey's gamekeeper and the estate bailiff, Jack Pickering, was PC Douglas Foster, who lived in a police house near the village green where he had a small office. He patrolled the village and the surrounding land, most of it belonging to William Ramsey's large estate, on his bicycle, reporting to a larger police station in the nearby market town of Alford. He was a benevolent man and tried to be a friend to those under his watchful eye rather than an enemy.

William's Ramsey's estate covered just over two thousand acres of farmland, woodland, parkland, streams and lakes. The farmland was divided into three small farms. One, Home Farm, was managed by William with the help of his estate bailiff. The other two, Bluebell Farm and Blackberry Farm, were run by tenant farmers. During his lifetime as a poacher, Sam had visited all corners of the land belonging to William Ramsey and would do so again, but tonight he would stay close to home. He and Rosie would venture into the wooded slope just above and to the east of the village. Beyond that, the land sloped down again through cornfields to a huge lake, overlooked by Thornsby Manor, a grand mansion in the vale where the Ramsey family lived.

Sam had learned his dubious profession as a boy from the local poacher at the time, nicknamed Little Titch, and now he planned to pass on the tricks of his trade to his daughter, Rosie. Sam's wife, Agnes, had died giving birth to a stillborn son when Rosie was two. Sam had never remarried after his wife's death, preferring to concentrate on bringing up his daughter, but he had received a lot of help from the villagers, many of whom were grateful to the poacher. Without him, they might well have gone hungry during hard times. Sam, still a comparatively young

man at thirty-four, had one special friend; Nell
Tranter, a widow who lived about half a mile from
Sam's cottage on the outskirts of the village with her
son, Nathan. He was a year older than Rosie. Nell's
husband had been killed in an accident at threshing
time on the estate only a year after Sam's wife had
died. To avoid an inquiry and a scandal, William
Ramsey had made over the cottage to Nell and he
paid her a small pension. And if the whispered
rumours were to be believed, there had been bribery
in other quarters too.

'I know it's hush money, Sam,' Nell had said tear-
fully at the time. 'But what can I do? I've a son to
bring up.'

'Aye, I know, lass, an' it's not easy, I can tell you.
But if you need owt, you only have to say. Me and
Jim were good mates.' It had been Jim Tranter who
had often found casual labouring jobs on the estate
for Sam when work was plentiful.

Nell had smiled through her tears. 'And if I can
do anything to help you with Rosie, you must tell
me. There'll be times when she's growing up she'll
need a woman to talk to, just as I'm sure Nathan
will need a father-figure in his life.'

Sam had chuckled. 'I don't know that I'm a very
good role model for him, Nell, but I'll do me best.'

She had touched his arm. 'That'll do for me, Sam.'

And so, with the friendship between Sam and
Nell deepening, the two youngsters were thrown
together. Not that either of them minded. Nathan
grew tall and strong, with broad shoulders, brown
hair and warm brown eyes. Even from the time they

were in the school playground together, Nathan was Rosie's champion. Not that she needed him. With her fiery temper, she was a match for anyone and it was often she who gave someone a tongue lashing on Nathan's behalf, saving him the bother of using his fists.

As daylight began to fade, they got ready. Queenie, Sam's lurcher, wagged her tail furiously in anticipation.

'Now, just after harvest, is a good time for you to start,' Sam explained. 'Partridge are ground-roosting birds and can no longer hide in the corn. Even rabbits and hares are more visible.'

It was a mild night, a little windy, with the clouds scudding across a bright moon as they set out.

'It's not a perfect night,' Sam continued, beginning his first practical lesson. 'Bad weather's the poacher's friend, especially if you're using a gun, though a misty night's the best time for that. It muffles the sound.' Sam was thin and wiry but stronger than he looked. His face was tanned from being out in all weathers and his curly hair was still the same vibrant colour as his daughter's. Tonight, he was dressed in his poacher's garb: a dark shirt, black jacket and trousers, the latter secured around the waist with binder twine. On top, he wore a voluminous coat with several deep pockets for carrying the equipment he needed for setting snares and traps. Beside him, Queenie trotted obediently.

'You used to have two ferrets. I remember them. You used to carry them in the pockets of your coat.'

'Aye, and I did well with them, but they can be a lot of trouble. I'd rather it be just the two of us and Queenie now.' As they came to the edge of the woods, Sam whispered, 'No more talking now. Quiet as you can. Poachers need to move like ghosts.'

Rosie had fastened her long hair beneath a russet-coloured velvet hat to prevent it being caught by thorny brambles. Wearing a similar-coloured coat and carrying a leather bag over her shoulder, she trod carefully, trying not to make the undergrowth snap beneath her feet. The noise, in the black night, would sound like a gunshot. The trees rustled above her head, the moonlight, fitful between the branches, cast eerie shadows. Damp bracken brushed against her skirt. Scurrying animals and an owl's hoot were the only sounds to unsettle her. But she was undaunted; Rosie was used to the woodland at night. Maybe tonight was to be her first lesson in poaching, but it was by no means the first time she had ventured among the trees after dark.

They came out of the far side of the woods and stood looking down the gentle slope of the recently harvested fields, the stooks still standing awaiting collection.

Rosie gasped at the sight in the moonlit field. 'Just look at all the rabbits. There's dozens of them.'

Beside her, Sam chuckled. 'What did I tell you? Now, we've got to find a run. Let's start here and work our way round the edge of the field.'

'What am I looking for?'

'Rabbits are creatures of habit and always use the same route. They run at nightfall and daybreak.

10

You look on the ground for signs where they've hopped along.'

When the clouds uncovered the moon, he squatted down and pointed to the ground. 'See, here and here – the flattened grass.'

From his pocket he pulled two sticks joined together with a piece of string. To the end of one of the sticks was attached a loop of wire with a slip knot. He dug both sticks into the ground, carefully placing the loop of wire over the path the rabbit would take. 'Mind you get it at the right height. About six inches off the ground.'

They caught four rabbits, resetting the snare each time.

'That'll do for tonight. I don't need to start feeding half the village yet, not while there's still plenty of work to be done on the farms. But come winter . . .'

Her father didn't need to say any more. When harsh weather came, the need for farm workers on the estate lessened and many, who were only casual labourers, found themselves out of work with only parish relief or the workhouse to turn to. That was when they looked to Sam for help.

As they retraced their steps through the woods, Rosie heard voices. Beside her, Sam hissed, 'Down. Get down. Not a word.'

Queenie whined softly but Sam put his hand on the dog's collar to quieten her. Rosie crouched behind a bush, straining to hear the words. There were two of them; two men. She managed to stifle the exclamation that rose to her lips as one spoke, for now she recognized his voice. Byron Ramsey. Rosie held her breath but then, as the other man spoke, she let it out slowly in a sigh of relief. She recognized his voice too.

'There's nowt to see tonight, Mr Byron.' Amos Taylor's voice drifted through the trees. The estate's gamekeeper was getting on in years now and rumours were rife in the village that William was planning to retire him. Amos had served the Ramsey family all his life and was respected by everyone in the neighbourhood. The keeper wondered why Master Byron had suddenly shown an interest in coming out into the woods tonight. He'd never done so before. Amos hoped Sam was not about, as he remembered the whispered conversation he had had some years earlier with the poacher in a secluded corner of the village pub, the Thornsby Arms.

'As long as you only take rabbits and hares and birds like rooks and pigeons, we'll get along very nicely, Sam. And even a few fish from the stream, but mind you never touch his game birds and stay away from the lake itself. The old man' – he'd referred to William as old, even though his employer was actually a year younger than he was – 'has no idea of what goes on, but he trusts me. As a young man, I worked for his father, Edward Ramsey. He knew that the local poacher – which in them days was Little Titch – kept the poorer folk in the village fed when labourers' jobs were scarce in the winter. Mr Edward was a kinder soul than his son, I have to admit, but Byron's more like his grandfather.' Amos had wandered a little, reminiscing about what he remembered as the good old days. 'But I know you do the same for the villagers as Little Titch did, so, as long as you stick to the rules, I'm willing to turn a blind eye. Don't let me down, Sam, else it'll be my livelihood and your freedom gone.'

Sam had nodded as if giving his word, but he knew that when times got really hard, he would not stick to such a promise. He was not averse to shooting pheasant or partridge alongside rooks and pigeons if the opportunity came along. But shooting was a precarious way of poaching. The echo of a shotgun in the blackness of the night could bring the gamekeeper and his dogs running. And Amos would be honour bound to investigate the sound of a shotgun.

Now, crouching in the darkness of the woods, they heard the voices grow fainter until Sam said softly, 'Time we was going home, lass. The daylight's no friend to the poacher.' Luckily, they had already collected up their poaching equipment and were ready to leave.

They paused briefly at the edge of the woods furthest from their home to watch the two figures moving away from them towards the manor, the huge lake in front of the mansion glistening in the early morning light.

'I'm going to live in that house, Dad. One day I'll be mistress of Thornsby Manor.'

'Aye, an' pigs might fly. No one in yon house would ever look at the likes of us, so don't you go daydreaming, lass, for summat you're never going to have.'

He'd turned away, but his dismissive words had

not been able to wipe the smile from Rosie's face or to destroy her hopes. 'One day, Dad,' she'd murmured. 'One day, you'll see.'

Two

By the time Rosie went to bed, as the daylight crept across the fields, her head was buzzing with all that she had learned. But there was one secret that she did not share with her father: her meeting with Byron Ramsey. Her night vigil with Sam, however, had taught her one important lesson; caution.

'Trust no one, not even the villagers who seem friendly. And 'specially not the keeper.' Sam was referring to Amos.

'Does he know what you do?'

'Oh yes, though up to now, he's not been able to catch me.' His face sobered. 'I won't tempt fate by saying "never" because there's time yet, but Amos is getting old and he likes to be in his warm bed at night instead of tramping the fields looking for the likes of me. I wonder why he was out tonight?' He frowned and a worried note crept into his voice. 'We have an understanding of sorts, but he still has to do his job. His first loyalty has to be to William Ramsey. He gives him his livelihood and a roof over his head.' Then Sam chuckled, a deep, infectious sound, as he added, 'He nearly had me once, years ago now.'

'What happened?' Rosie whispered, almost as if

15

she feared the walls of their cottage were listening. She pictured the gamekeeper in her mind. He was tall and thin and stooped now. His grey, almost white, hair was thinning but his weather-beaten face still broke into a smile whenever he met Rosie. If she could have got to know him better, she was sure she would have liked him, but, sadly, Amos was her enemy.

'I was hedgin' and ditchin',' her father went on, 'and I'd set a couple of snares an' caught two hares. I'd taken up the snares and hidden them and the hares in the hedge further along from where I was working. Amos comes up behind me with his two dogs and they were sniffing around. I was sure they were going to find the hares and me snares, but, as luck would have it, I disturbed a rabbit in the hedge bottom and the dogs gave chase.'

'Have you ever been caught?'

Sam shook his head. 'No, lass, but I'm not daft enough to think I couldn't be. It's dangerous to get complacent.'

'But the villagers know you're a poacher, don't they?'

Again, Sam chuckled again – a low rumbling sound deep in his chest.

'They'll not give me away. They've too much to lose themselves if they do.'

'What d'you mean?'

'I never *sell* what I catch. I give away anything we don't want to the poorest in the village. Any money we need, lass, I earn from the little jobs that Jack Pickering puts my way. Selling owt – especially to

16

dealers – can be dangerous. If you don't take the price they offer – say for a brace of pheasants – they'll turn you in to the police.'

Rosie's eyes widened. 'Will they really?'

Sam nodded. 'Little Titch got caught that way.'

Tales of the legendary 'Little Titch' had peppered Rosie's childhood. He'd lived all his life in a small hovel at the edge of the wood about a mile from where Sam and Rosie lived now and further still away from the village. He'd had a tiny patch of ground where he'd grown vegetables and kept chickens and even a pig. After his parents had died, he'd continued to live there on his own. He'd never married; indeed, he was a recluse, but he never shunned the villagers' kindness to him and in return he, too, had kept many of them fed through hard times. And, Rosie had been told many times, he had taught Sam Waterhouse all he knew about poaching. But, despite Sam having kept him supplied with food as he'd become too infirm to go out for himself, the old man had died alone in his hovel one harsh winter a few years ago.

'He'd dealt with a butcher in the next village for years.' Sam went on with his story. 'And then suddenly the feller wouldn't pay a fair price and when Little Titch refused his paltry offer, the butcher told the local bobby that Little Titch had offered him a brace of pheasants.'

'What happened?'

'He was up before the magistrate, who happened to be old man Ramsey.'

Rosie's eyes widened. 'Mr William?'

'No, no. His father. Edward Ramsey.'

'Was Little Titch sent to prison?'

'No. He made a grovelling apology, telling them about the hard time he was going through and promising it would never happen again.'

'And did it?'

'What?'

'Happen again?'

'No.'

'So, Little Titch gave up poaching?'

Sam laughed. 'Nah. 'Course he didn't. He just minded he never got caught again.'

A week after her first meeting with Byron, Rosie hid in a thicket of small trees and bushes on the bank of the stream close to where she'd been fishing. Although Byron had been so kind, she was remembering her father's motto. Trust no one. She heard the horse's hooves long before she saw him. He dismounted just in front of the thicket, but he did not see her, for Rosie kept still and silent; she just watched. She saw him glance about him as if looking for her. Then she saw that he was carrying a pole with a sharpened hook on one end. He let the horse loose again, but the animal stayed close, grazing contentedly. Byron sat down on the bank, still glancing to his right and left every so often. Rosie left the thicket on the side furthest away from where he was sitting and approached him from several yards away as if she had just arrived.

'There you are,' he said, standing up. 'I thought you'd forgotten.'

Rosie shook her head. 'No, I wouldn't forget,' she said simply.

'I've brought you this,' he said, holding out the pole. 'I'll show you how to use it.' For the next hour they fished in the river, catching three fish. It was a much easier method than with a crooked branch, a piece of string and a hook.

Rosie carried home the fish with pride, but her pleasure soon evaporated when her father saw them.

'You didn't catch these with your bit of string and a hook,' he said sharply. He examined the fish more thoroughly. 'You've caught these with a gaff. Who's taught you how to do that, because I haven't?'

Suddenly, Sam – her kindly, loving father – was very angry. 'Sit in that chair, girl, and don't you dare leave it until you've explained yourself.'

But Rosie did not sit down. She stood on the hearth, planted her feet firmly on the rug and stood facing him with her arms akimbo. 'Byron Ramsey brought me a pole with a hook on it and showed me how to use it.'

Sam gaped at her. 'He – he helped you to poach his father's fish?'

'Yes, he did. He caught me one day last week fishing in the stream with my string and hook, so he brought me a gaff. And he's promised to teach me how to tickle trout, an' all.'

'Why? Why would he do that?' Sam's eyes narrowed. 'What did he want in return?'

Young though she was, Rosie knew the facts of

life. Nell had explained it all to her at Sam's request.

'I can't talk to a young lass about that sort of thing, Nell. Will you do it?' he'd said.

Nell had laughed. ''Course I will, Sam, but on one condition.'

'What's that?'

'That you have a man-to-man chat with my Nathan.'

Now, Rosie blushed at her father's blunt question. And then indignation swelled in her. 'Do you think I would let anything happen?'

'You'd have no chance if he wanted to – to . . .'

'He's a gentleman,' Rosie snapped.

'There's no such thing. All he sees is a young girl he could have at will. You'd not stand a chance against him. That's all village girls are to young men of his class. They'll use them and then cast them aside.'

Rosie felt the tears prickle. 'You're wrong, Dad. I know you are.'

'Then he's leading you on to trap you as easily as I snare rabbits and hares. He wants to catch us out and report us as poachers. Both of us, but he's trying to do it through you to get at me. You'll see, Rosie, we shall have the local bobby knocking at the door.'

Rosie said no more, but, stubbornly, she refused to stop meeting Byron. She was more careful now, though, about what she told him. When he asked her to show him how to set a snare, she lied and said she didn't know. Byron smiled. He didn't believe her, but he was a kindly young man who guessed the reason for her reticence. He said no more, but he was careful never again to ask her to show him the tricks of her father's trade; a trade that would probably become hers as time went by.

'And now,' he said the next time they met. 'I'll show you how to tickle trout. We need to look for big rocks in the stream. Maybe we can find one close to the bank, so we don't have to go paddling.'

They walked together along the bank, always careful to stay hidden beneath trees or behind bushes from anyone who might be watching.

'There's a big stone there,' Rosie said softly, pointing to the middle of the stream, 'but it's not very near the bank.'

Byron nodded. 'It'd be a good one, but I'd like to find one close to the bank for your first try. Ah, look, here we are . . .' He glanced around, making sure they were still hidden.

'Now, lie down on your front, with your hands in the water.'

Rosie hesitated for a moment, remembering her father's warning, but then she shrugged and did as Byron suggested. He lay down beside her and dabbled his right hand in the water. 'Now,' he said softly, 'very slowly and gently, feel right under the rock to see if a trout is hiding there.' He demonstrated as he spoke. Rosie watched as he felt beneath the rock. 'No,' he said, 'nothing there just now. Let's try further down the stream, but not too far. They won't go where it gets really shallow.'

For the next hour, they searched for rocks close to the bank. 'Now you try,' Byron said at last. Rosie lay on her stomach, slowly putting her hand into the water and feeling beneath a rock. 'I – I think there's some-thing there.'

'Careful, then. Put your fingers beneath his belly and stroke him gently.'

'He moved,' she whispered.

'But he's still there?'

'Yes, he's – oh!' There was a sudden movement and the brown trout darted away. 'Oh, I lost him.'

Byron chuckled. 'You did very well. If he'd stayed a little longer and submitted to your gentle stroking, once you could feel your fingers beneath his gills, you could have taken hold and brought him out of the water. You'll soon get the hang of it. But now, sadly, I must go. I'll see you again.'

And they did meet again – often. He would appear silently beside her as she picked berries or mushrooms in the woods, always helping her, guiding her. Sometimes, he brought her a gift from the orchards at the manor. Pears, apples, raspberries and goose-berries that Rosie would carry to Nell, who wisely never asked how she had come by such luxuries. And Sam, even if he guessed, now never said a word, at least not to Rosie, but he did confide in Nell.

'I'm worried about her. I know she's meeting Master Byron, but what I don't understand is what his intentions are.'

'Master Byron must be a lonely young man. He's never been away to school – he always had tutors at home. He doesn't seem to have any friends either. Maybe, Sam, it's all very innocent.'

Sam glanced at Nell, doubt in his eyes.

'You trust her, don't you, Sam?' Nell asked quietly.

'Yes, yes, I do, but I just don't want her to get hurt. It can never come to anything – I'm sure of that – and if the master gets wind of it, he could turn us out of our cottage. And then where would we be?'

Even through the winter, when the snow lay thick on the ground and Sam was hard pressed to help the poorest in the village as well as keeping himself, Rosie, Nell and her son fed, Rosie and Byron still managed to meet. Their encounters were never by arrangement, but Rosie knew where Byron liked to ride and she would wait for him in the shadows of the trees at the edge of the woods whenever she could sneak away from home. And Byron knew where she waited. There was a wariness on both sides now. They no longer caught fish together, though Rosie would venture to the stream alone. Now, she could catch a brown trout whenever she could find one sheltering beneath a rock. Byron never referred to Sam's night-time excursions and he certainly never asked if she went out with her father. He didn't really want to know. As winter turned into spring, they met beneath the shade of the trees, unseen by prying eyes – or so they hoped. Byron tethered his horse out of sight and they talked and laughed together.

'What do you want to do with your life, Rosie?' he asked gently one day.

It was early May now and she had just passed her fifteenth birthday. Beneath the trees, the ground was carpeted with bluebells and above them birds were finding a mate and building their nests. Buttercups were beginning to flower among the daisies. Rosie began to make a daisy chain.

'Get married, I suppose, and have a barrow load of kids. But first I'd have to find someone who loved me.'

'That won't be difficult,' he said softly. 'Have you anyone in mind?'

Rosie kept her gaze firmly fixed on the daisy chain. She had, but she could hardly tell him. Instead, she diverted his question. 'What about you?'

Byron pulled a face. 'My future is all mapped out for me. I have no choice but to carry on running the estate after my father.'

'We were all surprised that you didn't go away to boarding school. People of your class usually do.'

She saw Byron wince. 'I don't like the word *class*,' he said. 'We're all the same.'

Rosie laughed wryly. 'No, we're not, Byron. You know we're not.'

She looked up to see him staring intently at her. 'We are to me,' he whispered.

There was a rustling in the undergrowth and Queenie appeared, her tongue hanging out, her tail wagging at seeing her young mistress. Rosie scrambled to her feet. 'I must go. Dad must be about if Queenie's here.'

'I'll see you again soon,' Byron said, as she scurried away.

Neither of them knew it, but this was to be their last meeting. Memories of that warm spring day, the scent of bluebells and Rosie's daisy chain would stay for ever in their memories. As she hurried away through the trees, Byron picked up the daisy chain and tucked it carefully into his pocket. At home, he would press it between the pages of his favourite childhood book.

The rumours of the secret, yet innocent, meetings and the growing friendship between the two young people had reached William.

Three

It was the custom at Thornsby Manor to dress for dinner each evening, even if there were no guests. So, when the gong sounded, the three members of the family met in the dining room. The conversation usually centred around matters of the estate, with William's wife, Grace, feigning interest, though taking little part. Her time was taken up with organizing the running of the household and socializing with the ladies of the county who ran worthy charitable causes. In her spare time, she embroidered or played the grand piano in the drawing room. The only time she involved herself in estate matters was if she heard that a villager was ill. She would then send her lady's maid, Sarah, with a basket of fruit for the invalid. She would have liked to have become more involved personally, to have visited the sick and taken a more active part in the affairs of the village, but William would not allow it. 'You keep your place,' he had told her in the early days of their marriage. The only time she ever had a chance to speak to any of the villagers was at church on Sundays and at the harvest festival each September. And then the conversation was always stilted. They were in awe of her; she was the wife of the man who ruled their lives. Only one,

Nell Tranter, spoke to her with friendly ease. But William frowned on that.

'Just because I was obliged to give her the cottage to avoid an inquiry into her husband's unfortunate accident, the woman thinks herself an equal. You will ignore her, Grace.'

But Grace took no notice of her husband's demand and still greeted Nell and the other women every Sunday with a smile and a few words. William glowered, but said no more. In the early days of their marriage, he could not afford to offend his young bride; he still needed an heir. Through the years, Grace continued to acknowledge the village women but was careful not to engage in lengthy conversations, even though she would dearly have liked to have done so. Sadly, Grace came to realize that William was not the man she thought she had married. She would do her duty and be a loyal wife to him, but now her happiness was bound up in her son and his future.

One evening towards the end of May, when they rose from the table after dinner, William said, 'I would like to see you in my study, Byron.'

Byron glanced between his parents. His father's face was serious and his mother was avoiding her son's gaze.

'Of course, Father. Shall I come now?'

'If you please.'

Byron followed William from the dining room across the wide hallway and into his study, wondering what this was all about. William sat behind his desk, leaned back in the swivel chair and linked his fingers in front of him. William was a corpulent man, the result of good living and self-indulgence. Once he had been a handsome fellow even into middle age when he had won the hand in marriage of a woman twenty years his junior. With dark hair and an athletic figure, he had been the catch of the county as a still relatively young widower. But now his round face was florid and though he still rode around his estate, he needed help from his groom to mount his horse. But his mind was as sharp as ever and nothing concerning his lands or his family escaped his notice for long.

He looked up at his son, his expression unreadable. Tellingly, he did not invite him to sit down so Byron remained standing in front of the desk. The silence lengthened uncomfortably between them until Byron said at last, 'Is something wrong, Father?'

'I sincerely hope that is not the case, my boy, but I have heard some disturbing reports about you meeting with a young girl from the village. Now, I am not against a young man sowing a few wild oats before he settles down. Even an unwanted pregnancy can be paid off and hushed up, but I believe this girl is under age. You're playing a dangerous game there, Byron. You could end up in gaol and your reputation would be in shreds.'

The colour flooded Byron's face. He was well aware of the age gap between them but he also knew that, given time, Rosie would grow into a beautiful young woman. Anger surged through him to think that his father had so little faith in him. 'I would never hurt Rosie or any young girl.'

William's eyebrows rose. 'Ah, so it is true, then? Not just idle or malicious gossip.'

Byron clenched his fists at his side, realizing he had fallen straight into the trap his father had set. 'It's not like that. We just meet . . .'

Bluntly, William demanded, 'Have you had your way with her? Have you – deflowered her?'

'No – no, of course I haven't.'

'There's no "of course" about it.'

Byron's mind was in turmoil. Who had seen them together? Who had told his father? But his attention was brought back swiftly to the harsh words his father was uttering. 'I will evict them from their cottage and send them packing.'

'No, no, please, Father, don't do that. I give you my solemn promise I will not see her again.'

'We'd be well rid of the pair of them. Her father's the local poacher – we all know that – and I've no doubt he'll be teaching her the tricks of his nefarious trade. I've allowed them to carry on living there, at times against my better judgement. But Taylor has always said the man is useful too; that he keeps the vermin down and that he's cheap casual labour when needed. And Taylor assures me he never touches my game birds, although I'm not sure I believe him.'

'Amos Taylor is a loyal gamekeeper, Father. He's worked for the estate since your father's time, hasn't he? I'm sure what he says is true.' Now Byron held his tongue. He so wanted to point out that Sam Waterhouse helped to keep the villagers fed during hard times, but William was not the philanthropic type. He was utterly selfish and self-serving. His only concern was for himself, the future of his estate and his position among the county's gentry. Silently, Byron resolved that when he was in sole charge, things would be different. He would care for his tenants and workers.

'So, you give me your word, do you?'

Byron had no alternative but to agree. He knew that his father would have no compunction in carrying out his threat if he did not obey him. The young man felt a deep weight of sadness settle inside him as he gave his promise. He would not break it, but he needed, somehow, to get word to Rosie. He couldn't just abandon her without explanation. He would write a letter to her and explain everything. But how he would get it safely to her, he didn't yet know. He couldn't go to the cottage where she and her father lived; he might be seen. Nor could he risk meeting her again. He was sure his father would put a watch on him. Nor did he dare approach her father, Sam. That might cause trouble for Rosie. But then he thought of someone: Nathan Tranter. He knew that he and Rosie had been friends since childhood. He was a likeable young man and Byron felt he could trust him.

Byron composed his letter carefully but with each difficult word he felt as if another little piece broke away from his heart.

My dear Rosie,
    It is with a heavy heart that I am compelled to write this letter to you. My father has found out about our meetings and has forbidden me

*to see you again. I am entrusting this letter to
Nathan, who I know is your friend. I shall
miss seeing you and talking to you and please
believe me when I say that I shall watch over
you from a distance and – as much as it is in
my power – I will endeavour to see that no
harm comes to either you or your father.*

*Have a good life, Rosie, and take care in all
that you do. I am your devoted friend, Byron.*

He reread it three times before sealing it in an envelope and placing it in the inside pocket of his jacket.
He felt a strange prickling at the back of his eyes and
a lump in his throat. Byron Ramsey had been brought
up in the tradition that boys and men should never
cry, but at this moment he felt the closest he had ever
come to shedding tears.

It was two days before he saw Nathan working
in the fields and was able to approach him to speak
to him without the danger of being overheard. Byron
dismounted and, leaving his horse to graze at will,
approached the young man.

'Hello, Nathan. How are you?'

'Good morning, Master Byron. I'm well, thank
you. And you?'

'Well enough, thank you.' He paused realizing that
he was taking a huge risk. Could he really trust this
young man? He looked into Nathan's open, honest
face, into his dark brown eyes and took a deep breath.
'Nathan, can I trust you with a very delicate and
confidential matter?'

'Of course, Master Byron. How can I help you?'

'You're – you're good friends with Rosie, aren't you?'

Nathan smiled and his whole face seemed to light up. 'I like to think so. We've been friends since we were nippers.'

'Did you – has she told you that she and I meet occasionally?'

'She's not told me, no, but I do know because I've seen you together.'

Byron stared at him, suddenly unsure now whether to trust Nathan. 'Did you – did you tell anyone?'

'Lord, no, Master Byron. I would never tell tales on Rosie, though I have to admit to being a little concerned. You being so – far above her – if you get my meaning. But Rosie's her own person, even though she's still young. She wouldn't take kindly to me interfering.'

Byron sighed. 'I would never hurt her, Nathan. I want you to know that, but I fear I may have to. Word has reached my father of our meetings and he has forbidden me to see her again. I have been obliged – no, forced, if I'm honest – to give him my solemn promise and so I cannot even meet her one more time to explain. He has threatened to evict them if I do. But I – I can't bear for her to think badly of me, so I have written her a letter. Will you take it to her, Nathan? And can I trust you to tell no one about it?'

Solemnly, Nathan met Byron's troubled gaze. 'You can, Master Byron. I will give it to her personally as soon as I can catch her alone.'

Byron handed over the envelope.

'I am indebted to you, Nathan.'

He turned away abruptly, mounted his horse and rode away, spurring the stallion into a gallop. Nathan watched him go with mixed emotions. He had sympathy for the young man. It was obvious that Byron had feelings for Rosie. But she was young – only fifteen – and not born into the same society as Byron Ramsey. And, to make matters even worse, she was the daughter of the local poacher, who took his living illegally from William Ramsey's estate. It was not a match that could ever meet with the master's approval. But what would happen in a year or so's time when Rosie was older? Would Byron rebel against his father and his class? Nathan looked down at the letter he held. How he wished he knew what was inside it, but he was too honourable to think seriously of opening it. After finishing his day's work, Nathan went home by way of Sam's cottage.

'Hello, Nathan. How lovely to see you.' Rosie greeted him with a wide smile. 'Come in. The kettle's on the hob as always.'

'Is your dad at home?'

'No, but he shouldn't be long. D'you want to see him?'

'No – yes, I mean . . .'

Rosie laughed. 'Well, which is it?'

'It's you I want to see, but it'd be best if your dad's not around.'

'Oooh, this sounds very mysterious.'

Nathan fished the letter out of his pocket. 'Byron gave me this and asked me to give it to you in secret.'

Rosie looked startled and then reached out to take the letter. Nathan noticed that her fingers were trembling.

'Thank you,' she said huskily as she slipped it into the pocket of her apron. 'I'll – I'll read it later.'

'Of course,' Nathan murmured and glanced away. He'd hoped she would open it while he was still with her. Not that he wanted to pry; he already knew the gist of its contents, but he rather thought she might be upset and he wanted to be there to comfort her. They talked for a while until Sam arrived home carrying two rabbits.

'Tek one of these to your mam. She meks the best rabbit pie I've ever tasted.'

'Thanks, Mr Waterhouse. If I take both I'm sure she'd be happy to make a pie for you an' all.'

'No need.' Sam winked at his daughter. 'Rosie is getting almost as good with her pastry.'

Rosie chuckled. 'Well, I should be, since it's your mam who's taught me.'

'I'll be on my way, then,' Nathan said.

It was not until they had both retired for the night that Rosie was able to open the letter and read it by candlelight. She read it through three times, committing every word to memory before she crept down the ladder by which she reached her bedroom and burned it in the dying embers of the fire. She watched his writing disappear as the letter crinkled and smouldered until there were only tiny brown shards of shrivelled paper left. She lay awake far into the night; thankfully, it was not a night for poaching. Her mind was full of the two young men in her life. One was her true childhood friend and she loved him dearly, but the other was the one who made her heart race and whose image, his voice, his laughter, filled her waking hours and her dreams too. But now Byron was gone from her life. Now she would only see him from afar. No longer would she be able to speak to him, to laugh with him or to poach fish with him from his father's stream. It had been a wonderful time; they had met often through the months since that first encounter and had believed themselves safe from prying eyes. But someone had seen them; someone who felt Byron's father should be told. And now, it was over. She repeated the words of his letter over and over; she would never forget them. She would carry them in her heart for ever but she had not been able to keep the letter. She couldn't risk her father finding it. She remembered his words. 'No one in yon house would ever look at the likes of us.' It seemed he had been right and her girlish fantasies were in tatters.

Rosie buried her face in the pillow to muffle her sobs.

Four

Now that he believed he had settled the unsavoury matter of Byron meeting Rosie Waterhouse, through the summer months that followed William turned his attention to the other matter uppermost in his mind.

'My dear, I need your help,' he said, as he entered the morning room after breakfast. This was Grace's private sitting room where even William knocked before entering.

Grace raised her eyebrows. 'Really, William. In what way?'

'We need to find a suitable wife for Byron. He has just turned twenty-one and it's high time he was married and producing an heir.'

Grace stared at him for a moment, her mouth tight, but all she said was, 'And have you anyone in mind, William?'

'No, I was hoping that was where you might come in.'

'I see. You want me to find a wife for him, is that it?'

William failed to notice the hint of sarcasm in her tone. 'I just thought,' he said, 'that among all the ladies of the county with whom you lunch quite often and meet when attending the various committees you're on, there might be a suitable daughter or relative they could vouch for. Some young lady who is a debutante, who has been presented at court and moves in the right circles.'

It was on the tip of her tongue to retort, 'And you think such a young woman would be willing to bury herself in the countryside as Byron's wife?', but she bit back the words. Not every young girl today was as foolish as she had been. She thought back to the time when her own mother, desperate for her only daughter to marry well, had pushed her towards the wealthy widower.

'He's old enough to be my father,' Grace had wailed.

'He's still a fine figure of a man,' her mother Eliza Parker had snapped. 'Once you've been presented at court and had a Season, you will be well equipped to enter the county's society as Mrs Grace Ramsey. You will be set up for life if you marry William Ramsey.'

'All he wants is a brood mare,' Grace had said morosely.

'Don't be coarse, Grace. It's unbecoming. Of course he wants a son as an heir to his estate. You're fortunate he has even looked at you. Your father is nothing special. It's only because my dear friend was willing and able to act as your sponsor that you're to be presented at court. Without Helene's help, you would never have attracted such a suitor.'

Grace had said no more, but she was saddened to hear her mother speak of her father in such a derogatory manner. Gregory Parker was a lawyer in Lincoln and was well thought of but he did not have the standing in the society circles to which her mother craved admittance. He was kind and gentle, though Grace had heard he could be fearsome in a law court. She was surprised that he was allowing Eliza to push their daughter into marriage with someone who was almost as old as he was, but then she realized that men tended to leave such matters to their wives.

Now, as she faced her husband, she shuddered. Although William was so much older than she was, he had seemed – during their courtship – to be charming and kind and she had believed that that was what he would be to her and any family they had. She had never realized what a harsh and ruthless man he was. Somewhere, some poor girl was going to be offered up as a sacrificial lamb to Byron whether she wanted it or not. And whether *he* wanted it or not. She understood the reason for William's sudden interest in Byron's marital state – or rather the lack of it. From her own lady's maid, Grace too had heard the rumours about Byron's meetings with a village girl. Sarah, a plump, rather plain woman was the proverbial fountain of knowledge when it came to local gossip. She was, however, utterly devoted to her mistress and totally discreet when it came to anything regarding the Ramsey family. Grace treated all her staff kindly and fairly and they all loved her. Byron too was popular with them, although they were all a little afraid of William. It was he who ruled their lives.

'I'll have a word with Helene,' Grace promised her husband now. She had kept in touch with the woman who had been such an influence in her young life. Indeed, Helene had been the one to organize Grace's

Season and to introduce her to William. After Grace's marriage, Helene had helped her become acquainted with the landed gentry of Lincolnshire society. 'I'm seeing her for luncheon on Wednesday.'

'Thank you, my dear.' William smiled at her. 'I knew you'd have the right connections.'

Two days later, Grace sighed as she sat down at the table in the restaurant of The White Hart Hotel in Lincoln to wait for Helene to join her. The hotel was just along the street from the cathedral. Whenever she came here for luncheon, Grace always allowed an extra hour after her meeting before her carriage collected her. She liked to spend time in the cool, quiet interior of the beautiful building, alone with her own thoughts. Three-thirty was the time she had told Monty to pick her up, leaving ample time for her to have a leisurely luncheon with Helene and also to get home before she had to change for dinner. Monty was the stable lad at the manor, who usually drove the carriage to take Grace wherever she wished to go. While she waited for her friend to arrive, she thought over how she should phrase her request. She did not want to imply in any way that her own marriage was not what she had hoped it might be; Helene had been instrumental in introducing her to William and the woman had been a dear friend to her ever since. The conventions of the time and Grace's own mother's driving ambition had hardly been Helene's fault.

Lady Helene Montague swept into the restaurant in a flurry of silk, white fox fur and expensive perfume. The attentive waiters soon came hurrying.

'My dear Grace, how wonderful to see you. You are looking as lovely as ever. Do the years never touch you? No one would believe you have a son of one and twenty. How is my handsome godson, by the way? Has he found himself a suitable wife yet? Thank you, George.' She glanced up at the waiter as he held the chair for her.

'Helene . . .' Grace smiled at her. It was impossible not to smile when Helene was around. She was so vivacious and gregarious. She was tall and slim and always elegantly dressed. While she paid Grace the extravagant compliment, it was Helene herself who never seemed to age. She looked now – more than twenty years later – just the same as when she had found Grace a husband.

'It's strange you should mention Byron,' Grace said as her friend and confidante took her seat. 'I should like your advice.'

'Oh dear. I'm not sure I like the sound of this. He's all right, isn't he? He's not in trouble?'

'William has heard that Byron has been keeping unsuitable company with a girl from the village.'

'He's told you that?' Helene raised her eyebrows. 'William, I mean.'

Grace hesitated. It was hurtful to her that her husband never took her into his confidence about anything. Not even about their son.

'No,' she said shortly, 'but I heard about it myself.' She tapped the side of her nose as she added wryly, 'I have my sources.'

Helene laughed. 'Don't we all? Your lady's maid, I suspect.'

'Quite.'

'So, how can I help?'

'Are there any daughters of about Byron's age among your many friends and acquaintances? Anyone you know who would be deemed suitable, in William's eyes, of course.'

Helene was thoughtful for a few moments. 'There are one or two who might fit the bill,' she said slowly.

Grace felt relieved. She hadn't wanted one particular girl to be thrust at Byron. If there were a few, he would have some choice and perhaps, with luck, he might fall in love with one of them.

'Are you able to hold a ball or a party at Thornsby Manor?'

Suddenly Grace was animated by the thought of organizing a social gathering. It would take a lot of planning, but she would love that and, with Helene's guidance, she was sure she could make a great success of it. William had never liked entertaining, except for his shooting parties, but now he could not demure at holding a lavish ball.

'Oh yes. I know we live in the middle of nowhere, but we have plenty of bedrooms. Guests could stay for the weekend and, if we hold it at the right time, William would arrange a shooting party for the gentlemen.'

Helene's blue eyes twinkled at Grace. 'I do hope I'm going to be top of your list of invitations.'

'Of course. I'll not be able to manage without you.'

'Have you heard about this grand ball they're holding at the manor?' Nell asked, as the four of them sat down around her table for Sunday dinner in early October.

Deliberately, Rosie kept her eyes downcast but her heart started to beat a little faster.

'Aye, I had heard summat,' Sam said. 'Evidently, there'll be guests arriving early on the Saturday morning for a shoot and then the ball will be in the evening.' He glanced at Nathan. 'We'll mebbe get a chance to work as beaters for the shoot.'

'What's it all for, then?' Nathan asked. 'Mr Ramsey isn't a great one for entertaining.'

'Rumour has it that they're inviting some suitable young ladies for Byron to find a wife.'

Rosie's heart felt as if it had skipped a beat and it began to hammer twice as quickly as normal. Suddenly, she wasn't very hungry. She kept her head down and picked at her food. She didn't want to offend Nell, who had cooked them a wonderful meal. But now the conversation went on just between Nell and Sam. Even Nathan fell silent. Later, as they walked down the lane back towards the cottage where Rosie and Sam lived, Nathan asked, 'You all right, Rosie?'

She smiled up at him, once again in charge of her wayward heart. It had been a shock to hear that a wife was being sought for Byron, even though common sense should have told her it was bound to happen one day. 'I'm fine, Nathan. That was a lovely dinner your mam cooked. She spoils us.'

'It's the least she can do after all the stuff your dad brings us. I don't know where we'd be without him and neither would a lot of folks in the village. But I do get anxious about him – and you, Rosie. Because if I'm not mistaken, he's teaching you his poaching ways. I just don't want to see you get caught – or him.' Including Sam was almost an afterthought. Rosie's father had been a poacher all his life and he was wily. As far as Nathan was aware, he'd never been caught. But Rosie was a different matter. Although Sam would have taught her well, Nathan feared for her. And he was also concerned for her in other ways too. He'd never liked to pry about the letter he'd carried to her from Byron but he still wondered what exactly it had contained.

'I won't, Nathan.' She smiled up at him impishly, her good humour restored. She would show a brave face to the world – especially to her father and their friends. And Nathan – and his mother – were certainly her friends. No one must ever guess the secrets of her young heart. Fortunately, Rosie was not only pretty, vivacious and daring; she was also very sensible. She knew she could never be Byron's wife, knew, deep down, that her romantic notions of one day living in Thornsby Manor were unrealistic, but anyone could have their private dreams, couldn't they? But they must remain private dreams.

'And nor will Dad,' she went on. 'He knows when old Amos is tucked up safely in his bed.'

'Ah, now there you have it. *Old* Amos. He won't be around for ever and a new, younger man won't keep to his bed to suit you and your dad.'

'I don't think Amos does. It's just on certain nights of the week – he doesn't come out.' Rosie knew nothing of the arrangement between the keeper and her father.

'But don't you see, Rosie, Amos is a creature of habit? Another gamekeeper might not be. Probably *won't* be.'

'We'll worry about that when it happens, Nathan. Now, I've got to get home to make up the fire. There'll be no going out tonight. Not the right weather for it, so Dad likes to toast his toes.'

She kept up her cheerfulness until bedtime, but then, in the privacy of her tiny room, she allowed herself a few tears. 'Oh Byron, Byron, why did I have to fall in love with you?'

Five

There was great excitement at the manor. There was to be a shooting party for the men and a grand ball in the evening for everyone on the third weekend in October. Several guests would be staying overnight and although there would be a lot of work for the staff, they were all caught up in the fever.

'It's mainly for Master Byron,' the young maids whispered to one another. 'There are going to be suitable young ladies for him to choose a bride.'

'Oh, don't you just wish you could be one of them,' Elsie Warren, the kitchen maid, said dreamily.

Overhearing her, Cook said sharply, 'And why would a handsome young man like Master Byron look at the likes of a scruffy kitchen maid? Now get on with your work, Elsie.' But even Cook's sharp reprimand could not dampen the girl's anticipation of such a wonderful event.

'When the dinner's over and the dancing begins,' one of the older housemaids, Lucy, said, 'We might be able to go up to the balcony and take a peek at the dancers in the ballroom. But don't let Cook or Mrs Frost know' – she was referring to the house-keeper – 'or they'll stop us.'

'Master Byron wouldn't mind and I don't think madam would either. They're both so kind.'

'But the master would,' Lucy said. 'We'd be dismissed on the spot without a reference if he caught us.'

The thought was a sobering one, but could still not quell their eagerness to witness such a grand event.

'Dad! *Dad!* Quick, get your gun,' Rosie dashed into the shed at the bottom of their garden. 'The geese are coming. I can hear them.'

Migrating from the north, wild geese flew to the marshlands on the east coast of Britain around October. Sam snatched up his gun and followed her out. They stood in their vegetable garden, their gaze scanning the sky.

'There they are,' Rosie pointed to the north-west. 'There're hundreds of them and they're coming this way.'

'They'll be on their way to the Wash, more'n' likely,' Sam remarked. 'Get my cartridges out of the shed, Rosie. I might be able to reload a couple of times.'

As the skein of geese came closer, Sam raised his gun. As they passed overhead, he managed to shoot three. Queenie raced away to find them.

In the distance, they heard the echo of two more shotguns.

'That'll be Amos taking a pot shot. Good lass.' Sam bent to pat Queenie's head as she arrived back carrying the last of the birds.

'Take one to Nell. She'll tell you how to cook ours.'

'What about the other one?'

'Take that down to Mrs Merryweather.'

Rosie nodded. Emily Merryweather lived near the

village green. She was a widow with one young son and times were often hard for her even though she worked on Jez Crowson's farm in the dairy.

'And take her one of the rabbits we caught last night, an' all. She'll make good use of it or give it to someone else who will be glad of it. We won't need it now we've got a goose.'

'I'll be as quick as I can but I've got some bread proving and it needs to be baked soon.'

She picked up two of the geese and collected the rabbit from the shed.

'My word,' Nell exclaimed when she saw what Rosie was carrying. 'This is a rare treat and no mistake.'

'There's a goose for you, and Dad said to take the other goose and the rabbit to Mrs Merryweather.'

'A' you going there now?'

Rosie nodded.

'Right, you can take this cake I've baked this morning to her. Call on your way back, 'cos there's one for you and your dad.'

'Ooh lovely. I will.' Rosie grinned. 'And I need you to tell me how to dress and cook the goose. But I can't stop now. I've got bread waiting to go in the oven.'

'That's all right. Come here later. I'll show you then. In fact, bring your goose and you can do it alongside me. That's the best way to learn.'

Rosie grinned at her and then hurried away on her errand.

'Byron, please come in and sit down.'

Grace had sent for her son to join her in the morning room where they could talk undisturbed.

With an inward sigh, Byron crossed the room and kissed his mother's cheek, then sat down beside her.

'My dear, you must know that this shooting party and the ball is to introduce you to suitable young women. Although your father is keen for you to marry and produce an heir, I want you to know that I do not wish you to marry a girl you don't love. So, all I am asking you to do is to meet the three young women Lady Helene and I have chosen to see if you like any of them enough to want to get to know them better. You do understand, don't you, that *I* am not trying to force you into marriage for the sake of the Ramsey lineage?'

Byron could not fail to understand her meaning. His mother was merely carrying out her husband's wishes, but she was also making it quite clear that she was not in favour of an arranged marriage. She wanted, as far as was possible, Byron to have a free choice in his future wife.

He took her hand and raised it to his lips. 'Darling Mother, I know you have my best interests at heart and you want me to be happy. But perhaps duty to my father and the desires of my own heart do not coincide and I fear I will be obliged to choose between the two.'

Grace caught her breath. 'Oh Byron. Have you met someone? Have you fallen in love?'

Byron hesitated for a fraction of a second, but it was enough to tell his mother, sensitive to her beloved son's feelings, that there was something he was holding back. 'No, Mother. It's just the way this is being done. It's like a cattle market with suitable heifers being paraded in front of me.'

Grace winced but did not reprimand him for his coarseness of language, for there was truth in what he said.

'My dear, this is the way things are done in our society.'

'I know, I know.' He pushed the image of the red-haired girl with shining green eyes out of his mind and forced a smile and a brightness into his tone that he didn't feel. 'So, tell me about these three delectable young ladies whom you and my godmother have chosen for me to meet.'

'Well, let me see now. There's Pearl Anderson. She's a nice, quiet girl. I have met her mother, Bella, once or twice and her father, Henry, is an estate owner in south Lincolnshire, near Stamford. He doesn't own as much land and property as we do, but they are a well-respected family in that area. As for the other two girls, I have to admit I don't know them. They are Helene's recommendation but she tells me they are lovely girls. They live in Lincoln and their fathers are gentlemen of means. They are both very active in the Church and in the community life of the city.'

'Then I am sure they will be more than suitable. So, do I have free choice among the three?'

'Of course, but if none of them appeal to you, you must say so.'

'I'm sure they will all be charming and I shall be spoiled for choice. But will they like me?'

'Oh Byron, my darling boy. How could they not?'

The three young women had been primed by their ambitious mothers that they were there to make Byron Ramsey fall in love with them.

One, a feisty young woman called Harriet, declined to participate. 'I'll go to the ball to please you and Aunty Helene but I will not be married off to a country yokel and buried in the wilds of Lincolnshire.'

'Oh, but he's a very handsome young man by all accounts,' her mother said persuasively. 'And in line to inherit a large estate in time.'

'I don't care if he's a veritable Adonis or as rich as Croesus. I will choose my own husband in my own good time.'

Her mother had sighed and hoped that on seeing Byron she would perhaps change her mind.

The third 'candidate' was Beatrice. While she was not quite as pretty as the other two, she was already in possession of a large fortune which had been left to her by a childless uncle.

The menfolk, who were to take part in shooting game the following morning, arrived in time for dinner on the Friday evening. Their wives and daughters would arrive the following day in time for the grand ball in the evening. Byron was introduced to the fathers of the three girls but all of them declined to get involved. 'We leave all that to the women,' one declared, slapping Byron heartily on his shoulder. 'Let us just enjoy a day's shooting.'

They were gone for most of the following day, with the servants carrying huge hampers into the fields at lunchtime. The villagers wisely kept out of the way, though several of the men were employed as beaters.

'I'll be out till nightfall,' Sam warned Rosie. 'Amos Taylor has asked me to join the beaters and the money's good. Now you be sure to stay indoors or go to Nell's.'

'Can't I work in the garden, Dad?'

Sam shook his head. 'Best not. You know what these city types are like. Some of 'em have probably never held a gun before and can't be trusted to take aim properly. No, stay inside, lass. Just for today. And keep Queenie indoors with you. I don't want her getting hurt. All this fuss,' he muttered as he readied himself. 'Just to find a young man a wife.'

Rosie said nothing, but her heart was like a heavy weight inside her chest.

By the time all the wives and daughters had arrived at the manor, the excitement had reached fever pitch. The three girls, who all knew they were there on approval, eyed each other jealously, though outwardly, not wanting to appear peevish in front of their hosts, they chatted together with superficial friendliness.

Byron was scrupulously fair. He danced an equal number of times with each girl and forbore to take any of them into supper. Instead, he escorted his grandmother, Grace's mother. His grandfather had come to take part in the shoot, but the day had tired him and he had retired to bed.

'You must choose wisely, Byron,' his grandmother, Eliza Parker, whispered. 'A girl who will be a suitable mother to the heir of the Thornsby estate, but you don't have to be madly in love with her. Once you have produced a male heir – and perhaps a spare – you can take a mistress, though you should always be discreet. There shouldn't be any scandal attached to the Ramsey name.'

Byron was stunned into silence. He didn't know what to say. Neither his mother nor even his father had hinted that this was the way things were done in their circles. He realized now how he had been kept in ignorance deliberately. Sheltered from the real world, he was unbelievably naive for a young man of twenty-one. Perhaps, if he had attended boarding school or even gone to university, his outlook and his knowledge of the way of the world would have broadened, but his father had insisted that he be tutored at home, that he should not be exposed to the wild ways of young men liberated from the constraints of parental control. While his thoughts were running riot, Byron merely murmured, 'Of course not, Grandmama.'

'The one called Pearl,' Eliza went on, blithely unaware of the shock she had delivered to her grandson, 'is a pretty little thing with that blond hair and blue eyes, and she seems biddable. You don't want a harridan for a wife, Byron. She must know her place within the household, even though one day she will be mistress of Thornsby Manor. But that time is far off, God willing.'

Byron glanced down the table towards where his mother was sitting between the fathers of two of the girls. And across the table from her was the third father. She paid them all equal attention, giving no indication that any one of their daughters was emerging as the favourite.

Keeping her voice low, Eliza went on. 'Harriet seems to have a mind of her own. She will not be easy to control, I fear. And as for the other one, well . . .' Eliza shrugged and said no more.

Byron's gaze was still on his mother. He adored her. Her face, beautiful in the soft glow of candlelight, was animated as she charmed her guests. He had always believed his parents were a happily married couple who loved each other, but his grandmother's next words belied this.

'Your mother was very fortunate that your father considered her worthy of his attention and to be the mother of his heir. My friend, Lady Helene, had much to do with that. Our family is nothing special. We do not move in the upper echelons of society, but Helene's support was invaluable. My only sadness is that Grace has not given your father another son. The heavy burden to produce an heir now rests with you and you alone. So, you must do the honourable thing, Byron, and choose a wife without delay.'

The weekend of entertainment at the manor was deemed a great success by all who attended but Grace had only one thing on her mind.

'So, Byron, which of the three lovely young ladies Helene introduced you to did you like the best?'

He bit back a sharp retort. He really didn't like what was happening, but he was powerless to prevent it. Feigning a calmness he didn't feel he said, 'They were all lovely, Mother. Very pretty and two of them were' – he paused, searching for the right word to describe the young women – 'effervescent. The third, I felt, was a little quieter. Shy, perhaps. I think I liked her the best. Her name was Pearl. I don't think,' he went on slowly, 'that the other two would fit into country life very well, do you?'

'No, you're right about the other two. What shall we say to be kind? I think they were seeking the limelight – wanting to be noticed. And Harriet? Well, I found her voice rather strident. She was very opinionated for a young girl. No, I liked Pearl too, though sometimes you have to be wary of the quiet ones. And she's very young. Still only seventeen.'

'Perhaps she will be the one most used to rural life, having been brought up on her father's estate.'

'There is that,' Grace agreed, trying to keep her tone non-committal. Silently, she thought, *I hope she is, for her sake.* She remembered only too well how she had felt being taken from the elegant house uphill in Lincoln and all that the city had to offer and plunged into the wilds of Lincolnshire. She had been very lonely at first with only her husband and the servants for company. She had written copious letters to her mother and to Helene but got little sympathy or understanding from either of them. They constantly pointed out how lucky she was to have such a wealthy and influential husband. Byron's birth had rescued her. She had doted on the baby, doing far more for the child than a woman in her position would normally do. There had been many a battle royal between her and the nanny that William had hired. But Grace had won each and every round. She was, after all, the mistress of the house and the child's mother.

Speaking again to Byron, she said, 'Then you'll have no objection if I invite Pearl and her parents to stay with us? Just a small party this time. A weekend's shoot, I think. I understand that her father enjoyed the shooting immensely.'

'No, Mother, I have no objection,' Byron said dutifully, but his tone was flat, devoid of any enthusiasm. He turned away, 'I'm going riding. I'll be back for luncheon.'

Minutes later he was galloping over the fields, the horse's hooves pounding out the rhythm of the words running through his mind.

She's not Rosie. She's not Rosie.

Six

'Sit yarsen down, Sam,' Nell said, smiling. 'And have a slice of my chicken and leek pie.'

'Chicken, eh? I don't recall bringing you a chicken.'

'You didn't.' Nell's grin widened as she teased him. 'Jez Crowson brought one over.' Jez was one of the estate's tenant farmers.

Sam raised his eyebrows. 'Should I be worried?'

Nell chuckled. 'Not in the slightest.' Her hazel eyes twinkled with mischief. 'I don't reckon his wife'd be too pleased if he was to come a-calling on me, d'you?'

Sam snorted with laughter as he picked up his knife and fork. 'Couldn't blame the poor chap, I suppose, if he tried to look elsewhere for a bit of comfort. That wife of his is a shrew if ever there was one.'

Nell tweaked his ear playfully. 'The only man I give "comfort" to is you, Sam Waterhouse, and don't you forget it.'

As she sat down on the opposite side of the table, Sam said solemnly, 'I don't, lass, believe me, I don't.'

They ate in silence for a while until Nell said. 'I expect we set the tongues wagging – have done for a while now, I shouldn't wonder.'

'None of their business. We're very discreet, Nell. Not even our own kids know.'

Nell laughed loudly. 'You're wrong there, Sam. They're not daft, either of them.'

For a moment Sam looked nonplussed, then, with a sigh, he shrugged his shoulders. 'Oh well, they were bound to catch on sooner or later.'

'Of course they were. They're adults now. Well, almost.' There was a short pause before Nell, changing the subject, said, 'Have you heard the latest gossip? I heard it from Ivy next door. We don't need a news-paper or a town crier when she's around. She's a good sort and I'm very fond of her, but I certainly wouldn't trust her with my secrets. Though, credit due to her, she's raising two fine lads all on her own since her hubby died.'

Sam wiped the last of the rich gravy around the plate with a hunk of bread. 'No, I haven't heard owt, but I expect you're about to tell me.'

Nell leaned towards him, even though there was no one else in the room to hear her. 'They're saying that Master Byron has a young lady now. A girl from Stamford way. That's what the grand ball was all about. To introduce him to young women of his own class.'

Sam smiled. 'Not before time, I'd say. How old is he now? Twenty-one? Good luck to him. I bet his father will be pleased.'

'Only if she's suitable,' Nell said sagely, rising to clear away the plates.

Sam wrinkled his brow. 'There is that, of course, in their circles.'

'In *anybody*'s circles, Sam,' Nell said sharply. 'Now you wouldn't want your Rosie to take up with a wrong 'un, would you?'

Sam regarded her with amusement. 'And you don't think some'd look down on the daughter of a poacher?'

Nell wriggled her shoulders. 'Only them that don't know you. You do a lot more good in the world than you do harm. But since you mention it . . .' She hesitated only briefly. Nell Tranter was not one to be afraid to speak her mind. 'Mebbe you shouldn't be teaching your ways to your lass. It'd be better if she got herself a proper job.'

'They're a bit scarce around here, Nell, love.'

'Mebbe she could find work on one of the farms. She could learn dairy work or—'

'She's tried,' Sam cut in. 'But as soon as they hear her name . . .'

'Ah, I see. Like that, is it?'

"Fraid so.' He paused and then added, 'And there's summat else, Nell. There's a rumour that old Amos will be pensioned off before long and if he is, a new gamekeeper will be found.' They stared at each other. 'And what will happen then?' Sam added quietly. 'He might not be as' – he paused again, searching for the right word – '*regular* in his hours as Amos has been in recent years.'

Now, not even Nell had an answer for him.

As the weather worsened and available work on the estate and its farms lessened, Sam was needed more than ever to provide food for the villagers.

'We'd best get out there, Rosie, before he kills all his game birds. He's had more shoots already this year than I can remember. I expect he's wanting to impress Byron's future in-laws. I hear they're spending more time at the manor than in their own home. 'Specially the girl. We'll go out tonight. It's wet and blustery. Old Amos won't be patrolling the grounds in this weather.'

His words about Byron were like a knife through her heart, but Rosie made ready for their night-time foray into the woods.

'We'll go further away,' Sam said. 'We'll go north to the woodland on the edge of his lands. I won't take me gun tonight. It's near one of his farms, Jez Crowson's place, and he has sharp ears. Bring your catapult.' Sam had made a catapult for Rosie when she was seven and she had practised shooting tin cans from the fence ever since. He grinned at her. 'Let's see how good a shot you are now.'

As darkness fell, they walked stealthily through the woodland near their home and turned northwards, passing Home Farm and then Jez Crowson's, skirting the farmyard so they didn't rouse the two dogs Sam knew had kennels outside the back door of the farm-house. Sam kept his hand on Queenie's collar. They entered another patch of woodland at the northern end of William's estate and searched the branches above them. A fine drizzle wetted their upturned faces. Through the murk, Sam spotted a roosting pheasant. He touched Rosie's arm and pointed upwards. She aimed her catapult at the bird and brought it down with one shot. At once, Queenie retrieved it, but the other roosting birds had been startled.

'Wait a bit,' Sam whispered. 'They'll come back if we keep quiet.'

Over the next few hours of darkness, and moving quietly through the trees, Rosie bagged three pheasants and four pigeons with her catapult and Sam snared three rabbits.

'That'll do us for tonight, Rosie. Time we was making our way home.'

After another weekend visit by Pearl and her parents to the manor, Byron began his courtship of the young woman in earnest. They both knew what was expected of them. He visited her home and took her out to dine in Stamford. He spent Christmas with Pearl and her parents. In the New Year, Pearl visited Thornsby Manor again and they took long carriage rides in the countryside, Byron showing her the extent of the land his family owned.

'Although she doesn't mix socially with them, my mother takes an interest in the welfare of our tenants and their families, both on the two farms and in the village. Would you feel able to do that?'

Pearl smiled, her cheeks dimpling prettily. 'Of course, Byron. I want to be a good and dutiful wife to you. But' – she lowered her head demurely – 'our first duty is to have children, isn't it? Hopefully a son.'

'But I want you to be happy, Pearl.'

'Oh Byron, I'm sure we'll do very nicely together.'

'My mother is arranging to set rooms aside for our personal use, but we will be expected to dine with my parents every evening after – after we're married.'

'Of course, Byron.'

Over the next few weeks, Pearl seemed to say 'Of course, Byron' quite a lot. She charmed William and was easy company for Grace.

'So, my boy, have you proposed yet?' William asked Byron over dinner one evening in February when Pearl was not visiting. 'I thought a June wedding would be nice. It gives us plenty of time to prepare and—'

'I think Pearl's mother wants us to be married in Stamford . . .'

'Oh no, I won't hear of it. We were married here in the village church belonging to the estate, as was my father before me. I'm afraid that won't do. It won't do at all.' William paused a moment and when neither Grace nor Byron spoke, he added, 'I shall write to her father. You are not to propose officially to the girl, Byron, until this matter is settled.'

The reply to William's letter came a week later.

'Her father has agreed,' William told them, 'albeit reluctantly. Evidently, it is the mother who is the most upset. She had envisaged a grand wedding that the whole of Stamford would turn out to see. Pearl, it seems, is quite happy with the idea that you should be married here. So, on your next visit, my boy, you will propose.'

Byron glanced at his mother, but she was avoiding his gaze. He sighed inwardly. 'Yes, Father. Of course.'

The following morning, he rode out on his favourite horse from the stable and followed the path of the stream as it ran from the lake in front of the manor to the border of his father's land and beyond. Just near the stepping stones was where he had first met Rosie, but today she was nowhere to be seen. He toyed with the idea of visiting the cottage where she lived but knew that he would no doubt be seen and tongues would start to wag. The last thing he wanted was to bring trouble to her. He just wanted to see her one more time, to speak to her, to explain, before he made the irrevocable step of proposing to Pearl. But if he was honest with himself, he knew that if he did see her, then he would not make the journey to Stamford, he would not propose to Pearl and then all hell would break loose.

With an ache in his heart, he turned his horse back towards the manor where he readied himself for his journey to the south of the county.

The wedding took place on the second Saturday in June 1912, a fine, warm day when all the villagers turned out to line the path from the manor to the church. One day, they told each other, he'll be our master. We'd do well to be seen supporting him and toasting his future happiness.

It was the last thing Rosie wanted to do, but she felt she would be conspicuous by her absence if she did not join the other well-wishers. So, alongside her father, she stood in the shade of a tree beside the path winding up the slope to the small church at the opposite end of the village to Sam's cottage. The villagers, lining the route, waved and clapped as the guests arrived, even those they didn't know. It was almost like a royal procession. Then came people they recognized:

the servants from the manor, William Ramsey and his wife, a carriage bearing three bridesmaids and the bride's mother and then the bridegroom, supported by his best man, whom no one recognized.

'Who's he?' Nell asked as their carriage went by.

'No idea. Some pal of Master Byron's, I expect.'

Rosie shrank back beneath the shadow of the branches but Byron wasn't looking. He neither smiled nor waved to acknowledge the good wishes. He was staring straight ahead, looking neither to the right nor left.

'Well, he dun't look very happy,' Sam muttered.

'Poor feller looks as if he's going to an execution,' Nathan said and his mother added, 'Maybe that's what it feels like. It's an arranged marriage, when all's said and done. You can't deny that.'

'You'd have thought a handsome young chap like him would be spoiled for choice,' Nathan went on, 'that he'd have all the girls in the county trying to catch his eye.'

'He never went out much, though, did he?' Nell said. 'His father kept him on a tight leash.'

'Didn't want him mixing with the wrong company, I should think,' Sam added and, though the day was warm, Rosie shivered as she remembered every word of his letter to her.

'The bride! The bride – she's coming,' the cry went up as an open-topped carriage bearing the bride and her father came down the track.

'Oh, isn't she pretty?'

'She'll make a lovely wife for him and future mistress of the manor.'

The remarks flew around Rosie's head. She felt Nathan come to stand beside her.

'You all right, Rosie?' he whispered.

Not trusting herself to speak, she nodded.

They watched as the final carriage drew up outside the church gate and the bride alighted.

'What a beautiful dress,' cooed the women as Pearl walked into the church on her father's arm.

Those standing near the church could hear the music but not the words of the service spoken in hushed, reverent tones.

Nathan glanced down at Rosie's white, strained face. He cleared his throat and tried to sound jovial as he said, 'Well, I don't know about you lot, but I've had enough of this. I'm ready for me dinner.'

'Stew's on the hob,' Nell murmured. 'I'll just see 'em come out . . .'

'Right you are, Mam. You coming, Rosie?'

'Yes, yes. I'll come back with you.'

Together they turned and walked back towards Nell's cottage.

The wedding party emerged from the church about half an hour later. They stood for several minutes while a photographer performed with a box-like contraption on a spindly tripod and then the carriages returned to the manor, with the bride and groom's now leading the way. Pearl waved gaily to the villagers, smiling and bowing her head in acknowledgement. Byron did not wave, but this time, he looked about him, his gaze searching the faces of those standing alongside the track. Then he glanced at the happy face of his pretty bride and felt a stab of guilt.

He shouldn't be searching the crowd for the face of the girl he loved when he was sitting beside the woman who was now his wife.

Seven

'Your mam makes the best rabbit stew I've ever tasted,' Rosie said, forcing a brightness she wasn't feeling as she ladled a generous helping onto Nathan's plate. 'What's her secret?'

Nathan chuckled. 'I really have no idea. You'll have to ask her. I'm sure she'd share it with you. You're like a daughter to her.'

'And she's the mam I never had. And you're like a brother.'

As they sat down, Nathan reached across the table and took her hand. 'You're right, Rosie. What we have between us is a brother and sister affection, isn't it? I love you dearly but it's not the sort that one should feel for the person they want to marry. Do you know what I mean?'

'I know exactly what you mean because I feel the same way about you.'

They smiled at each other, a new understanding bringing them even closer together.

'But – there is someone you love in that way, isn't there?'

Rosie dropped her head and whispered, 'Oh Nathan, don't ask me. Please don't ask me.'

He gave her hand a quick squeeze and then let it

go. 'All right. But just know that if you ever want to talk about it – or anything else, if it comes to that – I'm always here for you. I will *always* be here for you and all your secrets are safe with me.'

Rosie nodded but could not speak for the lump in her throat. If only, she thought, she and Nathan could love each other like that, what a perfect match they would be. But she was glad that he felt the same way as she did. It would have been disastrous if he'd wanted to marry her and she'd refused him. It would have spoiled a beautiful friendship and also, more than likely, damaged the closeness between Sam and Nell.

They ate in companionable silence until Nell and Sam came in through the back door.

'I hope you two haven't eaten all the stew. Me and Sam are starving.'

Rosie laughed as she got up to serve them. 'I think we could have done, Aunty Nell. I don't know how you make it, but it's lovely. Will you share your secret with me?'

Nell was thoughtful for a moment then said slowly, 'Aye, I will one day, lass. I promise. But not yet, eh? It was my granny's recipe and she didn't like anyone outside the family knowing it.'

Nathan laughed. 'Well, Rosie's the closest you'll ever come to having a daughter, Mam.' And before either Nell or Sam could get the wrong idea, he added, 'And me a sister.'

They all laughed and spent the rest of the afternoon together until Sam got up and said, 'Come on, Rosie. It's a good night. Time we were in the woods. They're all busy celebrating up at the manor, so I don't reckon old Amos will stir far tonight. I reckon I dare risk taking me gun with me. They say there's to be fireworks after dark. No one will take any notice of an extra bang or two if I time it right.'

'Do be careful, Sam,' Nell warned.

The June night was warm but, being almost midsummer, they had to wait until it was almost dark for them to venture out.

'Rabbits run at twilight and daybreak,' Sam reminded her. 'We'll set the snares and Queenie will chase them towards them. I reckon I saw a roe deer the other night. Now, if I could catch it, we'd be fed for weeks. They're the tastiest venison you can get. Best time for that is just after sunset.'

As the light faded, they set out. Beneath the trees it was even darker. They caught several rabbits with Queenie's help. And then they crept through the woods to the place where Sam had spotted a deer a couple of days earlier. Rosie clutched his arm and whispered, 'There he is. My, he's a fine buck. It's a shame to kill him.'

'Don't start going soft on me, lass,' Sam chuckled softly. 'Just think of all that fine meat Nell will show you how to cook.'

'We'd be best to wait a little longer until the fireworks start.'

'You're right, but we might lose him.'

'Better that than getting caught,' Rosie said tartly.

They waited ten minutes until, in the distance, they heard the sound of fireworks bursting with bright-coloured lights into the night sky. As the buck raised his head, startled by the noise, Sam raised his gun and fired. The animal dropped to the ground with a thud and did not move again. Sam and Rosie did not move either for several minutes until they were sure no one else was about. It was a heavy beast to carry home, but they managed it between them with Queenie running excitedly beside them.

'I can't remember you ever killing a deer before. Do you know how to cut it up?' Rosie asked, as they stood looking down at the animal. In the darkness of Sam's shed in the back garden, it looked even bigger and the task even more daunting than when they had carried it home.

'Little Titch taught me years ago. I think I can remember. Nell will tell you how to cook it.'

'Should we really be involving Aunty Nell? Ivy Bates, next door to her, is the biggest gossip in the village and if she were to find out . . .'

'Then Nell can come here and show you what to do. We'll leave it for tonight, but tomorrow I want you to watch how I butcher it. You need to learn that too.'

Rosie felt a quiver of apprehension and guilt. Deep down, though she could never admit it to her father, she hated killing anything and the thought of butchering this lovely creature lying at her feet sickened her. But, she comforted herself, they only killed for food for themselves and others. They did not kill for sport like William Ramsey and his cronies.

Byron's and Pearl's honeymoon was in the south of France, courtesy of her generous father. They were away for a month, at the end of which they returned home to take up residence in the rooms which Grace had set apart for their use.

'Welcome home, my dears,' she greeted them, holding out both her hands. Then she linked her arm through her daughter-in-law's and led her into the morning room. 'I haven't presumed to furnish your rooms for you. I thought you and I could have great fun selecting whatever furniture and decorations you would like. We'll take a trip into Lincoln and—'

'I would prefer my mother's advice. She has such excellent taste.' Pearl glanced around the morning room and Grace was sure that the corners of the girl's mouth turned down as if she disapproved of what she was seeing. Grace was shocked. The girl was bordering on rudeness; she was certainly being ungracious. Suddenly, she was nothing like the acquiescent and polite girl she had seemed to be during Byron's courtship of her. How had everything changed so swiftly? Had something dreadful happened on the honeymoon? As Pearl spoke, she moved away, breaking Grace's affectionate gesture. Swallowing the hurt of Pearl's rebuff and aware that Byron was listening to every word, Grace said, tactfully, 'Of course, I understand. Perhaps you would like your mother to come and stay for a few days?'

'That would be nice, but first I want to go home for a week. I'll be leaving in the morning.'

'But—' Grace began and then stopped. She glanced at Byron but his expression was stony, his jaw set in a hard line. He kissed his mother's cheek.

'I'm going to the stables. I'll see you at dinner.' He turned to his wife. 'I'll ask Monty' – he was referring to the young stable lad who was called upon to do all sorts of jobs – 'to come and help Baines carry the luggage up to our room for you and I'm sure my mother will find one of the maids to help you.'

'I thought Lucy could be your lady's maid,' Grace began. 'She's young but very willing and you could train her to your ways.'

'There's no need. I intend to bring my own lady's maid from home back with me. I expect you could find a room for her in the servants' quarters, though I wouldn't expect her to have to share. She's used to being on hand whenever I need her.'

Grace inclined her head. 'I'll see what I can do, though perhaps your maid should wait until all the rooms are ready before coming to Thornsby.'

Byron left the room without another word while Pearl feigned a yawn. 'I will lie down until I need to dress for dinner. Perhaps you would ask your man to bring up the trunks and Lucy to attend me for the time being?'

Without waiting for an answer Pearl left the room leaving Grace staring after her in stunned silence. 'My poor boy,' she whispered at last. 'What have we done to you?'

'Good morning, Brown,' Byron greeted the head groom. 'Could Monty saddle up my horse, please? And then could he go to the house and help Baines take our luggage upstairs? I'm afraid there's rather a lot. My wife enjoyed buying gifts for everyone.' Quietly, he added, 'Though most of them were for herself.'

'Of course, Master Byron. At once.'

Lucas Brown had worked for William for over twenty years. He lived above the stables. He had never married and his whole life was devoted to serving his master to the exclusion of any friendships either with any of the other staff or anyone in the village. His only recreation was to visit the pub in the village every Friday and Saturday night where he sat alone in a corner watching and listening to what was going on around him. Anything he thought his master should hear about was faithfully reported to William. Though no one else knew it – only William and Lucas – he had been the one to spy on Byron's and Rosie's meetings. Monty, the stable lad, who also had a room above the stables, was at his beck and call day and night. Lucas was a harsh taskmaster, taking the lead from his own master, but the boy who had come from the workhouse as a twelve-year-old knew no different. He was grateful to have a home, employment and a little bit of money in his pocket, even though his wage was meagre. Despite the harshness of his early life, however, Monty had learned the meaning of loyalty and responded to those who were kind to him. He worked hard, always following the orders of his immediate superior, Lucas Brown, and of his lord and master, William, but they did not earn his respect and affection. That he gave to Master Byron. As for the mistress, Grace, he secretly adored her and would willingly have laid down his life for her if it had been necessary. Although he had had little education, he had an innate common sense and intuition. As he helped his young master to mount, he knew that Byron wasn't happy. He stood watching him ride away.

'You've no time to stand idling, Brat,' Lucas shouted across the yard. 'There's work to be done. You're needed at the house.'

Monty turned towards Lucas, ignoring – as he always did – the cruel name Lucas had bestowed upon him when he had arrived two years earlier. At first it had been 'Workhouse Brat' but over time it had been shortened to just Brat. Smiling, Monty walked towards the man. Whatever Lucas Brown did, he would never break the lad's spirit. If life in the workhouse hadn't done that, nothing would.

Byron galloped up the gentle slope out of the vale where the manor nestled and towards the woods. He slowed his mount to a walk as he entered the cool shade of the trees. He paused a moment, listening, but there was no sound except the rustling of the leaves above him. He rode through the woods, his horse surefooted, until he came to the far edge of the trees overlooking the village. His glance took in the small houses and cottages clustered together around the village green and moved left to take in the Tranters' cottage on the outskirts and then further left to the lone cottage, standing about half a mile away from the other dwellings, where Sam and Rosie lived.

'Rosie, oh Rosie. Where are you? If only I could just catch sight of you.'

He rode a little closer until he was on the slope just above their cottage. But there was no movement below him, no sign of either Rosie or her father. The whole village seemed quiet; no doubt the menfolk were all at work in the fields and the womenfolk busy with their household chores. Reluctantly, he turned back to return the way he had come. Emerging from the woods again, he passed the place where they had met for the very last time, where Rosie had made a daisy chain. It was still safely pressed between the pages of his childhood copy of *Robinson Crusoe*. He rode down the slope and alongside the stream until it left the Thornsby estate. He recalled the happy hours he had spent with the young girl on its banks, laughing and talking. Nothing untoward had ever happened between them; they had just enjoyed each other's company. But now she would be a grown woman with a woman's body, her face still beautiful – but mature. He wondered if she had a young man courting her. Perhaps Nathan and she were now more than the good friends they had been through their childhood. He'd heard the rumours about Sam and Nell and wondered if they'd pushed their offspring together. No, not pushed. They wouldn't do that. Not like his father had pushed him into marriage. But no doubt they would have encouraged – yes, that was the word – a romance between Nathan and Rosie.

With a sigh, he turned towards the manor. He should seek out his father; he hadn't seen him since their arrival home. It was a meeting he dreaded. He didn't like lying to William, but he would have to do so. He would have to pretend that all was well in his marriage. But he knew he wouldn't be able to hide it from his mother; Grace would see through it all.

*

Rosie was in the washhouse at the back of the cottage, singing softly to herself. She glanced out of the small window and saw, a little way to the left, a movement at the top of the slope, near the trees. Moving closer to the window to peer through the grime, her heart seemed to skip a beat.

'Byron!' she breathed.

The door of the washhouse opened, making her jump. She leapt back from the window, feeling ridiculously guilty. 'Nathan. You made me jump.'

He stood in the doorway for a moment, before saying softly. 'Byron's back home. He's up there. Near the woods.'

She stared at him and then, realizing there was no need to lie to Nathan, she sighed, 'Yes, I saw him.'

'Do you – want to go and speak to him?'

She paused for a moment. The desire to go to him was overwhelming, but she glanced away from Nathan's gaze and shook her head. 'There would be no point. I haven't spoken to him for years. Not – not since you brought me that letter from him.'

He waited but she still didn't tell him what had been in the letter. Instead, she smiled and, turning her back on the window, plunged her hands into the soapy suds in the wash tub. 'One day some handsome young man will sweep me off my feet and if they don't' – she grinned saucily at him now – 'then I'll marry you.'

Nathan threw back his head and guffawed loudly. 'Well, I suppose we could both do worse.'

They laughed together, their easy friendship restored and both deliberately ignoring the still figure on horseback near the woods.

'Mam sent me to ask you and your dad to have supper with us tonight. She's made jugged hare.'

'We'll be there.'

'Right. See you later, then.'

After he'd gone, Rosie finished the washing, the rinsing and the mangling and carried the heavy basket out of the washhouse to hang the wet clothes on the line stretched across the backyard. She couldn't stop herself glancing towards the trees again, but Byron had gone.

Eight

'Byron! My dear boy, come in, come in,' William said jovially welcoming his son into his study. 'How are you? How was the honeymoon?'

'Fine, Father, on both counts, thank you.'

'It's good to have you home, though your mother tells me that Pearl wishes to go home to see her parents. It's only natural, I suppose, but I hope you won't stay away too long. I need to bring you up to date with all that's been happening on the estate while you've been away. You are aware, aren't you, that I want you to take over the reins by degrees so that by the time you are twenty-five you will be in sole charge.'

'Yes, Father, I do. But I won't be going with Pearl.'

William raised his eyebrows. 'I'm not sure I like the sound of that. Is everything all right between you?'

Byron sighed inwardly. Sometimes his father was far too astute. 'Of course it is, Father, but I think Pearl wants a little time with her mother.'

'Ah – ah, oh I see,' William mumbled. But he didn't see at all. He was appalled that the young couple wanted to be apart even for a day, let alone a week or more. 'Well, just make sure it's for no longer than a few days. I'll be blunt, Byron. You need to get her with child and you can't do that if you're miles apart.'

Byron winced but merely inclined his head.

Pearl was away for two weeks and when she returned, she brought her mother with her.

'I do hope you don't mind my coming, Grace,' Bella greeted her, holding out both her hands towards her hostess. 'But Pearl so wants me to be involved in choosing the furnishing for their rooms. I thought perhaps the three of us could have such fun shopping in Lincoln together.'

Bella had lectured her daughter, quite severely, on the need to keep on the right side of her in-laws, particularly her mother-in-law. 'You must involve her, Pearl. After all, they will be paying for everything and, although I'm sure they want you to be happy, you must remember that the house and all the lands are still theirs. Not yours. Not yet.'

'Mother,' Pearl had wailed, 'they could live for years.'

'Grace might well live for a long time yet, but when anything happens to William – and he is much older than her, don't forget – then Byron will be running things and *you* as his wife, will have the responsibility of all that that entails. Make a friend of his mother, my dear, not an enemy.'

'Of course not, Mrs Anderson,' Grace said now. 'I'm delighted to see you.' Her sentiment was genuine; she was hoping that the girl's mother might instil some common sense in her.

'Oh, do call me Bella, and may I call you Grace?'

Bella leaned closer, as if sharing a secret. 'I think you and I need to help the young ones settle in together, don't you? Marriage is a big step and I'm sure you will understand that Pearl is still only young and moving away from home is such a big wrench for her.' Artfully, Bella added, 'You must have felt something similar when you married Mr Ramsey.'

Grace thought back and remembered how lonely and isolated she had felt. She'd missed her parents, she'd missed the city. Byron's birth had been her salvation. She smiled at Bella.

'I did,' she confided. 'But after Byron was born, it all changed and hopefully it will for Pearl too.'

The trips to Lincoln over the following two weeks were a revelation to Grace. She marvelled at how Bella managed her self-centred daughter. The girl – an only child – had been spoiled, but with gentle suggestions and persuasion, Bella manipulated Pearl into her own way of thinking without the girl realizing what was happening. Grace watched – and learned. But she was not blind to the fact that the girl was strong-willed and occasionally defiant. Pearl was certainly not the quiet, biddable girl Grace had believed her to be. It was becoming quite obvious to her now that Pearl had been putting on a very clever act to ensnare Byron and to charm her future in-laws. Now, with a wedding ring safely on her finger, there was no further need for pretence. Her true colours were showing and, sadly, Grace did not like what she saw. Despite her disappointment in her daughter-in-law, Grace could not help liking her mother, Bella.

The decorators moved into the manor to paint and wallpaper the rooms which had been designated for Byron and Pearl. A drawing room and a small morning room for Pearl's use and a study for Byron on the ground floor on the west side of the house. A bedroom, bathroom and nursery on the first floor and rooms on the second floor to house whatever personal servants the young couple would need. It had been agreed that Pearl should be allowed to bring her own lady's maid from home. The girl would arrive when all the rooms were ready.

'If you find you need more space,' Grace said to both Pearl and Bella, 'we can soon make more rooms available for you. We have two dining rooms on the ground floor. The small one is used when it's just the family present and the larger one for formal occasions. You're welcome to use that any time, if you wish to entertain.'

'That's very kind of you, Grace. Isn't it, Pearl? Of course, I'm sure it won't be long,' Bella added coyly, 'before you'll need to engage a nanny. They might need a little more room then, Grace.'

Grace inclined her head. 'Of course.'

Bella had returned home after a month at the manor.

'I must go home,' she had said. 'I've left poor Henry for far too long to cope with matters on the estate on his own. And before we know it, Christmas will be looming. There's always so much to organize. I'm sure you understand that, Grace dear.'

Grace had smiled and said with genuine feeling, 'I shall miss you, Bella, but I do understand. I must start to make my own preparations too very soon. Perhaps Pearl would like to help me?'

'I'm sure she would,' Bella had replied, smiling. The two women had become good friends. They had a mutual interest in helping the young couple settle down together but besides that, they had found that they actually liked each other.

The day after Bella left, Jane, Pearl's lady's maid, arrived. Grace was greatly relieved to find that the young woman in her late twenties stood no nonsense from her young mistress and she got on well with all the staff at the manor, particularly Grace's own lady's maid, Sarah.

'She fits in with us all lovely, madam,' Sarah told her. 'She's very fond of Mrs Pearl, but she's not blind to her faults.'

Pearl seemed a great deal more settled now that she had her own maid with her. She even began to involve herself with the plans for Christmas.

'Would you like me to invite your parents to spend Christmas with us, Pearl?' Grace asked her. 'They'd be most welcome.'

'I'd love that, but I know my father wouldn't come because of his responsibilities on the estate. And it wouldn't be fair to ask Mother to come without him.'

'I quite understand. I think my husband would feel much the same.' Grace remembered the lonely Christmases in the early days of her marriage when William would not leave Thornsby.

They all spoiled Pearl over Christmas, buying her lavish gifts and allowing her to dictate how the days should be spent, eating, drinking and playing parlour games. The event that William insisted should still take place, as tradition at Thornsby Manor dictated, was the Boxing Day shoot. But even then, Pearl joined in with the wives of William's guests and appeared to enjoy the day, probably because she was the centre of attention and speculation. The time after the festivities was a little flat. Around the middle of January, there were heavy snowfalls, making travel difficult and the residents of Thornsby Manor felt even more cut off. Pearl was pale and listless and irritable. So much so, that one morning at the beginning of February her maid, Jane, sought a conversation with Grace in the privacy of her morning room.

'Madam, Mrs Pearl is being sick first thing in the morning.'

Grace's eyes widened. 'Oh, do you think . . . ?'

Jane nodded. 'I do, madam, and there are other signs too, if you know what I mean.'

'Oh, yes, of course. I understand. We must get the doctor to call. I'll ask Brown to tell Monty to take a message. Does Byron know?'

'I believe so, madam.'

When Grace told William, he jumped up from behind his desk. 'We must get the doctor straight away to advise us. She must have the very best care that money can buy.'

'I've already sent a message to Doctor Wren, but she says she wants to go home to be with her mother when she gives birth.'

William stared at his wife. 'Oh no, she can't do that. My grandson must be born here at Thornsby Manor. I won't hear of such a thing. If she wants her mother with her, then Bella must come here. She can come for as long as she likes, but the child must be born here.'

'I will write to Bella myself and suggest the idea. I will make the blue bedroom available and turn the bedroom next to it into a small sitting room for her. I have a feeling she might be here for some weeks.' Instead of being annoyed, Grace welcomed the idea of another prolonged visit from Bella. She left her husband's study to return to the morning room to make plans. *Thank goodness*, she thought, *that we have plenty of rooms*. On her arrival at the manor she had been appalled at the vastness of the house and how many servants it took to run it properly. Now, however, she was glad of its spaciousness. The expanding family could all live in harmony without getting in each other's way. There was only one thing that saddened her; she didn't see as much of Byron as she had done before his marriage. She saw him at dinner each evening, but that was the only time in the day, and in front of William and Pearl she did not feel able to talk freely. She didn't even see him at breakfast; indeed, she often ate alone at that time of the day. William and Byron ate early and were out and about around the estate and Pearl had taken to having her breakfast taken up to her on a tray, excusing herself on account of the morning sickness. Grace was sorry too that the bond she had hoped to develop with a daughter-in-law just wasn't happening. The girl only sought her out when she wanted to speak to her about something. Usually, it was a litany of complaints against the servants.

'They're not washing my clothes properly. One of my silk dresses is ruined.'

'The lunch which the maid brought up to me yesterday was just inedible. Oh, how I miss our cook from home.'

Occasionally, she even moaned about Byron. 'Where does he go to all day? I hardly see him.'

At last, almost in desperation, Grace said, 'Perhaps you would like your mother to come for a week or so.'

Suddenly, Pearl's face became the most animated Grace had seen it in recent weeks. 'Oh yes. I'll ask both of them to come for two weeks. I'm sure Papa will come too, if I ask him expressly.'

The visitors were much easier to deal with than their daughter and their presence lightened her mood.

Bella and Grace had already formed a strong bond of friendship and Pearl's father, Henry, enjoyed being shown around the Thornsby estate. Once a horse had been provided for his use from the stables, he was happy.

'I have a very reliable bailiff,' he told William. 'I don't mind being away for a week or two.'

'He's quite a knowledgeable man,' William confided in Grace. 'I must say I enjoy our discussions about running an estate. His isn't as big as ours, but he manages it well, I can tell. He has asked us to visit, Grace, and I would like to go.'

'Of course, my dear,' Grace said, obediently.

'Have you heard the news from the manor?' Nell asked as the four of them sat down to eat.

'About the baby, you mean?'

'Well, yes, that, but the latest gossip is that the master and the mistress have gone on a visit to Stamford. To Pearl's parents' home, leaving Byron in charge of running the estate.'

'Good practice for him, I suppose, but we'll have to watch oursens, Rosie lass,' Sam said. 'Master Byron might have ideas about getting a new gamekeeper. A younger feller. Even I have to admit that Amos is getting too old for the job. I'm surprised the master hasn't put him out to grass before now.'

'D'you think he'll let him keep his cottage?' Nell asked.

'Nah,' Sam said scathingly. 'Old Amos'll be for the workhouse.'

Nell was shocked. 'The master wouldn't do that to him, would he? Amos has worked for that family all his life.'

'William Ramsey is ruthless when it suits him, Nell. He would turn any of his tenants out without batting an eyelid if they crossed him. I'm surprised me and Rosie haven't been shown the door before now.'

'There's no one else who'd take on keeping the vermin down on the estate, Sam. You know that. You might do a bit of poaching, but he must be willing to ignore that if you keep the rats and the moles down. Even the rabbits and hares are pests to farmers. As long as you don't touch his game birds, he'll tolerate you.'

Sam chuckled. 'I think you're right there, Nell. Though I do take the odd pheasant or partridge now and then.'

Though life continued in much the same way for the villagers, it had changed considerably at the manor. Pearl no longer allowed Byron to sleep in the same bed or even in the same room.

'You don't want to harm the baby, do you?' she'd said, putting her hands against his chest and looking up at him with tears in her blue eyes. 'And Dr Wren says I'm not strong – that I ought to be very careful.'

'Of course not, Pearl. I quite understand.' Byron had kissed her gently and stroked her hair, feeling guilty because her request was actually a relief to him. He was thankful that her recent happier mood had resulted in pregnancy and that she was content for their love-making to cease, at least until after the child was born.

May the Good Lord grant me a son, Byron prayed fervently.

Nine

The weeks and months passed and Bella moved into the manor to stay for several weeks. Grace was delighted. She found it comforting to have another woman of her own age to chat to and to share confidences with. Bella's presence in the house made life easier for all of them, especially the hardworking servants, who had found themselves constantly at the beck and call of Byron's wife. And now they had a mutual interest in the arrival of a grandchild. Bella would join Grace for afternoon tea each day while Pearl rested. They shared, it seemed, an interest in cross stitch and spent the time when Pearl did not demand her mother's company, sitting companionably together with their embroidery.

Meanwhile, Byron had moved back into his old bedroom and while the servants raised their eyebrows, nothing was said. Even William accepted the news when told that it was for the sake of the health of the mother and baby and that the doctor had endorsed the decision.

'Just so long as she gives us a boy,' was all he had muttered.

Pearl grew larger and more petulant and demanding.

'She'll be better once the baby is born,' Bella tried to excuse her yet again. 'It's a difficult time for her and she is still very young.'

The Ramsey family demurred. They crossed their fingers and hoped. Byron rode out each day around the estate, but he never again went to the far side of the woods. If he were to see Rosie now, he couldn't trust himself not to go to her, to take her in his arms and declare his love for her. Nor did Rosie see him. Her hunting ground was with her father in the dead of night.

Early in September, when the doctor declared that Pearl's child would be born within two weeks, great preparations were made at the manor. A nurse was hired to stay with the expectant young mother until the birth and for a few weeks afterwards. A nanny moved into the rooms set aside as a nursery and a bedroom for her. And Bella was still there. The two grandmothers grew even closer as they decorated and furnished all the rooms in readiness. Pearl, weary with her increasing bulk, left everything to her mother, but Bella was wily enough to consult Grace on everything. Besides, she, perhaps even more than Grace, valued the other woman's friendship. Pearl's father visited often, but could not stay for weeks on end; he still had his own lands and employees to supervise, although he enjoyed visiting the manor for he and William shared interests in farming and wildlife.

It seemed that the parents of the young couple were on friendlier terms than the pair themselves.

Byron tried his best – and for the main part – succeeded in pandering to his wife's wishes. He sat with her when she demanded his company and disappeared when she wanted only her mother. Tellingly, she never asked for Grace to sit with her.

The pains began in the middle of the night and within minutes the whole household was aware that Pearl had gone into labour. Byron washed and dressed and went down to the breakfast room where the butler served him tea, cereal and toast, even though it was three o'clock in the morning.

'You shouldn't be doing this, Baines.'

'The servants are all up, Master Byron. This is an exciting day for all of us and we only want to serve you and the young mistress in any way we can.'

'That's very good of you. Of you all. I appreciate it.'

At that moment, William came into the room. 'Ah, there you are, Baines. Tell Brown to send young Monty to fetch the doctor. Dr McKenzie, that is.'

Byron stopped munching his toast. 'Dr McKenzie? From Louth?'

'That's right.'

'But what about Dr Wren? He's been attending Pearl.'

'He's a country bumpkin. I want the best for my grandson's birth. Wren can be present if he wishes, but McKenzie must take the lead. I have his word that he will come.'

'You've – you've already arranged it?'

'I have. Months ago. What are you waiting for, Baines? Go and find Brown.'

By four o'clock in the morning, everyone in the household was up and dressed and beginning their usual work, albeit over two hours earlier than normal. Breakfast was served and then the waiting began. The only placid person seemed to be the nurse who, until the doctor – or doctors – arrived, was in charge.

'Now, Mrs Ramsey, try to do the breathing exercises we have been practising and you, Mrs Anderson,' she addressed Bella, who was fluttering about the bedroom like a distressed butterfly, 'must calm yourself if you want to stay here. I must have a peaceful atmosphere for Mother,' she added, referring to Pearl.

'She's not to go,' Pearl cried. 'She must stay with me.'

Nurse Banton moved to the side of the bed. 'She can if she does exactly as I tell her.'

'She will – she will. Mother' – Pearl reached out – 'sit beside me. Hold my hand . . .'

Two hours later, both doctors arrived. They knew each other well and often acted as locum for one another, but they had never before been summoned to attend a patient together.

'Wren! Good to see you, but what are you doing here?'

Dr Wren, an elderly man who lived in the next village to Thornsby and who had served the locals for over thirty years, chuckled. 'I could ask the same of you, McKenzie, but I rather think I know the answer. The birth of this child is the most important thing to happen to William Ramsey since the arrival of his own son. To tell you the truth, I am rather relieved to have you here.'

'That's all right, then. I wouldn't want to interfere . . .'

'My dear fellow, you won't be doing so, I assure
you.'

As they mounted the stairs together, Dr Wren
confided, 'They've got Nurse Banton in attendance.'

'Ah good. I know her. She's a bit of a dragon, but
she knows her stuff. That's very good.' He smiled.
'No expense spared, then?'

'Absolutely not.'

They knocked on the door of the room and waited
until the nurse herself opened it. She blinked, taken
aback to see the two doctors, both of whom she
knew very well, standing there. She at once felt as if
her professional capabilities were being questioned
but she was astute enough not to let it show. Indeed,
if she thought about it, Dr Wren's competence was
also being doubted. So, Nurse Banton smiled a
welcome and bade them enter the room, just as Pearl
shrieked as another contraction overwhelmed her.

Nurse Banton hurried to the bedside. 'Breathe,
my dear, breathe like I've told you.' She turned back
to the doctors and swiftly explained to them the
stage that Pearl had reached.

'Why are there two doctors?' Pearl demanded as
the pain subsided temporarily. 'Is something wrong?
Have you sent for them, nurse?'

Dr McKenzie moved closer and said smoothly, 'No
cause for alarm, dear lady. Dr Wren and I are old
friends and colleagues.' He turned back to his associate
and gestured towards Pearl as if inviting Dr Wren to
step forward.

'No, no, McKenzie you do the honours. I'll just observe.'

Bella had the sense to sit quietly beside Pearl, who was still clutching her hand like a drowning woman.

'Just relax, dear lady. You're very tense.'

'Oh – oh,' Pearl began to wail as another contraction began.

Dr McKenzie glanced at Bella. 'You are her mother, I presume.'

'Yes, doctor.'

'Then continue to hold her hand, but please try to tell her to relax. You must not grip each other's hands.'

The four of them – Bella, Nurse Banton and the two doctors – worked together to help Pearl bring her child into the world.

By evening, the news had spread through the whole village.

'It's a boy!'

'The master will be thrilled. That's his little empire safe, then.'

'They say he's splashing the champagne around like there's no tomorrow and there's to be fireworks tonight on the village green for us all to celebrate.'

'What are they calling him?'

'William Albert. But he'll be known as Albert.'

'Or Bertie, more likely.'

'They're good names. William Albert Ramsey. Yes, it has a ring about it, but I hope it's not an ill omen for the little chap.'

'What d'you mean?'

'His initials spell WAR.'

Sam, who had no such superstitions, would celebrate the child's arrival in his own way. With fireworks and music and dancing on the green, there would be plenty of noise. He would be out with his gun. Even William Ramsey would not mind losing a few of his game birds on the night his grandson had been born.

'I expect you've heard then?' Nathan said gently to Rosie.

She managed to smile. 'Of course. I don't think there's a soul in the village who hasn't heard, especially when Mrs Bates gets going.'

Nathan pulled a face and then said softly, 'Are you all right?'

Rosie took in a deep breath. 'Yes, Nathan, I am, but thanks for asking. Dad and I are very close but this is something I can never talk to him about.'

'I'm always here for you, Rosie. You know that.'

She nodded. 'Yes, I do.'

He sighed. 'I suppose the main poaching season starts soon.'

Now Rosie grinned at him. 'Yes, it does.'

'Do be careful.'

'Dad's showing me how to use his gun.'

'Oh no! That's far too dangerous for a—'

Rosie wagged her forefinger in his face. 'Don't you dare say it. For a girl.'

Nathan smiled sheepishly. It had been exactly what he had been going to say. 'All right, but how's he going to teach you when shots can be heard miles off?'

'The shooting season's started and the master will be holding regular parties. Quite probably more than normal in celebration of his grandson's birth.' Rosie found she was able to speak of it now without her voice wobbling. 'We plan to go to the far end of the estate, well away from where they are, but a distant shot or two won't be noticed among all the others.'

Nathan still looked doubtful. 'But your father usually goes as a beater when there's a shoot, doesn't he?'

'Oh, he will be going,' Rosie said airily, 'once he's taught me to how to handle a gun.'

'Confident, aren't you?'

Rosie shrugged. 'What's so difficult? I've got excellent eyesight, a steady hand and I know to aim where they're going, not where they've been.'

Christmas was always a hard time for the villagers as there wasn't enough work on the land to employ all those who needed it. Sam and Rosie found themselves busier than ever providing food not only for themselves and the Tranters, but also for the poorer members of their community. Whenever the weather was right, they went out into the darkness of the night.

At the manor, William raged, 'My game birds are disappearing. It must be that wretched Sam Waterhouse and his girl. I've a good mind to evict them.'

Byron felt a stab of fear. He was careful not to let it show. Instead, he said mildly, 'Amos always says he does such a good job keeping the vermin down, that losing the odd game bird now and again is a small price to pay.'

William made a gesture of impatience. 'Taylor is an old dodderer now. It's high time I found a replacement. I've never been sure where his loyalties truly lie. I'll start putting some feelers out and by spring, I'll have a new gamekeeper.'

Byron shivered, feeling, as the saying went, as if someone had just walked over his grave.

Ten

In May 1914, as the farming world sprang into life once more and everything seemed to be running smoothly on his estate, William smiled at his wife across the breakfast table.

'My dear, I have a wonderful surprise for you,' Still, after over twenty-five years of marriage, he never tired of looking at her. Grace was still a beautiful woman even though she had just celebrated her forty-fifth birthday. She had smooth porcelain skin, blond hair without a hint of grey, and she dressed elegantly. She ran his household with a firm but fair hand and entertained his guests with charm. He owed her a lot. She had given him the son and heir he'd craved but he still felt guilty because he could not love her with the devotion he'd felt for his first wife, Florence. Theirs had been a true and passionate love affair. Her death at the age of twenty-eight had left him devastated and still without an heir. He'd had to marry again. There was no choice, for there was no one else he wanted to inherit his estate other than a child of his own. Even a daughter would have been better than nothing. But Grace had given him Byron; a fine, handsome son of whom they were both justifiably proud. It was their son who had held their marriage together. They were both sure he would never disappoint them, though there had been a worrying few months when they'd thought he was getting entangled with a girl from the village; a poacher's daughter, no less.

'Byron turned twenty-four last month,' William went on. 'And next year, I intend to make over the estate entirely to him. In the meantime, I want to give him full responsibility of running things to see how he shapes up.'

Grace regarded him steadily. 'That's hardly a surprise to me, William. It is no more than I expected, especially now he is safely married and has already given you a second heir.'

William's smile broadened. 'No, my dear, that is not my surprise. I thought you deserved a little treat. In two weeks' time we will be setting off on a world tour.'

Suddenly, Grace's face was more animated than he had seen in a long time.

'Oh William. How wonderful.'

'We shall be away for about six months, so, in the meantime, I am sure you will enjoy yourself buying a whole new wardrobe to suit all occasions.'

Grace crossed the space between them and kissed his cheek.

'Hello, Nathan.' Rosie smiled up at the young man who opened the door in answer to her knock. She held up two dead grey rabbits, their hind legs tied together. 'For your mam.'

'Come in.' He stood back, holding the door open for her to enter and then swiftly closing it. 'You really shouldn't be bringing those here in broad daylight.'

Rosie arched her eyebrows. 'Surely everyone around here knows what we do by now.'

'Not the new gamekeeper, though. If you were to bump into him . . .'

Now, Rosie's eyes widened. 'Is he here, then? We hadn't heard.'

'Oh aye. Mr Ramsey has given him Amos's cottage at the edge of the woods and I've heard he's due to get married in a few months' time and then he'll be bringing his new wife here and settling in.'

'What about Amos? What's going to happen to him?'

'I've heard he's staying at the pub at the moment, helping out to earn his keep. But it's heavy work for him at his age. Long term' – he shrugged – 'I've no idea.'

'I don't think Dad's heard about the new game-keeper,' Rosie murmured. 'He's never said anything.'

'Then you should tell him. And you'd better both be careful.'

He touched her arm and his voice was husky. 'I – I wouldn't want anything bad to happen to you, Rosie. Or your dad.'

'We'll watch him for a while. See what his routine is.'

'He might not stick to a routine. Mebbe he'll go out all times of the day and night. Especially if he's looking for poachers.'

Rosie chuckled. 'A young married man won't want to be out at nights looking for the likes of me an' my dad.'

Nathan smiled, though the worry didn't quite leave his eyes. 'Just be careful, Rosie, that's all.'

*

Sam and Rosie stood at the edge of the woods, careful to stay within the shelter of the trees in broad daylight.

'So, the new gamekeeper's moved into Amos's cottage, has he?' Sam pointed at the thatched dwelling a few hundred yards away.

'That's what Nathan said. Mr Ramsey arranged it all before he and Mrs Ramsey went on their long holiday. The gamekeeper's cottage is a bit too close to the woods for my liking. It was all right when Amos was there, but this one'll likely have a dog penned in the backyard. It'll only have to get wind of us and start barking and out he'll come.'

'Aye, lass. We'll have to be even more careful than usual. Come on, we'd better go home.'

'I just wanted to see him. Get a look at him. See what we're up against.'

Sam sighed heavily. 'Times have changed, lass. It's not going to be the same anymore.'

Just as they were about to turn and melt away among the trees, they saw a figure emerge from the cottage.

'That must be him,' Rosie whispered.

'It is.'

'How d'you know?'

'He was in the village pub last night. Landlord introduced him to us all.'

Rosie stared at him. 'Did – did he find out who you are?'

Sam laughed. 'No, lass. Villagers won't give us away.'

'No, I don't suppose they will. Not deliberately. But he'll find out somehow. What's he like?'

'Tall, fair-haired. Mid-twenties. Young for a game-keeper, I'd say.'

'Where's he from?'

'Dunno. But I dun't reckon he's from Lincolnshire. Someone said they thought he'd got a Norfolk accent. Now, come on, we'd best be getting home.'

Rosie stood for a few moments, her gaze still on the figure in the distance. She would have liked a closer look at the man who could have a huge effect on their lives.

'So have you heard from your mother and father?' Pearl asked Byron as she sat down at the breakfast table opposite her husband.

Out of politeness, Byron folded the newspaper he had been reading and laid it aside. 'Yes, they sound as though they are having a wonderful time. They're in Italy at the moment and hope to go into Germany soon.' It was unusual for Pearl to join him at break-fast; she didn't usually rise until halfway through the morning, but he made no comment. He was, however, about to find out the reason for her early rising.

'I shall be leaving today to go home for a couple of weeks. I'll be taking the baby and Nanny with me. My mother is longing to see him again. He's growing so fast and altering so quickly.'

'Are you sure you're well enough to travel?' Byron tried hard to keep the sarcasm from his tone. Marital relations had ceased soon after Pearl had found she was pregnant and they had not slept in the same room since then, even though it was now eight months since she had given birth.

'I felt as if I was being torn asunder,' she had explained soon after the birth. 'I couldn't possibly go through that again. You have your heir, Byron. Please don't demand any more of me.'

Strangely, for a virile, recently married young man, the fact that his wife's bed was denied him didn't bother him unduly. There was only one woman he desired to take into his arms and make love to, but he would never treat Rosie in that way. He loved her too much to make use of her. So all he said now was, 'Please don't stay away too long.' He did not explain that it was his son he would miss far more than his wife.

Pearl smiled at him. 'I won't, Byron. I promise. I'll just stay until the end of June.'

Pearl kept her promise and arrived back at the manor on the same day that the news broke that Archduke Franz Ferdinand, the heir to the Austro-Hungarian throne, and his wife had been assassinated in Sarajevo. As they sat down to dinner that same evening, Byron said, 'I'm worried for my parents' safety.'

'Are you? Why? They're not planning to go anywhere near there, are they?'

'No, but peace in Europe has only been maintained because of several alliances between the different countries. This could upset the balance completely. It could escalate into war.'

Pearl's eyes widened. 'But it wouldn't involve us, would it? This country, I mean.'

'It might, but all I'm concerned about at the moment is getting my mother and father home safely.'

*

101

'Hello, Nathan. Do come in.'

'Is your dad in?'

Rosie blinked. 'Is something wrong? You look worried.'

Nathan stepped across the threshold. 'I am a bit, Rosie, to tell you the truth. Mam's heard rumours in the village so I thought I'd better come and have a chat with your dad.'

'Come in. He's sitting in front of the range.'

'Hello, lad,' Sam greeted. 'Sit yarsen down. Rosie, find Nathan a glass of our blackberry wine. Is your mam all right?'

'Yes, she's fine. A bit – a bit – well, worried, like.'

'What about? Anything I can do to help?'

Nathan sighed. 'Folks are saying there's going to be a war in Europe and that we might get dragged into it.'

Rosie stared first at one and then the other, fear in her eyes but she said nothing.

Sam sighed. 'Aye, there was talk about it in the pub last night. In fact, the talk was about nowt else. It's all because of the assassination of this archduke.'

'Why? Why did someone kill him and what's it got to do with us anyway?' Rosie spoke at last.

'It's all very complicated, lass. It's all to do with alliances between countries. If one country is threatened, then others are either on their side or on the side of the aggressor and then things can escalate into a war.'

Rosie blinked. She had never taken much interest in international politics. People in her position had enough to worry about in their own little corner of the world. But she was sharp and intelligent when things were explained to her and she knew that Nathan always read the newspapers. So, now she looked to him.

'So has someone threatened someone and whose side are we on?'

Nathan ran his fingers through his hair and then accepted the glass of wine Rosie handed to him. 'I got talking to the local school teacher last night in the pub. He always comes in on a Friday night for just one pint. He's a very knowledgeable man. I only wished I'd listened to him more when I was at school. Anyway, he was telling me that at the present time an alliance exists between Austria-Hungary and Germany and there's a completely different one between Russia and Serbia.'

'So, it's nothing to do with us?'

'Not at the moment, but because the assassination was carried out by a Bosnian Serb nationalist, it seems that Austria believe that Serbia was behind the plot to kill the archduke and if that's proved to be the case, then—'

'Then Austria will retaliate against Serbia.'

Nathan nodded.

'So how could we possibly become involved?'

'Because Russia also has an alliance with France, so they could get pulled into a war and we . . .' He paused briefly before adding heavily, 'have an alliance with France, and Belgium too, as it happens.'

Rosie thought quickly. 'So, if France goes to war, then we have to. Is that right?'

Sam and Nathan exchanged a solemn glance.

'That's what it looks like.'

She glanced between them again, her mind working furiously. 'And your mam's worried because you might have to go. Is that it?'

Before Nathan could answer, Sam said, 'Oh, I don't think that will happen. You work on the land, Nathan. The nation still needs to be fed.'

'We don't know that, though, do we, Mr Waterhouse? Besides, I would never want to be thought a shirker.'

'I doubt anyone would ever think that of you, Nathan.'

There was silence between the three of them until Sam said softly, 'You know I wouldn't mind volunteering if war does come. I always fancied being a soldier and I'm not too old at thirty-eight.'

Not really listening to her father's musings, Rosie said, 'I wonder if it will cause Mr and Mrs Ramsey to return home sooner than they would have liked.'

Eleven

Later that night, Sam and Rosie crept out into the dark night. It was a perfect night for poaching. After several days of summer storms, the weather was still unsettled.

'There's still a rumble of distant thunder. I'll take me gun tonight, but we'll have to be extra careful,' Sam said before they set out. 'The new keeper might be about. Keep Queenie close to us. She'll give us a sign if she hears anything. Her hearing is much sharper than ours.'

'What's the new gamekeeper's name? Have you heard?'

'Wilfred Darby. That's what he introduced himself as when he came into the pub that night. Now, a' you ready? Time we was off.'

The summer was not the best time of year for poaching, but there were still rabbits and hares to be had and a few birds. Sam set a few snares on rabbit runs and they moved further into the woods. Queenie ran ahead, even though Sam had tried to keep her close.

'Drat the dog,' Sam muttered. 'Here, girl, heel . . .'

Before the words had left his mouth, there was loud clang of something metal. Queenie's howl of pain echoed through the night as Sam and Rosie hurried forward.

'My God! The bastard's set a man trap,' Sam muttered. Poor Queenie was caught in the trap's vicious jaws, designed to catch a man by his leg. With a supreme effort, Sam managed to prise the trap open while Rosie picked up the dog. She was whimpering pitifully.

'Let's get home and see how bad she is,' Sam muttered. 'Here, I'll carry her. You bring my gun.'

'What about the snares?' While she was desperately worried about Queenie, who was more to them both than just their working dog, Rosie had to think about their own safety. If their snares were found . . .

'I'll come back for them,' Sam said. 'You stay with Queenie and see what you can do for her.'

But at home, in the light of the lamp, they saw that Queenie's injuries were too severe for the poor animal to have a chance of survival. They were both covered in her blood.

'Kindest thing I can do is put her out of pain,' Sam said, with a catch in his voice.

'I know,' Rosie whispered, the tears running down her face.

'You stay here, lass, while I do it.'

'No, Dad. I'm coming with you.'

They laid her on the ground in their back garden. They both stroked her in a last goodbye and then Sam raised his shotgun and fired. As he lowered the gun and looked down at the animal that had been his constant for companion for some years, he muttered, 'I'll have the bastard for this. He's no right to set a man trap. They've been illegal for years.'

'I know,' Rosie said softly, 'but you can't do anything. You can't report him, else you'll put yourself in danger. You know you will.'

Sam grunted but did not reply. Instead, he said, 'When I come back, I'll dig a hole near the back fence under the willow tree and we'll bury her together.'

'Dad, do be careful. That shot might have fetched Darby out.'

Sam turned away towards the woods, disappearing into the darkness. Anger burned in him, but he was sensible enough to know that what Rosie said was true. The gamekeeper might well have been alerted by the shot ringing through the night air.

Rosie sobbed as she waited. She was angry too, but she was also fearful; terrified now for her father's safety. And for their future. This new man meant business; he wasn't going to turn a blind eye to his master's game being poached. He was determined to stop them or to catch them, even if it meant using illegal means. He was going to be a ruthless enemy.

It seemed an age before Sam returned. Rosie ran to him and flung her arms around him. 'Oh, thank goodness.'

'All right, lass. I'm all right. Let's get these put away.' He was carrying four rabbits and his snares. They put everything in the shed at the end of their back garden and then went to the willow tree where Sam dug a hole. They both stood a moment looking down at poor Queenie before Sam laid her gently in the ground and shovelled the earth back on top of her. Back in the cottage, Rosie roused the fire and made a pot of tea. An extravagance that they both needed this night.

'Did you hear or see him?'

'Nah,' Sam said scathingly. 'He's safely tucked up in his bed leaving his sadistic weapon to do the job for him.'

'I was sure he'd hear your gun.'

'We were right to bring poor Queenie back here. If Darby's at home and asleep, the sound wouldn't have been loud enough to wake him on the other side of the woods.'

'But he'll know, won't he? When he sees the trap's been set off.'

Sam shrugged. 'Mebbe so, but what can he prove? If he reports it, then it will come out that he's been using illegal methods.'

'D'you think Mr Ramsey knows what he's doing?'

Sam made a dismissive noise in his throat. 'I wouldn't be at all surprised. The man is as unscrupulous as his new gamekeeper.'

Rosie said no more but to herself she thought, *Byron would not approve. I know he wouldn't.*

While the inhabitants of Thornsby village were shocked by the events in a faraway country, they were more concerned about the gossip in their own community. News of the man trap set by the new gamekeeper was soon being talked about.

'How they've got to know, I don't know,' Sam said. 'I've not said owt – not even to Nell. Have you?'

'No, Dad, I haven't. Maybe they heard the shot in the night and someone went to investigate the next day and found the trap.'

'Well, I hope they report him, that's all.'

'I doubt they will. They don't want to get on the wrong side of the master any more than we do. He rules their lives, considering he owns almost all their homes and employs them too. He still owns our home, an' all. He could turn us out any minute.'

Sam sighed. 'That's true.' He pondered for a moment and then, to her surprise, added, 'I don't reckon young master Byron would like it.'

'Perhaps someone could have a word with him. He's in charge while his father is away, isn't he?'

Gloomily, Sam shook his head. 'He was, but Mr and Mrs Ramsey are due back tomorrow. They've cut their holiday short because of the unrest on the continent now. More's the pity, because I think Master Byron might have listened.'

Ted Roughton, the enterprising landlord of the local pub, the Thornsby Arms, began to buy three copies of a daily newspaper, which he left on the bar for his customers to read. He was astute enough to know that the villagers would not waste their precious money on newspapers and yet the menfolk would certainly want to keep up with events. His clientele had almost doubled during the days and weeks after the incident in Sarajevo. Nathan was a regular visitor to the pub for his customary one pint and came home each evening with the latest information. Sam went occasionally to the pub himself, but usually waited eagerly at home to hear what Nathan had learned each day. One evening towards the end of July, his face was sober when he arrived home to find his mother, Sam and Rosie waiting for him.

'Austria has sent a humiliating ultimatum to Serbia for restitution for the events that happened in Sarajevo, demanding a reply within two days. Evidently, Germany's behind the suggestion but now Russia has come down on the side of the Serbians.'

'It's not sounding good,' Sam murmured. 'It's like a tinder box. Just one spark and . . .'

Two days later, Nathan reported that the Serbians had agreed to all but one of demands, but, at the same time, they were mustering their armed forces.

'But according to what the papers are saying, that's still not enough for Austria-Hungary's emperor, so he's ordered the mobilization of his own forces.'

'What about Russia?' Rosie asked, remembering that Nathan had said that country was Serbia's ally. 'Are they doing anything?'

'Partly mobilizing, evidently, and Germany has sent orders to its navy to be in readiness.'

'It'll escalate into an all-out war, if they're not careful,' Nell muttered. 'What is the British Government doing?' She didn't take part in a lot of the discussions and theories but she was just as anxious as any of them. More so, perhaps; if Britain became involved in a war, her son might be called up.

Nathan pulled a face. 'Not a lot on the surface, but I suspect there's a lot going on that doesn't get into the papers.'

The first shots were fired on 29 July when Austro-Hungarian warships on the Danube opened fire on Belgrade and Serbian artillery retaliated. Over the next few days, the four of them kept abreast of the news until on the Sunday evening, Sam said, 'I'm fed up with all this talk of war. Come on, Rosie, you an' me are going out tonight.'

'But it's Sunday, Dad. We don't reckon to go poaching on a Sunday.'

'That's why we're going, lass, and it's a bank holiday tomorrow. Darby won't be expecting us to be out tonight.'

Nell looked even more troubled. 'Oh, do be careful, Sam. He might have set more traps.'

'We will, Nell,' Sam promised as he gave her a peck on the cheek, while Nathan and Rosie exchanged a smile. Their parents' friendship was becoming more open now.

Sam laid his gun on the ground while he set a snare. Rosie eyed the weapon fearfully. Even though he'd taught her how to use it, she still didn't like it. She wished her father wouldn't bring the gun out at all, but since the arrival of the new gamekeeper, he seemed to carry it more often – and especially since the loss of their beloved Queenie. As she crouched by his side, she heard rustling in the undergrowth only a few yards from them. She laid a warning hand on her father's arm and they both stayed very still, straining to hear through the darkness. The sound, which they now both recognized as the footsteps of a man, came nearer. Sam gripped Rosie's arm, drawing her close to him so that he could whisper in her ear.

'Go,' he urged.

Ever since Sam had started taking his daughter out poaching with him, there was one thing he had instilled into her. 'If I tell you to go, Rosie, you obey me at once, without question. Do I have your word?'

'Of course, Dad,' Rosie had promised and now the moment had come. She didn't want to leave him, but she knew she had to obey. Sam had his reasons. She rose and crept silently away through the woods towards their own cottage. She was about halfway home when she heard a shot echo through the night air. She caught her breath and turned back at once, not taking care now to be stealthy. She pushed her way through brambles and bushes, not heeding the scratches.

'Dad. Oh Dad,' she sobbed.

Twelve

There was someone crashing through the under-growth towards her but she made no effort to hide herself; she didn't care if she was caught now. If her father had been injured or even killed . . . As the figure came close, she called out. 'Dad, oh Dad. You're safe. Oh, thank God.'

He gripped her arm so hard his fingers dug into her flesh. 'Dad—' she began but he cut her off. 'Here,' he said, thrusting the gun into her hands. 'Get rid of this. Throw it in the lake. Anything. Just get rid of it so it won't be found.'

'What's happened?'

'I've shot the gamekeeper. I reckon I've killed him. I'll have to leave, Rosie. They'll guess it was me and I'll hang. I've got to get away. But you stay here. They won't come for you, but just get rid of that. You've got a bit of time before someone comes looking for him.' He gripped her arm again and gave her a push. 'Go. Fling it in their lake. It's deep enough.'

Rosie's heartbeat was fast and her legs trembled. Had her father really killed the gamekeeper or was he just panicking? But she couldn't stay to find out. She had to do his bidding. But if she were found with the gun . . .

'I'll see you back at home.'

'No, you won't. I'll be gone.'

'Where are you going?'

'I don't know yet and it's best you don't either.'

'But—'

'No "buts", Rosie, lass.' He touched her cheek. 'Take care of yourself and – and don't think too badly of me. It was an accident. I swear to you it was an accident – whatever others might think.'

Before she could utter a word, he was gone, disappearing into the darkness, but moving more quietly now. Feeling the weight of the gun, Rosie shuddered. She stood for a moment listening until she could hear no further sounds other than the wind rustling the leaves above her and the sound of scurrying animals around her feet. But they were safe tonight, she thought. In fact, probably for several nights to come.

She set off in the opposite direction from where they had heard the sound of the gamekeeper moving towards them. She came out on the opposite side of the woods overlooking the slope down towards Thornsby Manor. The huge lake in front of the house glistened in the fitful moonlight. She paused again, listening intently. But if anyone was watching for any movement, they'd be keeping motionless until she showed herself. If she was caught with the gun . . .

Still hesitating, she laid the weapon under a bush and taking a deep breath stepped from beneath the trees. She stepped further and further out from the shadows until she was standing fully on the open ground. She walked a little further, but all around her was only silence. She turned, went back to retrieve the gun and then set off again towards the lake, running this time as fast as she could. Rabbits and hares feasting in cornfields scuttled away at the sound of her pounding feet. What a haul she and her dad could have had tonight. Reaching the edge of the lake, she took hold of the gun by the barrel and swung it round and round with all her might, releasing it to fly high over the water, pivoting as it went. When it was almost over the centre of the lake at its deepest point, it fell into the water with a splash, the ripples spreading out all the way to the banks. She stood listening again, but still no one came running. Then she turned and fled back towards the shelter of the trees, dodging between them until she came to the other side of the woods and her home was in view. She paused again, panting hard and listening. Then she approached her home cautiously. Were they waiting for her? But the cottage was in darkness. She crept forward and only breathed easily when she pushed open the door. Inside, she found a note on the table:

Sorry, lass. I've got to go. Take care of yourself.

So, her father was gone and she had no idea where. Would he ever dare to come back? Would she ever see him again? She went up the ladder to the space where she slept under the eaves. She undressed swiftly and got into bed, but sleep eluded her. She was trembling and wide awake with fear. Any moment, she expected a knock on the door, but no one came. She lay awake wondering and worrying what else might betray her father. She sat up suddenly as she remembered the cartridges and other paraphernalia belonging to the gun. She must get rid of it all. But how? And where? Would it be safe to drop them down the well in their back garden? But, if they suspected her father – as they surely must – they would most likely search there. They'd come and search the whole cottage. She couldn't bury them because they'd dig the garden over. They might even search the woods for a sign that earth had been disturbed recently. And the fields were no good. She couldn't dig a hole deep enough to avoid the constant ploughing. The big river – the River Trent that bordered the west of the county – perhaps . . . And then she remembered a day trip to the seaside – to Skegness with its long pier that stretched right out into the sea. That would do. It was a long way to walk, but she'd done it before. She and her father had walked there one bank holiday. She'd only been about ten but her determination to see the sea for the first time had kept her walking. Only on their way home had her father carried her the last few miles as she slept against his shoulder. And it was Bank Holiday Monday again tomorrow – or rather today now.

Rosie made up her mind. It was her only option. She dressed, packed a piece of bread and a hunk of fat bacon in a piece of cloth, then found everything she could think of that would give away the fact that her father had owned a gun. Packing it all into a sack, she set off once more as the first fingers of dawn crept across the fields. She avoided the woods but picked up the stream some distance from the manor. She knew that it flowed towards the sea.

She walked for several miles, keeping close to the water whenever she could, but she knew that at some point she must take to the road and turn to the south-east to get to Skegness. Walking along the road was easier than tramping through rough ground. One or two carts passed her, but going the opposite way. Then she heard the rattle of wheels behind her and stepped onto the grass verge out of the way. But the carrier's cart drew to a halt beside her.

'That looks like a heavy bundle, miss,' the carrier, sitting high on his seat, called. 'Can I give you a ride anywhere?'

Plastering a smile on her mouth, even though at this moment she didn't feel like smiling at all, Rosie said, 'That'd be grand. Thank you.' She climbed up beside him clutching her bundle as tightly as if it held the crown jewels.

'Where are you heading?' he asked as he flicked the reins and the horse plodded on.

'Skegness. I've a mind to see the sea.'

'Where're you from?'

'Louth,' she answered promptly, having decided not to give her true location.

'Mablethorpe would have been nearer, lass, if it's just the sea you want.'

'I want to see the pier at Skegness. My dad' – she almost choked on using his name – 'took me when I was little.'

'Aye, aye,' the man said. He must have heard the catch in her voice because he asked gently, 'Lost him, have you?'

Rosie hesitated and then said huskily, 'No, no. I was just thinking back to that time, that's all. We had such a lovely day.'

'Aye, remember the good times, lass.'

He took her right to the seafront and set her down near the clock tower. She climbed down and thanked him.

'Think nowt of it. I'll be going back to Louth tonight, if you want another lift.'

'I'd be very glad of it, thank you.'

'Be here about four o'clock, then, and I'll pick you up.'

The cart trundled away and Rosie looked about her. She walked down to the beach and looked out towards the sea. The tide seemed a long way out. She glanced to right and left and then saw the pier stretching out into the water.

She walked along the seafront until she came to the entrance. Keeping close to a family of four when they entered the pier, as if she were one of their party, she hoped not to draw attention to herself and the bundle she carried. About halfway along, she dawdled, allowing the family to move ahead of her. Then she strolled along casually, watching the children playing on the beach below and listening to the cries of the seagulls wheeling and diving overhead. But she was fascinated too that through the loosely fitting boards of the walkway she could see the sea below. She walked right to the end until there was nothing to see but the stretch of the North Sea and the sky. She had to wait for almost an hour until there was no one else near her. She wasn't sure, either, how to judge if the tide was in or out or even which way it was going, but when she thought the water off the end of the pier looked deep enough, she flung

118

everything she had brought in different directions, glancing round every so often to make sure no one was watching her. But they were all intent on enjoying their own day. When she'd got rid of everything, she walked back along the pier. There was still some time before she was due to meet the carrier again so she wandered up and down the main street, marvelling at all the goods in the shop windows; the pretty dresses and shoes, the food – some of which she'd never seen before. She smiled to see a row of rabbits hanging in a butcher's and wondered who kept his shop supplied. She sniffed the air outside a baker's and felt suddenly hungry. Then she wandered along the seafront and watched all the holidaymakers enjoying the freedom of a day's holiday.

She was waiting near the clock tower at the appointed time when the carrier drew up and she climbed up to sit beside him.

'I'm surprised you're working on a bank holiday,' she said as they rattled along the seafront and took the road out of Skegness.

'Well, when you run your own business, so to speak, you have to work any day and every day. What do you do, lass, if you don't mind me asking?'

Rosie smiled inwardly. She did mind, in a way, for there was no way she could tell him the truth. But she had decided long ago what she would say if she was ever asked.

'I keep house for my father. My mother died when I was two.'

'I'm really sorry to hear that. Hard for you growing up without a mam. Is your father good to you?'

119

Tears prickled Rosie's eyelids but she managed to keep her voice steady. 'He's a wonderful father,' she said. 'We get along very well together.'

'That's good.'

There was silence between them until the carrier suddenly said, 'Do you read the newspapers?'

Rosie was startled by his unexpected question, but she decided to be careful how she answered. 'No – not very often. Why?'

'Because it looks as if there's a war coming and I just wondered if your dad was still of an age to be called up.'

'I – I don't know.'

'What does he do?'

Promptly, Rosie said, 'He works on the land.'

'Ah, that's good, then.'

Rosie could not stop herself asking, 'Why?'

'Because I don't reckon they'll call up agricultural workers. They're too valuable, see. For feeding the nation.'

On a normal day, Rosie would have been smothering her giggles, but today, laughter did not come easily. Oh, her father fed folk all right, but not in the way this man was thinking. But his words had given her an idea; a way she might explain her father's absence from home when the police came asking. As they surely would.

As they neared Ulceby crossroads, Rosie said, 'I'll get off here. I have an aunt who lives in Alford and I'd like to take the chance to see her now I'm this close.'

'If you're sure lass. You'd be late getting back to Louth.'

'I'll probably stay the night.'

'Won't your dad worry where you are?'

'No,' she lied again. Wasn't it always the case? If you told one lie, more had to follow to keep up the pretence. 'I told him I might call to see her. He won't be worrying.'

No doubt he would be thinking about her, but she was far more worried about him than he needed to be about her. The carrier pulled to a halt. She thanked him for his kindness and climbed down, standing to wave to him as he trundled away. Then she set off down the hill towards the market town of Alford, but at about the halfway point she turned to the right towards the village where she lived. It was very late by the time she arrived at the cottage and she paused some distance away to see if there was any sign of activity. All was in darkness, but were they waiting for her? Would a burly policeman jump out at her as she approached? All was silent, though she didn't breathe easily until she was inside and had locked the door. Although it was dark now, she checked through the cottage for anything incriminating. There were only two rabbits hanging in the larder and no sign of pheasants or their feathers. Everyone knew that her father snared rabbits; that was hardly a secret and no one could prove whether he caught them on the estate's lands or not. Not unless they came upon him in the act. She checked the shed in the back garden where he kept his poaching tools. She bit her lip. Should she try to get rid of anything else? She decided against it, hoping she would be able find reasonable answers to their questions. To move everything now would look as if she had something to hide. With a sigh, she closed the door of the shed and went back inside the cottage. Even though she had not eaten much that day, she was still not hungry, so she drank two tumblers of water and then climbed the ladder to her bed. She had not expected to sleep, but the weariness of the day claimed her and she slept deeply until the early morning. She awoke slowly and then the memory hit her. She felt sick to the pit of her stomach but she knew she must get up, dress and try to carry on as normally as possible. Tuesday passed by without her seeing anyone. She stayed inside the cottage deliberately, but no one came and she began to hope that her father had been mistaken. The gun had gone off, and, in a panic, he'd thought he'd killed the gamekeeper, but perhaps he hadn't after all . . .

Just when she had begun to hope that everything might be well, a knock came on the back door the following morning. Her heart began to hammer painfully as she went to open it and her legs were trembling. It was not the local policeman but Nathan who stood there. She stared at him. She could see he was very worried.

'Is yar dad in?'

Rosie took a deep breath. This was where the questions started. For the last two days and three sleepless nights she had pondered the questions that might be asked, but still she had not come up with any plausible answers apart from one which the carrier had unwittingly given her. But that depended . . .

'Have you heard the news?'

Rosie held on to the doorframe, her legs feeling as if they were going to give way. 'What – what news?'

'Well, there's two bits of news, really. The first is that Britain's ultimatum to Germany that they should withdraw their troops from Belgium was due to expire at eleven o'clock last night. We haven't heard officially yet, of course. We won't know till the papers get here, but it seems likely that we are now at war with Germany. The other news is' – he took a deep breath – 'even more important to us in a way. The new gamekeeper was found dead in the woods early this morning.'

Rosie gripped the wooden doorframe until her knuckles showed white.

'He'd been shot,' Nathan said bluntly. 'So, Rosie, where's yar dad? Because if I know our local copper, he'll be round to see him afore very long, I reckon.'

'He's gone,' she whispered. Now that her worst fears had been confirmed, she had no hope left that her father had made a mistake.

Nathan's frown deepened. 'Gone? Gone where?'

'He's gone to volunteer. I know it. He's been saying it ever since war was likely.'

But Nathan still looked sceptical.

'Look, I'll show you.'

She left the door standing open and moved back into the kitchen. The note her father had left was still lying on the table. She pointed at it. 'See.'

Nathan picked it up, read it and then dropped it back on the table.

'Where's his gun, Rosie?'

'Gun? What gun?'

'Aw, now don't lie to me, Rosie. Not to *me*. You told me not long ago that your dad was going to teach you how to use a gun. It worried me then, but it worries me even more now. We need to get rid of it before PC Foster comes calling, as he surely will.'

'Nathan, there's no gun here.'

He stared at her for a long moment before asking quietly, 'Has he taken it with him?'

'I don't know what he's taken with him.' This at least was the truth, though there was food missing from the larder and some of his clothes had gone.

Nathan took her hand and looked into her eyes. 'Rosie, whatever's happened I'm on your side. I'll *always* be on your side and I'll help you in any way I can. Now, we ought to have a look around before the police come, because when they do, they'll likely ransack the place looking for evidence.'

'You – you mean they'll think it was Dad?'

Nathan sighed. 'Of course they will. He's the local poacher. Everyone knows that. And if I know this village, the rumours will be rife, especially' – he added ominously – 'after Darby killed your dog. Well, as good as. Even PC Foster will think that. So, I'm sorry, but they'll come for him. And they'll likely question you, an' all.'

Rosie felt the bile rise in her throat. Now, it was all too real.

'You'd better get your story ready.'

Rosie said nothing. The less Nathan knew, the better. It wasn't that she didn't trust him. She did, but she didn't want him to be put in the awful position of lying to the police on her behalf. She'd have plenty of that to do for herself.

Thirteen

'They've found Darby's body in the woods,' William said over lunch that same day. When the unrest in Europe had escalated, William had decided that they should return home. They had arrived back at Thornsby Manor during the week before Britain had declared war. 'He'd been shot and I have a shrewd idea who might be the guilty party.'

'Really, Father?'

'Waterhouse. He's well known around here for being a poacher. Or maybe even his daughter.' He cast a sly glance at his son, but Byron managed to keep his expression impassive. 'I understand he's been teaching her his nefarious trade.'

It was Pearl who gave a dramatic shudder and said, 'Oh, how barbaric. Teaching a girl to poach. Have they caught him?'

Byron said nothing. He was remembering the bright sunlit days sitting on the banks of the stream or in the shadows of the woods, alongside the flame-haired girl. He could still hear her laughter and see the mischief in her green eyes. He had only seen her from a distance since then, but he guessed she had grown into a lovely young woman by now. All the promise had been there.

'Not yet,' William was saying. 'But they will. I understand from Taylor that the police will be visiting Waterhouse's cottage today.'

Amos had stepped back into his previous role. It was as if he had never been away, but it was too late to help Sam.

Oh Rosie, Rosie, Byron was thinking. *Run away. Run and hide. Don't let them catch you. They'll hang you for sure.* How he wished he could play the part of the knight in shining armour. He would ride up to her door, sweep her onto his horse and gallop away, carrying her to safety. But Byron couldn't move. He had to stay the dutiful son, husband and father. How, in that moment of supreme danger for Rosie, did he berate himself for having been such a coward. If only he had stood up to his father three years ago, even if it had meant he would have been disowned.

He felt Pearl's touch on his arm. 'Darling, I think we should take little Bertie and go to stay with my mother and father for a while. I can't bear to think of such a criminal being on the loose around here. We're not safe.'

'You're perfectly safe, my dear,' William said smoothly before Byron could answer. 'I've no doubt the police will apprehend him.'

'But he could be anywhere. Hiding in the woods or – or . . .' She turned pleading blue eyes towards Byron. 'Byron, please take us home.'

They all noticed how Pearl still referred to her parents' house as 'home' but no one commented. Byron glanced at his father briefly, but then patted her hand. 'Very well, my dear. When can you be ready?'

'Oh Byron, *thank* you. We can leave early tomorrow morning. My maid can pack everything we'll need by then. She and Nanny will come with us, of course, so we'll need the carriage.' She rose from the table and hurried from the room. William and Byron rose too out of politeness but when Pearl had gone, they sank back into their chairs.

'You really shouldn't indulge her, Byron. I'm afraid your young wife has not turned out to be the woman I hoped she'd be. She has been spoiled and indulged all her life.' He glanced at his own wife sitting passively at the opposite end of the tale. 'Your choice of a wife for our son, my dear, was not what it might have been.'

Before Grace could answer, Byron said at once, 'Mother's not to blame, Father. She put three suitable young ladies before me and I had the choice. I had thought Pearl was shy and biddable. It seems we were all wrong, but we were not to know that at the time. She was, after all, very young and her character not fully formed. She is, I'm sorry to have to agree with you, like a spoiled child. As you rightly say, things have not turned out the way we had all hoped. And I feel sure they haven't for Pearl either, but at least she has given us a fine and healthy son and heir. And I must do my duty and take care of them both.'

He did not add, though he was thinking it, that if anyone was to blame it was him, for being weak in allowing himself to be railroaded into an unsuitable marriage. A marriage he certainly had not wanted. Byron knew he would regret his cowardly inaction for the rest of his life.

He stood up and, in so doing, for the first time in his life, Byron stood up to his father metaphorically also. 'I will allow Pearl and the child to go for a short stay with her mother. Bertie should see his other grandparents from time to time anyway. But I will make sure she understands that this is only a temporary arrangement until things are settled here. Her home – and her duty – is here at Thornsby Manor. I will do my best to make sure she understands that.'

William grunted reluctant approval. 'Just make sure that you don't promise her that she can stay away until the murderer is caught, because I fear the wretch is long gone from these parts. We may never catch him. But,' he added with a gleeful glint in his eyes, 'we will still have his accomplice.'

Byron shuddered inwardly but managed to keep his expression impassive.

The knock, which Rosie had been expecting, came just before tea time. With trembling hands, she opened it to see PC Foster standing there. The constable was a well-built middle-aged man who had known the Waterhouse family for many years. Through all that time he had expected to be called to arrest Sam but it had never happened. Until today.

He watched Rosie carefully. She was a fine-looking lass, the constable thought, but then reminded himself firmly that he was here on police business. A man – the new gamekeeper – had been found shot dead in the woods this morning and he was charged with investigating the death until, that was, senior police officers should arrive from Louth. Then, no doubt, he would be side-lined, but for the time being, he was in charge.

'Now then, Rosie, lass. Have you heard about the new gamekeeper being found shot dead?'

Rosie nodded. 'Yes. Nathan told me.'

'Is yar dad at home?'

Rosie kept her gaze direct and her voice firm, but she couldn't stop the trembling in her knees. Thank goodness they were hidden beneath her long skirt.

'No, Mr Foster. He isn't.'

The constable frowned. 'Do you know where he is?'

'No, but he's left a note.'

'Have you still got it?'

Again, Rosie nodded and opened the door wider, silently inviting the officer to step inside. 'It's on the table, just where I found it.'

Douglas Foster removed his helmet and stepped inside. He bent over the note on the kitchen table but did not touch it.

In the darkness of the previous night when sleep had eluded her, Rosie had practised her answer about her father's disappearance so that now the lie came out unhesitatingly. 'I'm sure he's gone to volunteer. He's been talking about joining up ever since the rumours of war began.'

Douglas blinked and the startled look on his face showed his disbelief. 'Volunteer? Whatever would he want to do that for? War's only just started. They reckon it'll all be over by Christmas anyway. Just a storm in a teacup. Besides, they say that agricultural workers' – Douglas allowed himself a sardonic smile when thinking of the man everyone knew to be the local poacher; although, to be fair, he did work on the land legitimately sometimes – 'probably won't have to go anyway.'

Rosie kept her expression impassive. What she said next was easier, for there was some truth in it. 'Dad often said he wished he'd been a soldier and especially when the Boer War happened, he used to tell me. But by then my mam had died and I was only small.'

'Aye, lass.' Douglas's tone was gentler now. 'I remember.' Then he cleared his throat and his tone was formal once more. 'Well, I'm sorry, Rosie, but your dad has to be the prime suspect.'

Rosie's heart hammered inside her chest. Now, it would not be out of place to look worried and nervous. 'A suspect? What for?'

Solemnly, Douglas explained, adding, 'Doctor Wren thinks the gamekeeper had been dead at least a couple of days by the time he was found. So, that'd make it sometime during Sunday night.' His tone hardened. 'Was your father out that night?'

Now came another deliberate lie and this was harder. 'No.'

'Think carefully, Rosie. A' you sure he wasn't?'

Rosie thought quickly. There was no use denying the fact that her father was a poacher; everyone knew it. 'But it was *Sunday*, Mr Foster.' Her face was a mask of innocence.

It was a known fact that some poachers never went poaching on the Sabbath, whatever the weather. It was not a tradition to which Sam Waterhouse adhered rigidly. He would go out when the conditions were right whatever the day – but Rosie was counting on the policeman not knowing that.

Douglas grunted. 'Where was he on Monday?'

'I don't know. I went out for the day to Skegness.'

Now he raised his eyebrows. 'On yar own?'

'Yes.'

'How did you get there?'

'I walked.'

'All that way?'

Rosie nodded.

'And when did you get back?'

'Late last night.' Another lie was necessary. She could not admit to having arrived home late on the Monday night. Luckily, no one – not even Nathan or Nell – had seen her on the Tuesday. She had deliberately remained indoors and no one had called.

'And was your father here then?'

'I don't know. I didn't see him. I went straight to bed. I was tired.'

'So, when did you find the note?'

'This morning.'

'So, you don't actually know exactly when your father left?'

Rosie shook her head.

There was silence between them until Douglas said, 'Look, Rosie, I'm sorry about this, but I have to do my job. I'll need to make a thorough search of the house, the garden and the shed. You do understand, don't you?'

'Of course.'

'And what am I likely to find?'

132

Now, she had to be honest. She sighed heavily. 'Snares, nets and a fish hook and mebbe some other bits and pieces.'

'No gun?'

Rosie forced a smile. 'No, Mr Foster. No gun. Far too noisy.'

He nodded and turned away to start his search. Pausing briefly, he pointed to the note on the table. 'And don't touch that. Leave it exactly where it is. My superiors will want to see everything.'

'Yes, Mr Foster,' Rosie said meekly.

While PC Foster rummaged his way through the cottage and the shed, Rosie sat near the range, twisting her fingers together nervously, trying to think whether she had missed removing something incriminating. Through the window she saw him prodding the earth in the vegetable patch. *He must think I've buried the gun*, she thought.

At last he came back into the cottage and sat opposite her across the hearth. 'Well, I can't find owt, lass, I have to admit, but you do realize that my superiors will want to carry out a thorough search, don't you? They'll likely send a team of men to go through everything with a fine-tooth comb, as they say.'

Rosie nodded again. 'Would you like a drink, Mr Foster?' She was surprised how steady her voice sounded and wondered if she ought to be showing a bit more concern. Perhaps being too calm was a giveaway in itself.

She stood up to go to the scullery but paused to look down into the policeman's face. 'He hasn't got a gun, Mr Foster.' This at least was the truth now. It was at the bottom of Byron's lake. She always thought of everything as belonging to Byron already. Not his father, not William Ramsey, but Byron. In her mind the manor, the lake, the stream and the estate, all were Byron's.

They sat together in front of the fireplace, but conversation was awkward and stilted. At last, PC Foster said, 'I'd best be going, but be prepared for another visit later. I'll try to come with them, but I might not be allowed. My superiors' – there was a hint of bitterness in his tone – 'have a habit of wanting to take all the limelight from a simple copper such as me.' He picked up his helmet from the table, glancing once more at the note. 'Anyway, lass, I hope all goes well. Let's hope they don't find owt, eh?'

'They won't, Mr Foster. There's nowt to find.'

Douglas Foster eyed her keenly and then nodded. 'Aye, well, lass, I hope you're right, because now he's gone off – for whatever reason – you're the one they'll be looking to. Someone shot that gamekeeper on Sunday night and, as far as I know, there's only you and your dad who are known poachers around here.'

A shudder of dread ran through her.

Fourteen

Britain had declared war on Germany at 11 p.m. on Tuesday, 4 August. On the Friday morning, Byron stood at the top of Steep Hill in Lincoln looking down over the city. To his left was the cathedral, to his right the castle. Slowly he turned to the left and walked towards the towering building. Inside it was gloomy, but peaceful. Oh how he needed peace; peace from the disaster his married life had become, peace from the turmoil in his heart and mind over Rosie. He had delivered his wife and son to her parents' home in Stamford the previous day, had stayed the night and was now travelling back and had called into the city as he returned home. He loved the cathedral and, if ever he'd needed some moments of solitude and tranquillity, it was now.

'They must stay here as long as necessary, until that dreadful man has been caught,' Pearl's mother had said. 'Are you sure you can't stay too, Byron? You're very welcome.'

Byron had shaken his head, pretending reluctance and citing his duties at home helping his father run the estate. But they all knew this was an excuse; William still held the reins firmly in his grasp despite his promise to hand everything over to his son.

Admittedly, he involved Byron much more now in the organization and running of the estate, but nothing had been put down on paper yet. William was still the legal owner and there was Jack Pickering, the estate bailiff, too, overseeing everything. The Thornsby estate did not, at the present time, need its heir.

He sat in a pew, but couldn't think how to form a prayer, though he badly needed to pray. He needed guidance because he didn't know what to do. He couldn't think how he could reach out to help Rosie without innocently making things worse for her. He was sure she hadn't actually shot the gamekeeper herself, but if she had been with her father that night, she could be considered an accessory. Now, Byron shivered in the coolness of the cathedral's cavernous interior. He wasn't aware of how long he had been sitting there, but at last he rose stiffly to his feet. Dropping a few coins into the offertory box, he went out into the bright light of the day and walked along the road to where Monty was waiting with the carriage. He was about to climb in when he saw a group of men walking together, laughing and joking. A little way behind them there was another group and beyond them yet more, all walking in the same direction.

'What's going on, Monty? Do you know?'

'It's been going on for over an hour, sir. There must have been a hundred men or more gone by me.'

'Why? Where are they all going?'

'I stopped one of 'em and asked him. The army barracks is along the road there, sir. They're going to make enquiries as to how they can volunteer. It's been in the newspaper today that the new Secretary for – for—' Monty hesitated.

'For War?' Byron offered helpfully.

'That's it, sir, yes. That he's calling for one hundred thousand volunteers to join the army. That's an awful lot of men, isn't it, Master Byron?'

'It is, Monty,' Byron murmured. He was silent for a long moment before saying, 'I know I've kept you waiting a long time already and I'm sorry, but would you mind waiting a little longer?'

'Of course not, sir, though could I ask a favour?'

'Do you need money to get something to eat?'

'No, no, sir. It's not that. It's just that when we get back, Mr Brown'll likely clip my ear for being away so long. Would you explain to him?'

'Of course I will. I'll try not to be too long,' he said, as he turned and began to follow the men all walking in the same direction.

At the same time that Byron was walking towards the barracks, a knock came at the door of Rosie's cottage. Douglas Foster stood there again, but this time he had a plain clothes officer with him.

'Rosie, lass. A team of detectives have come from Lincoln to investigate Darby's death. They're going to search your place again and you'll have to come to the police station in Alford for a formal interview. I've told them I've already questioned you and searched your cottage, but they want to do it for themselves. I'm sorry about this, lass.'

'Am I being – arrested?'

'Only if you don't co-operate,' the other man said sharply. He had fair hair and piercing blue eyes which, she was sure, never missed a thing. Dressed in a smart suit, his manner was superior and Rosie felt he looked down his nose at her. To him, she was nothing more than a country girl, who was known to be a poacher and might well be a murderess too.

'This is Detective Inspector Cowley,' Douglas Foster said. 'If you'll come with us, Rosie . . .'

As she left her home, four police officers moved into the cottage to begin their search.

Surprisingly, Rosie had never been inside the police station in the nearby town. Douglas Foster lived in the village and, if they needed his help or advice, all the villagers would traipse to his front door. He had always been a friendly, caring community policeman and this was the biggest case he had ever had to manage. In truth, he was quite relieved to be able to hand it over to his superiors, and yet, he was worried for Rosie. He looked upon the local inhabitants of Thornsby and its estate as his 'flock', in much the same way as he believed the vicar did.

Arriving at the police station in Alford, Rosie looked about her with interest. She was not in the least fazed or frightened. She would stick to her story – the same one she had told PC Foster. Much of it was the truth and the one or two lies were easy to remember. She had repeated the details to herself so many times now that she almost believed it was all true. Even so, as she sat in the cold, stark interview room with the detective and Douglas sitting on the opposite side of the table, she couldn't stop her heart beating faster; it felt as if there was a bird fluttering inside her chest.

'Now, Miss Waterhouse. Some of my questions will perhaps be the same as PC Foster has asked you, but I need to hear them for myself.'

'Of course,' Rosie answered as calmly as she could.

At first, he did just that; asking the same questions as Douglas had done. Now and again, however, he threw in an additional one but Rosie was ready for them.

'So you went to Skegness early on the morning of Bank Holiday Monday.'

Rosie nodded.

'Did you see your father that morning?'

'No, I went out *very* early. I didn't want to miss all the excitement and fun.'

'Did you look in on him?'

'No, I didn't want to disturb him.' She forced a cheeky grin. 'He might have tried to stop me going.'

Douglas smiled a little, but Chris Cowley remained stony-faced. 'You say you got back late on the Tuesday night? So, did you stay two days in Skegness?'

'No. I left late on Monday night' – she recalled that Douglas had only asked when she got back home, not how long she'd stayed at the seaside town – 'to walk home, but I got very tired. There was a barn in a field on the road coming out of Skegness with a hay loft.' She sighed expressively. This was a new lie she'd invented in the darkness of a sleepless night. 'I know I was trespassing, but I was so tired. I didn't do any harm.'

'So, then, you walked the rest of the way home on the Tuesday. Is that right?'

'Yes. I'd slept a long time so I was late getting back here and I went straight to bed.'

'Wouldn't your father have been worried about you being away for two days?'

Rosie hadn't thought she might be asked this. She hadn't practised an answer. For a moment, she was at a disadvantage. Then she smiled. 'I've always been allowed a lot of freedom. He knows I can look after myself.'

Again, the inspector repeated Douglas's questions about finding the note.

There were a few more questions which Rosie answered easily before she was taken to a cell to await their decision.

'What do you think, Douglas?' The two men had known each other for several years. They'd trained together, but while Douglas had happily remained a 'country copper', Chris Cowley had risen through the ranks.

'You know these people better than I do. Is it true her father is a poacher?'

'Yes, it is, but he's not a killer. Not of people anyway.'

'Did he have a gun?'

'He may have done, but not that I know. They're noisy things for a poacher in a small community like ours. Using one might well have brought the game-keeper running.'

'You searched the house on Wednesday? Is that right?'

Douglas nodded. 'Yes, straight away after Darby had been found.'

'And d'you believe her story of walking all the way to Skegness?'

'Yes, I do. I've asked around and no one has said they saw her on Monday or Tuesday.'

The inspector sighed. 'But they'll cover for one of their own, won't they?'

'Aye, I don't doubt that. And no one admits to hearing a shot on Sunday night either.'

'Not even Mr Ramsey at the manor?'

'No, but then if there was only one shot fired, it's believable,' Douglas said.

'Yes, I know what you mean. It might have wakened them but they wouldn't be sure. So, no one suspected foul play or carried out a search until Darby was reported missing.'

'And because he lives alone at the moment, he wasn't missed until' – Douglas wrinkled his forehead – 'Wednesday morning. Ted from the pub got in touch to say that Darby hadn't been into the pub since Saturday night and although he was new to the area, it was unusual. Ted said the new gamekeeper went in most nights for a pint and' – he chuckled – 'to pick up the local gossip.'

'Darby wasn't married, then?'

'About to be, I understand.'

The inspector pulled a face. 'That's sad.'

They were silent for several moments until the inspector said slowly, 'I don't think there's much more we can do. I'm inclined to believe *most* of her story.'

'We're not going to break her. She's a tough little nut, is Rosie.'

'Is the note in her father's handwriting?'

'I believe so, but he could just as easily have been leaving because he'd killed the gamekeeper or, like she said, he'd decided to volunteer.'

'And that's the bit I don't quite believe, Douglas. It's a bit too convenient.'

'Aye, well, he won't be the only one to volunteer from the village. There's a lot of excitement among the young fellers.' His kindly face fell into lines of sorrow. 'I only wish they realized what they're letting themselves in for.'

'So are you inclined to believe that her story about her father volunteering might be true?'

'If what I've heard is to be believed, Sam did want to join the army some years ago, just after he lost his wife, but he had the bairn to look after by then.'

'Mm.' Chris Cowley was thoughtful for a few moments again and then seemed to come to a decision. 'I'll put out a "wanted" notice on Sam Waterhouse. He's definitely the one we really need to find. We'll release the girl from custody but keep an eye on her. If she stays around, then I think she's innocent, but if she leaves suddenly, then . . .' He shrugged his shoulders, but Douglas understood exactly what he meant.

Exhausted by the questioning, the hours in the uncomfortable cell and the constant anxiety, Rosie knocked on Nell's door and fell into her arms.

'Come on, lass. Sit yarsen down. I've a nice stew on the hob.'

'I couldn't eat a thing, Aunty Nell.'

'You should try. I bet you haven't had anything all day, have you?'

Nell fussed around the girl, as much to keep her own mind off Sam as wanting to take care of his daughter. When the plate of steaming meat and vegetables was placed in front of her, Rosie found that, after all, she was hungry.

'I'm not going to bombard you with a lot of questions. I bet you've had enough of them today. Just tell me about it when you're ready.'

They both ate in silence and then sat by the range. Rosie leaned her head back and closed her eyes.

'Have a sleep, lass. I can see you're shattered. You can stay here the night, if you want. Sleep in Nathan's bed. He won't mind. He'll sleep in the easy chair by the range.'

Rosie opened her eyes and sat up. 'I will, if you don't mind – stay with you tonight, I mean. I can't face going home yet. They've searched our cottage again. Four great clod-hopping constables. I bet the place is a right mess.'

'I'll come and help you tomorrow. We'll soon have it ship-shape.'

'What on earth do you mean, you can't find any evidence to arrest her?' William Ramsey stormed at the inspector standing in front of him. He didn't even ask the officer to take a seat or offer him refreshment. 'The girl is as guilty as sin.'

Calmly, Chris Cowley said, 'That's as may be . . .' Reluctantly, he added a courteous 'sir', though he was averse to pandering to the likes of

William Ramsey. Just because the man had a few bob, owned some land and held sway over people's lives and fancied himself as the local 'squire', it didn't make him a gentleman in the policeman's mind. That was one thing about being an upholder of the law; it gave him authority over others, no matter who they were – or who they *imagined* they were. The only people for whom Chris Cowley had deference were his superior officers. 'But,' he went on now, 'we have to have evidence before we can arrest someone and the girl answered all my questions to my satisfaction.'

'If it's not her,' William growled, 'then it's her father.'

'Quite possibly, sir. But he's not here.'

'Then find him, dammit.'

'I have circulated a "wanted" notice to other forces, but I fear that if what the girl says is true and he has indeed volunteered, then it might not be so easy to extricate him from the army.'

'But he's a murderer. Of course, the army will release him to stand trial.'

The inspector said nothing. Did the blustering man in front of him not understand that perhaps at this very moment Sam Waterhouse was being trained to kill other human beings in the name of war? Of course, it was a very different situation; Chris understood that. One was unlawful killing, the other was sanctioned by the government of the day in defence of the realm. But arguing with William Ramsey would serve no purpose and might get him into trouble with his superiors.

'I'll see what I can do, sir,' was all he said.

'Mind you do,' William said curtly and Chris found himself dismissed.

Fifteen

The following day, Rosie and Nell tidied the small cottage.

'At least they haven't broken anything,' Nell said, as she washed all the pots and pans and placed them on the shelf in the scullery.

'Actually, they've been very good.'

'I expect Douglas was in charge of them and, despite him being the local bobby, he's one of us. Mebbe he told 'em to be careful.'

Rosie sighed. 'He's been very fair with me, really. He was only doing his job.'

'Aye well, he can't show favouritism, lass, not when there's wrong been done.'

Silence fell between them. They were each thinking about Sam in their own way.

'You're going to do *what*?'

Calmly, Byron faced his father. 'I am going to volunteer for the army.'

William stared at his son, his expression thunderous. 'Then you're a bloody fool.' He was silent for several long moments, seeming to struggle with his son's proposal.

'What's brought this on?'

146

Byron explained how he'd followed the lines of men heading for the barracks in Lincoln and how he'd felt the compulsion to help defend his country.

'You've no need to go,' William argued. 'You're running a big estate . . .'

Byron raised his eyebrows. 'Not exactly, Father. You haven't really let go of the reins yet, have you?'

'Then I will.' William sat bolt upright. 'I'll sign everything over to you this very day. I'll send for my solicitor now.' He half rose, as if to pull the bell to summon a servant.

Byron was shaking his head. 'Father, I have given my word that I will return on Monday and sign up properly. I can't – and won't – go back on my promise. They'll be forming some sort of service battalion in answer to Lord Kitchener's request for volunteers. No doubt I shall be drafted into that.'

Grace's reaction, however, was not what her husband had expected. William burst into the morning room with Byron following more slowly. 'Do you know what this young fool has done?'

Grace looked up calmly from the sheet of paper on which she was compiling a list of meals for the coming week. 'No, but I'm sure you're going to tell me.'

'He's promised to volunteer for the army. Given his word to sign on properly on Monday without even telling me first. But I'm going to put a stop to it. I'll get my solicitor on to it. I'll sign the whole estate over to him. Then he won't be able to go. He'll have an estate to run and people's lives depending on him.'

Grace laid aside her paper and rose. She crossed the room towards Byron and stood close to him, putting her palms on his chest. As she looked up into his eyes, tears were glistening in hers. 'My darling boy, I don't want to lose you, but I want you to know that I am very proud of you.'

Byron put his arms around her and held her close. 'Thank you, Mother.'

'Grace, what on earth are you saying?' William blustered, his florid face growing even redder. 'You can't mean it. You can't take his side in such a reckless, thoughtless act. You can't possibly.'

Mother and son ignored him. Grace drew back a little and reached up to touch Byron's cheek. She didn't need to say any more; the loving gesture said it all. She cleared her throat and stepped away from him. 'Does Pearl know?'

'No. It was a spur-of-the-moment decision after I'd left Pearl and Bertie . . .' At the thought of his little boy, Byron faltered. He loved his son dearly and would hate to leave him fatherless, but he also wanted Bertie to have cause to be proud of him. 'I came back via Lincoln. I wanted to visit the cathedral—' Mother and son exchanged a look. They were both fond of the magnificent building. They both found peace and contentment there whenever they visited. 'And there were all these men heading in the same direction. To the barracks. And I – I just felt I had to join them.'

'There you are, you see,' William spluttered. 'A ridiculous impulsive gesture. Swept along on a tide of misplaced patriotic fervour. I expect you tagged on to a hoard of men all rushing to be heroes. Well, all I can say is they'll likely end up dead heroes and you along with them.' William paused again, struggling with himself before saying gruffly, 'I hope that at least you're going to have the sense to sign up for officer training.'

'No, Father, I shall not,' Byron said quietly. 'I shall join the rank and file. I have no experience of leading men. Not even,' he added pointedly, 'on the estate.'

William's face reddened again as he blustered, 'If you hadn't been so headstrong, I would have made everything over to you. I'd planned to do it when we came back from our tour, hadn't I, Grace?'

Grace inclined her head. 'That is true, yes. But perhaps if you had told him of your plans before we went away . . .' She left the end of her sentence hanging in the air, turned and walked from the room, her shoulders back, her head held high. Only in the privacy of her own bedroom did she let the tears of fear for her beloved son's safety fall.

News spread very quickly around the small community. In the local pub that Saturday evening, the men discussed the two pieces of news they had heard. One was surprising, the other, shocking. Nathan stood at the end of the bar, his hands around his pint of beer. His neighbour, Dan Bates, stood next to him.

'They're loving this,' Dan muttered, but Nathan didn't answer. He was listening to what was being said, ready to step in to defend his friends.

'Have you heard,' one of the drinkers at the opposite end of the bar said, 'the police took Rosie to

149

Alford yesterday for questioning while four coppers searched the cottage? They say they even dug up parts of the garden. Looking for the gun, I expect.'

'I heard Sam's disappeared, though. He wouldn't have gone if he'd been innocent, now, would he?'

'Rosie's adamant he's gone to volunteer.'

This was greeted with a derisive laugh. 'Volunteer to fight? Him?'

'Of course, it could have been Rosie who pulled the trigger.'

'Nah, I don't believe that. Oh, she poaches alongside him, I'll give you that, but I don't think she'd ever use a gun.' The speaker grinned. 'Too noisy for one thing.'

'So why did Sam use one?'

'We don't know he did. Police haven't found anything. Not a trace. Not even an empty cartridge case. Not in his cottage, anyway.'

'What about at the scene of the crime?'

'They're still searching the woods. But if whoever it was had any sense, they'd have picked up anything incriminating, now wouldn't they?'

'S'pose so.' There was a pause and then, 'So, where's young Rosie now?'

'Back home, isn't she, Nathan? They can't prove anything against her.'

'Aye, she is. They've no reason to hold her,' he defended her stoutly. 'Rosie hasn't done owt.'

'Poor lass.'

'Aye, well, I won't be turning against her, that's for sure. Her and Sam kept my family fed last winter and I never forget a good turn.'

'D'you reckon she'll carry on with the poaching even though her dad's gone?'

'Couldn't say. Mebbe not. It'll be even more dangerous now. I've heard it said that old man Ramsey is out to get her one way or another. She'll have to be careful.'

'Mebbe he will, but he'll have more to worry about now, won't he?'

'What d'you mean?' All eyes turned to look at Ray Chambers, the son of the village wheelwright and carpenter.

'Young Monty was telling me that Master Byron visited the barracks in Lincoln yesterday.' He paused, waiting for the rest of the bar to fall silent as he delivered the surprise. 'He gave his word that he will go back on Monday and enlist.'

There was a shocked silence and then everyone began talking at once. Ray moved along the bar to stand next to Nathan and Dan. Quietly, he said, 'Me and the lads have been talking about volunteering and Nick and Geoffrey are up for it. What about you two? What say you we all go together on Monday? The five of us. It'd give this lot summat else to natter about other than poor Rosie.'

Nathan and Dan glanced at each other.

'I'm game,' Dan said. 'I've been thinking about it, an' all. But what about your mam, Nathan? You're all she's got. It's a bit different for me. Although she's a widow, my mam's still got our Joey at home. He's far too young to even think about volunteering. If owt happened to me, she'd still have him, but your poor mam'd have no one.'

'She won't stand in my way if it's what I want to do.'

'And do you?'

Nathan raised his head and glanced between them. 'Yes. Yes, I do.'

Ray slapped him on the back. 'Right, we'll meet on the green at midday on Monday to hitch a ride with the carrier. I'll go and tell Monty. He's sitting outside with his beer.'

The three young men smiled. On William Ramsay's orders, Monty was too young to be allowed to enter the pub, but the locals saw to it that the lad had a pint of beer whenever he visited. 'He does a man's work,' they said. 'He deserves a man's drink.'

As Nathan was deciding his future, Nell and Rosie were seated either side of the table in Nell's cottage eating rabbit pie with rich, tasty gravy.

'Dad would have loved this,' Rosie murmured huskily. 'I just wish I knew where he is and if he's all right.'

Nell's eyes were red from shedding tears and lack of sleep. 'Best you don't know, lass. And *you* will have to be careful, Rosie. Mebbe you ought to give up the poaching all together.'

Rosie gave huge sigh. 'I'd thought that myself, but how would I earn a living?'

'One of the tenant farmer's might employ you . . .' Nell put in, but her tone didn't hold out much hope.

Rosie laughed wryly. 'I've tried before. They don't want to know me. I expect they think their chickens might start disappearing. No, I've had a lot of time to think these last two or three days. If I can't find work locally, I'll go further afield. To one of the towns or even to Lincoln, where no one knows me.'

'They'll likely want references,' Nell said softly.

'Perhaps they won't be so fussy now we're at war. With the men going off, they'll need women to take their place.'

'And the hospitals will always want staff.'

'But I'm not trained to nurse . . .'

Nell was shaking her head. 'That won't matter. They'll want ward orderlies – cleaning staff. All sorts.'

Rosie sighed. 'I expect it'd be for the best.'

'Just one thing, lass, if you'll take my advice, don't leave suddenly, else everyone – including Douglas Foster – will think the worst. We'll look after you, Rosie, love.'

They sat together until darkness fell. Rosie was reluctant to go back to the empty cottage, but she couldn't keep taking Nathan's bed from him. He worked hard in the daytime on the estate and needed his rest. She was about to leave, when the back door rattled and he came in.

'I'm just on my way,' she said, getting up to give him his chair by the range.

'Don't go yet, Rosie. I've summat to tell both of you.'

Rosie sank back down and Nathan pulled out a chair from under the table and sat down between them.

He glanced from one to the other. They were both watching him intently, guessing, from his serious face, that this was something they were not going to like.

'There's no easy way to tell you this, so I'll just say it straight out. I'm going to Lincoln with four other lads from the village on Monday to volunteer.'

For a brief moment, Nell stared at him and then dropped her head.

Shocked, Rosie said, 'Oh no, Nathan. Why? Surely, there's no cause for you to go. You're needed on the land.'

He shrugged his broad shoulders. 'I – I don't want to be seen as a coward.'

'You wouldn't be. No one could ever think that of you.' She turned to Nell. 'Can't you stop him?'

Slowly, Nell raised her head and said sadly, 'No, lass, I can't. And besides' – she hesitated, then lifted her head higher and added bravely – 'I wouldn't if I could. He's a man now and must make his own decisions.'

'But he's—' Rosie began and then stopped abruptly. She had been going to say, 'But he's your only son.' It was stating the obvious and it wasn't her place to interfere with Nathan's decision.

'Who else is going?' Nell asked.

'Dan from next door, Ray Chambers, Nick Gill and Geoffrey Porter and, from what I hear' – he paused a moment, knowing that what he was about to say might hurt Rosie even more – 'Byron Ramsey is going to volunteer on Monday too. Monty was full of it in the pub . . .'

'Monty? In the pub?' Nell cut in. 'He's not old enough to be frequenting a pub.'

Nathan laughed. 'He sits outside and we keep him supplied. He's a good lad. He's had a rough start in life and Lucas Brown doesn't make it any easier for him now, though from what Monty says, Byron's kind to him and as for Mrs Ramsey, he worships her.'

'You want to be careful Douglas Foster doesn't catch him.'

'He won't. We all see to that. Anyway, as I was saying, evidently Master Byron went to the barracks in Lincoln yesterday and he's planning to go back and sign on properly on Monday. So, we've all decided that we're – we're going at the same time.'

Although her heart began to beat faster, Rosie managed not to let her feelings show on her face. However, she could not prevent her hand trembling. Nathan noticed, but said nothing. He was sorry to have been the one to give her more pain. She would find out soon enough and perhaps it was better coming from him. But Nell, still partially lost in her own thoughts, merely murmured, 'I expect Master Byron's going for officer training.'

'No, I don't think he is. Dan' – their neighbour, who was apprenticed to the village carpenter, Ray Chambers's father, was, apart from Rosie, Nathan's best friend – 'said that Monty told them he's determined to join up with the rest of us. Just as an ordinary soldier. Maybe we'll all end up in the same training camp and, if we do, it's likely we'd be sent out there together.'

Rosie said nothing. Now she could not trust herself to speak.

'This war isn't going to be over by Christmas like they've all been saying,' Nathan remarked. 'I'm very much afraid it's going to go on a lot longer than that.'

Sixteen

When Byron heard from Monty that others beside himself were joining up, he instructed the stable lad to make ready the carriage for Monday morning. Lucas Brown grumbled that he had not been consulted, but there was nothing he could do to contradict the young master's direct order. They drew up on the village green at midday, where already the group of other volunteers was waiting to get a lift with the local carrier into the city. Instead, at Byron's invitation, they piled gratefully into the Ramseys' carriage.

'This is very good of you Master Byron,' Nathan said. 'We heard you were going today too, but we hadn't expected this.'

'Please don't mention it. I expect we're all on our way to join the Lincolnshire Regiment, so we should all stick together.'

'Are you going to be an officer, Master Byron?' Dan asked.

Byron shook his head. 'No, Dan. I'm sticking with all of you.'

The other five men glanced at each other and then, with one accord, stuck out their hands to shake Byron's. 'Glad to have you with us, sir.'

'Please – no more "sir". It's Byron from now on. Though I expect we'll all be addressed by our surnames.'

'We'll stick together if they'll let us,' Nathan suggested. 'We'll watch out for each other.'

The others all nodded their agreement.

'Are we going to the barracks up the hill?' Nathan asked.

'No,' Byron said. 'They told me on Friday to report in the first instance to the Drill Hall. They'll tell us if we need to go anywhere else. Monty knows where it is.'

For the six recruits from Thornsby, the rest of the day was filled with medical tests, which they all passed, and form filling. It was a busy day as more and more volunteers queued outside.

'We're got so many coming forward,' one harassed officer told them, 'I'm afraid you'll have to take the oath in a group instead of individually.'

The six stood together and solemnly swore on the Bible their allegiance to the King.

'You'll receive a letter in a week or two's time to report to a training camp.'

'Is there any chance we would be able to stay together, sir?' Byron asked.

The recruiting officer smiled. 'Every chance, soldier. Since you've joined up together, it's likely you'll stay together, at least for training. After that, I can't say for definite at this time but men who have some sort of bond – like where they live, their work or even their hobbies – are being encouraged to enlist together. It will be noted that you all come from the same village and, if at all possible, you will serve together.'

The six young men emerged from the hall a little mesmerized by the day's events.

'Well, we've done it now, lads,' Ray Chambers said. He put his hand on Dan's shoulder. 'My dad's not going to be too pleased to learn that his son and also his best apprentice are leaving together.'

'He might like to consider taking on my young brother, Joey,' Dan said. 'He's dead keen to learn the trade.'

'Won't he want to join up?'

'He's too young. He's only fifteen.'

'Aye,' Ray said, 'but he'll grow, won't he? What then?'

Now, no one had an answer.

Outside the building, still waiting patiently, was Monty. 'You've all got in, then?'

'We have, Monty lad.' Nick Gill, who, like Nathan, worked as a labourer on the estate, slapped him on the shoulder. 'Are you coming with us?'

'I only wish I could.' Monty glanced at his employer. 'I'd lie about me age, but then Master Byron knows exactly how old I am.'

'Indeed, I do. He's the same age as your Joey, Dan. He's fifteen.'

'Well, that is too young. Mebbe he could have sneaked in at seventeen, but not at fifteen, no.'

'Your Joey's a strappin' lad, though,' Geoffrey Porter, the son of one of the estate's tenant farmers, said. 'I reckon he could pass for seventeen. Sorry to say it, Monty lad, but you only look your age. No offence.'

Monty grinned. 'None taken, Geoffrey.' After years in the workhouse, the boy was thin and small even for fifteen. There was no way he could pretend to be old enough to join up.

'Don't put ideas into our Joey's head, Geoffrey,' Dan said. 'Me mam's going spare at the thought of me going, let alone her baby boy.'

They all laughed as they climbed into the carriage. It was a merry party, keen for adventure, that rattled its way back to Thornsby.

'I never thought I'd see the day when I called my own son a fool,' William Ramsey raged. 'But that's what you are, Byron. An absolute fool. To volunteer is bad enough, but to join the rank and file is just plain stupid. At least as an officer, you'd have some position – some reputation. But this' – he waved his hand and made an explosive noise –'is sheer madness.'

'I'm going with friends, Father.'

'Friends? With the village country bumpkins? Whatever are you thinking, boy? Trouble is,' he went on without even giving Byron the chance to reply, 'you're not *thinking* at all. You did it on a whim – on the spur of the moment. Caught up in a fever of excitement.'

'Yes, I did, but even though I've had time to think about it more rationally since, I still don't regret it. I've given my oath to serve the King and that's what I'm going to do. I shall hear in a week or so, but first I'm going to Stamford to say goodbye to Pearl and to Bertie.' At the mention of his son's name, Byron had to stiffen his resolve, but he did not allow his voice to waver.

*

It seemed as if the whole village had turned out to wave their six menfolk off to war. They gathered on the little patch of grass laughingly called the village green to watch their heroes board the canvas-covered army truck that had come to take them wherever they were going.

Ray Chambers, standing next to Nathan, nudged him. 'Look who's joining us.'

Nathan glanced up the road and saw Byron marching towards the gathering on the green. 'I'd've thought—' he began and then hesitated, but Ray, guessing what was in his friend's mind, took up his words.

'That his papa would have driven him to wherever we're headed in style. No such luck for the poor young feller. Amos was telling us in the pub last night that his father is livid, not only at him joining up in the first place, but also at his volunteering to serve with the likes of us.'

The other three young men standing with them had all been present for a final drink together the previous evening. Only Nathan had not been there, choosing to stay with his mother. Nell had had so much sorrow in her life. She had lost her husband in a tragic accident and then, just recently, her dear friend Sam Waterhouse had disappeared under a cloud of suspicion. And now she had to wave her only son – her only child – off to war, not knowing if she would ever see him again. So, Nathan had decided that his last night should be spent at home.

'But we *all*,' Ray continued, emphasizing the last word, 'admire him for what he's doing. He's not setting himself up above the rest of us and he could easily have done so. No, he's mucking in with us, so we'll mek him welcome like we did the day we all volunteered together.' Without waiting for any answer from Nathan, Ray pushed his way out from the throng and strode to meet Byron, his hand outstretched in welcome.

'Good to have you with us, Master Byron,' Nathan heard Ray say.

'Just Byron.'

Ray chuckled. 'I'll do me best. We all will, but it'll take a bit of getting used to.'

Byron moved among them, shaking hands until at last he stood before Nathan, who returned his warm handshake and grinned. 'You're going to have to be patient with us. Using your name like this doesn't come easy.'

Byron laughed with him. 'I can understand that, but please try. I don't want to get off on the wrong foot with all the other lads we're going to be with.' Then Byron glanced around him at the groups of villagers, mostly women, waiting to wave their menfolk off.

'Is—?' Byron stopped, aware of what he had been about to say and how it would sound. He had never forgotten the letter he had entrusted to Nathan. He had no idea of knowing whether the young man had read it. He had trusted him to deliver it and though he had never asked him, he knew he would have done so, but had curiosity overcome him? Had he actually read the letter? Byron had been going to enquire if Rosie was there, but now he changed it to, 'Is your mother here?'

'Yes. Over there under the shop's awning.'

Byron glanced to where Nathan pointed and felt a jolt in his chest as he saw Rosie standing quietly beside Nell Tranter. It had been a long time since he had seen her this close. She hadn't changed, except to grow more mature. Her figure was perfect, her beautiful hair flying loose and free. He couldn't see the colour of her eyes from this distance but he knew their bright greenness would still be sparkling with mischief and the joy of life. Though perhaps not so bright these days with all that she must be going through. How he wished he could hold her, tell her everything would be all right. Tell her how he would protect her and save her from the clutches of the police and, it had to be said, from his father's wrath. But he could say nothing to her.

Perhaps understanding something of Byron's longing, Nathan suddenly said, 'Come and say goodbye to her.' Though which "her" he meant, Byron didn't know.

Slowly, Byron, almost in a trance, allowed himself to be led towards the two women until he was standing in front of them. Mindful of appearances, he forced himself to look into Nell's eyes first and hold out his hand to her. She took it and held it for a long moment between both of hers.

'God bless you, Master Byron. May He keep you and all you boys safe.'

'Thank you, Mrs Tranter. I'll do my best to look out for Nathan. You have my word.'

'And he'll look out for you, Master Byron.' With tears in her eyes, Nell released her hold on him and turned away, hurrying through the crowd.

'Mam—' Nathan began and tried to follow her but at that moment a whistle, blown by the driver of the army vehicle, shrilled. 'We'll have to go,' he murmured. 'Rosie, please look out for Mam, won't you?'

'Of course I will.'

He put his arms around her and hugged her, then he turned away and went towards the truck. 'We'd better go, Master Byron.'

Byron did not follow immediately. At last he allowed himself to look into Rosie's eyes. They gazed at each other and the rest of the world around them faded away. They saw their love for one another reflected in the other's eyes. There was no mistaking it. Not now, when they might be parting for ever.

He wanted to say so much to her. He wanted to tell her how he felt. He wanted to tell her that she could go to his father for help, but he knew that was the last thing she could do.

He put his arms around her and held her close for a brief moment, not caring now who saw them.

Close to her ear, so that no one else could hear, he whispered, 'I still have your daisy chain. I'm carrying it with me. It's my good luck charm to keep me safe and every time I look at it, I will think of you.'

Then, abruptly, he stepped back, turned, picked up his bag and followed Nathan. Rosie watched him until he climbed up into the back of the vehicle.

He did not look back.

Seventeen

Rosie went in search of Nell, to find her standing at the back of the crowd milling around the village green. She stood with her, her arm about the older woman's waist, until the young men had all scrambled into the back of the truck and it had chugged away along the road out of the village and disappeared into the distance.

'Come back to my place, Rosie love. I don't want to be on my own.' What she was saying was true, of course, but her heart went out to the young girl. Nell had seen the hug that Byron had given Rosie, had seen them gazing at each other. Now, she knew the truth; the pair were in love and probably had been for years.

Nell and Rosie sat together over a strong cup of tea, which was normally only kept for special occasions. Tea was expensive for the likes of Nell Tranter. But today, they both needed it.

'What shall you do now, lass?'

Rosie sighed heavily. 'I don't know. I can't get a job locally. No one will take me on and I – I don't think I dare carry on with – well, you know. They'll be watching out for me.'

'Aye, an' likely arrest you.'

'But if I leave, it'll make me look guilty, won't it?'

Sadly, Nell nodded. 'Gossip is rife in the village. A lot of them believe it was your dad.'

'I suppose they don't believe the story about him volunteering.'

For a moment, Nell frowned. 'Some of 'em might. Years ago, he wanted to go and join the fight in South Africa and he made no secret of it, but you was a bairn and yar mam had just died. He couldn't leave you, though, could he? Some might remember that.'

Rosie said nothing, but she felt a burden of guilt. It was not really her fault and yet, but for her, he might have joined the army instead of leading the life of a poacher.

'I'll stay a while,' Rosie murmured. 'See – what happens.'

A week later, Nell and Rosie both received a letter from Nathan on the same day. Although they read each other's, the news was much the same in both letters, though in Rosie's letter Nathan gave her brief news of the other young men, including Byron.

We're all still together and settling down
nicely. The other chaps here are a great
bunch. We're still in training and expect to
be for several more weeks. It's pretty tough.
I can't tell you exactly where we are –
everything has to be very hush-hush – but
we're still in the county. We haven't got

*proper uniforms and weapons yet, so I don't
think we're likely to be sent abroad any time
soon. We're all well and in good spirits,
though Byron has a nasty blister with all the
marching. We tease him that he's a softie but
he takes it in good part and teases us in
return. He's a grand chap. He's really one of
us now. He sends his kindest regards . . .*

A month since the dreadful night of the murder passed
and still Rosie stayed in the cottage she had shared
with her father.

'No one around here will give me work, Aunty
Nell. I'll have to leave,' Rosie said to Nell one day.

'Don't do owt hasty, lass. Nathan sends me money
from his pay and I've started to take in washing. It's
not much, but it helps a little.' She laughed wryly.
'Most villagers do their own but I had a spot of luck
last week. Sarah, Mrs Ramsey's lady's maid, came to
see me to ask me if I would take in the servants'
washing from the manor. It seems that Mrs Portus,
who works in the laundry there, is getting on a bit
now. Her legs are troubling her. Mrs Ramsey doesn't
want to replace her, Sarah says. Poor old thing has
nowhere to go, only the workhouse, and madam won't
hear of that happening. Mrs Portus can still manage
all the washing for the family, but everything for the
servants as well is just getting too much for her.'

'Don't they have younger maids who would do
it?' Rosie asked.

'One or two of the girls are leaving to go and do

war work.' Nell pulled a face. 'It's a lot better paid than domestic service. So, you can help me with that, if you like. No one else need know.'

'Oh, I couldn't take your money . . .'

Nell flapped her hand. 'Nonsense, Rosie. There were times when we wouldn't have survived if it hadn't been for your dad bringing me and Nathan food.' Suddenly, her face dropped into lines of sadness and her voice quivered. 'I miss your dad, Rosie. I'll always miss him.'

Impulsively, Rosie put her arms round her. 'I know you do.'

In charge of her emotions again, Nell patted her shoulder and said briskly, 'Well now, lass, let's give this joint venture a try shall we?'

'If you're sure . . .'

'I am.'

'You see, I could go out poaching, but—'

'You'll do no such thing. If they catch you – and mark my words, they'll be on the look-out for you now more than ever – they'll have you back in for more questioning before your feet touch the ground. No, lass, you'll stay well clear of that way of life, if you take my advice.'

Solemnly, Rosie said, 'I will, Aunty Nell.'

The weeks went by and their new arrangement worked well, but Rosie was aware that there wasn't really enough work for both of them and that she was – quite literally – eating into Nell's own meagre income.

'Have you heard about Tilly Baxter?' Nell said one day at the beginning of October as they toiled together over the wash tubs. It was a good time of year for poaching, but now Rosie stayed safely at home every night. Tilly lived with her parents at the opposite end of the village. She was the same age as Rosie. They had attended school together.

'Oh, don't tell me she's in trouble.'

'No, lass, far from it. She's gone to volunteer to do some kind of nursing for the wounded soldiers coming back from the front.' Nell's face creased in anguish. 'And, from what the papers say, there's a lot of them.'

Nell got a newspaper each day from her neighbour, Ivy Bates. Young Joey, Dan's brother, scrounged it from the pub when everyone had finished reading it. Although the news was always at least a day late, Ivy and Nell still read it avidly, searching, always searching, the casualty list.

'But she's not trained as a nurse,' Rosie said now.

'No, but they need women and girls to support the nurses. Washing, cleaning, maybe even moving the patients around. You know, helping with anything that's not exactly nursing.'

Rosie was thoughtful. 'I could do that. I'm strong.'

'Think about it, lass. But if you do decide to go, be sure to go and tell Douglas Foster yourself. Just so they don't think you've disappeared an' all.'

By a strange twist of fate, that same night, just as she was about to go to bed, a soft knock sounded on Rosie's door. Her heart skipped a beat and then began to hammer in her chest. 'Oh no, not again. Not more questions,' she muttered. But then she realized. The police did not knock softly; they banged

on the door or even barged their way in uninvited.
She crept quietly to the door. Peering through the
little window at the side of the door, all she could
see was the dark shape of a man standing there, but
she couldn't recognize him. Rosie stood a moment,
biting her lip, unsure what to do. She took a deep
breath, drew back the bolt and inched the door open.

'Let me in quick, lass,' the man whispered.

'Dad!' Rosie breathed and opened the door wider.
He stepped inside and she closed and bolted the door.
Then she flung her arms around him. 'Oh Dad! Are
you all right? You shouldn't be here, but I'm so glad
to see you.'

'I mustn't stay long, Rosie.'

'Sit by the fire and I'll get you something to eat.'

She stirred the dying embers in the grate into a
warm glow and set the pan of stew she'd made earlier
in the day to reheat.

'I'll light the lamp . . .' she began, but he put out
his hand to stop her.

'No, lass. The candle's enough. Just a bite to eat
and then I must go. I mustn't be seen.'

'Oh Dad—' Tears brimmed in Rosie's eyes and she
clung to his hand. As her glance roamed over him,
she gasped. 'You're – you're in uniform.'

'I've joined up, but not under my real name. I
enlisted as Samuel Skelton. That was your mother's
maiden name.'

'I never knew that,' she murmured. 'I've never
known much about any of my family.'

'There's something I need to tell you, Rosie lass.
If anything happens to me . . .'

'Don't, Dad. Please don't say that.'

'Rosie, we must face the truth. We could be sent out to France at any time.'

'Oh no. No!'

'Rosie, listen to me, love. If I stay here, I'll be permanently on the run. Better I go to serve my country and take my chances. If I survive, well, I'll never be able to come back here.'

'But you'd let me know, wouldn't you? I could come to you.'

'We'll see when that time comes.' The unspoken words hung between them: *If it ever does.*

'But you'll keep in touch? You'll write to me?'

'I can't, Rosie. You know I can't.'

Her voice trembled as she whispered, 'What about Aunty Nell?'

His face was bleak in the candlelight. 'I daren't risk trying to see her. Her cottage is too close to the village. I might be seen. I've come through the woods to get here and I'll go back the same way.'

'Oh do be careful.'

He chuckled softly. 'I haven't forgotten how to move silently through the woods, Rosie. And the game is safe from me tonight.'

'And from me too, now,' she told him. 'Aunty Nell thought it best I stopped.'

'She's a good woman. Listen to her, Rosie. She'll give you good advice. And Nathan too. He'll look out for you.'

'Nathan's gone,' she blurted out. 'He's enlisted. He went with – with Byron Ramsey. They left together with four other lads from the village.'

'The young master? He's gone to war? Whatever for? He'd no need to go. Neither had Nathan, if it comes to that. He works on the land.' Sam shook his head sadly. 'All these fine young men rushing to be heroes – a whole generation of them.' He sighed. 'Let's just hope I don't run into anyone who knows me.'

'I think they're all in what Nathan told me is a service battalion in answer to Lord Kitchener's call for volunteers.'

Sam's worried expression lightened a little. 'I might be safe, then. I've joined the regular army, signing on for several years, not just for the duration of the war.'

At that moment a gust of wind rattled the door and they both jumped. 'I must go, Rosie, but there's one more thing I have to tell you. Under my bed you'll find a box with some personal papers in it. If you ever need to prove that you're my daughter, the proof is in there. And remember my new name. Skelton. Sam Skelton. And please, give my love to Nell. And I really mean that. My love.'

They stood by the door for a long moment, holding each other close. As he released himself from her arms, he gave a soft laugh. 'I've joined the Lincolnshire Regiment, Rosie, and you'll never guess what their nickname is. It's The Poachers. You're still a poacher's daughter.'

Eighteen

There was only one person Rosie told about her father's fleeting visit: Nell.

Tears filled the older woman's eyes. 'Why didn't he come here?'

'He wanted to. He really did, but it was too dangerous. For both of you.'

Nell wiped her eyes and nodded. 'I expect you're right, but oh, I so wanted to see him.'

'You know what I've been telling everyone about him going away to join up? Well, it happens to be true. That's exactly what he has done.'

Nell stared at her. 'Never!'

'Yes, he has. And' – even amidst their sadness, she laughed – 'he's joined the Lincolnshire Regiment and their nickname is The Poachers.'

'No!' Even Nell smiled through her tears now. 'Well, I never.' Her smile faded again and she sighed heavily. 'I suppose it was the best thing he could have done in – in the circumstances, but I fear for him, Rosie. I really do, and for all the fellers that have gone.'

They exchanged a sorrowful glance. Both of them were thinking about the other two men who were so important in their lives and whom they'd waved off: Nathan and Byron.

*

Time passed and the investigation into the murder of Wilfred Darby had ground to a halt. There were no witnesses and no useful evidence had been found.

William was growing impatient. 'If they're not going to arrest the Waterhouse girl, then I want her out of that cottage and gone from here altogether.' Although William would never admit it, he was secretly afraid that Byron would begin meeting Rosie again. The girl was grown up now and certainly attractive. And while he was loath to acknowledge it, even William could see that Byron's marriage was not a happy one.

'Is that really necessary, William?' Grace asked, greatly daring.

William frowned. 'I don't know who actually pulled the trigger of the gun that killed Darby, Grace, but it was one of them and because he's done a bunk, it rather looks as if it was the father. However, she's as guilty as he is in my eyes, but I just can't prove it. If nothing else, she's a poacher like her father. So, I want her gone.'

'But she has nowhere to go.'

Now William glowered at her. 'That is hardly my problem. And if anyone in the village tries to help her, they'll be out too.'

'But where could she go?'

'There's always the workhouse.'

Grace pictured the bright-haired girl with shining green eyes and shuddered inwardly. The grim building – a last resort for many – would likely kill her. It would certainly kill her spirit. Grace had always known her husband was a hard taskmaster. His tenant farmers, his workers – all those he employed in one way or another – even his own wife, had to obey his rules and demands, but she had never thought him to be a cruel, vindictive man. He had even forced his will on their own son, driving Byron, when he was little more than a boy, into a disastrous marriage, all for the sake of his progeny. She regretted now the part she had played in assisting him.

For a while, Grace watched William, seeing him as he was now. Overweight, florid and ill-tempered. She herself had been pushed into marrying him by her ambitious mother, but when she had married William, he had still been a fine figure of a man, albeit some years older than her. Not until later had she seen the streak of ruthlessness in him. She loved her son devotedly and feared for him, but part of her was glad that he had stood up to his father in volunteering. It would be the making of him. She just prayed that he would come back safely.

For the rest of the day, Grace sat quietly in the morning room with her cross stitch, but her mind was busy. She knew more about her husband's tenants in the village than he did. She felt isolated and lonely for much of the time – apart from her lunches with the 'ladies of the county', many of whom she wouldn't trust with her secrets. But there was one person within the household who she knew she could trust implicitly. Her lady's maid, Sarah. A little older than her mistress, Sarah had been appointed when Grace had arrived as a young bride and had soon become Grace's confidante. Sarah was well liked by the other members of the household staff and while she never reported tittle-tattle to the mistress, if there was a problem brewing among the staff, a discreet word with Grace often quietly solved the problem without it escalating into something serious. So, William's household ran smoothly without him ever realizing the reason why.

When the afternoon light began to fade, Sarah entered the room and gave a little bob. Despite their closeness, Sarah never forgot her place and was happy in it. She always maintained the mistress-and-maid relationship.

'Good evening, ma'am. It's almost time to dress for dinner. I've laid out your blue silk. Is that all right?'

'Perfect.' Grace smiled as she looked up.

'If you want to carry on with your embroidery a while longer, I can get Mr Baines to come in and light the lamp.'

'No, don't worry, Sarah. I've done enough for today.' Grace laid aside her work and patted the couch beside her. It was the cue for an off-the-record chat. No one else, not even William, would come into what was regarded as Grace's private sitting room without knocking. The unusual intimacy shared between mistress and maid would not be discovered.

'I want you to do something for me but this must be just between ourselves.'

'Of course, ma'am.'

'Do you know Rosie Waterhouse?'

'By sight, ma'am, but I do know Mrs Tranter and she is very close to Rosie.'

'Nell Tranter who does the servants' washing for the manor now?'

Sarah nodded. 'That's right, ma'am.'

Grace was thoughtful. She had kept the domestic arrangement a secret from William. No doubt he would have insisted that she dismiss the elderly woman and employ a fit, strong girl. Mrs Portus was a widow. The manor was her home and the only place she could have gone in her declining years would have been the workhouse. William wouldn't have hesitated in sending her there, but Grace would keep her here for as long as she could.

'And' – Sarah was saying, bringing Grace's wandering thoughts back to their conversation – 'I do know that although Rosie is still living in her own cottage, she helps Nell out with the laundry. She can't find any other work. None of the tenant farmers will employ her. I expect they fear upsetting the master if they did.'

'Is she still poaching?'

'No, she isn't.'

'I don't think we'll ever know the truth about what happened that night, but I don't think Rosie had anything to do with the actual shooting, do you?'

Sarah shook her head. 'No, I don't, ma'am. But I think a lot of folks think that if she was with him, then she's as guilty as him.'

Grace sighed heavily. 'It's what my husband thinks. Sarah, I want you to go and see Nell Tranter. You can make an excuse to visit her about the laundry, can't you?'

Sarah nodded. 'As it happens, there's a bundle to go tomorrow. I'll take it first thing before you're ready to get up, ma'am, if you like.'

'If you would, Sarah, thank you. I want you to tell her that my husband is planning to evict Rosie from her cottage.'

Sarah drew in her breath sharply, but made no comment.

'So, they need to plan what Rosie is going to do,' Grace went on. 'I rather think that he wouldn't be too happy if Rosie moved in with Nell Tranter either. Although he doesn't own Mrs Tranter's cottage now, he'd find a way to stop Rosie living with her.'

'I'll sort it out for you, ma'am. Don't you worry no more.'

The following morning, Sarah walked along the path through the woods to get to Nell's cottage, wheeling a heavy load of washing in an old perambulator.

'What are you doing here, Sarah, and this early too?' Nell greeted her. 'Not that I'm not pleased to see you, but usually the kitchen maid brings the washing. But come away in and have a cup of tea with me.' Nell dismissed the expense of drinking tea; a visit from Mrs Ramsey's lady's maid was something special.

'I won't say no to that, Nell. I've come this morning because the mistress has sent a private message to you.'

Nell's face fell. 'Is she going to stop sending the washing to me?'

'No, nothing like that. She is very happy with your work. It's about Rosie.'

'Rosie? Do you want to see her? She's in the washhouse across the backyard. We start early on a Monday.'

'I think it would be best if you were to pass the message on. But you must both say nothing to anyone. The mistress is taking quite a risk, I might tell you. If the master were to find out . . .'

'Ah,' Nell said, catching on, even before quite understanding what the message was.

'The master is going to evict Rosie from her cottage.'

'Then she can come and live with me—' Nell began, but Sarah was shaking her head.

'No, I don't think that would be a good idea. He'll be vindictive towards anyone who tries to help her. He's said as much.'

Nell's face was bleak. 'So, what you're telling me – what the mistress is telling me – is that Rosie ought to go away?'

Sarah nodded.

'So, I'm to lose everyone I've ever cared about, am I? My husband, my son, my – my friend and now Rosie too.'

Sarah said nothing. There was nothing she could say.

Flatly, Nell said, 'I'll talk to her.'

'Don't leave it too long, Nell,' Sarah said.

Later that day, when they had both spent a hard day at the wash tub and hanging clothes on the line in the garden behind the cottage, Nell ladled rabbit stew onto two plates. Although Rosie no longer ventured into the woods or onto the farmland to poach, any creature who dared to venture into their gardens or onto the common land was fair game for her poacher's snare.

Nell cut off a generous hunk of bread and they sat down together. Both were tired; they just wanted to eat and go to their beds. The dried washing lay in neat piles around the kitchen awaiting ironing the next day. Once again, Rosie would come to help.

When they had finished eating, Rosie stretched and yawned. 'I'll be off home, then, Aunty Nell. I'll see you in the morning.'

'Just stay for a cup of tea, Rosie lass. We've earned a special treat. There's something I have to tell you.'

Rosie's eyes widened. 'It's not about Nathan, is it?'

'No. He's fine. At least, he was the last time I heard.'

When they were seated by the fire, Nell explained swiftly what Sarah had told her that morning. She wiped a tear away with the corner of her apron. 'Oh lass, I don't want to see you go, but I think it would be for the best.'

'I'm not surprised and I've been thinking about what you said about Tilly Baxter. I'd almost decided to do the same thing.'

'It'd be the best thing for you, but like I said before, go and see PC Foster. The police are obviously not interested in you anymore, else they'd have been back before now. But the master – he's not going to forget.'

'Oh Aunty Nell. I don't want to go – I don't want to leave you.'

'And I don't want you to, lass, but I think you should.'

'You'll be all right?'

'I'll manage. I've got the washing from the manor and a few other bits and pieces from the village now and again. That'll keep me going. Don't you worry about me, Rosie. Just look after yourself. And don't worry about the ironing tomorrow. I'll cope. Just get your things together and get off as soon as you can. The carrier comes to the village tomorrow dinner time. He'll give you a lift into Lincoln, I don't doubt. Look, I've got an old carpet bag I'll give you . . .'

The decision made, even though it was one she was loath to do, Rosie slept well for a few hours and was up early the next morning to gather her few belongings together. By eleven-thirty she was ready, the cottage left tidy. Even the garden, which she had tended regularly, was neat. With a last glance around her, she left the only home she had ever known and went to Nell's door.

'I'm off, then. I'm going into the village. I'll call at PC Foster's and then wait for the carrier on the green. That's where he always stands for the villagers to come to him. But I just wanted to tell you to help yourself to all the vegetables in our garden before a new tenant is likely to come. It's a shame for them all to go to waste and I'd rather you had them.'

'I'll see they're used, Rosie. I'll preserve what I can and give the rest away. I know some folks are having a hard time already with their menfolk away. You and your dad will be sorely missed through the winter months, I can tell you. There'll be many a mouth go hungry because you're not here.'

Rosie sighed. 'Things can never be the same again, though, can they? And it's best we've both gone. There's just one more thing, Aunty Nell. Will you look after this for me? It's a box with my father's papers in it. He told me to take care of it just in case

I ever needed it. I've had a peek. It's got several certificates in. You know, births, marriages and that.'

'Of course I will, lass. I'll put it under my bed. It's where I keep my own precious papers.' She smiled wryly. 'Specially the one where Mr Ramsey signed over this cottage to me after my Jim was killed on his land. It'll be Nathan's one day, God willing, but he might have to prove it.'

Nell clasped Rosie tightly and then with a voice that was none too steady, said, 'Take care of yourself, lass. I'll miss you so much.'

'I'll miss you too, Aunty Nell. You take care, an' all.'

Rosie picked up her bag and turned away. As she walked towards the village centre, she turned round once or twice to wave to Nell, who was still standing at her gate watching Rosie until she was out of sight.

That night, Nell wrote a letter to Nathan, sending it to the address he had given her.

Rosie has left the village. I don't know where she's gone and it's best I don't, though she made sure Douglas knew she was leaving. Nathan would know that his mother was referring to PC Foster and she knew he would also tell Byron. *I think she's going to try to find work in a hospital somewhere to do her bit for the war effort too . . .*

Nineteen

'So, you have no nursing experience?'

'No, ma'am. I'm sorry . . .'

'Don't be. There are plenty of jobs here for a strong young woman, though the work is rather menial.'

Rosie had left the village at the beginning of October. She'd headed towards Lincoln, learning on the way that a school on Wragby Road was being turned into a military hospital. She'd found the building and now she stood facing a tall, thin, middle-aged woman dressed in some kind of uniform, though she wasn't quite sure what it represented; a navy-blue dress with stiff, white cuffs and a white cap.

'What is your name?'

'Rosie Skelton.' She had decided to call herself by the same name which she knew her father had adopted.

'Have you any references?'

'No, I'm sorry, I haven't.'

The woman looked her up and down with a searching glance. 'Come into my office and we'll have a little talk.'

Inside the small room the woman sat down behind a desk and indicated for Rosie to sit down in front of her. 'I am Miss Archer and I am the matron of this recently opened hospital. We are known as the Fourth Northern General Hospital.' She smiled and the severe lines of her face relaxed. 'You might have guessed the building we are occupying was a school before the start of the war. The Lincoln Grammar School. The pupils have, of course, been sent elsewhere for the duration of the war. Additional huts for our use are being erected on the playing fields. So, tell me about yourself, Miss Skelton.'

Rosie licked her lips and began the speech she had rehearsed. She'd decided to stick to as much of the truth as possible.

'I'm from a small village in Lincolnshire. I lived with my father, who used to work on the land, but when the war started, he volunteered. It was difficult for me to stay on in our cottage – I don't think the master would have granted me the tenancy to stay there on my own after my father had gone. So, I decided to do the same – to volunteer for some sort of war work.'

'Very admirable,' the matron murmured. 'You look like you're a strong young woman and if you're honest and hardworking, I can certainly find work for you. I'll give you a one-month trial as a cleaner to start with. If you do well, you may be transferred to being a ward orderly.' She paused and then added, 'And even beyond that, if you prove yourself suitable, I might consider putting you forward to become an assistant nurse. You're not squeamish at the sight of blood, are you?'

Rosie thought of all the rabbits and hares she had skinned, the fish she had gutted, the birds she had plucked and drawn. 'No, ma'am, I am not.'

'You would receive some basic training in first aid and nursing and would work under the trained nurses. We have a few already and they are invaluable in assisting the experienced nurses who, when we have a convoy arrive, can be quickly overwhelmed.'

Rosie beamed. 'Thank you, ma'am . . .'

'You address me as "Matron". The woman in charge of you will be Mrs Duncan. She oversees all the auxiliary staff. She will put you with someone who will show you the ropes.'

Mrs Duncan was a buxom woman with a broad, welcoming smile. She reminded Rosie of Nell.

'Now then, duck.' She looked Rosie up and down and her smile widened. 'You look a strong, healthy lass. Matron ses to give you a try, so that's what we'll do.' Then her face sobered. 'The work's hard and you'll see some horrible sights, so I hope you're not squeamish. You don't faint at the sight of blood and gore, do you?'

Rosie swallowed the laughter that bubbled up in her throat but she managed to keep her expression serious. 'No, ma'am. Not at all.'

'Call me Mrs Duncan, duck. Right, I'll put you to work with Anna. Anna Dawson. She's not been with us long but she's a good lass and will show you what to do. You do whatever she tells you and you won't go far wrong. Any questions?'

'Only one, ma'am – sorry, Mrs Duncan.'

The woman laughed. 'About the pay, is it?'

'No. I was just wondering where I could sleep.'

Mrs Duncan blinked. 'Ah. You don't live in the city, then?'

'No. I've walked here from the country. My dad volunteered and I'm on my own now so I wanted to help with the war effort.'

'Most of our manual workers live locally but we'll talk to Anna. She came to us from the work-house, so she has a little room in the attic here. She might have an idea. Come along, we'll go and find her.'

Anna was working in one of the wards, sweeping under the beds and wiping down the iron bedsteads. She didn't, Rosie noticed, touch the patients at all, not even to straighten their rumpled bedding. Rosie glanced at the patients and drew in a sharp breath. There were about a dozen wounded soldiers in the ward; several were heavily bandaged about the head and were lying perfectly still, their eyes closed. One or two were sitting up and looking about them. Another had a cage over his left leg and yet another was propped up against pillows. His eyes were closed and his breathing was a harsh rasping sound.

'Anna? A word, if you please?'

The girl stopped her sweeping and came towards them. She was painfully thin with a sallow complexion, lank brown hair and huge brown eyes that held a depth of suffering. Beside her Rosie was the picture of robust health.

'This is Rosie, Anna. She's on trial for a month. Can you take her under your wing and show her what to do?'

'Of course, Mrs Duncan.' The girl cast a swift, almost frightened glance at Rosie.

'Rosie has nowhere to stay, Anna. She's not from

around here. Do you know if there are any spare rooms in the attic where you are?'

Anna shook her head. 'I don't think so, but – but . . .'

'Go on.'

'There's a spare bed in my room. She – she could share with me, if she doesn't mind.'

Rosie smiled. 'Of course, I don't. As long as *you* don't mind.'

A small smile flickered on the girl's mouth. 'Oh, I'm used to sharing, miss. In the workhouse we slept in dormitories. Twelve to a room. I've liked having my own room, but I do get a bit lonely at times. It'll be nice to share with you.'

'Right, then,' Mrs Duncan smiled at them both, 'I'll give you ten minutes to take Rosie upstairs, Anna, where she can leave her bag, and then if you could get her kitted out with an apron and what-ever else she needs, she can start work alongside you now.'

'The room's bit small,' Anna said, as she led Rosie up the flights of stairs and into the attic. 'I don't know what you're used to, miss.'

'This is fine, Anna. I lived in a cottage in the countryside and my bedroom was under the eaves, reached by a ladder, and was no bigger than this. And, by the way, please call me Rosie.'

'Right you are, then, Miss Rosie.'

'No, no, just Rosie.'

The work was hard and Rosie was amazed at how strong Anna must be beneath the waif-like appearance.

'My word,' she said as they finished for the day and she eased her aching back. 'You must be a lot stronger than you look, Anna.'

The girl smiled. 'The workhouse was exactly what its name implies. We all worked hard, those of us who could, that is. Now, let's go and get summat to eat. I'm always hungry, but the food's lovely here.'

While they ate, Anna introduced Rosie to a few of the other workers, including one or two nurses. 'They're ever so nice,' Anna whispered, referring to the young women dressed in smart uniforms, who came to sit at the same table. 'You'd think they wouldn't want to mix with the likes of us but—'

'Hello, there,' one rosy-cheeked nurse, with blond curls peeping from beneath her cap, smiled at Rosie. 'You're new, aren't you? My name's Vera. What's yours?'

'Rosie.'

'You're very welcome, Rosie. We all muck in together here. No pulling rank. We' – she waved her fork at a few of her colleagues who were collecting their meal and sitting nearby – 'all consider that we need you lot to help us do our job. We're all in the same boat and we all have to paddle together.' She leaned a little closer to Rosie and Anna. 'And I'll tell you something else. If you do well, Mrs Duncan and Matron will get their heads together and might let you do a bit more than just the cleaning. Not nursing, of course, if you haven't had any training, but things like bed making, helping the patients to move, even writing letters home for them. That sort of thing.

But, in time, you might be taken on for training and become an assistant nurse.'

'I'm willing to do anything asked of me,' Rosie said and was rewarded by a beam of delight from Vera and nods of approval from one or two others.

As they left the dining room, Rosie asked Anna, 'Is there anything else we have to do? I'm whacked. I'm for bed, if you don't mind.'

'No, we're done for today but we have to start at six in the morning, so we have to be up and to have had our breakfast to report for duty by then.'

Rosie nodded and yawned. 'I didn't get much sleep last night. The barn where I slept was cold and very draughty.'

Anna gaped at her. 'A barn? You slept in a barn?'

Rosie giggled. 'Yes, but I had to be up and away before dawn in case the farmer caught me.'

'But – but . . . Oh my. A barn! And I thought the workhouse was bad. Haven't – hadn't you got a home, then?'

'I had to leave. My father volunteered and, as it was a rented cottage, I heard that the landlord was going to turn me out, so I left.'

'So – where did you live?'

'A little village in the middle of nowhere.' Rosie smiled. 'I don't expect you'd know it.'

'No, I probably wouldn't. I never got outside the workhouse gates until I came here.'

'Were you in the workhouse long?' Rosie asked tentatively. She was careful not to pry too much; she didn't want to have to answer awkward questions about her own past.

'All my life,' Anna said simply. 'I was born there and my mother died at my birth. I – I have no idea who my father was.' Her head drooped. 'I think I'm what they call a bastard.'

Rosie was suddenly aware of how lucky she'd been in her life. True, she'd lost her mother too, but her father had cared for her even though he'd brought her up to live close to the edge of the law. Luckily, until recently, she'd never even been questioned by the police. But she was thankful to have left that life behind and to have been given a chance to do something useful. But oh how she missed her dad, Nell and Nathan. And most of all, she missed being close to Byron.

She wondered where they all were now. Only Nell would still be safely in her little cottage. She hoped her neighbours would be good to her and watch out for her and that Sarah from the manor would keep bringing the servants' washing to her, giving Nell a small income. And it was Mrs Ramsey and Sarah whom Rosie had to thank for giving her a warning about the master and his intentions to have her thrown out. Because of them both, Rosie had been able to leave of her own accord.

'So, that wretched girl has escaped retribution, has she?' William glared at his wife. 'Did you have anything to do with it?'

Grace regarded him steadily. 'My dear, I don't know who on earth you're talking about.'

'Waterhouse's brat. She's left the cottage. I sent Pickering to evict her, but she's gone.'

With a supreme effort, Grace managed not to smile. She was pleased that the girl had thwarted her vindictive husband. She was sure in her own mind that Rosie had had nothing to do with the tragic events, though she wasn't sure about Sam. And, of course, she was sensible enough to realize that Rosie could well have been with him that night. But, whatever the truth, Grace couldn't help herself feeling glad that the girl had escaped. She would ask Sarah to talk to Nell the next time she saw her.

'Anyway,' William was saying, 'at least I can re-let their cottage now. I'll have Pickering burn any belongings they've left. Good riddance. Sam Waterhouse has been a thorn in my side for years.'

'So why did you not get rid of him?' Grace asked mildly.

William gave a wry laugh. 'I have asked myself that many times, my dear. The truth is that although he was a poacher on my lands, he was still useful. Amos swore to me that Waterhouse was a good worker at busy times when extra hands were needed and would do jobs that others hated. He was the local rat catcher. He kept the moles down and he would clean out sewers and drains. As for his poaching, yes, he did trespass on my land and kill my game and I'm sure, over the years, he's had a few pheasants, partridge and such, but my father turned a blind eye to Little Titch, who was the poacher here in his day, and so I decided to do the same with Sam Waterhouse. But only to a point, mind you.'

Grace pursed her lips to stop the ready retort that

sprang to them. William was trying to make out he was a philanthropic landlord and employer when the opposite was the truth. If anyone had 'turned a blind eye' to Sam's poaching, it had been Amos Taylor – not William. She hesitated before saying any more; she didn't want William questioning how she came to know such things. And yet . . .

'I'm sure you know,' she began carefully, 'that I hear the servants' gossip now and again and rumour has it that Sam never *sold* what he caught. What he didn't need for himself and his daughter, he gave to the villagers during hard times, especially during harsh winters.'

William's answer was surprisingly mild. 'Yes, old Amos used to tell me that too.' He sighed. 'My father was too soft. I think Little Titch appeared before him in court once and, as a magistrate at that time, he let him off.' He smiled smugly. 'But I let it be known that if Sam was ever caught red-handed, he'd be up before the magistrate. And considering *I* am now a local magistrate, he wouldn't have stood much of a chance if he'd appeared in front of me, now, would he?' He paused and then added, 'I think Byron takes after his grandfather rather than me. He'll be far too lenient. He'll let them get away with—' He stopped suddenly, realizing what he had been about to say. He grunted and rose from his chair. 'I'm going for a ride around the estate. I'll see Pickering about getting another gamekeeper. Amos can't go on any longer.'

'Will it matter now?' Grace murmured. 'Your poachers are both gone.'

'Huh! Don't you believe it. There'll always be someone to take their place. You mark my words.'

Grace gazed at the door after her husband had left the room. Then she rang the bell for Sarah.

Twenty

'Morning, Nell,' Sarah greeted her on the following Monday. 'How's things?'

Nell shrugged lethargically. She was missing Rosie and was desperately worried about Nathan. She hadn't had a letter for two weeks. The last time she'd heard from him, he'd still been in the training camp, but now she wondered if he'd been moved elsewhere. She just prayed that he – and the rest of the young men who had gone with him – had not been sent abroad yet. Her neighbour, Ivy, hadn't heard from Dan either. Both women were very worried.

When Nell didn't answer, Sarah, who had become very fond of the woman who was probably only a few years older than herself, put her arm around her shoulders. 'Come on, Nell. You can tell me. It won't get back to the mistress – and certainly not to the master – if you ask me not to say anything.'

'It's no secret really, Sarah. I miss my lad.'

'That's only natural. All the mothers whose sons have gone are worried sick – including, I might say, Mrs Ramsey.' She paused a moment and then added softly, 'But you feel like you've lost a daughter, too, don't you?'

Nell nodded and wiped her eyes with the corner of her apron. 'Yes, yes, I do. Rosie was the daughter I never had.'

'D'you know where she's gone?'

'No, Sarah, I don't and, in some ways, I don't want to know. I'd just like to know she's all right, that's all.'

'I'm sure she will be. She's a resourceful girl and there'll be plenty of jobs going for young women now that all the menfolk are rushing to volunteer.'

'How's Mrs Ramsey coping? She seems a nice woman.'

'She is, Nell, take my word for it. Too good for the likes of *him*.' She laughed. 'But please don't quote me on that, else I'll lose my job.'

'I wouldn't, Sarah. I know how to hold me tongue when I have to.'

'I don't suppose you've heard anything of Sam either, have you?'

Now Nell, much as she liked Sarah, who she felt was fast becoming a friend, was wary. She wanted to trust her, wanted to believe that anything she said to her would not be repeated back at the manor, but this could be Sam's life at stake. So, she was thankful to be able to say just what Rosie had told her and everyone else in the village. Of course, they all had their own ideas about what had happened that night, but no one actually knew. Only, perhaps, Rosie, and now she had left too. So, Nell was able to say quite truthfully, 'No, Sarah, I haven't. All I know is what Rosie told all of us. He left to volunteer.'

'But didn't he come to say goodbye to you? You were very close, weren't you?'

Nell smiled wryly. So the village gossip had reached the manor, then. There was no point in denying it – and she had no wish to either. 'Yes, we were.' She avoided saying whether or not Sam had bade her farewell. 'But I miss all of them.'

'If it's any consolation, Nell, Sam and Rosie are best out of the way. The master is still gunning for Rosie even though he can't prove anything.'

'I know and it was good of you to tip us the wink.'

'He's on the look-out for another gamekeeper now.'

'What about poor old Amos?'

'It'll be the workhouse for him this time, I shouldn't wonder. The master doesn't believe in his retired workers taking up a valuable property he can rent out. He's not like his father was. He was a nice old boy from what everyone tells me, though I never knew him. He wouldn't see any of his old retainers put in the workhouse. But this one . . .' Sarah shook her head.

Nell said no more, but a plan took root in her mind.

'Come in, Foster.' William waved the policeman into his study. 'That will be all, Baines,' he added, dismissing the attentive butler. Douglas Foster stood in front of William's desk, his helmet under his arm.

'You wanted to see me, sir?' he said with as much politeness in his tone as he could muster. If there was one man on his patch whom he hated, it was William Ramsey. The policeman had witnessed at first hand the poverty and suffering this man caused by his selfish, ruthless ways. He was every bit as bad as a dictator in Douglas's eyes. He reckoned William could give old Kaiser Bill a run for his money.

William leaned back in his chair and linked his fingers across his ample stomach. 'Indeed I do, Foster. I am about to set on a new gamekeeper and I have dismissed Taylor. Hopefully, this time he will not have the chance to take up possession of his cottage and his job again if I were to find myself temporarily without a gamekeeper. This time, I want him gone for good. You will escort him to the nearest work-house, Foster. I think my trust in him over the years has been badly misplaced. I allowed him to persuade me, against my better judgement, I might add, to allow that wretched Waterhouse to carry on living here. He was forever bleating on about how Waterhouse did the jobs that no one else wanted to do. I should have evicted him and his daughter years ago. But, out of the goodness of my heart' – Douglas had to stifle a wry chuckle – 'I allowed them to stay on after his wife died. I regret that decision now. I should have been tougher.'

'I'll see what I can do, sir.'

'You'll do better than that, Foster. You will carry out my orders or I shall make sure your superiors hear about your insubordination.'

The policeman kept his face deadpan and his eyes fixed upon a point on the wall just behind William's head.

'And there's another thing. I want you to find out if it's true that Waterhouse volunteered. If he did, I want him cashiered so that he can stand trial.'

Now, Douglas had to press his lips together to stop himself retaliating. Instead, all he said was a stiff, 'Sir.'

'And have you any idea where the girl's gone?'

'No, sir, I haven't.' Although he had seen Rosie as she left the village, she had not told him where she was going. He hadn't wanted to know either because he knew he'd be asked questions at some point.

'Well, find out, if you can. I want her in gaol too.' He paused briefly and then added, 'That will be all, Foster. I trust you can see yourself out? I'm hardly afraid that you're going to steal the silver.' William laughed at his own joke and waved the man away.

Douglas rode his bicycle away from the manor and up the slope towards the far end of the woods where the gamekeeper's cottage stood. He was seething. The arrogance of the man! He enjoyed ruling people's lives and, it seemed, ruining them on a whim. It wouldn't have hurt him or his pocket to have found the poor old man a cottage somewhere on the estate. There was at least one standing empty now that Rosie had left.

Douglas came to a halt outside the keeper's cottage and leaned his bicycle against the fence. Amos was in the front garden hoeing. He wouldn't have to do this for much longer, Douglas thought. There was a definite autumnal chill in the air that would soon turn to wintry weather and, sadly, the old man wouldn't be *able* to do it for many more days; he wouldn't be here.

Amos looked up. 'Come to tell me to pack me bags, have you, Mr Foster?'

'No need to be so formal, Amos. It's always been "Douglas" to you, now hasn't it?'

'Not when you're on official duty, as I expect you are now.'

'I've been put in a very awkward position. Sometimes, Amos, I hate my job.'

Amos leaned on his hoe and looked Douglas straight in the eyes. 'Aye well, I'll not make it any harder for you. You're a good man and a fair one when you're able to be. We all know you've done your best to help young Rosie, though if her old man was still around, you wouldn't be able to turn a blind eye then, would you?' He laughed throatily. 'Like we've both done over the years, eh?'

'Aye, well, we both knew what they were doing to help the villagers when times were hard,' Douglas said.

'He never sold anything, y'know. Just gave it to those in most need.'

'To be honest, Amos, I hope they both stay well away from here because that old bugger down there in the vale is determined to get his hands on them. Both of 'em, if he can.'

'Now, now, Douglas, language like that coming from an upholder of the law.'

'I could think of worse to say about him, Amos. Believe me.' There was a long pause before Douglas said quietly, 'So, what, my old friend, am I going to do about you?'

A month after Rosie had arrived at the Lincoln hospital and had begun to work alongside Anna, the matron called them both to her office.

198

'Have we done something wrong?' Anna whispered, her brown eyes wide with anxiety as they hurried to answer the summons. The girl had altered even during the short time Rosie had known her. She was no longer the little waif from the workhouse. She had put on some weight and her skin was a healthier colour. Her brown hair – with Rosie's help – now shone. Though most of the time imprisoned beneath her cap, when loosened, it curled prettily around her elfin face.

'Not that I can think of.' Rosie was worried too. She liked this job and was happy here – at least as happy as she was able to be when she could have no news about her father, nor even of Byron and Nathan. She had not dared to write to Nell to let her know where she was; she was so afraid that news would get back to William Ramsey and that he would come looking for her.

They stood meekly before the matron, but felt some relief when they saw that the woman was smiling at them.

'You've both done so well in your work as cleaners. You've both been so willing to take on extra duties whenever you've been asked. Usually, the next step would be for you to become ward orderlies, but from all the reports I hear about you, my senior staff think you should be tried out as assistant nurses now. You're badly needed on the wards. You will wear a uniform and a white apron with a red cross on the bib. This will distinguish you from the ancillary workers and yet also show that you are not trained nurses. We'll see how you do. You will not, of course, be able to carry out any actual nursing tasks – you are not qualified or experienced – but there are so many jobs you could do for the patients that would free up my nurses. I am going to try you out in the ward where the casualties are first admitted. I must warn you that it is not a pleasant place to be. The men have some dreadful injuries but it is the ward where the nurses are most under pressure to attend to wounds as quickly as possible and then assign the patients to other wards. Your help in keeping the beds changed, moving the patients, helping them wherever and whenever you can, will be invaluable. And I'd also like you to observe the nurses carefully at all times. As you progress, you may be able to undertake simple nursing tasks. And in the future, well' – she paused – 'who knows what the future holds for any of us? So, will you do it?'

'Oh yes, Matron,' they chorused.

'You will move to the nurses' accommodation, but I will ensure that you stay together as I would like you to continue to work together on the wards, so you will be on the same shifts.'

The room they were given was, to the two girls from such humble backgrounds, palatial.

'There's so much room,' Anna whispered, almost fearful that she was dreaming and that suddenly all this would be whipped away and she would wake up in the attic bedroom, or, worse still, back in the workhouse.

'Look,' Rosie said, 'we have a proper wardrobe.'

'And a chest of drawers.'

'We're to be given two sets of uniform with two extra aprons, which we must keep clean at all times.'

Anna's face sobered. 'We're going to see some dreadful sights, Rosie. I just hope I'm going to be up to it.'

Rosie put her arms round the girl. She had become very fond of Anna. 'We'll be fine. We've seen quite a lot already. I think the secret may be to concentrate on the patient and trying to help them as best we can and not dwell on how *we* feel.'

'I'll try.'

Sister Makepeace was in charge of the ward to which they were assigned. It was perhaps the busiest ward where the patients were first admitted. She was plump and kindly, but expected the very best of all her staff.

'If you work well, we shall get along fine,' she told them with a beaming smile, 'but if you don't, I can be a veritable dragon.' Her face sobered. 'Seriously, we are dealing with some very poorly men, many of whom, sadly, are going to die. But you must always try to be cheerful and optimistic. They will pick up on your mood very quickly and we don't want any of our patients to lose hope. Sometimes, that's all they have. They have, of course, been in field hospitals in France and some have been in hospitals in the south of England, but many have come here straight from abroad. They will be the worst cases for us to deal with because they might not have had proper treatment and their wounds may be more serious because of it.'

The work was hard and soul-destroying, as they had been warned. Male orderlies carried the patients into the admissions ward. Each time a new batch of wounded arrived, Rosie went among them, searching their faces, dreading to see someone she knew . . .

Twenty-One

'When is that wretched girl going to do her duty and bring my grandson back home where he belongs?' William raged several times a day. Since Pearl had taken Bertie to her parents for what had turned into an extended stay, and since Byron had left, William's temper had deteriorated so that he was in a foul mood most of the time. 'I've a good mind to take the carriage and fetch him home myself.'

'That, my dear, would be tantamount to kidnapping,' Grace pointed out calmly.

'He's my grandson,' William growled. 'He should be here – with me – learning how to run the estate.'

'My dear William,' even in the face of his wrath, Grace dared to say, 'the child is only just over a year old.'

'Yes, and we missed his first birthday too. Anyway, that's beside the point. He should be here with me, absorbing the way of life he will one day lead. His future. He needs to be under *my* guidance.'

'Perhaps Henry Anderson feels the same way. It is probable that Bertie will be his heir too. Pearl is an only child and – sadly – our grandson may well be Byron's only child too.'

William grunted. It was a statement he could not refute but it did not please him.

'I think she may be enjoying herself a little too much at home. I've a good mind to have her watched.'

Deftly, Grace changed the subject, but her next words angered him even more.

'Lady Helene has invited me to stay with her in Lincoln for a few days. She is organizing a fundraising event for the local hospital and would appreciate my help. After all she has done for this family, I feel I cannot refuse.'

'Must you go?'

'I feel obliged, William.'

'Well, don't stay away too long.'

'She has organized for us to visit the hospital for which she is raising funds. I believe it is called the Fourth Northern General Hospital and is housed in what used to be a boys' school. It was requisitioned early in the war and the pupils were moved out. She wants to raise money for extra treats at Christmas for the wounded.'

Uninterested, William turned away with a grunt.

Grace left home the following morning with relief. She knew her duty lay with her husband but just sometimes it was good to be separated from him for a short while. She was looking forward to spending time with Lady Helene and to helping her with the fundraising.

As they sat down to dinner that evening, Helene said, 'The event will take place on Saturday in the hospital grounds, my dear, but I have arranged a private visit there for tomorrow afternoon. I thought you would like to see what the money raised will be for, but I must warn you, the visit will be quite harrowing. There are some very sick and wounded men there.'

'I'll cope, Helene. My focus will be on them and how we can help. I will not give way to my sensitivities, I assure you.'

'You're a very strong woman under that serene exterior, aren't you, Grace?'

Grace inclined her head at the compliment, but did not reply.

The following afternoon the two women arrived at the hospital to be met by the matron. She escorted them through the wards where they spoke to the patients who were well enough to respond.

'And now, if you're sure, I'll take you to the admissions ward. This is the hardest place to visit and certainly to work. The nurses and their helpers see some dreadful sights. But all my girls rise to the occasion. I am fortunate to have a dedicated team right through from the cleaners to the sisters in charge. Please, follow me.'

They stepped into the ward behind the matron and glanced around them. The sight which met their eyes looked, to their inexperienced eyes, like a battlefield. Just as they entered the ward, a batch of new arrivals were being brought in. Men with torn uniforms, filthy bandages and their faces contorted with suffering. Some were crying out in pain, others gasped for breath and clawed at the air.

A young girl, with bright red tendrils escaping from her cap, her apron soaked in blood, stood up from the wounded man she'd been helping to lift onto a bed. 'I'll fetch—' she began as she turned towards them. She stopped, her eyes wide and staring as she caught sight of the matron and her two visitors.

'Oh – oh! *Ma'am* . . .' she whispered.

Grace too stared back. Even though she had never seen her close up before, she knew at once who she was. 'Rosie,' she breathed, but not loud enough for either of her companions to hear. Then, deliberately, she looked away and moved aside for Rosie to go wherever she had been going. Rosie scuttled away on her errand to fetch a bowl of clean water and more bandages for the nurse who was attending to the badly injured patient. Her heart was pounding. Mrs Ramsey was the last person she had expected to see in this place. Byron, yes, though she had feared that happening, but not his mother.

As she filled the bowl with warm water, she felt tears prickle the back of her eyelids. She would have to leave. She would have to flee somewhere else. Somewhere where the Ramsey family wouldn't be able to find her. She'd been foolish to stay as close to home as Lincoln, but she was loving it here. She felt that, at last, she was being really useful to others. She'd wanted, more than anything, to leave her past behind and make a fresh start. But now it seemed as if that was all in ruins. No doubt, Mrs Ramsey would already be telling the matron exactly who one of her nursing assistants was. With shaking hands, she carried the bowl and the bandages back to the ward. The patient's need was greater than her own fears. Whatever happened to her, she must carry on with her duties. At least, for now.

The matron and her two visitors had moved further down the ward. Rosie tried to concentrate on the job in hand, but her ears were straining to hear their conversation.

'May I talk to the nurses?' Grace was saying.

Matron inclined her head. 'Please don't interrupt them if they are attending to a patient. These men coming in today need urgent care and attention.'

'Of course.'

Out of the corner of her eye, Rosie watched Mrs Ramsey move back along the room, coming ever closer. At last she stood beside her. Rosie looked up to see that Grace was smiling at her as she whispered, 'It's all right. I don't know you.' Then, in a louder voice, she added, 'I understand from the matron that you are not qualified, but that you are doing sterling work assisting the experienced nurses.'

'Yes, ma'am,' Rosie whispered hoarsely. What had she meant when she'd said she didn't know her? Surely, she didn't mean . . . ?

'I'm so glad you've found such a rewarding job, my dear.' Lowering her voice, Grace added, 'You will be quite safe here.' She smiled and raised her voice again to say, 'My son has joined up and I would like to think that if he were wounded, he would come to a hospital like this to be cared for by all you wonderful young women.'

Rosie drew in a sharp breath and stared at Grace. She had the feeling that the woman was trying to tell her something. Her next words confirmed it. 'My son volunteered and left with friends from the village where I live. As far as I know, they're still in England at the moment. I get a letter once a week. Anyway, it was good to meet you, my dear. Take care. Goodbye.'

As Mrs Ramsey turned away to join her friend and the matron, Rosie stared after her. Surely, she would go back home and tell her husband that she had found the runaway poacher's daughter? And yet, would she? It was obvious that she'd been trying to tell Rosie that both Byron and Nathan were still safe at present.

The fundraising event in the grounds of the hospital the following Saturday afternoon was a great success. Luckily, it was a fine November day.

'I couldn't have done it without you, Grace,' Helene said. 'And all that lovely money will go to the hospital possibly to buy extra Christmas treats for the wounded. Every penny of it will go there. I'll make sure of that.'

'Will any of it be spent on the welfare of the nurses and their helpers? I thought one or two of the girls looked exhausted.' Grace was careful not to mention anyone by name. She didn't want to draw anyone's attention to Rosie.

'That's a very good suggestion. After all, if the staff don't keep healthy, they can't look after their patients properly, can they? I'll talk to the matron myself and see what can be done. Perhaps we could arrange charabanc trips for them when they are off duty. A day at the seaside when the warmer weather comes would do them the world of good.'

Grace returned home, satisfied that she had been useful in a small way, but the visit to the hospital had left her feeling restless. Her mind kept returning to the scenes she had witnessed; the hard-pressed nurses, the wounded men. She wanted to do more than just raise money, badly needed though it was. She would give the matter serious thought, but for the moment there was something else she had to do. Grace visited the village more often now than she had done in the past. She felt an affinity with the women whose menfolk had gone to war. She'd always been a good and dutiful wife to the owner of the estate and had always taken an interest in the welfare and wellbeing of all her husband's tenants, albeit rather a distant one. Recently, however, she had decided to disregard her husband's demands and to keep in touch with the villagers personally. In truth, she cared for them and about them far more than William did. Normally, she got Monty to drive her there in the pony and trap while she visited. Grace had never learned to ride or to drive the trap, but today she wanted to go alone. She didn't want anyone to know where she was going; not even Sarah. Dressed in her walking clothes and taking one of her husband's stout sticks from the hall stand, she set out towards the lake. She often walked around the grounds, down to the lake and the stream. If anyone saw her from the house, they would not think it unusual. She followed the path of the stream until she came to the stepping stones. She glanced back towards the house, but trees obscured the view so now no one would be able to see her either. Picking up her skirts she crossed the stream, stepping carefully onto each stone. Safely on the opposite bank, she climbed the slope to the trees at the top, glancing back every so often to make sure she was not being watched. Beneath the shadow of the trees, she felt a little safer, but now she was exploring new ground. She had never been into the woods before but her sense of direction was good and she emerged on the far side just above the now-empty cottage where Sam and Rosie had lived. She glanced to her right and saw the cluster of cottages and houses that made up the village of Thornsby, many of which she now visited more regularly. And then, on the outskirts of the village nearest to where she was standing, she saw the dwelling she sought: Nell Tranter's cottage. She set off towards it.

When she opened the door in answer to Grace's knock, Nell was startled. 'Oh, madam. What are you doing here? Is Sarah ill?'

Grace smiled. 'No, Mrs Tranter, but I wanted to see you privately. I don't want anyone to know, not even Sarah.'

'Come in, madam. Come in. Will you take a cup of tea with me?' Nell didn't mind the expense when she was being visited by the mistress from the manor.

'That would be lovely.' She laughed. 'It's a longer walk than I'd thought.'

'Come and sit down while I make it.'

When they were seated together on the opposite sides of the hearth, Grace said, 'I knew you'd want to know this but I don't want anyone else to hear what I have to tell you. I've seen Rosie.'

Nell gasped and her cup rattled in its saucer. 'Oh madam . . .'

'It's all right. She's well. She's working at the military hospital in Lincoln and because she lives there too, I think she's reasonably safe.' Grace related the story of how she had come to meet Rosie. 'She's doing remarkable work, Mrs Tranter.'

'But – but what about the master? When he hears, he—'

'He won't hear. At least, not from me.'

Now Nell's mouth dropped open and she gaped at Grace. 'You mean – you mean – you're not going to tell him?'

'I most certainly am not. Look, whatever happened that night – and perhaps we'll never know – I don't think Rosie is guilty. Oh, she might *know* what happened, but no one in their right mind would expect her to give her father away, now would they, even if indeed he was the one who shot Darby? And if he did, I am sure in my own mind, it must have been a terrible accident.'

Nell winced at Grace's bald statement. 'She never said a word, madam. Not to me, or even to Nathan.' She bit her lip. Even though she trusted Grace, she wasn't going to tell her about Sam's clandestine last visit to see his daughter. That was their secret. Hers and Rosie's. Even Nathan didn't know.

'Do you hear from Nathan?'

'Now and again, madam. He's not much of a letter writer.' She smiled fondly, but there was a deep sadness in her smile.

'Byron writes every week. They're still together and they're still in this country at the moment, though he can never tell me exactly where.'

211

Nell let out a huge sigh. 'Oh, that's a relief. Thank you.'

Grace leaned across the hearth and touched Nell's hand. 'But we have to brace ourselves that they will probably be sent abroad at some point.'

Nell nodded and tears filled her eyes. 'I know,' she whispered. 'I know.'

'And there's one more thing you just might be able to help with. My husband is turning Amos Taylor out of his cottage any day now and PC Foster has been charged with the awful task of escorting him to the workhouse.'

Nell nodded. 'You leave that with me, madam. I've got an idea.'

Twenty-Two

Later that afternoon, after Grace's unexpected visit, Nell donned her hat and her warmest coat against the November chill and followed the same pathway through the woods that had brought her visitor, but on reaching the far side, she turned to her left towards the gamekeeper's cottage.

'Now then, Amos,' she greeted him as he straightened up from digging in his vegetable patch.

'Mrs Tranter. To what do I owe this pleasure? But first, come and sit yarsen down. You've had a fair walk through the woods.'

They sat together on a bench seat near his front door, facing down the slope towards the manor. Nell looked about her. The garden was well kept, not only with vegetables, but also flowers, which, in summer, created a colourful display.

'You've got a lovely little cottage, Amos, and you keep the garden grand, whatever the time of year. It's always a picture. I wish I had green fingers but all I seem to have is two dirty great thumbs.'

Amos looked sorrowful. 'Aye, I've liked living here, but it won't be for much longer.'

'How's that? I thought you were back here since – well, you know.'

213

'It was only temporary, until the master found another gamekeeper, and from what Pickering told me yesterday, he has.'

'You lodged at the pub when you moved out before, didn't you? When Darby came?'

'Yes, I did, but it wasn't ideal. No garden to tend, see. I was lost with nowt to do. I tried to help out with the pub work, but it was far too heavy. All them barrels.'

'So, where will you go this time?'

'There's only one place I can go, Mrs Tranter. The workhouse.'

Nell took a deep breath. 'How would you like to be my lodger? I'm on me own now since Nathan went.' She rushed on, her words tumbling over themselves to make her meaning clear from the outset. 'And I could do with a man about the place and – and the company. But I'm not suggesting you should take Sam's place. I'm sure the village gossips know that me and Sam were close. No, this would be a purely business arrangement. Bed and board in exchange for you keeping me garden nice and doing a few tasks around the place that I find hard now Nathan's gone.'

'But he'll come back. What then?'

Nell was silent for a moment as her greatest fear surfaced. Nathan might not come back. But she voiced none of this to Amos. 'We'll cross that bridge when we come to it. I don't think this war's going to be over very quickly like they're all reckoning. I think we've all got to deal with the here and now and right at this moment, you need a home and I need some help.'

'Well, I thank you, Mrs Tranter, and gladly accept your offer. And you've nowt to fear from me trying to take Sam's place. I promise you that.'

Nell nodded. 'We understand each other, then. And the name's Nell, by the way.'

'There'll be tongues wagging though.'

Nell laughed and flapped her hand as if batting away irritating flies. 'Think I'm not used to that, Amos? When would you want to move in?'

'When the new feller gets here. I think he's coming on Saturday.'

'That'll be fine. Just gives me time to get Nathan's room ready for you. And don't you worry about what happens when he comes home on leave. I'm lucky. I've got a nice little cottage with a front parlour I only ever use on high days and holidays. Just Christmas and maybe Easter. It's got a nice comfy couch. He can sleep in there.' She stood up. 'Right, that's settled then. I'll be off now. See you Saturday.'

Nell walked back through the woods with a satis-fied smile on her face. She had been very lonely since Nathan, Sam and, lastly, Rosie had all left. She wasn't in the least fazed by the gossip that would run riot through the village, no doubt started by her neigh-bour, Ivy Bates. Her smile broadened. In fact, Nell realized, she actually enjoyed causing a bit of a stir.

Grace was feeling very unsettled. And she was lonely too. She hardly saw William. He'd left the house by the time she came down to breakfast. She lunched alone, so she only saw him at dinner. And more often than not he was silent and withdrawn. When he did

215

engage in conversation, it was usually to rant about Byron's foolishness and the continuing absence of his grandson from what William considered to be the boy's rightful home.

'She'd never have gone if Byron had stayed at home instead of rushing off to play the hero. What if he's killed and doesn't come back? What then? You tell me that?'

A tremor of fear flooded through Grace at the mere thought of losing her beloved son, but she kept her voice calm. 'Bertie will always be your heir wherever he is.'

'Of course he will, but he should be here – with me.' He grumbled and groused for a while longer before saying, 'The new gamekeeper arrives on Saturday,' and adding sarcastically, 'let's hope this one doesn't get shot.'

'What about Amos?'

'Oh, he knows to move out that morning.'

'Where will he go?'

'I really have no idea.' William feigned disinterest, although he believed there was only one place the elderly man could go. The workhouse.

Grace stared at him. How could he be so callous about a man who had given him – and his father before him – loyal service the whole of his working life? Greatly daring, she said, 'I understand from Bella that Henry Anderson has built a row of small cottages on his land to house his old retainers when they can no longer work.'

William grunted. 'More fool him, then. A waste of good money when there's a perfectly good workhouse in the district.' He rose from the table. 'I'll see you in an hour.' It was his way of saying that he would visit her bedroom that night. Grace shuddered. She was a dutiful wife and would never refuse his needs, but it was a long time since she had actually enjoyed his attentions. But perhaps, she thought, as she too rose and went to her room, there was another way.

The following morning, Grace sat down at her small writing desk in the morning room and began a letter.

Dear Matron,
I was much impressed by my visit to the hospital and would like to do something more practical. I have no nursing experience, but I would like to help in the wards as an orderly. I would be willing to do anything asked of me, however menial. I would also be willing to share accommodation, if necessary. There is just one thing I would ask of you in return; that no one at the hospital should learn about my background. If you think I could be of service, I want to be accepted as one of your workers with no special treatment or favours. If you do have a space for me, I would like to start with you in January.

Grace paused and bit her lip. There was one person already working there who knew exactly who Grace Ramsey was, but she was sure that Rosie would say nothing; she had too much to hide herself.

The matron's reply came by return of post.

Dear Mrs Ramsey,

We would be delighted to have your help in any capacity you feel able to undertake. Accommodation would be available and you would be paid as a ward orderly. I respect your request that your fellow workers should know nothing about your background, except for what you decide to tell them yourself.

We have been having a steady flow of wounded arriving and if you could start on the first Monday in January, that would be a huge help to us.

I look forward to welcoming you to the hospital in the New Year . . .

Now, Grace thought, folding the letter, *all I have to do is to tell William.*

Amos leaned against the bar, his pint next to him, and surveyed the room. He had been living with Nell for a week. They had settled down very well together, but he still liked to have a pint in the pub now and again. Despite his position in the community, he had always been made to feel welcome. There was the usual crowd in the public bar: the two tenant farmers and one or two of their employees and other workers from the estate, as well as Terry Chambers and the owner of the one and only village shop, Ben Plant. It was his shop where the local women gossiped, but it was the pub where the menfolk exchanged their news; news that was far more important in their eyes than women's chit-chat. So, one way or another, the shopkeeper heard it all, for he made sure he was a regular patron of the pub.

Ben sidled up to Amos. 'See yon feller sitting in the corner on his own?'

Amos nodded.

'He's the new gamekeeper.'

'So I believe.'

'Ralph Carter's his name. D'you know owt about him?'

'Not yet, but I intend to find out. If you'll excuse me, Ben, I'll make a start right now. D'you know what he's drinking?'

Ben shook his head. 'No, but Ted will know.' Ted was the pub landlord, who was serving behind the bar.

Moments later, Amos crossed the room, set a pint down in front of the man sitting alone and sat down. He held out his hand.

'Evenin'. I'm Amos Taylor. Pleased to meet you.' Amos wasn't being entirely honest; this was the man who was the cause of him being turned out of his job and his home. If it hadn't been for Nell's kindness, he would probably be in the workhouse by now. But it wasn't this feller's fault, Amos told himself. He doubted he knew anything about it.

The young man – fair-haired, with hazel eyes and dressed in workaday clothes – had a pleasant, friendly face. Ralph took the proffered hand and shook it warmly. He was not, Amos thought, what he imagined the master would look for in a gamekeeper. He had expected a sour-faced, ruthless-looking man. The previous gamekeeper who had taken over from Amos briefly – the one who had been shot – had been exactly like that. But Ralph Carter was neither.

'You're the old gamekeeper, aren't you?'

Amos nodded. He felt Ralph appraising him. At last the young man said, 'I'm not too sure whether I shall be staying here long, Mr Taylor.'

'Amos, please. Why is that, then?'

Ralph glanced down at the pint in his hand and swirled the amber liquid in the glass. 'I can't go to war, Amos. I volunteered the week the war started, but was refused on health grounds. It seems I have some sort of heart trouble, which I didn't know about.'

'I'm sorry to hear that, young feller.' He paused and then asked, 'So, why do you say you might not be staying?'

'May I speak freely? Can I trust you?'

'You can, Ralph, yes.'

Ralph still hesitated for a moment, but then his words came out in a rush. 'I've been told in no uncertain terms by the locals that I'm the cause of you being turned out of your home. I'm sorry for that. It's not how I would have expected any estate owner to treat a faithful and long-time employee. So, I'm not sure I can work for Mr Ramsey. He seems heartless in other ways too. He was telling me about the poacher that used to be here. How he shot my predecessor and escaped justice by volunteering.'

'That's what the rumours say,' Amos said. 'If they're true, the master can't reach him now wherever he is.'

'No, but he's still bent on catching his daughter, isn't he?'

Amos raised his eyebrows. 'Ah, so he's told you all that, has he?'

Ralph nodded. 'My previous employer – where I trained to become a gamekeeper – was entirely different. As long as the local poachers didn't touch his game birds, he was happy.'

'That's how it used to be in William Ramsey's father's day. It was him I first worked for and it's what I've always done, though William's never liked it. Sam Waterhouse – the chap he's been telling you about – would do all the unpleasant jobs that no one else wanted to do and, with his poaching, he kept the villagers fed through hard times. You see, he never took money for anything he caught. There's many a family who would be in the workhouse now if it hadn't been for Sam and his daughter. Mr Ramsey is not the most benevolent of masters.' Amos's tone was laced with sarcasm.

'I gathered that.'

Amos's eyes narrowed as he assessed the young man sitting in front of him. 'So, what you're saying is that you'd prefer to carry on the way I did, but that the master is not going to allow it.'

'That's about the size of it, yes. I can't stand by and see folks go hungry when there's wildlife running free that would feed them. Oh, I know it's not what a gamekeeper should be, but it's the way I feel.' He swirled his pint again and added, mournfully, 'Mebbe I'm in the wrong job, Amos.'

Amos laughed wheezily. 'Now look, young feller,

we've only just met, but I've taken a liking to you and I'm going to trust you with a little secret.'

He looked into Ralph's steady gaze and liked what he saw. The young man's face was open and honest. 'You can trust me, Amos. Like I say, I might not be here long.'

'Well, now, perhaps what I'm going to say will help you decide one way or the other.'

So, for the next half an hour, Amos told Ralph all about his life as William's gamekeeper and how, when he'd grown old, the man whom he'd tried to serve well had just dismissed him without a thought as to how he should live. 'He's like that with all his tenants. If they can no longer pay the rent, out they go.'

'And you're one of them, aren't you?' Ralph pulled a face, then asked with genuine concern, 'So where are you living now?'

'I'm lodging with a Mrs Tranter who lives on the outskirts of the village. A little further along the lane from the cottage where Sam, the poacher, and his daughter used to live. Mrs Tranter and Sam were very close after Sam's wife and her husband died, if you get my meaning.'

Ralph smiled and shrugged his shoulders. 'Why not?'

'Nell Tranter is one of the few people in the village who owns her cottage.' He leaned closer. 'Her husband was killed in an accident on the estate and to avoid an inquiry, the master gave her the cottage and a small pension to keep her quiet. We all knew about it at the time but no one begrudged her. She'd lost her husband and had a young lad to bring up on her own. By the way, in case you're getting any ideas, I'm not taking Sam's place. I'm just a lodger. But she's a good woman and didn't want to see me end up in the workhouse; that's where I would be, if it wasn't for her.'

'So, is that your secret?'

'No, no, I'm coming to that.' He chuckled again. 'Me and Nell have had a good laugh about this. You see, with winter coming and the privations this war is bound to bring sooner or later – I reckon they'll have to start some sort of rationing before it's all over – folks in the village are going to go hungry, so—'

'You're going to become a poacher.' Ralph finished his sentence for him.

Amos nodded and watched the young man's face for a reaction. Just how was this newcomer, whom he'd only just met, going to respond to what had just been said?

'It's funny you should bring the subject up, because I had a surprise yesterday.'

Amos said nothing, but just waited and watched Ralph swirling his beer again. It seemed to be a habit with the man when he was thinking. 'The master called me into his study and told me – no, ordered me – to arrange a shooting party for the first week in December and then, he said, "Of course, there'll be the usual shooting party on Boxing Day." I don't mind telling you, Amos, I was shocked. I thought at least he'd suspend shooting parties while the war is on. It doesn't seem right, somehow, does it? Besides, all the birds that have been reared could be distributed among the villagers, because times are going to get hard for them this year. I even had the gall to suggest it . . .' Ralph smiled wryly. 'He went red in the face and I thought I was going to be sacked on the spot.'

Now, Amos's mouth actually dropped open. 'You dared to say that to him? You're having me on.'

Ralph shook his head. 'No, true as I'm sitting here with me pint.'

'Well, his reaction doesn't surprise me. He's a mean old so-and-so. And yes, you're right, it's always difficult for folks during the winter when there isn't much work on the land, so I expect it's going to be even tougher this year. If the war goes on much longer, I fully expect we'll be getting all sorts of shortages.'

There was silence between them for several minutes until Ralph said quietly, 'So, if you want to do a bit of poaching, I won't be out looking for you. Not while the war's on, anyway.'

Amos grinned, but leaned towards him. 'Just one thing. Don't look now, but you see yon feller sitting on his own in the corner? Don't let him know owt about our little arrangement. You've probably noticed no one goes near him. And there's a good reason for that. He's Lucas Brown, head groom at the manor and the master's eyes and ears for everything that goes on in this village. As you can see, everyone knows and avoids him like the plague.' Amos chuckled. 'I'm taking a bit of a risk talking to you. He'll no doubt report back to the master that I'm still living on the estate *and* getting friendly with his new gamekeeper.'

Ralph raised his glass to his lips and smiled over the rim. 'Thanks for the tip, Amos. Now, let me buy you drink. Same again, is it?'

Twenty-Three

The first Christmas of the war was a strange one for the people of Thornsby. Though there hadn't been any casualties that affected them, they were appalled by the lists that appeared in the newspaper. Thousands of men on all sides had been lost already and a steady flow of wounded came back home to be nursed back to health and returned to the fighting, or to go home to their loved ones, broken and unfit ever to work again. The war that had been predicted by many to be 'over by Christmas' showed no sign of coming to an end. All those who had volunteered with such enthusiasm and hope now realized it was no way to 'see a bit of life'. It was more likely a way to face death.

The villagers tried to carry on as normally as they could for Christmas, but no one was feeling particularly festive. They attended the church services; they decorated their homes and exchanged small, inexpensive gifts, and they packed parcels to send to the six soldiers, who had gone from their community. Letters were spasmodic and not one of them had come home on leave for Christmas. Only Grace knew why. Byron had written to her.

My dearest Mother,

None of us will be coming home at Christmas. It is not encouraged because it might tempt chaps to go AWOL (Absent Without Leave) or even to desert. The six of us have had a serious talk and have all agreed that we won't come home – not even for an embarkation leave when it comes, as it surely must. We think it would be too painful for all concerned. Leaving the first time was hard enough. Now, it would be a hundred times worse . . .

Grace kept her son's confidence She didn't even tell William.

Knowing nothing of Byron's letter to his mother, the villagers could only wonder.

'We don't even know where they are,' Nell moaned to Ivy as they put together a parcel for their boys.

'I hope they're still all together,' Ivy said. 'They'll be able to make a bit of a Christmas if they are. I'll tell you summat for nothing, Nell. Folks are missing Sam Waterhouse and Rosie, especially those who can't find work on the land at the moment.' She sighed. 'Hardship's always happened in winter, but now there's no one to catch a few rabbits for them, is there?'

'No,' Nell said firmly, 'there isn't.' She was not going to let it be known – and especially not to Ivy Bates – but there was one person who was prepared to steal out into the night and set a few snares at the far extremity of the woodland where the new gamekeeper rarely ventured: Amos. In the confines of Nell's cottage, the two of them laughed together at the irony of the turn of events.

'Gamekeeper turned poacher,' Nell teased him. 'Who'd have thought it?'

'Not that old bastard down in the vale, that's for sure.'

'Don't get caught, Amos, that's all I ask.'

'I'll do me best, Nell, 'cos I know I'd get no mercy.' He tapped the side of his nose, 'but you see I have an advantage. I know the sort of weather that's best for poaching, so I know when a gamekeeper would go out looking. I don't go out on them nights. I go when the weather's *not* right, but the rabbits and hares are still running.' He said nothing about his little arrangement with the new keeper. Not even to Nell. The fewer people who knew about that, the better.

No one else, apart from Nell and Ralph Carter, knew about Amos's night-time excursions onto the land he had once protected, and when Nell took a rabbit or a hare or even a pheasant or partridge – to a family in need, they all had the good sense not to ask how she had come by it, but accepted it gratefully.

It was an even stranger time in the trenches near Ypres, in Belgium. On the Western front, following an offensive action lasting ten days in appalling weather, the guns on both sides fell silent on Christmas Eve. The British in their trenches heard the sound of carols echoing across the wasteland between them and the German trenches. Cautiously they climbed their ladders to peer over the top and saw candles and small Christmas trees had been placed along the enemy line. And then, to their amazement, German soldiers climbed out and called to their enemy to come to meet them. Cautiously, at first, and then with growing confidence, the British soldiers scrambled out of their trenches too and crossed the space between them. For the rest of the day – and in some places for most of the following week – the two sides exchanged gifts, chatted and even played football. When the authorities got to hear what was happening, they attempted to stop it immediately.

On New Year's Eve, the men of the village pored over Ted's newspaper in the Thornsby Arms.

'Have you seen this?' Terry Chambers jabbed at the page. 'On Christmas Eve our lads heard the Hun singing and then one of 'em shouted across, daring one of our lot to go over for a bottle of wine.'

'D'you mean one of our lads from the village?'

'Nah, just one of the British soldiers.'

'Oh, right. Go on. Did he go?'

'Aye, he did and he took them a cake.'

'Then what?'

'A lot of them on both sides climbed out of their trenches and met in the middle. That's what they call no-man's-land, isn't it? Our lads even helped the Germans bury some of their dead.'

'Never!'

'That's what it says here.'

Someone laughed wryly. 'I bet the officers didn't like it. They wouldn't approve of fraternizing with the enemy.'

'No,' Terry said slowly, 'I don't expect they did. But it proves one thing, doesn't it?' The faces around him were blank until he smiled grimly and added, 'The ordinary German soldier doesn't want this war any more than we do.'

Christmas at Thornsby Manor was a very subdued affair. No Byron, no Pearl and no grandson to spoil, and the shadow of the war hung over the whole community. The staff cared for their employers as they always had done, but everyone lacked the heart for merrymaking. Grace said nothing of her plans to anyone but on the day after New Year's Day, she dropped her bombshell.

'You're going to do what?' William spluttered.

Calmly, Grace repeated what she had just said. 'I'm leaving on Monday to go to work in a hospital for the wounded coming back from France and Belgium.'

He gaped at her. 'You'll do no such thing. I won't hear of it.'

'And how are you going to stop me?'

'Lock you in your room, if I have to.'

'The servants will release me . . .'

'No, they won't, if I tell them not to.'

Grace rose from her place at the table. 'Oh, I think they will. You seem to forget that the person who runs this house, who employs all the staff, and who pays their wages, is me.'

'Then I'll sack the lot of them and employ my own.'

Grace smiled down at him, rather pityingly. 'I think you'll find, William, that there is now a dearth of domestic staff. In fact, we are lucky that so many have remained with us and have not volunteered.'

Now he too rose and shook his fist at her. 'Go,

then, if you must. I give you a week. In fact, I guarantee that you'll be back home in a few days, realizing just how foolish you have been. And also appreciating just how lucky you are.'

Grace inclined her head. 'We shall see, William. We shall see. Now, if you will excuse me, I have some packing to do.'

'Oh madam, are you sure?' Sarah said, with tears in her eyes when Grace asked for her help to sort through her clothes.

'I am, Sarah. This is something I have to do – something I *want* to do.'

'Then I'm coming with you.'

'Oh but – I don't want anyone to know who I am. I mean—'

'Then I'll come as your friend. There's going to be nothing here for me, if you go, madam. Please . . .'

'Well, all right, but if the matron can't take you . . .'

'She will. They're always on the look-out for good workers, I bet. Now, let's sort out your plainest clothes . . .'

Despite the gravity of Grace's decision and the work they would face, the two women had great fun sorting out the clothes they would take.

'Oh, I can't take that, Sarah, it's far too fancy. Where's that old grey morning dress that I was going to throw out? Has it gone already?'

'No, madam. It's with a pile of other clothes that the servants have discarded since you bought them all new outfits last May Day.'

'Perfect! Let's have a look at their clothes too . . .'

By the time they had finished, they were both kitted out in the servants' cast-offs and one or two of Grace's plainer dresses.

Sarah giggled. 'Even they're a bit grand, madam. You'll have to say that your former mistress gave them to you.'

'How are we going to get there?' Grace pondered. 'We can't be seen arriving in a carriage.'

'We could get Monty to take us to a short distance from the hospital, madam, and walk the rest of the way.'

But Grace was shaking her head. 'I don't want Monty – or anyone else – to know where we're going. We need to take the carrier's cart into Lincoln but your idea about getting off a distance from the hospital is a good one. But there's one other thing, Sarah. You must stop calling me "madam".'

'Oh dear,' Sarah said with a comical expression. 'Now that is going to be difficult.'

Twenty-Four

They arrived at the hospital in the late afternoon. After being greeted by the matron, who was very happy to receive Sarah as a new recruit too, they found their way to the dining hall just as the evening meal was being served. Grace searched for sight of Rosie; she had to speak to her and explain what was happening.

'No one must know where she is,' Grace had impressed upon Sarah. 'We must act as if we don't know her. We must keep her secret, just as I hope she will keep ours.'

Grace spotted Rosie and Anna as they took their place at a table. Touching Sarah's arm and nodding towards the two girls, Grace weaved her way through the dining room until she was standing near Rosie. The girl looked up and, startled, opened her mouth to speak, but swiftly Grace put her finger to her lips. Aloud, she said, 'May we join you? We're new here and don't know what we're supposed to do. My name's Grace and this is Sarah.'

'Oh – er – yes. I'm – I'm Rosie and this is my friend, Anna. Please do sit down. I'll – er – get you something to eat.'

'That's kind of you, Rosie. Thank you.'

Grace and Sarah sat on the opposite side of the table to Anna while Rosie fetched two plates of hot food.

'We've volunteered to work as ward orderlies,' Grace told the two girls as they all ate together. Sarah kept quiet. She was so afraid that she would say the wrong thing, so she just smiled and nodded.

'We were cleaners to start with, but now Matron has let us start working as assistants to the nurses,' Anna said. 'We're not fully trained, of course, though we've had a bit of first-aid instruction. It's heart-breaking to see all the soldiers' terrible injuries, but we do feel we're helping.'

'We'll show you the ropes,' Rosie said. 'It's hard work but the patients are lovely and the nurses will be so glad of your help.'

'You'll see some very upsetting sights,' Anna warned, 'even as ward orderlies.'

Grace's face sobered. 'Yes, I think we're prepared for that. We just want to help in any way we can.'

'Have you got a relative or someone out there?' Anna asked innocently.

Grace heard Rosie breathe in sharply, but she had prepared her answer to such a question. 'Yes, I have. That's why I've volunteered, I suppose, though I'm praying I don't see him brought in here.'

'Oh, so who—?' Anna began, but Rosie dropped her fork on the floor with a clatter.

'Oh sorry, Anna, it's gone under your chair. Can you . . . ?'

Anna bent down and retrieved the fork. As she sat up again, Rosie said, 'Oh thanks. Clumsy me.' Then, turning back to Grace and Sarah and deliberately changing the subject, she said, 'Have you been allocated a room yet? We'll help you settle in and then, tomorrow morning, we'll find out where you're working and take you there.'

'You're very kind.' Grace was tempted to ask more questions, but in so doing she might invite further probing from Rosie's friend.

'Well, well, well, Nell Tranter, you're a fast worker and no mistake. You've kept that quiet. Even I didn't know about it until I saw him in your garden yesterday.' Nell's neighbour sounded quite upset that a juicy bit of gossip had escaped her notice. 'Your Nathan gone to war and Sam run off to God knows where and you move another feller in. Have you no shame?'

'Not a lot and not that it's any of your business, Ivy Bates.' Nell paused on her way to the village shop to face the woman who stood with her plump arms folded across her ample bosom.

The two women grinned at each other. They'd been friends since girlhood and neighbours since they'd both married. Their husbands had worked side by side on the estate until Jim Tranter's sad accident. And then only a short time after that, Ivy's husband had died of tuberculosis.

'You're a good sort, Nell.' Ivy nodded and her three chins wobbled in unison. 'Goodness knows where poor old Amos would have ended up.'

'The workhouse,' Nell said bluntly. 'And I know that for a fact, 'cos I asked him where he was going and that's what he said.'

Ivy frowned. 'He's a mean old bastard is William Ramsey. Not to look after them that's worked years for him. He could at least have offered Sam and Rosie's cottage to Amos now it's standing empty. But have you heard the latest? Mrs Ramsey's up and left him.'

Nell gaped at her. 'Never. Where's she gone?'

Ivy shrugged. 'Nobody knows. And her lady's maid – Sarah, is it? – she's gone with her.'

'Ah, that explains that bit of a mystery, then.'

'What?'

'Why Sarah didn't bring me any washing yesterday.' She sighed. ''Spect I've mebbe lost that bit of income, then.'

Ivy sniffed. 'Well, you'll have Amos's board and lodging instead, won't you?'

Nell laughed loudly, the sound carrying on the breeze. 'Oh, I ain't charging him owt, Ivy. He's going to keep me garden nice and do a few jobs about the place for me. You know.'

Now Ivy laughed raucously too. 'Oh, I know all right, Nell Tranter. I know. Keeping ya bed warm an' all, is he?'

Nell winked saucily. 'That's for me to know and you to find out, Ivy Bates. Now, I must get on. Can't stand here gossiping all day with the likes of you.'

The two women laughed together again but just as Nell turned away, Ivy said softly, 'Have you heard from Nathan?'

Nell stopped and was very still for a moment before saying, 'No, I haven't. What about your Dan?'

'No, me neither. I'll tan his hide for him when he gets home for not writing. That I will.'

Nell nodded and moved on, the merry banter between them dying in seconds.

Much to Nell's relief, Elsie, the kitchen maid from the manor, appeared at her back door the following morning with a huge bundle of washing.

'Sorry this is a day late, Mrs, but we're all at sixes and sevens at the manor. The mistress had gone away suddenly and taken Sarah with her and we've no idea when she'll be back, but she instructed Mrs Frost that everything should carry on as normal.'

'That's all you can do, love,' Nell said. 'Come away in and I'll make you a hot drink like I always did for Sarah.'

'Ooh ta. That'd be ever so nice. This lot's right heavy.'

'Mebbe she's gone to see her grandson down in Stamford, has she?' Nell said conversationally.

Elsie shook her head. 'We don't think so. She's not taken any of her best clothes.' She leaned closer to Nell, even though there was no one else to hear; Amos was already at work in the back garden. 'We reckon the master knows, but he's saying nowt.'

As they sat together, the young maid with the older woman, Nell asked. 'Anyone else left from the manor? To go to war, I mean?'

'Mr Brown is too old and Monty is too young, but one of the housemaids has gone to work in a factory somewhere making shells, I heard. The pay's much better than we get, but then you have to find yarsen somewhere to live, don't you? I won't be going. The staff at the manor are me family, see? I ain't got no one else except—' She paused a moment and blushed slightly.

'Go on, love. Your secrets are safe with me.'

'Well, there's this lad in the village. We aren't really allowed followers, y'know, but me and him meet up on me days off. It's quite harmless. I'm a good girl, Mrs Tranter. I won't be getting mesen into trouble. We're both only fifteen, so he won't be going to war yet and I'm hoping he never does.'

'Does he work on the estate?'

'For one of the master's tenant farmers. He lives next door to you. It's Joey Bates.'

'Ah, yes, Ivy's youngest. He's unlikely to be called up because of his age and as he's a farm worker too, but then' – she sighed heavily – 'some of 'em still want to volunteer.'

'Like your Nathan and Master Byron. And Joey's brother, Dan, has gone, hasn't he? And I don't reckon any of 'em *had* to go, did they?'

Nell shook her head, not trusting herself to speak as the anxiety that always lay deep in the pit of her stomach threatened to surface.

Elsie jumped up. 'I'd best be getting back or Cook'll have me guts for garters. 'Bye for now, Mrs Tranter. I'll pick up the clean laundry on Thursday, if that'll be all right.'

Nell levered herself out of her chair. 'That'll be fine, lass. See you then. And now I'd better get cracking.'

*

The work on the wards, as they had been warned, was hard and distressing. Sarah coped very well and to everyone's surprise – including her own – so did Grace. After two months, both women had fitted in very well. Surprisingly, no one, apart from those who already knew her, had found out Grace's true identity and by now both the lady of the manor and her lady's maid were accepted for themselves and the work they did. Although she wasn't as physically strong as the other women and girls, Grace made herself useful in other ways. She talked to the men, comforted them, wrote letters home for them and held the hands of the dying. The sight of the dreadful wounds, the rasping breathing and the blood didn't faze her. She managed to bury, deep within her, the ever-present fear that, one day, she would come across Byron being admitted to the ward on a stretcher. But, as far as she knew, he was still in England. Before he had left, they had made an arrangement that he would send messages to her in his letter in some way that would be unintelligible to the censors. When she had arrived at the hospital, Grace had written to him telling him what she had done.

Send letters to me here at the hospital, but please continue to write home as if I am still there. I don't want your father to find out where I am. He would only fetch me back . . .

In April a letter arrived telling her that they were moving somewhere else for final training; she guessed it was still somewhere in England. Hearteningly, he added: *The six of us are all still together.*

She hurried to find Rosie to tell her.

'How I wish I could let Aunty Nell know, but I daren't write to her.'

'But I can,' Grace offered at once. 'I won't say where I am, or mention you, but it will give her a few more weeks' peace of mind. And she can tell the other mothers in the village too that our boys are still together.'

Through the months that followed, while concentrating on doing all she could to help the nurses care for the casualties that arrived in ever-increasing numbers, Grace could not forget the words in Byron's letter: *for final training*. She made little of it to Rosie or to Nell, but she guessed what it meant. Soon, they would be shipped overseas.

And then, during August, the letter she had dreaded arrived.

We are going to the theatre, Byron wrote. By that, Grace knew he meant they were going to the 'theatre' of war. Her fingers trembled as she read the rest of the letter. A little further on, he wrote: *How I miss my gallops with my friend Oli*. And then she knew. Byron and his friends were going to a place called Gallipoli. It had been much in the news since February and they had already had a few casualties from there arrive at the hospital.

With a heavy heart and leaden feet, she went to find Rosie.

'What do I do now, Rosie?' she asked in anguish. 'Do I tell Nell?'

Rosie chewed her lip. 'I don't think it's fair to keep her in ignorance, but I wouldn't say *where* you think they've gone. Just – just tell her you think –

from one of Byron's letters – that they have now gone abroad.'

'Yes, yes, you're right. That's what I'll do. Thank you, Rosie.'

The days and weeks turned into months and the summer passed almost without the busy nurses and their helpers noticing. The hospital continued to receive casualties from all theatres of war. Grace devoted herself to doing whatever was asked of her and the matron, Connie Archer, decided to promote her and Sarah to be assistants to the nurses, alongside Rosie and Anna. Grace wore the apron with the red cross on its bib with pride. Now, she became even closer to the wounded, the sick and the dying. She was able to help those who were well enough to get up each day to get dressed in the blue uniform and red tie that the patients wore. Her calm presence eased many a young man's passing and gave hope to those who could be saved. Grace began to take a particular interest in one young soldier who arrived at the beginning of September. He reminded her vividly of Byron. Although he had no visible physical wounds, he was now a broken shell of the man he must once have been. He could no longer speak and the whole of his body shook constantly, making walking almost impossible. Grace prayed every night that her son would not end up like this and she persevered in trying to help the recent arrival. He was someone's son and she hoped that if ever Byron was lying injured somewhere another mother would help him too. No one knew his name because when he'd been found in a shell hole, there was no identification on him. All they knew was that he was from one of the battalions in the Lincolnshire Regiment and so he had been sent, eventually, to the Lincoln hospital.

'He's been fortunate not to have faced a firing squad,' the matron told Grace. 'The military view this sort of thing as cowardice.' The two women – of a similar age and background – had become friendly during their off-duty time and the matron often invited Grace to have tea with her, recognizing that Grace was not the sort of woman ever to take advantage of a show of friendship. On duty they both remained professional at all times.

'Is there no one in the medical profession who could make a study of it?' Grace asked as Connie poured tea for them both in her private sitting room that had once been the headmaster's study.

'We do have a very go-ahead young doctor here,' Connie Archer said. 'He's always looking for something to make his own particular project. Leave it with me, Grace, but don't be surprised if one day you get a visit to your ward from a bouncy, ginger-haired young doctor. His name is Simon Oldfield. He's a wonderful man and very, *very* clever. I prophecy that he has a brilliant future ahead of him.'

'As long as he doesn't get drafted into the war.'

The matron shook her head. 'I don't think he will. He's doing sterling work here. I would fight to keep him here, if necessary.'

The visit happened the following day and Grace recognized him the moment he came into the ward

like a whirlwind, his white coat flapping, his stetho-
scope clinging on for dear life around his neck, his
hair a shock of vibrant ginger.

'Ah . . .' He came to a sudden halt beside the
patient's bed where Grace was sitting. 'Is this the
patient Matron was telling me about? And you must
be Nurse Grace Ramsey.'

'I'm not a nurse, doctor. Just an assistant.'

'Ah yes. The red cross on your apron. I should
have known, but you're every bit as important, Grace.
The qualified nurses couldn't do half what they do
without your backing. Now, let's have a look at this
young man. Do you know his name?'

'Sadly, no. He doesn't speak.'

'Can he walk?'

'A little, but only with help. He's very unsteady.'

Dr Oldfield gave the young soldier a thorough
examination and then stood at the end of the bed
observing him. 'Is he the only patient like this?'

'So far, doctor.'

'Mm. I fear we'll get more. Interestingly,' the young
doctor said, almost more to himself than to Grace,
'there was an article in last month's *Lancet* about a
condition they're calling shell shock. Actually, it's the
soldiers themselves who have coined the phrase. I
think that this might well be what we have here.'

Grace felt a touch on her arm and turned to see
Rosie standing there. The girl had been working on
another ward and, at the moment, they only met up
at mealtimes and before and after their shifts.

Grace turned. 'Hello, Rosie, what . . . ?' She stopped
mid-sentence. Rosie was staring transfixed at the

soldier in the bed; her eyes wide, her mouth half open in shock. 'What is it, Rosie? Do you know him?'

Dr Oldfield said nothing, but he was listening intently.

Rosie nodded, her gaze still on the young man. Even though she might be risking revealing her true identity, she could no longer keep silent. 'Hasn't he told you his name, Grace?'

'He can't speak, Rosie. We don't know who he is.'

'I hardly recognized him,' Rosie whispered. 'He – looks so – so different.'

'He's very ill,' Grace whispered. 'Who is he?'

'It's Dan Bates. Ivy Bates's eldest son. They live next door to Mrs Tranter.'

At the sound of his name the soldier looked up and, although he was still shaking, a small smile curved his mouth.

'Ah,' Dr Oldfield was smiling broadly, 'now that's a step in the right direction. Well done, Rosie.' Dr Oldfield ignored the tradition of calling the nurses and other staff by their surnames. If he knew their Christian names, that was what he called them. Even the matron could not get him to conform. 'We've got something to work on now,' he went on. 'Spend as much time with him as you can, Rosie. I think it will help him enormously and if we can get his family to come and visit him, so much the better.'

Both Grace and Rosie froze at the thought of discovery, but they were both forced to understand that it was necessary for Dan. Grace put her hand on Rosie's shoulder and murmured, 'Don't worry. We'll work something out.'

Later, after they had finished for the day, Rosie said, 'Whatever can we do? I know Dan ought to have his family visit him – it'd probably do him the world of good – but if Mrs Bates comes to visit him and sees either of us . . .'

'I'm not so worried on my own account. My reason for my anonymity was that I wanted all the staff here to accept me as one of them and not some condescending posh woman. I think they have already done that, but I am concerned for you, Rosie. I wish I'd recognized him. I should have done, but then I didn't get to know the young men of the village like I did their mothers. Would Mrs Bates keep your secret, d'you think?'

Rosie laughed wryly. 'Hardly. She's the biggest gossip in the village. Don't get me wrong, she's a nice woman, kind and generous, but keep a secret? Never. Not even if you paid her.' Rosie nibbled nervously at her lip. 'But I must do what is right for Dan. I'll go and tell Matron I have recognized him and give her his home address so that she can write to his mother. I'll just have to take that risk.'

'Ironically,' Grace said, 'I think the only person who is determined to find you is my husband. I don't even think the police are interested in you any longer.'

'No. I saw PC Foster before I left. I didn't want him to think I was running away.'

'That was sensible of you, but your father, I'm afraid, would be a different matter.'

Rosie said nothing; whatever remark she made in answer might incriminate her father even more.

'We'll just have to keep you working on another ward when Mrs Bates visits Dan,' Grace went on.

'We should be able to wangle it. At least we'll know when she's coming.'

'There's only one thing I would like to find out for definite,' Rosie murmured.

'What's that?'

'Where he's come from – if it is that place you thought – because that's where they all might be.' She met Grace's glance with a steady, unapologetic gaze. 'It's where Byron might be.'

'I'll ask Matron if she knows.'

Twenty-Five

On the day in late September when they heard that Ivy would be visiting Dan, and knowing that the matron disliked anyone working on the wards with an infection that could be passed on to the already seriously ill patients, Rosie told everyone that she felt as if she were starting a cold.

'I can't do this every time she comes, though, can I?' she said to Grace, sniffling realistically.

'No, but I don't think the poor woman will be able to come very often. It's a long way for her to travel – and expensive. We'll just have to deal with it, Rosie, whenever it happens.'

Grace was tending Dan when his mother, accompanied by Nell Tranter, arrived in the ward. Grace hurried to meet her, anxious to forewarn her about her son's condition.

'Oh Mrs Ramsey – madam,' Ivy exclaimed. 'Whatever are you doing here?'

Smiling, Grace put her fingers to her lips. 'You'll both have to be let into my little secret. I wanted to come and help out here, but I don't want any of the staff here to know who I am. The matron knows, of course, but I want everyone else to accept me as one of them. Do you understand?' Her pleading gaze took in Nell too. 'Just call me Grace – or even Mrs Ramsey – but please, no more "madam".'

'Well, if you're sure . . .'

'I am. Now come and see Dan. You must understand that he is very poorly, but he has a wonderful doctor looking after him and he is starting to improve, though it's going to take a long time.' She put her arm through Ivy's and smiled fleetingly at Nell, who followed them down the ward.

Ivy stood at the end of her son's bed and put her hand over her mouth. Tears flooded down her cheeks. 'Oh Dan,' she whispered. 'My poor, poor boy. What have they done to you?'

'Dr Oldfield believes it is the shock from the incessant pounding of the guns while at the front. He is studying your son very closely. Dan is in the best possible hands, Mrs Bates, please believe me.'

Ivy clutched at Grace's hand. 'Oh, I do, I do. And if you're looking after him too . . .'

'I'm only an assistant to the nurses here, but they are wonderful, so dedicated and kind, and I do what I can for him too, outside actual nursing care.'

As Ivy sat down at her son's bedside and took his hand, Grace drew Nell a little away to whisper, 'Rosie wanted me to tell you that she's working here.'

Nell's eyes widened. 'Is she all right?'

'She's fine. She's doing valuable work but she's keeping out of the way today. She didn't want Mrs Bates to see her.'

'Best not. Ivy's a good sort but she'll be telling all and sundry about Dan and our visit here when we

248

get home, and no doubt it would slip out about Rosie, even unintentionally.'

'Perhaps, if you come again, you could let me know. Just drop me a note care of the hospital. It'll find me.'

'I'll do that – if I can, but if she decides to come on the spur of the moment . . .'

Grace shrugged. 'Then that can't be helped.'

They both glanced back towards Dan. 'The boys who went on the same day from the village had hoped to stay together,' Nell said softly. 'I haven't heard from Nathan in weeks. Do you think they are still together?'

Grace hesitated. 'I don't know, but I think they went out to Gallipoli together.'

Nell nodded towards Dan. 'Is that where he's come from?'

'We think so.'

'Then may the Good Lord help them all.'

Nell gripped Grace's hand briefly and then returned to sit with her friend beside Dan's bed. They stayed for two hours but before they left, they were able to speak to Dr Oldfield.

'This is a new and unusual illness to the medical profession, Mrs Bates, but I intend to make a study of it. Your son is my first patient with such symptoms, but sadly, I don't think he's going to be the last.'

'Will – will he be able to come home soon? I can look after him, if you tell me what I should do.'

Simon Oldfield's freckled face smiled. 'As soon as I think he's well enough, I think love and care in his own home would be the best possible treatment, but it might not be for a few weeks yet. Matron has your address, hasn't she?' Ivy nodded. 'Then I will write to you every week and tell you about his progress.'

'Perhaps Mrs Ramsey—' Ivy began but stopped when she felt a warning touch on her arm from Nell.

'We'll not take up any more of your time, doctor,' Nell said. 'Thank you so much for all you are doing for him. I'm Ivy's – Mrs Bates's – neighbour, so I'd be able to help her when he comes home.'

'I'm delighted to hear it. Mrs Bates will need all the support she can get. It won't be easy.'

As they bade the doctor goodbye, Nell said, 'We'll come again when we can.'

Rosie had stayed in her room the whole day, but the following morning she was back on duty, her head cold having miraculously disappeared.

'I don't like pretending to be ill when I'm not,' she told Grace. 'I'm *never* ill.'

'It was for the best,' Grace soothed.

'Well, I won't do it again. I'll just have to take my chances of being seen. And I don't believe the villagers would tell on me and anyway; I told PC Foster I was leaving, although I didn't tell him exactly where I was going.'

'I think you're right. I don't think they would give you away,' Grace said. Then, grimly, she added, 'The only person you have to fear, I'm afraid, is my husband.'

Ivy and Nell visited three more times before, at the beginning of December, Dr Oldfield deemed Dan well enough to go home. Each time, by working on a different ward, Rosie was able to avoid being seen by them.

'I'll send for Monty to fetch him in the carriage,' Grace told Rosie. 'It'll be much more comfortable for him. Sarah's agreed to go home to arrange it and then to travel back in the carriage when it comes to fetch Dan. She'll bring Ivy – and possibly Nell too – so they can look after him on the journey back.'

'Won't the master . . . ?'

'No,' Grace cut in. 'If we can do it the way I've instructed Sarah, he'll never even know.'

Dan Bates came home early in December to a hero's welcome. Over the days following his arrival, all the villagers came in ones and twos to greet him. They went away shaking their heads.

''Tis a terrible business, this war.'

'Poor fellow. I've never seen owt like it before.'

'Will he get better, d'you think?'

'Mrs Bates says he's improving a little . . .'

'But that's his mother talking.'

'Aye, it is. He might, given time, but I don't think he'll ever be the strapping young feller he was.'

Joey stood looking down at the brother he loved and admired. He watched the shaking, the saliva dribbling from the corner of his mouth, and heard his rasping breathing. He turned away with a grim, determined, look on his face and went back to his work on Mr Ramsey's land. At the end of the day, he did not go home. Instead, he walked to the nearest town where there was a recruiting office and volunteered.

Because he was tall and broad-shouldered, no one even bothered to ask his age.

*

When Elsie had delivered the washing to Nell the following morning, she called next door to see how Dan was. Ivy was in tears. The young girl put her arms around her. 'Aw, Mrs Bates. He'll get better now he's home. I'm sure he will . . .'

Ivy wept even harder. 'It's not that – it's not Dan. It's Joey.'

Elsie stepped back. 'What's happened?'

'He's only gone and volunteered, that's what!'

Elsie's mouth dropped open as she stared at the older woman. 'Why? Why did he go and do a stupid thing like that?'

'Because – because of Dan.'

'But – but that doesn't make sense.'

'It does to him. He said "they're not getting away with injuring my brother like that. I'll show 'em".'

Elsie was dry-eyed; she wasn't a girl given to shedding tears, but she was angry. So angry, that if Joey had been standing in front of her at that minute she would have slapped his face – hard.

She frowned. 'But he's not old enough. He's only just turned sixteen.'

'Huh! That didn't stop them taking him. Besides, I don't think they asked and he certainly didn't tell them.'

'Then I will. I'll go to the recruiting office – wherever it is – and tell them myself.'

Ivy was shaking her head. 'It wouldn't do any good, love. I know you mean well – and I want to do the very same thing myself – but it would shame him. We can't do that, Elsie love. He's a man now.'

'But – but . . .'

'There're no "buts", lass. It's done and can't be undone. He's taken the King's shilling and there's no going back.' Ivy wiped her tears away and took a deep, steadying breath. 'We've just got to get on with it, Elsie lass, but you can come and talk to me any time you want. I've taken a liking to you and my Joey could do a lot worse for himself. So, we'll help each other through this and pray for his safe return. Me and Nell have been doing that ever since both our lads went. And now she's got old Amos living with her, he's a big help, an' all. He's started doing a few little jobs for me too, so I reckon he'll be on hand when Joey goes.'

Elsie's mouth was a thin, tight line. 'You're right. I know you are, but Joey'd better watch out when I catch up with him. I'll give him what for.'

Even through her sadness, Ivy couldn't help smiling. 'I wouldn't be in his shoes when you do.'

The big row between Elsie and Joey took place that evening on the village green, observed by all the villagers within earshot.

'How could you do it, Joey? How could you do it to your mam? Even if you didn't think about me, what about her? She's got poor Dan like he is and the same thing could happen to you – or worse. What if you don't come back at all? Have you actually thought about it from anybody's else's point of view except your own selfish need to be a hero?'

'I can't sit by and see what they've done to our Dan,' Joey shot back, 'without wanting to take revenge.'

'And that'll be your "revenge", will it? To get yourself maimed or killed? Fat lot of good that'll do your Dan – or your mam. You'd've done better to stay here and help look after him. And how's he going to feel when he finds out you've only gone because of him?'

'He won't understand,' Joey muttered.

'I reckon he understands a lot more than you think he does. He can't talk at the moment, but if you look into his eyes, you can see he knows what's going on.'

Joey stared at her. 'D'you really think so?'

'I'm sure of it.'

'And – and do you think he can keep getting better?'

'Yes, I do,' Elsie said firmly as if, by the strength of her will, she could make it so.

Their quarrel had subsided now and Elsie's anger fell away from her, leaving her deeply saddened. She stepped closer to him and looked up into his face. 'Joey Bates, God help me, but I love you. I will always love you, but you can be stupid at times. And this is the stupidest thing you've ever done. But, like your mam says, it's done now. An' I'll tell you summat else. I'm going to volunteer.'

'Wha—?'

'Oh, not to fight. I'm not that daft, even if women could. But your mam's been telling me about the hospital your Dan was in. It sounds as if they could do with all the help they can get. So, on me next day off, I'll be going into Lincoln to see if they want another pair of willing hands.'

Twenty-Six

'Nell! *Nell!*'

'Oh Ivy, whatever's the matter? Is it Dan?'

'No, no, it's Elsie.'

'What's happened?'

Ivy flopped down at the kitchen table, her hand to her chest, breathing heavily. 'She's going to volunteer to work at the Lincoln hospital. Oh Nell, I'm sorry. Me an' my big mouth. I was telling her all about it and how kind they all were to Dan and how Mrs Ramsey was working there . . . Oh I shouldn't have. If *he* finds out, he'll fetch her back, won't he?'

Nell was thoughtful. It wasn't Grace Ramsey she was worried about; it was Rosie. 'Don't worry, love,' she said, putting her hand on Ivy's shoulder. 'I'll have a chat with Elsie when she collects the washing.'

When the girl came back the following day to collect the laundry, Nell sat her down at the kitchen table, poured her a cup of tea – the occasion warranted a special treat for both of them – and said, 'Now, Elsie, love, you're a sensible girl and—'

'Don't try to stop me going, Mrs Tranter, because—'

'I wouldn't dream of it, Elsie. I think it's a grand idea. But there's just something you ought to know before you go.' Nell gazed at the girl, trying to decide

255

if she could be trusted. She sighed. Really, she had no alternative. 'Elsie, I need to be able to trust you. Can I do that?'

'Of course, Mrs Tranter. I know how to keep me mouth shut when it matters.'

'Well, this really does. It's about someone who already works at the hospital.'

'Oh Mrs Ramsey. Yes, I know about that. Mrs Bates told me, but I haven't said a word back at the manor. I would never let madam down. I really like her. All the staff do. We miss her.'

'It's not about her. There's someone else there too and we must all keep her secret, because if the master found out where she is—'

For a moment Elsie looked puzzled and then she whispered, 'Rosie? You're talking about Rosie Waterhouse, aren't you?'

Nell nodded.

'I won't say a word to a soul. I never thought she was involved with that awful business anyway. Her dad, yes, I think he might have done it, but not Rosie.'

'You mustn't tell Mrs Bates – she doesn't know – or even Joey.'

'No, I won't. I promise. I always liked Rosie. We were at school together. I'm glad she's all right. And you're right. Word's filtered down to the kitchen that he's still trying to get her arrested. Mr Baines was saying that when PC Foster visited the master a while back, he listened at the keyhole.' She giggled. 'Who'd have thought it, eh? Mr Baines listening at keyholes? Anyway, the master wasn't trying to keep his voice down and he was telling the policeman that he wanted inquiries made about Sam Waterhouse and about Rosie too. I'm glad she's safe.'

'But to keep her safe, no one around here must know where she is.'

Elsie nodded solemnly. 'You have my word, Mrs Tranter.'

Nell smiled and touched the girl's cheek. 'Good lass, and I wish you well. It'll be nice for you to have both Mrs Ramsey and Rosie there if they take you on.'

Elsie decided not to go to Lincoln until after Christmas. The staff at the manor was already depleted and even though neither Mrs Ramsey nor Master Byron were at home, William still demanded that the usual customs be followed. The second Christmas of the war was, however, very different. There was the constant worry over their loved ones as three more young men from the village, including Joey Bates, had volunteered. The optimism, still present that first Christmas, had evaporated as the casualty lists had grown longer with each passing month. The sight of poor Dan had devastated the whole community and doubled their fear over those who were still in the thick of the fighting.

As he had agreed with Nell, Amos went out poaching whenever he thought the new keeper would not be out and about. While work on the land was a little more plentiful through the winter for the men who were left in the village, there were still widows and poor families to be fed and Sam and Rosie were no longer there to help out. Although he had developed an understanding with Ralph Carter, Amos didn't want to get the young feller dismissed. He felt no animosity towards his replacement. The older man was, in fact, enjoying his 'retirement'. He had settled in very well with Nell. He enjoyed her company and, best of all, he was no longer answerable to the master. He realized that should he be caught poaching, the punishment would be harsh, but Amos had an advantage because of his years of experience as a keeper and he soon became an even better poacher than Sam had been. If the villagers guessed what might be happening when Nell brought them food during the winter months, they were wise enough not to ask questions as to how quite so many rabbits, hares and even game birds were trespassing into her garden. Nor did they discuss it in the pub. Lucas Brown still sat in his lonely corner watching and listening.

Just before Christmas, when harsh winter weather seriously affected many of the men, it was decided that the British troops should withdraw from the Gallipoli campaign.

'All those young lives wasted and for what?' The men, poring over the newspapers in Ted's pub, were angry and disillusioned.

'We mustn't lose hope,' Ted's calm voice encouraged. 'We have to go on. We have to win in the end, else it'll *all* have been in vain.'

At the hospital, Grace received a letter from Byron telling her that they were 'on the move', but he couldn't as yet give her any hint as to where they were heading. *We've been lucky so far. Only poor Dan out of our number has been a casualty.*

When she wrote back, she told him briefly that Dan was improving slowly and was back home with his mother. She did not, however, tell him that, as a consequence, young Joey had enlisted.

On 2 January 1916, Elsie bade her farewells to her colleagues at the manor.

'Now, if things don't work out,' Cook told the girl, 'Mrs Frost says you can come back. She's not going to tell the master that you've left yet, so he won't know for a while. Lucy's volunteered to take the washing to Mrs Tranter each week, so if you have any messages you want to reach us, you can write to her and she'll pass them to Lucy, I don't doubt. Now, take care of yourself, lass.'

The matron was delighted to receive another strong and willing country girl. 'We're getting busier and busier. We're getting more and more casualties every day. They're still arriving here as a consequence of the Gallipoli campaign and, of course, from other areas too. I'll start you on the cleaning and then, if you're suitable, you might progress to becoming a ward orderly.'

'Thank you, Matron,' Elsie said politely. 'I'll work hard at whatever job you give me.'

'Do you know anyone already here?'

Elsie licked her lips not wanting to risk saying anything she shouldn't. 'I'm not sure, but I make friends easily.'

Connie Archer stood up. 'I'll take you to meet Rosie

Skelton. She and her friend, Anna, will look after you. They both started as ward cleaners and progressed very quickly to becoming assistants to the nurses. They're both very able.' She sighed. 'It's a shame we haven't time to train them up properly as nurses. They'd both make excellent ones.' She smiled at the willing girl. 'Maybe you will follow in their footsteps in time.'

The matron took Elsie into the ward where Rosie was working.

'Skelton,' Connie Archer said as she approached the bed where Rosie was bending over a patient. 'We have a new recruit. I would like you to take her under your wing . . .'

As Rosie turned, her eyes widened and a look of fear crossed her face. Elsie moved forward swiftly. 'Hello, my name's Elsie Warren. I'm very pleased to meet you.'

Rosie blinked as Elsie chattered on. 'I used to work in a big house in the country as a kitchen maid, so I'm used to hard work. You just tell me what to do and I'll do my very best.'

'I'll leave you with Skelton, then,' Matron said. 'Can you sort out accommodation for her?' she asked Rosie.

Rosie cleared her throat and tried to calm her nerves. 'Of course, Matron, and we'll show her around and help her settle in.'

As the matron moved away, Elsie whispered, 'Mrs Tranter told me you were here and swore me to secrecy. I've told no one, Rosie, not even Mrs Bates.' She frowned. 'But I thought Mrs Ramsey was here. Hasn't she said anything to her husband about you?'

Rosie, fully recovered now from the shock of seeing Elsie, giggled. 'No, she's been brilliant.' As they walked together out of the ward, Rosie explained all that had happened, ending, 'I think she wanted to get away from home and feel that she was helping soldiers like her own son.'

Elsie sighed. 'It's the same for me in a way. You know what happened to Dan Bates, don't you?'

'Yes, I helped to nurse him but every time his mother visited, I made myself scarce.'

'You did right. His mam's a lovely woman, but couldn't keep a secret to save her life.' Then her face fell. 'But when Dan came home, my Joey took one look at him and went off there and then to volunteer.'

Rosie stopped walking and stared at her. 'But he's not old enough.'

Elsie shrugged. 'It seems they didn't even ask him. He's a big lad, as you know, and I expect they're taking anyone they can get now, whatever their age.'

'I'm sorry to hear that, Elsie, but in a way I'm glad it's brought you here.' She laughed. 'And you'll never guess what? Although we all have to call each other by our surnames when we're on duty, Mrs Ramsey has told us to call her "Grace" when we're off duty.' She laughed again at the amazement on Elsie's face.

'Oh heck!' the young girl said. 'I don't reckon I'll ever manage that.'

'Rosie, there's a badly wounded soldier shouting out your name. I don't know if he means you or just someone he knows. He's probably delirious,' Anna said, only a week after Elsie's arrival at the hospital. 'He's just been brought in. Half his face is bandaged and I think he's lost a leg.'

'But no one—' Rosie began and then stopped. She felt as if her heart had stopped beating and then begun to thunder. 'Oh no,' she whispered. 'No. Not Byron!'

She hurried to the admissions ward. She had worked there previously but now she'd been moved to help the surgeons and nurses in the operating theatre. She stood in the doorway, her frightened glance searching . . . This was a bad intake. The sound of men groaning, crying and gasping for air made her shudder. Don't let him be here, she prayed silently. Don't let Byron be one of these poor men.

'Skelton! Over here. Give me a hand.' It was one of the nurses, but not one Rosie knew, struggling to take a filthy bandage off a soldier's leg; he was fighting her, his arms flailing, his head thrashing from side to side.

'We've got to get this wound cleaned up else he'll get sepsis.'

Rosie hurried to help her and breathed a small sigh of thankfulness when she didn't recognize the casualty. But there were still several others . . .

'Hold him down. You might have to lie across his chest. He's not wounded there. It's just his leg.'

Using all her strength – she was surprised how much fight the man still had – Rosie put his arms down by his side and then lay across him, while the nurse removed the blood-soaked bandage. The soldier yelled and then was suddenly silent.

'He's passed out. You can get up, Rosie. I think I can manage as long as he's out of it.'

'I'll come back if you need me. I'll be here for a few minutes. I'm looking for someone. Anna said someone's asking for me.'

'It's the feller in the corner over there. I warn you, he's in a bad way. Not expected to make it.'

Rosie's heart thumped in fear as she walked towards the soldier the nurse had pointed out. Her hands were clammy, her knees trembling. She held her breath as she drew nearer and then, as she recognized him, she was overwhelmed with a mixture of emotions; it was not Byron, but it was someone she knew, someone dear to her.

He was calling out her name and holding out his hand. She went to him and took his hand, holding it close to her chest.

'I'm here, Dad. I'm here now.'

That evening, when she had finished her day's work, she sat beside Sam, holding his hand.

'Rosie, lass. I want to see Nell one last time.'

'Please don't talk like that, you're—'

'I'm going to die. You've got to face it.' Rosie listened to his laboured breathing. He was fighting to pull in every breath. She was forced to believe him. 'And it's better this way – to die a hero rather than dangling at the end of a hangman's rope.'

Rosie held his hand against her cheek as tears ran down her face. She couldn't argue with him. If he lived and William Ramsey caught up with him, he would undoubtedly be thrown into gaol, tried and hanged. Though it broke her heart, she knew he was right.

'I'll get her here, Dad,' she promised in a broken voice. 'I'll send for Aunty Nell.'

That night, Rosie wrote to Nell, forming the wording of her letter carefully in case it should fall into the wrong hands. Letters were supposed to be private but she knew that the contents of a letter were often circulating through the village before they reached the hands of the true recipient. It had always happened and now, more than ever, people were nosy.

> *Dear Mrs Tranter,*
> *It's not Nathan – I'll say that straight away –*
> *but please come here as soon as you possibly*
> *can.*
> *Regards, Miss Skelton*

She was fortunate that Elsie was working on a different ward and was unlikely to see Sam, but Mrs Ramsey was another matter. She was hoping that she had never seen Sam close up and would not recognize him. But Grace was a lot sharper than perhaps even Rosie gave her credit for. She noticed Rosie frequently disappearing into Ward Four, where the most seriously wounded patients were moved to after their admission. Most of them were receiving end-of-life care. There was no more that the doctors could do for them and it was up to the nurses to ease their last days.

So, Grace made it her business to find out who the patient was.

'His name is Sam, but more than that I don't know,' the staff nurse in charge of the ward told her. 'He had no identification on him by the time he reached us. We don't even know where he came from, only that he was a Poacher.' The word startled Grace until she realized that the staff nurse was using the nickname for a soldier in the Lincolnshire Regiment. 'It's surprising he's lasted this long,' the staff nurse went on. 'I can only think it was sheer will power to get back home that's kept him going. One of the assistant nurses seems to know him. At least, she's spending a lot of her off-duty time with him and often seems tearful.'

'Which one?' Grace asked.

'Skelton.'

Grace nodded thoughtfully. Now she thought she knew who the new arrival was. The next time Rosie was on duty in another ward and she was not, Grace went to the wounded soldier's bedside. As she stood over him, he looked up at her and she saw the fear in his eyes. He recognized her and now she knew for definite exactly who he was.

He became agitated, his restless fingers plucking at the bedclothes and his breathing becoming rasping.

'It's all right, Sam,' she said quietly, sitting down beside him. 'You're quite safe here. No one is going to give you away, certainly not me.'

'Aren't you' – he spoke in short painful gasps – 'going to tell *him*?'

'Certainly not.'

'Why? I – deserve—'

She took his hand into hers. 'I'm sure that whatever happened that night was an accident but my husband and the authorities wouldn't see it that way. But you stay here until . . .'

'I die, Mrs Ramsey. I'm dying. I know that. And mebbe it's for the best but – I worry about Rosie.'

'Well, don't. She's a strong young woman who can fend for herself, but she is now my friend and I give you my word, I will watch out for her.'

He gazed into her eyes. 'You're a good woman, Mrs Ramsey. And I'll tell you something, so you'll know for sure. That night . . .'

'Don't—'

'Yes, I must. I never meant to hurt anyone.' He paused every so often to catch his breath, but his voice was surprisingly strong. This was a confession that had to be made before he could pass in peace. 'I was retreating quietly through the woods. I tripped over a fallen branch and, as I fell backwards, the gun went off. I suppose my finger must have jerked on the trigger as I fell. I swear to you that it was an accident. A terrible accident. But, in law, I killed him. I've cursed myself ever since for taking a gun out with me that night. I don't know to this day what made me take it, because I rarely used a gun.' When he had finished, he was exhausted. He lay back and closed his eyes. Grace wanted to ask more questions and yet, part of her didn't want to know any more. She was tempted to ask what had happened to the gun because it had not been found in his cottage or garden. Had he stopped to bury it in the woods? She doubted he would have risked doing that and besides, William had insisted that a thorough search be made. Nothing had been found and she rather thought that Rosie had disposed of it. But how? And where?

She sat holding his hand. Maybe it was best that she knew no more. She wanted to help Rosie and by remaining in ignorance of any part the girl might have played, she could do that.

After several minutes he stirred again and Grace whispered, 'Is there anything I can do for you?'

'I want to see Nell. I've asked Rosie . . .'

'Don't worry. I'll see to that for you. Now, you get some rest.'

She got up, leaving him to sleep while she went in search of Rosie. It wouldn't be a peaceful sleep, for his breathing was rasping and painful. She found her helping a nurse attend to a patient, fetching clean bandages and taking away the soiled ones. Grace waited until she was free.

'Rosie,' she murmured, taking her elbow gently and stepping to one side. 'I know who the solider in Ward Four is, but don't worry. He's quite safe here but you do know he's not got long, don't you?'

Rosie nodded, but was unable to speak for a moment.

'He wants to see Nell,' Grace said.

Rosie blinked in surprise. 'You've been talking to him.'

'Oh yes. I sat with him for quite a while.'

'I've written to Nell and asked her to come.'

'I can help with that. I'll ask Sarah to go and fetch her, like I did for Mrs Bates when she came to see Dan.'

267

'But then Sarah will have to know about my father. I know she's been ever so good keeping quiet about me, but Dad's a different matter.'

'Sarah is the most loyal friend anyone could have. She's been with me for many years and I no longer regard her as a servant. Now, she's my friend. I know she'll do whatever I ask of her.'

Rosie bit her lip. 'It's a lot to ask. She – she'd be breaking the law. As we all are.'

'We're in the middle of a catastrophic war, my dear. We've bigger things to worry about than that. For one thing, I'm worried sick about Byron every minute of the day. And then there's Nathan Tranter. He must be in Nell's thoughts constantly.'

Her blue gaze caught and held the look in Rosie's green eyes. 'And if I'm not mistaken, you think about them both a lot, don't you, Rosie?'

Rosie dropped her gaze but was obliged to answer truthfully. Huskily, she said, 'Yes, yes, I do. All the time. Both of them.'

Grace squeezed her hand. 'Leave it with me. I'll get Mrs Tranter here as soon as I can.'

Twenty-Seven

'Rosie, I need to talk seriously to you.'

Rosie sat down at the bedside and took her father's hand. 'Dad, please don't try to talk. It tires you so.'

'I have to, Rosie. I have to know what you did that night.' He paused, breathed painfully for a few moments and then carried on, but every word was an effort. 'I should never have asked you to get rid of the gun. It was wrong of me. I'm sorry. But I need to know – I have to know – what you did with it.'

'Exactly what you told me to do. I flung it right out into the middle of the lake.'

'No one saw you?'

Rosie shrugged. 'They can't have done. No one's ever asked me about it.'

'You've been questioned?'

Rosie hesitated. She didn't want to add to her father's suffering.

'Tell me!' Suddenly, his voice was surprisingly strong, as if, in the last few days – perhaps only hours – of his life he had to do this one thing. He had to know. 'Tell me everything you did that night and then what's happened since.'

Seeing that it was going to be the only way to get him to rest, Rosie recounted everything, ending with her leaving the village and arriving at the hospital. When at last she fell silent, Sam closed his eyes and slept.

As dusk fell, Grace came silently to Sam's bedside. He was awake.

'Sam, Mrs Tranter will arrive tomorrow. I have arranged for Monty to bring her.'

He gripped her hand. 'You're very good to me, Mrs Ramsey. I can't thank you enough.'

'Is there anything else I can do for you?'

'Just one thing. Could you find me a writing pad, an envelope and a pencil? I need to ask Nell to write a letter for me when she comes.'

'I can do that for you . . .'

Sam shook his head agitatedly, which set off a bout of coughing.

'No – no,' he wheezed at last. 'It's not fair for you to have to write down what I have to say. It's best that Nell does it.'

Guessing that perhaps it was something very personal between the two of them, Grace agreed. She had learned of the closeness between the couple and respected his wishes.

Nell arrived the following afternoon and sat beside Sam holding his hand, the tears running down her face.

'Oh my dear,' she whispered.

'Nell – I have loved you dearly. You must know that. I've nothing to leave you. Nothing to leave even to Rosie, but there is one last thing I need you to do for me.'

'Anything, Sam.' Nell wiped away her tears and

tried to be brave, but it was hard. She had only ever truly loved two men in her life and now she was to lose the second one too.

'There's a writing pad and pencil on the little table there. Mrs Ramsey got them for me but I didn't want her to write the letter, even though she offered.' He paused to catch his breath. 'She's a good woman, but it's not fair for her to have to write what I need to say. There's only you I can really trust, Nell.'

'Can't Rosie . . . ?'

'No. She'd refuse to do it. But it must be done.'

For most of the next hour, Nell sat by his bedside and carefully wrote down everything that Sam said. It took a while because he had to keep stopping to breathe and recover from coughing bouts. But, at last, it was done to Sam's satisfaction.

'I understand now, Sam, why you wanted me to do it.' Nell said at last. 'Can you raise yourself up a bit enough to sign it? You must sign it yourself and I'll witness it, though I think someone else ought to witness your signature as well as me.'

'Ask – Matron. She'll do it.'

Nell hurried away to the matron's office.

'Of course, I'll come at once,' Connie Archer said. 'Is it his will?'

'Not exactly, Matron, but it's a very important letter that he has entrusted to me to write for him.' Nell smiled sadly. 'It's lucky the village school was so good and I learned to read and write.'

'I see. Well, I have no need to read it. I just need to see him sign it and then you too, as you have done the writing of it.'

As the matron watched Sam write his name with painful slowness, she noticed that he wrote the surname 'Waterhouse'. But she made no remark. She was not going to question a dying man.

When it was done, Sam sank back against the pillows. 'Thank you. Both of you. It's for Rosie, just in case it's ever needed.'

'You want me to give it to Rosie?' Nell asked.

'No – no, you're to keep it, Nell. Rosie mustn't know anything about it. But you'll know what to do, Nell, if – if it's ever needed.'

'I don't know what it's about,' Connie said, 'and I'm not going to pry. We get all sorts of strange last requests in here, Sam, but I can see how important it is to you, so, Mrs Tranter, if you ever need me to verify that I have witnessed both your signatures to this – this – well, whatever it is, I am willing to do so.'

Nell thanked her, folded the letter, placed it in the envelope and sealed it. Then she put it carefully in the bag she was carrying.

As the matron left them, Nell leaned towards Sam again. 'Rosie has given me the box from under your bed, Sam, for safe keeping. I'll put it in there.'

'Thank you, Nell.'

With the last ounce of his strength, he squeezed her hand, lay back against the pillows and closed his eyes.

It seemed as though, once Sam had seen Nell, had dictated his letter to her, he gave up the fight. As dusk fell that evening, he slipped away still holding her hand.

'He's at peace now, Rosie love,' Nell said to her while the nurses reverently dealt with Sam's ravaged body and spared Rosie the ordeal. They all knew that he'd meant something to their colleague, but they weren't sure exactly what the relationship was, though one or two, knowing his surname, had guessed that perhaps he was her father. Not one of them, however, was tactless enough to ask. Only the matron, who had to fill out the details of his death for the registrar, learned his real name and therefore Rosie's too, but she was happy for the girl to continue to use the surname Skelton.

'It's no one else's business but yours, my dear,' Connie said to Rosie. Instead, she had a discreet word with Grace and learned about the tragedy that had happened in Thornsby. They had both agreed to shield Rosie from trouble.

'Yes, I remember reading in the local paper about a gamekeeper being shot. It was about the time that war broke out, wasn't it?'

Grace had nodded. 'None of it was Rosie's doing but, sadly, my husband is bent on someone paying the price and now that her father is out of his reach once and for all, I fear he may still want to take his revenge on Rosie.'

'Then we must see to it that he doesn't find her,' Connie Archer had agreed. 'What does puzzle me, though, Grace, is why you are deliberately defying your own husband.'

Grace smiled wryly. 'Oh, it's a long story, Connie. Maybe one day I'll explain, if you've time to listen.'

'I'm a good listener. If ever you feel you're ready.'

*

Rosie's emotions were in turmoil. She was saddened by her father's death and yet she couldn't help but feel relief, and then she felt guilty. But the truth was that, had Sam been caught, he undoubtedly would have been tried for murder and hanged. Rosie shuddered every time she thought about it. She knew her father had caused the gamekeeper's death, but she also knew that it had been a tragic accident. He would never have deliberately harmed another human being and yet he had been commanded by his country to do just that; to kill and maim the enemy. But they had got him first and now he was gone. In time Rosie would put it all aside and remember the good times; the dark nights creeping through the woods at his side, watching and listening and learning. She wondered if any of his stealthy ways had been useful in the trenches. Perhaps he had helped to save the lives of the men around him. She hoped so.

'D'you know, Rosie,' Grace said as they sat together over lunch towards the end of February. It was 1916 and eighteen months of war had passed. 'I can't make out where Byron and the other boys are now. I've always been able to make a guess from his convoluted messages, but this time I can't. All I know is that they've left Gallipoli, but where they've been posted, I just don't know. He's talking about looking after the boats going up and down the water.'

Rosie laughed. 'If you can't work it out, Grace, I really don't think I can.' She wrinkled her brow thoughtfully. 'Is he near a river somewhere?'

Grace was silent for a few moments and then her

face cleared. 'You've given me an idea. I wonder if they're at the Suez Canal? There was some action there a few weeks back. You clever girl, Rosie.'

'I can't take the credit for that; I don't even know where this canal you're talking about is.'

Grace laughed. 'Don't worry. It won't make you a better nurse knowing things like that.'

'Perhaps not,' Rosie said seriously. 'But I like to know where he – where they – are.'

Grace touched the girl's hand. 'I know,' she said softly. 'And I promise I will tell you everything he tells me. At least it sounds as if they're still together and all right.'

In May 1916, the newspapers, which the men in the Thornsby Arms read every day, reported that conscription, which had only been introduced in January that year, was to be extended to bring in all men between the ages of eighteen and forty-one. Even men who had previously been deemed unfit for service were to be re-examined.

'They're not getting the vast numbers of volunteers they had at the beginning,' Terry Chambers said.

'It's hardly surprising with all the casualties,' Ted agreed.

'I wonder if any of our lads regret going now,' Terry said thoughtfully. 'I know my lad doesn't. He actually sounds as though he's enjoying the life,' he added as if he couldn't believe what he was saying.

'We can't allow countries to threaten and invade each other,' Ted said, placing another pint in front of Terry. 'This one's on the house – for your lad.'

Terry smiled and picked up the pint, raising it in a silent toast.

'It's my opinion,' Ted went on, 'that the Hun would have overrun the whole of Europe if they'd been left unchecked.'

'They still might,' Terry said grimly. 'It's not over yet.'

Terry was proved right; indeed, the war was not over by a long way. The bloodbath at Verdun, which was mainly being fought by the French, had been going on since February, and the Allies planned a huge offensive around the area of the Somme. Through the last two weeks of June, they bombarded the enemy lines constantly, believing that they would obliterate any defences. But when the whistle blew on 1 July and lines of allied troops went over the top, they were mown down remorselessly by an enemy that had dug deep and had survived the onslaught of their enemy's guns.

It was utter carnage; slaughter on a scale never before witnessed in a war. On that first day alone, there were over 57,000 British casualties of which more than 19,000 had been killed. The battle of the Somme would become infamous in war, but for those at home the loss was far more personal.

Rosie stood at the end of the young soldier's bed looking down at him, feeling as if her heart was breaking. Facing her father's terrible injuries and death had been bad enough, but this was something else.

'Oh Nathan, Nathan, not you,' she breathed. 'However am I going to tell your mam?'

She felt an arm creep round her waist and Anna spoke softly. 'Is it someone you know?'

Rosie nodded. 'A lad from our village. We grew up together. We were – are – the best of friends.'

'Is he your young man?'

'No, nothing like that. We're more like brother and sister. My father and his mother were very close. They'd both lost their partners, you see.' Now that he was gone, Rosie felt she could mention her father freely.

But the young girl, brought up in a workhouse, had never experienced family life. She didn't understand how it worked, but she could see the distress in Rosie's face and feel for her.

'He's Mrs Tranter's son,' Rosie murmured.

'Oh no, not that nice lady who came to visit Dan and then came back again to sit with the soldier who died?' Anna still hadn't realized that that particular soldier had been Rosie's father.

'Yes, I'm afraid so.'

'How bad is he?'

'I don't know yet. I've only just found him. I came into the ward to change the jugs of water for all the patients and saw him. He must have come in late last night after I went off duty.'

'He's not moving. Is he unconscious?'

'I think he's just asleep.'

'Let's find Sister. She'll know.'

Nathan's injuries were not life-threatening but they might mean he'd got what the soldiers called a "blighty" wound.

'It's an awful thing to say, but, in a way, he's

been lucky,' Rosie was told. 'He's got a wound in his leg that will probably keep him out of the rest of the war.'

'I'll help you look after him, Rosie,' Anna said. 'We can't nurse him, but we can do anything else he wants. You must introduce me to him when he wakes up.'

'I must see Grace. Maybe she can help again to get his mother here.'

The following day, Sarah set off once more to Thornsby to fetch Nell. This time she was not so lucky; William was at home and from the window of his study, he saw her walking up the drive. He was waiting for her when she entered the kitchen by the back door.

'Oh, so you've dared to come back, have you? Well, there's no job for you here now, but you will' – before Cook or any of the servants realized what was happening, he stepped across the space between them and grasped Sarah's arm – 'tell me exactly where my wife is, because I'm sure you know.'

Sarah raised her chin. 'I don't work for you, sir. Not now. And I won't tell you where she is.'

William released his grip, drew back his hand and slapped her hard on the left side of her face. There was an audible gasp from Cook and her kitchen maid. Biddy, who had taken Elsie's place, had come from the workhouse too. Although she'd been used to blows, she hadn't expected to witness such treatment in a grand house like Thornsby Manor.

Now the butler stepped forward. 'There's no need for that, sir,' Baines said, placing himself between the master and Sarah. 'The mistress wouldn't tolerate it.'

'The mistress,' William said through gritted teeth, 'isn't here or is she so useless at running the household that none of you have noticed her absence?'

'Far from it, Mr Ramsey. We all miss madam and wish she would come home.'

'Do you know where she is, Baines, because if you do . . . ?'

'No, sir, I don't know.' He did not add: 'And if I did, I wouldn't tell you.'

William turned back to glare at Sarah. Her face was reddening and there were his finger marks imprinted on her cheek. 'Well, you can tell your mistress,' he spat, 'that her son is home, injured in the war, and that her duty is here with him. And you can also tell her that I shall be demanding that Pearl brings Albert back here where he belongs.'

William turned and left the room, slamming the door behind him.

Cook hurried to Sarah with a flannel soaked in cold water. 'Here, lass, put this on your poor face. He's always been a nasty man, but it's the first time he's struck one of us.'

'Not exactly,' Baines put in. 'He's taken his temper out on young Monty once or twice when his horse wasn't ready the minute he wanted it. And Lucas Brown takes lessons from the master. Poor Monty often feels the back of the groom's hand. I know that for a fact.'

'I never knew any of that,' Cook said, pursing her lips. 'I'd have put a stop to that, if I had.'

Baines laughed wryly. 'Oh yes, Cook, and how would you have stopped it, eh?'

'Told madam. She'd never have let any of us be mistreated. Just because he was a lad from the work-house, the master thinks he can treat him anyhow. But he's never laid a finger on us women before and I'm not going to stand by and see it happen now. If you are with madam, Sarah, you tell her what's happening here. And as for Mr Brown – well, I will have words with him.'

'Is it true? Is Byron back home?' Sarah asked.

The cook and Mr Baines exchanged a glance. It was Cook who answered her. 'Yes, he is.'

'Is he – is he hurt?'

'Not physically – but he just stays in his room all day.'

'He sits staring out of the window and won't talk at all.'

'He's not as bad as poor Dan Bates, but the local doctor thinks it's something similar, caused by being in the trenches.'

'But – but' – Sarah glanced wildly from one to the other – 'the army doesn't recognize it as an illness. The doctor at the Lincoln hospital had an awful job to persuade the army not to put poor Dan up against a wall and shoot him for cowardice.'

'Oh, so that's where you are, is it?' Mr Baines said softly. 'In the Lincoln hospital?'

Sarah's eyes widened and she clapped her hand over her mouth when she realized what she had done.

The butler smiled gently and put his hand on her shoulder. 'Don't worry, we won't give you away, but I think that once you tell the mistress about Byron, she'll come home anyway.'

'Yes,' Sarah nodded grimly, 'she will.'

'But you must tell her that he'll have to go back to the war. Even his father is saying that he must. He doesn't want any son of his shot as a coward, he says.'

'By heck, he's changed his tune, hasn't he? It's all about him and what *he* wants, isn't it?'

'It always has been, Sarah, and I suspect it always will be.'

'Well, I don't suppose I can ask Monty to take me and Mrs Tranter back to Lincoln in the carriage this time. Master'll have his beady eye on the lad. I don't want to cause him any more trouble.'

'You can catch the carrier's cart. He might not take you all the way, but he goes in that direction on a Wednesday.'

'That's a good idea, Cook. Thanks. And now I'd best get to Mrs Tranter's and give her the news. Oh, I hate being the bearer of bad tidings, but there's nowt else for it. She's got to be told. And then, when I get back, I'll have to tell Grace.'

'Grace!' Both Mr Baines and Cook spoke at once. 'You call her Grace?'

Despite all the worries and responsibilities she had on her shoulders at that moment, Sarah smiled. 'It's what she wanted. She wanted to fit in with everyone there and she has. She's just one of us now.'

'And who is "one of us" exactly?'

'She started as a ward orderly but she's an assistant to the nurses now.'

Scandalized, the cook repeated the words, adding, 'I thought at least she'd be a proper nurse.'

'She hasn't any training. Neither have I, but we

help the nurses so that they can concentrate on doing what they do best – caring for the patients.'

'And where does she sleep? Is she staying in a hotel?'

Now Sarah laughed out loud. 'Oh no. She sleeps with the rest of us.'

Now, both Cook and Mr Baines were speechless, their mouths dropping open.

'She's a lovely woman,' Sarah said gently. 'None of you got to know her like I did. She's far too good for the likes of *him*.' She jerked her thumb towards the door through which William had departed. 'Anyway, now I'd best get to Mrs Tranter's. I know she'll let me stay with her.' She glanced round. 'Goodbye, all of you. I don't know if I'll be seeing you again.'

'Good luck, Sarah. And give our best to Mrs Tranter too. We hope Nathan will be all right. And, of course, don't forget to tell the mistress about Master Byron.'

'Oh, you can be sure I won't forget that.'

Twenty-Eight

'Nathan,' Rosie whispered, sitting down beside his bed and taking his hand. 'Sarah's gone to fetch your mam. She'll be here soon. Do wake up.'

But there was no response from the sleeping man. The ward sister stood beside her, looking down at him. 'Dr Oldfield has examined him thoroughly and can't find any reason why he should not be awake. Yes, he has a nasty injury on his leg that's infected, but he thinks we've caught it early enough for it to be treated. He's no other visible injury. He's a puzzle. The doctor thinks someone sitting with him and talking to him might help. I can give you an extra hour off, Skelton, if you want to do that.'

'Of course. Thank you. And I'll come back in my off-duty time, if you'll allow it.'

'Of course.' The sister smiled. 'It's doctor's orders and when his mother arrives, she's to be given extra time with him too.'

Little by little, the gossip had permeated among all the staff. They now knew where Rosie, Grace, Sarah and Elsie came from and exactly who Grace was, but by this time she was well liked and respected for being herself and not because of who she was. As for Rosie, they'd realized that the older soldier who had died had been her father. What they had not yet learned was exactly who he had been and about the terrible shooting accident, because Rosie still went under the surname of Skelton.

'Nathan, dearest Nathan. Please wake up and talk to me. Sarah has gone to fetch your mother. Please wake up so you can talk to her.'

Dr Oldfield appeared at her side. 'That's very good. Keep talking to him. Talk about the past. What you used to do together as children. That sort of thing. Keep up the good work.'

'Do you remember, Nathan, when we were at school together? Do you remember little Elsie Warren? She's working here too. And now you'll never guess this – Mrs Ramsey's working here as well. We began as cleaners, or ward orderlies, but now we're all assistant nurses. You won't believe it, but she's fitted in with everyone and she insists we all call her Grace when we're off duty. What do you think of that?' On and on Rosie chattered until she almost ran out of things to talk about. The following morning – the day on which she hoped Nell would arrive – she sat down beside him once more. The nurses had finished changing his bandages and she and Grace had remade his bed, rolling him gently from side to side to change the sheet.

'Now, what shall we talk about today?' she began, but a sound from the bed interrupted her.

'Byron,' he whispered huskily. 'What's – happened – to Byron?'

'Oh Nathan – you're awake.' She squeezed his hand. 'Let me fetch Sister . . .

*

Sarah stayed one night with Nell and then the next day they set off together for the tortuous journey to Lincoln, arriving mid-afternoon.

When Sarah had left the hospital, Nathan had still been sleeping, but when his mother hurried into the ward, he was sitting up and watching the door for her arrival.

'I'll leave you with him, Mrs Tranter,' Sarah said. 'I must find Grace.'

'Oh son—' Nell sat beside him, her voice full of tears.

'Now, don't fuss, Mam. I'm fine. Just a bit of a scratch on me leg. I'll soon be as right as ninepence.'

Nell, who had been determined not to cry when she saw him, couldn't stop a tear of thankfulness from trickling down her cheek. Her boy was alive and she'd move heaven and earth to keep him with her now he was home. But she was sensible enough to know that the 'last word' did not lie with her.

'You've Rosie to thank for this,' he said, smiling weakly.

Nell gaped at him. 'For – for what?'

'The fact that I'm sitting up and talking to you. Evidently, she's been sitting here beside me, hour after hour, talking to me and bringing me back into the land of the living. From what they're saying, I was out of it for quite a time. Now, tell me all the news, but first I want to know if you've heard anything about Byron. We've been lucky to be able to stick together, you know. Right from when we volunteered. We fought side by side and it was him who carried me from no-man's-land back to our trenches when I got wounded. But for him, Mam, I wouldn't be here.'

'We've heard he's at home. He's not physically injured but' – she touched her head – 'he's damaged in here. A bit like Dan Bates, but not so serious.'

'Dan? What's happened to Dan? The six of us who went together stayed together as much as we could, but Dan and Ray got sent up the line somewhere and we got separated.'

'Oh dear. Didn't you know? The poor lad's in a terrible way.' She went on to tell Nathan all about his friend.

'This is a dreadful war, Mam. It should never have been allowed to happen. I hope it'll be the last one we ever have like this.'

'It's being called "the war to end all wars",' Nell said. 'Some writer put something like it in one of his newspaper columns. Anyway, Sarah's gone to find Grace to tell her about Master Byron. She'll go home at once, I'm sure.'

'Grace? Oh yes, now I remember, Rosie said something about that when I was half asleep. Fancy, who'd have thought it. Her working among the riff-raff. I bet her old man doesn't like it.'

Now that she had seen for herself that her son wasn't as bad as she had feared, Nell was able to smile. 'No, he doesn't. Sarah told me he's spitting feathers.' She sighed. 'Poor Grace. She'll have a hard time of it with him when she does get home. Now, Nathan, tell me honestly, how do you really feel?'

*

'Rosie – where's Grace?' Sarah asked. 'Have you seen her?'

'Ward Two. She's helping one of the nurses with a patient.'

Sarah hurried away to find her. She paused in the doorway to catch her breath. Grace was bending over a patient, smoothing his pillows, smiling down at him. Sarah took a deep breath, reluctant to break the moment, and yet . . .

'Grace,' she said softly, approaching her. 'Could I have a word?'

'Sarah! You're back. Did you bring Mrs Tranter? I heard that Rosie has done wonders. Nathan is awake and talking normally. Isn't that wonderful?' She came to Sarah. 'But you still look anxious. What is it? Have you hurt your face? It looks as if you've got a bruise on your cheek.'

'Never mind about that, but I have something to tell you. Byron's home.'

Grace's face lit up. 'Oh, how wonderful. Is he on leave? How long has he got?'

Sarah took both Grace's hands into hers. 'Grace – listen. He's not physically injured, but his mind is affected.'

Grace's smile died instantly. 'Oh no!' she breathed. 'Not – not like poor Dan?'

'Something similar, but not nearly as bad. He just sits in his room staring out of the window. He won't talk to anyone. He's hardly eating or drinking. And – and . . .'

'And what, Sarah? Tell me quickly.'

'Dr Wren says he can't make a case for him being

invalided out of the army. If they come to – to arrest him . . .'

'They'll judge it to be cowardice,' Grace finished her sentence for her.

'And – I'm sorry to tell you this – but your husband wants him to go back to the war. He – he says he doesn't want a son of his to be branded a coward.'

'Of course he doesn't,' Grace said, her tone heavy with sarcasm. She sighed. 'I must go home at once. And, very sadly, I don't think I shall be coming back. I must see Connie – Matron – and explain what has happened, but first there is someone else I must see.'

She found Rosie taking a well-earned break and having a cup of tea. She sat down beside her as Rosie smiled and began to pour a cup of tea for her.

'Rosie – Sarah has returned with Mrs Tranter but while she was home, she found out that Byron has returned to the manor.' She hurried on to explain all that she knew and ended, 'I have to go home.'

Rosie's face was bleak and if Grace had ever been in any doubt about the girl's feelings for Byron, there was no uncertainty now. Rosie was in love with Byron.

'How I wish I could see him,' the girl whispered, her words ending in a tearful hiccup.

Grace touched her hand and said gently, 'It's not possible, my dear. My husband would have you arrested.'

Rosie nodded, trying to stem her tears, but failing.

'But I will tell Byron about you, I promise, and I will write and let you know how he is.'

'Oh will you? Will you really? That would be so good of you.'

Grace nodded, unable to speak for the lump in her own throat. It was all she could promise Rosie. But as she left the hospital, Grace made another promise to herself; she would join forces with William to ensure that Pearl brought Bertie back to the manor. She was sure that the little boy's presence would help Byron.

'Ah, so you have condescended to come home where you belong, have you? You've been away for over eighteen months. Is that any way for a dutiful wife to behave? I could divorce you for desertion. Where have you been all this time? I demand that you tell me.'

William was playing games with her. He'd known all along exactly where his wife was; he'd made it his business to find out shortly after she'd left. He'd hoped she would come home when she found the work too onerous and realized how foolish she'd been in leaving her comfortable lifestyle. But in this he'd been thwarted; she'd only come back because her son needed her. William's pride, however, would never let him admit this so he decided to keep up the pretence.

'Divorce me if you wish, William, but I doubt you will. You wouldn't want the scandal, now, would you?' Grace said as she stepped into the hallway and peeled off her gloves. 'I have merely been doing what my conscience told me to do. To help out with the war effort.'

'Well, you're needed here now to get that coward of a son of yours to return to his duty. If he doesn't go soon, we can expect a visit from the military police, I shouldn't wonder.'

'Is he not on sick leave?'

'Pah! Sick leave, my foot. It's all in his mind.'

'Exactly, William. You can be sick in your mind just as much as you can have a wound in your leg. And now, if you will excuse me, I'll go and see Byron.'

As she mounted the stairs, William called after her. 'And none of your namby-pamby words. Get him back into uniform and returning to his regiment. The doctor has given him two weeks. After that – God knows what will happen. I have sent for Pearl and my grandson. They should be here. I have demanded that they come home.'

Grace carried on climbing the stairs and headed towards Byron's bedroom.

Baines, who had been hovering in the hall when Grace had arrived home, told the rest of the staff when he returned to the kitchen, 'She's back. At least for now because she won't tell the master where she's been. Cook, get a tray ready for her and I'll take it up to Byron's room. Make up a tray for him too. Maybe she'll get him to eat something.' There was a flurry of activity as they all scurried to care for the woman they all loved and had missed so much.

Upstairs, Grace opened the door quietly and crossed the room to where her son was sitting in a chair facing the window. His eyes were vacant, staring at the view yet not really seeing it. He was witnessing the horrific pictures being played over and over again in his mind's eye. Grace took hold of his cold hand.

'Byron, my dear,' she said softly. 'I'm home now. We'll soon get you well again.'

He stirred and shifted in his seat. His mouth worked as if he was trying to say something.

'What is it? Try to tell me.'

'Rosie . . .' he stuttered. 'I want – to see – Rosie.'

'Oh my darling,' she breathed. 'You know that's not possible. Rosie would come in a flash, but your father would have her arrested on the spot. She can't come back here, you know that.'

'Where – is – she?'

'She's safe.'

'You've – seen her?'

'She's safe and well and helping to care for the wounded. I've been working with her. More than that, I can't tell you. If your father were to find out . . .' She paused and then said, 'But your father has sent for Pearl and Bertie. Won't that be wonderful?'

But all Byron said was, 'I want to see Rosie.'

Twenty-Nine

Pearl arrived, bringing Bertie.

'I'll stay as long as Byron is here,' she announced, 'But then I'm going home.'

'This is your home,' William snarled. 'You should be here doing your duty as a wife and mother. This is where my grandson belongs. He is heir to my estate.'

'He is also heir to *my* father's estate,' Pearl countered. 'Which he is likely to inherit long before this one. Besides, why is the Thornsby estate more important than my father's, might I ask?'

'It's bigger,' William snapped. 'Albert should be here, learning how to run it.'

Pearl laughed. 'He's not even three. Besides, he will be going to boarding school as soon as he is old enough.'

'There will be no need for that. I will engage the best tutors for him . . .'

Pearl waved her hand dismissively. 'A boy needs to learn something of the world. He can't do that in the wilds of north Lincolnshire.'

'And I suppose south Lincolnshire is so much more civilized,' William said sarcastically.

Pearl glanced at him disdainfully, but did not

condescend to reply. Instead, she held out her hand to her son. 'Come, Bertie, we'll go and see your papa.'

The presence of his son did Byron a power of good. Within a week he was eating properly again and taking walks in the grounds with the toddler trotting at his side. He even taught the little boy the rudiments of cricket. But the welcome improvement in his health meant only one thing: Byron would have to report back for duty.

'Pearl,' Grace said, when they were alone in the morning room. 'I want to thank you for bringing Bertie. I don't think Byron would have recovered so well – or so quickly – if you had not.'

Pearl nodded and was thoughtful for a moment. 'I heard you'd been away. Nursing, was it?'

Grace smiled. 'Not exactly – I'm not qualified – but the work I did was useful.'

'Shall you go back once Byron has gone?'

Grace hesitated. 'I don't think so. I'd love to,' she added, 'but I can see that my duty is here. Standards have slipped while I've been away and I have to remember that years ago I made solemn marriage vows which, of late, I have not kept. As, my dear,' she added softly, 'did you. We have tried to be good to you and to give you everything you wanted.'

Pearl was silent for a long time, twisting her fingers in her lap. 'Mother and I are doing useful war work around Stamford. There's nothing for me to *do* here. I get so bored.'

Grace could not argue with that; she'd often felt much the same herself.

'It's just that – at home – and I'm sorry if this offends you . . .'

'It doesn't worry me, my dear, because I understand. Go on.'

'At home, Mother and I are doing our bit for the war effort too. We organize fundraising events and hold them in our grounds. We do at least one a month and if it's cold or wet, we use one of the big barns.'

'We could do that here. In fact, I think it's an excellent idea. We could do it together.'

Pearl smiled weakly. 'We *could*, I suppose.'

Grace thought quickly. 'May I make a suggestion? Why don't you come here for a few months each year and spend the rest at your parents' home.'

'Even when Byron comes back for good?'

Grace was heartened to think that the girl believed Byron would survive the war. 'That would be up to you and him to work out between you. Perhaps he could spend some time at your home with you?'

'Oh, I don't think that would be a very good idea,' Pearl said swiftly. A little too swiftly. Grace wondered if there was a reason behind it. She sighed inwardly. Instead, she suggested, 'Think about it. You could come here in the spring, say March or April and stay here until August or September. That way, you could be at home for Christmas.' Grace knew William wouldn't be happy with the arrangement, but surely to have Bertie at Thornsby for part of the year was better than nothing.

'I'll think about it,' was all Pearl would promise and, with that, Grace had to be content – for the moment. Grace was no fool and she was beginning to suspect that perhaps Pearl had formed a romantic attachment to someone in Stamford.

A week later, Byron was well enough to return to his unit and Pearl insisted on leaving on the same day. Byron hugged his son hard and the little boy wound his chubby arms around Byron's neck and rained kisses on this cheek. 'Bye, bye, Papa.'

Byron set him down and turned to Pearl and kissed her on her cheek. 'Thank you for coming, Pearl, and for bringing Bertie. Please come again, won't you, even if – even if I'm not here? Mother and Father would so love to see more of him – of both of you.'

'Yes, I will. I promise,' Pearl said.

They left in a flurry of goodbyes. William, Grace and Byron stood on the top step to see them off. They watched until they could no longer see Bertie's little hand waving.

'What a lovely child he is,' Grace said. 'I have to hand it to Pearl. She is certainly bringing him up well.'

'He should be here with us,' William growled and then turned to his own son. 'Can't you control your wife, Byron?'

Byron only smiled sardonically as if to say, 'it seems you can no longer control yours'. Instead, he said, 'And now, I'd best be on my way to Lincoln. I have to report back by noon.'

'I've already arranged for Monty to take you in the carriage,' William said and then glanced towards his wife, fully expecting her to say she was leaving too.

Guessing his thoughts, she turned to him. 'I will be staying at least for the time being. There is much I can do here now that many of our villagers are being affected by the war one way or another. I intend to do what I can to help them. And I shall expect your support, William. They are, after all, your tenants.'

William struggled to control the retort that sprang naturally to his lips. He had missed his wife more than he would ever openly admit and would do anything to keep her at home. If playing the philanthropist was what it took to keep her with him, then he would do it.

'Of course, my dear,' he said smoothly. 'I will help you in any way I can. What have you in mind?'

'My plans are not fully formed yet, William, but I will, of course, discuss everything with you before I take any action.' Grace smiled at him. For the first time in her life she had the upper hand. It was not a feeling she was used to, but she would make the most of the moment. As the carriage drew up in front of them, Byron put his arms round her and held her close for a moment.

'She's working at the Lincoln military hospital,' she whispered in his ear. 'But your father must not find out.' Louder she said, 'Take care of yourself, my darling boy, and come back safely to us.'

He drew back from her and although all he said aloud was, 'Thank you, Mother, I'll do my best,' the gratitude for her whispered words was in his eyes.

*

'Rosie,' Anna called. 'There's someone here to see you.'

Fear flashed in Rosie's eyes. 'To – to see me?'

'Yes. A man. A very handsome man in uniform, I might add.' Anna was smiling. The little orphan from the workhouse had blossomed into a pretty girl, despite all the long hours and the hard, often distressing, work. Half the soldiers were in love with her and one of them, it seemed, was Nathan. Rosie had watched the growing fondness between them with indulgence and took every opportunity to allow Anna to attend to his needs.

'Are you sure,' Anna had asked her worriedly in the privacy of the bedroom they shared, 'that Nathan's not your young man?'

'I promise you he's not. Never has been and never will be.'

'But – but you seem awfully fond of each other.'

'We are. Brothers and sisters usually are. Except,' she added, with a giggle, 'those who can't stand the sight of each other.'

'But you're not brother and sister, are you?'

'No, we're not, but that's the sort of relationship we have. I promise you, Anna. That's the truth. Ask him, if you don't believe me.'

Anna blushed. 'Oh, I couldn't. He – he might guess, then, how I feel about him.'

'Would that be so bad?'

Anna hung her head. 'Yes, it would, if he doesn't feel the same way.'

Rosie did not reply, but she understood how the girl felt. Perhaps . . .

'Well,' Anna was saying now, 'are you going to see

297

the young man who's asking for you, or not? He's waiting in the front entrance.'

Rosie bit her lip, so afraid it was someone sent by Mr Ramsey. As she walked through the corridors to the front entrance, her knees were trembling and she felt as if her heart was in her mouth. When she saw him standing there, silhouetted against the light, her legs nearly gave way.

'Byron!' she breathed. 'Oh Byron.'

He turned and saw her. He held out his arms and, without a moment's hesitation, she ran into them and was enfolded into his embrace.

'Rosie, my darling Rosie.' He touched her cheek with gentle fingers. 'How I've missed you all these years.'

She pulled back a little to look up into his face, but she did not leave the circle of his arms.

'Are you well again?'

He nodded. 'I don't know whether to be pleased or sorry, because now I have to go back to the horror.'

She nodded. 'I can't begin to imagine what it must be like, but we see so much suffering here.'

'I can't stay long.' His tone was urgent. 'We leave tonight . . .'

'Nathan's still here. Have you time to see him?'

'Yes, of course.'

'He'll be going home soon, but I don't think he'll ever go back to the front. The wound on his leg is taking a long time to heal. I'll take you to the ward, but I won't come in. I think it's best if we're not seen together.'

Byron nodded, understanding, but the thought saddened him. 'I'll go when I've seen him, but first there is something I must say to you, Rosie, just in case – in case I don't come back.'

She put her finger against his lips to still such words, but he was not going to be put off. Not this time. He caught and held her hand, holding it against his chest. 'I love you, Rosie. I think I always have done ever since I caught you poaching fish from my father's stream.'

'And I love you, Byron, but you know it was always impossible. We are from such different worlds. We could never have been together.'

'This war will alter things. It will be a great leveller . . .'

Rosie laughed ruefully. 'Not that much. Besides, you're married now.'

'Yes, and that was a great mistake for both Pearl and me. The only good thing to come out of that is little Albert – or Bertie, as we call him. I will never regret having him, not for a moment, but' – he groaned – 'if only he had been our child – yours and mine.'

'Just promise me you will come back,' Rosie whispered.

He smiled, but it was tinged with sadness. 'My mother asked me to promise the same thing, but all I can say to both of you is, I'll do my very best.'

'Your mother is a lovely person. We've been working here together. She was one of us.'

'There you are, then. It can work, you see. Our two worlds are not so far apart.'

'Oh Byron,' she said, her tone was sad and not without a little exasperation. Did all men think they could change the world to fit what they wanted? 'Now, come. I'll take you to see Nathan.' For a brief moment she held his face between her hands and kissed his lips. Just once and then she turned from him and led the way to Ward Four. As he approached Nathan's bedside and heard Byron say, 'Now then, old chap . . .' Rosie slipped away. She would not see him again before he left – she would make sure of that – but she would carry his loving words in her heart for ever.

Thirty

'So, my dear, what are these grandiose ideas you have?'

William, feeling secure in the thought that his wife had 'come to her senses' and had returned home for good, was beginning to allow his natural sarcasm and superiority over her to reassert itself.

Grace regarded him through narrowed eyes down the length of the dinner table. For the moment she said nothing, but he would soon find he could no longer control her every move.

'The sons of a few of your tenants volunteered at the beginning of hostilities and more have gone since.'

William grunted disapprovingly. 'Caught up in the wave of misguided patriotism that swept through the country. Our own son among them.'

'Sadly,' Grace went on as if he hadn't spoken, 'some will never return, but there are several who are coming back badly injured. They may be maimed for life.'

William shrugged as if he didn't care.

'I want to do something to help them.'

Now his head shot up. 'How?'

'I want to arrange fundraising events. We have large grounds and, if it's well advertised, I'm sure people will come from all around north Lincolnshire at the very least. And perhaps we could join forces with Pearl and her mother. They are already doing such work in south Lincolnshire.'

'Well, that would be all right, my dear. I thought for one dreadful moment you were going to suggest opening up Thornsby Manor as some sort of nursing home.'

'Oh William' – Grace clapped her hands – 'what a splendid idea. Now, why didn't I think of that?'

William gaped at her, scandalized, as Grace rose from her seat, walked the full length of the table to kiss his forehead, then left the room saying, 'If you need me, I'll be in the morning room. I have plans to make . . .'

William was left sitting at the table with his mouth open, staring at the closed door.

'What have I done?' he murmured.

As it happened, Grace was only teasing him. She didn't think Thornsby Manor would be a suitable location for a nursing home – although, the more she thought about it, she began to wonder if they could offer convalescence to one or two men at a time who no longer needed actual nursing care but just a peaceful place to recuperate.

'Is my horse ready, Monty?'

'Yes, Mr Ramsey. Ready and waiting. A good gallop will do him good.'

'Haven't you been exercising him?'

'Of course, sir, but with Mr Byron's horse and the other two to manage—'

'It's what I pay your wages for, boy, and why I give you a home. Where would you be now if I hadn't taken you out of the workhouse?'

Monty felt the colour rise in his face. Looking after the stables at Thornsby Manor almost single-handedly, for Lucas Brown did as little work as possible, was a huge responsibility for the young man. And always, the threat of being returned to the workhouse loomed large. William Ramsey would not hesitate to send him back to that awful place if he was displeased. Monty lamented the fact that now there was no Sam Waterhouse – or even Rosie – to help those who fell on hard times.

'I trust you delivered Byron safely to the barracks or wherever he needed to be?' William said as Monty cupped his hands to let his master mount his horse.

'I took him to Lincoln, sir, but not to the barracks.'

'Really. Why not?' William sat on his horse, looking down at Monty's upturned face.

'He asked me to take him to the hospital. I think he wanted to see his friend, Nathan Tranter.'

William nodded, but as he rode away, he was thoughtful. How had his son known where Nathan was? He knew that was where Grace had been working. No doubt she had told Byron that his friend was there. It fitted in with the trips that he knew Monty had been taking with the carriage at Sarah's instigation. They all thought they had kept him in ignorance, but William was more astute than they gave him credit for. He could see a lot more of the comings and goings from his study windows than they guessed. William Ramsey missed very little about what was going on in his house or on his estate, for that matter. But until now he hadn't been aware of exactly where the carriage had been going. Now, he thought he knew.

But there was still one person whom he couldn't find. The one person still escaping his clutches.

Rosie Waterhouse. Now where could the girl be?

'Nathan.'

He opened his eyes and they lit up when he saw who it was. 'Anna.'

'You're going home tomorrow. Matron has written to your mother and to Mrs Ramsey and she is sending the carriage for you.'

'How kind of her. It will be good to get home, but' – he reached for her hand – 'I will miss you.'

Anna smiled but her mouth trembled and tears filled her eyes. 'I – I will miss you too. You've been a model patient.'

'Will you come and see me?'

'I – I'd like to. Where d'you live?'

'A little village called Thornsby, but it's a long way for you to travel, especially in just one day. If you could get a few days off sometime, you could come and stay with us. I'm sure Mam wouldn't mind.'

'I'll try.'

'But we could write to each other.'

'All right,' Anna said shyly, 'although I'm not very good at letter writing.'

'Neither am I,' he grinned, 'but I just want to know you're all right.'

*

304

Rosie and Byron were not able to write to one another and while Rosie now carried in her heart his declaration of love for her, the days were long without receiving any news of him. Was he back in the thick of the fighting? Was he safe? Was he hurt? Was he still alive even? If Nathan had still been in the hospital, Byron might have written to him, but Nathan was going home now to be cared for by his mother. The days were long and lonely but Rosie filled them with hard work and there was plenty of that to do as more and more casualties arrived at the hospital. But how she wished she could hear news of Byron. Now that Grace had gone home too, she couldn't even ask her and there was no one to whom she dared write.

In Thornsby, Nathan was given a hero's welcome. Nell had rearranged her little cottage to accommodate both her son and Amos.

'I should leave,' the old man had said. 'Now Nathan is coming home.'

'You'll do no such thing, Amos Taylor. It will be good for Nathan to have another man to chat with. He'll miss male company after his time in the army – and besides, he won't be able to help me about the place like you do. So I don't want to hear any more of that sort of talk. I'm going to turn the front parlour into a bed-sitting room for him. I think he'll have difficulty climbing the narrow stairs for a while.' Her face saddened. 'The wound he's got will take a long time to heal, Amos.'

'Then I'll be glad to help you look after him, Nell.'

The three of them settled into a new routine and

there was a regular stream of visitors to see Nathan. Some came out of curiosity, but most were those who sincerely wished him well. Soon Nathan was able to walk a little way, leaning on Amos's arm and, on his first venture outside the cottage, he visited Dan next door.

He was shocked at the sight of his childhood playmate and army buddy. When Dan could not answer his questions, Nathan turned to Ivy. 'Is he getting *any* better, Mrs Bates?' His tone was doubtful as he watched his friend's uncontrollable limbs fluttering helplessly.

'Oh yes, he's a lot better than when he first came home. Even Dr Wren says so and you don't get doctors say that if they don't think it. It'll take a long time, but then' – she nodded towards Nathan's leg – 'your wound is going to take a while to heal too, from what your mam says.'

Nathan sighed. 'I'm afraid it will.' He said no more but he couldn't help thinking: *At least I'm not like Dan.*

The war ground on and still there was no sign of it coming to an end. More and more young women left domestic service to work in the munitions factories or in other jobs where they were now needed to replace the men who had gone to war. Thornsby Manor found itself with only just enough staff to keep the big house running.

As the first signs of autumn came, Grace entered her husband's study one morning in September. It was an unusual occurrence and William was immediately suspicious of her motives.

'Baines is bringing us refreshment, William. I need to talk to you about something which is troubling me.'

William laid down his pen. He had been compiling a plan for the running of the estate through the coming winter. While there would be less work on the land, he was troubled that one or two more young men had recently volunteered. Soon, there would not be enough labourers to work his land and he dreaded to think what would happen when spring came.

'How can I help you, my dear?' he said, feigning interest. 'Do you wish to hold an event to raise funds for Christmas?'

'I have been thinking about that, yes. I thought we could hold a harvest festival event in the big barn. All the produce could then be distributed among the poorest in the village.'

William kept his tone deliberately mild. 'Doesn't the vicar usually arrange that sort of thing in his church when he holds the appropriate services for "all is safely gathered in" and so on? The estate usually gives generously, I believe.'

'It does, William, and I trust it will continue to do so. No, this is something else.'

He waited, wondering what was coming.

'I want you to suspend your shooting parties until the war is over.'

William gaped at her, his face turning red.

'If I remember correctly, William, the shoot you held in the autumn of 1914 was poorly attended, even though the war had only just started. I think many thought it inappropriate in such troubled times.'

With great reluctance, William was forced to agree that his wife had a point. The shooting parties he'd held during the last two years had not been popular even with his regular cronies and he remembered the embarrassment among those who had shown up. It hadn't seemed right, some had muttered guiltily, to be killing innocent game when across the channel the lives of their boys were being taken with similar callousness.

He cleared this throat. 'So what do you intend should happen to all the birds? You'll have poachers from miles around coming here, once' – he added sarcastically – 'they find out we no longer have our own resident poacher.'

'I rather thought that your most recent gamekeeper – what's his name?'

'Ralph Carter.'

'I thought Mr Carter might be able to shoot some and distribute them among the villagers. Times are going to be hard for everyone, William.'

As her husband opened his mouth to protest against her largesse, Grace smiled and said smoothly, 'After all, you don't want to lose any more of your workers for any reason. Those who don't volunteer will, I fear, soon be conscripted and more jobs – good jobs in factories manufacturing war weapons and the like – will become available. So, my dear, it wouldn't do you any harm to *appear* generous to your workers and tenants.'

William, failing totally to hear the sarcastic emphasis she put on the word 'appear', grunted. 'I'll give it some thought,' was all he would say.

*

'Nell.'

Ivy was standing at Nell's back door holding a piece of paper in her trembling hand. Tears flooded down her face.

'What is it? Is Dan worse?'

Ivy shook her head and bit her lip. 'It's – it's Joey. He's been killed at a place called Thiepval Ridge. There's been a battle there, apparently. And – and' – she wailed – 'I don't even know where that is.'

'Oh no!' Nell put her arms round her friend and Ivy wept against her shoulder.

'They – they can't bring him home. They can't even bury him properly out there. He – he was blown up by a shell. Just – just blown to bits.'

'That's awful.'

Ivy lifted her head. 'I suppose I must take comfort in the fact that it would have been quick. He wouldn't have suffered.'

'No, he wouldn't have known anything about it. Now, come in, love. We must tell Nathan.'

Nathan was devastated. It was not the first time he'd lost a friend, a mate. One or two he'd become friendly with in the army had already been killed, but Joey was the first from the village to lose his life. True, he and Dan had been closer friends, but Joey, though younger, had often tagged along after them. They hadn't minded; he'd been a good kid.

'How's Dan taken it?'

'I don't know if he really understands.'

'I'll talk to him,' Nathan promised. 'And what about young Elsie? They've been childhood sweethearts. She ought to be told.'

'The new kitchen maid from the manor will be bringing the washing tomorrow,' Nell said. 'I'll write a note to Mrs Ramsey. I'm sure she'll help us if she can.'

'Perhaps she'd lend us the carriage. I could go and tell Elsie. And – and there's someone else I'd like to see there.'

Nell said nothing. She guessed it was Rosie he wanted to see, but she was careful to say nothing in front of Ivy. Fond though Nell was of her neighbour and heartsore for her at this moment, Ivy was a notorious gossip. She didn't mean any harm, but no secret was safe with her.

But Nell was wrong. It wasn't Rosie whom Nathan wished to see; it was Anna.

Thirty-One

The following day, after receiving Nell's note, Grace announced at breakfast, 'I shall be going into Lincoln today. I need to visit Helene for some advice about the charity event I'm planning for raising funds for Christmas. I'll be gone for the day.'

William frowned. 'Brown won't spare Monty for the whole day.'

'Then he can drive me into the village. I'm sure Nathan Tranter is well enough now to drive the carriage. I can ask him.'

'If he can do that, then he's fit enough to come back to work on the estate. Besides, I don't want an inexperienced hand driving my carriage and pair.'

'Oh, be reasonable, William. He has an open wound in his leg that he must keep scrupulously clean. If he doesn't, he risks sepsis and that's a killer. He can't possibly come back to work yet.'

'And you'd know all about that, would you?'

'A little now, yes.'

William's eyes narrowed as he kept up the pretence. 'So, you and, I presume, Sarah too, were working in a hospital, were you? Smoothing fevered brows? Lincoln, was it?'

Knowing nothing of William's devious ploy, Grace hesitated and thought quickly. Surely now there couldn't be any harm in him knowing where she had been? She was unlikely to go back there now that she had found another outlet for her energies at home. She still felt she was helping the boys at the front, one of whom was never far from her thoughts.

'Yes, it's a good hospital and they're doing sterling work there and need all the help they can get. That's why I still want to raise funds for them.'

'And is that how you've been scooping up injured soldiers like Bates and Tranter?'

'Yes.'

'So, what is it this time? Because I'm afraid, my dear, that I don't quite believe your story about visiting Helene. Ladies of your social standing don't just drop in without warning or an invitation.'

Again, Grace hesitated briefly. Surely, there could be no harm in telling him. 'It's about Elsie.'

'Elsie? Who is Elsie?'

'Elsie Warren. She used to work here as a kitchen maid but she left to work at the hospital when her sweetheart, Joey Bates, went to war.'

'I thought we never allowed our staff to have followers.'

'Officially, we don't, but you can't stop it happening.'

'I could if I knew about it. The workhouse is always a handy threat.'

'So I've noticed,' Grace remarked drily. In recent months she had looked at William with fresh eyes, seeing him now for the harsh, almost tyrannical, master that he was. If only she'd seen it before she'd married him. But she'd fallen for his charms and his promises and the expensive gifts he'd lavished on her. She could still hear her mother's voice ringing in her ears. 'You'll never want for anything, Grace. How fortunate you are.'

'So,' William interrupted her wandering thoughts, 'are you going to tell me what is so important about our former kitchen maid?'

'Joey Bates has been killed and Nathan wants to tell her himself.'

'So, there's no need for you to go. Visiting Helene was a lie, wasn't it?'

'No, I intend to go and see Helene while I'm there.'

'And does she know?'

'No, but the war has changed all the old niceties of social etiquette. Helene won't mind. It was through her I got to know about the hospital in the first place.'

They glared at each other, both of them unwilling to back down. At last, with a sigh, William said, 'Oh very well, you can have Monty for the day, as long as you promise me you won't stay, because I warn you, Grace, if you do, I shall come and fetch you home myself now I know where to find you.'

'I give you my word, William. It's just for the day, though I can't promise,' she added impishly, 'that I won't bring back some poor wounded soldier to nurse here.'

William's face was a picture.

*

As he stepped down from the carriage in front of the hospital, Nathan said, 'There's someone else I want to see while I'm here. Anna. We – we – er – got quite fond of one another while I was here.'

Grace smiled. 'Yes, I know. I saw it for myself. If she can get time off, bring her home with you for a few days. I am sure I can arrange to have her brought back here when she needs to be back on duty.'

'Oh thank you, Mrs Ramsey.'

'It's Grace. Remember?' she said, smiling.

'It doesn't seem right to call you that now you're back home as mistress of the manor.'

Now Grace chuckled. 'It still shocks my husband to hear Sarah calling me "Grace", I have to admit. Sarah insisted on returning home with me, much to the matron's disappointment. She was sorry to lose two of us at once. But I rather like her still calling me Grace. It causes amusement among the rest of the staff. However, you call me whatever you're most comfortable with, Nathan.' She turned to the stable lad. 'Now, Monty, you can drive me to Lady Montague's house.' She turned back briefly to Nathan. 'We'll be back for you at three o'clock.'

Nathan touched his cap as the carriage drew away.

The first person he saw on entering the hospital was Rosie.

'Nathan, what are you doing here? You're all right, aren't you? Not having trouble with your wound?'

'No, it's fine. Getting better gradually, I think, but it's a slow job. No, sadly I'm here to see Elsie. Joey's been killed and I thought I should come in person to tell her. Mrs Ramsey brought me. She's picking me up later this afternoon.'

'Oh, I'm so sorry to hear that. How dreadful for Mrs Bates and poor Dan too. Joey was a cheeky little rascal. What you'd call a loveable rogue. We were all very fond of him. How has Dan taken it – that is, if he understands? How is he?'

'We think he's improving a little but it's a slow job. We're not sure if he's taken it in about Joey. Did you know Dr Oldfield came all the way out to Thornsby to see him the other week?

'No, I didn't, but that sounds just like him. He's a dedicated doctor.' She sighed. 'But now I'll find Elsie for you. Go into the waiting room. It'll be quiet there for you.'

'And – er – is Anna about?'

Rosie smiled. 'Yes, I'll find her too, but I'll ask her to leave it a few minutes while you have chance to break the awful news to poor Elsie.'

Elsie came into the room a few minutes later. Her eyes were wide as if she already guessed that this was not a social call.

'It's Joey, isn't it?'

Nathan took her hands into his. 'Yes, I'm so sorry; it is. His mother had a telegram but they have told her it was very quick. He wouldn't have suffered.'

Elsie's mouth tightened but she remained dry-eyed. 'They say that to all the mothers, but we know differently, don't we, Nathan? Look at all the suffering we see here and they're the ones who don't die. What about all the ones who are badly wounded and linger in agony for days and weeks? Just look at his poor brother. How is Dan, by the way?'

He repeated what he had just told Rosie.

'It will be slow,' Elsie said. 'His wounds can't be bandaged. Still,' she stretched her mouth into a smile that did not reach her eyes, 'Dr Oldfield is winning his own little war to get Dan's condition recognized as a medical illness despite a lot of opposition among his colleagues.'

'That's good news.'

'Thank you for coming to tell me, Nathan. I appreciate you taking the trouble, but I have to admit it has not come as a great surprise. I have been expecting it ever since he went. And please thank Mrs Ramsey too. It was very kind of her to bring you. And now I'll go and let Anna come in. She's hovering about in the corridor. Good luck to the pair of you. I just hope you don't have to go back, Nathan. Keep out of it, if you possibly can.' Her voice broke and she hurried from the room, leaving the door open.

After a moment, Anna came in. 'Is Elsie all right? She rushed off before I could say anything to her. Rosie told me what's happened.'

'She was very brave but I think she may need some time on her own.' He held out his arms and Anna went into them without hesitating.

'Oh I've missed you so much,' he murmured against her hair.

'I've missed you too. How are you? Is your wound healing?'

'Slowly, but it would be better if you were looking after it. Mrs Ramsey brought me and she says if you

316

can get a few days off, you can come back with us and she'll see that you're brought back here later in the week. What do you say? Will Matron let you have a few days off at such short notice?'

Anna looked trustingly up into his face. 'I can only ask, Nathan. I'll go this very minute . . .'

Connie Archer was able to give the girl a week off. 'We are coping nicely just now, as long as we don't get another influx of wounded. You go, Anna. You've not had any time off since you've been here.'

Nell greeted the girl with open arms. She had met her briefly at the hospital, but not as a prospective daughter-in-law.

'It'll be a squeeze in my little cottage, lass, but you're more than welcome.'

'Anna can have my couch and I'll sleep in the armchair near the range . . .'

'That doesn't seem fair, Nathan,' Amos put in at once. 'You can have your room back and I'll take the couch.'

'Now, now, no arguments,' Nell said. 'If Anna doesn't mind, she can come in with me. I've got a huge double bed and, as far as I know, I don't snore, so is that all right, lass?'

'I don't want to be any trouble,' Anna said, blushing furiously.

'You're not. It'll be lovely to have you here.'

Nathan took Anna on gentle walks around the village.

'You really are improving, you know,' she said. 'You're so much better than when you left the hospital. Your colour is better and you've put on a little weight.'

'Yes, nurse. That'll be my mam's cooking,' Nathan laughed. 'She's forever feeding me up.'

On the night before she was due to return to Lincoln, Nathan took Anna to see Dan. She sat in front of him and took both his hands in hers.

'Hello, Dan. Do you remember me?'

'I don't think he'll know you,' Ivy said, fussing over her son and tucking a blanket around him. 'Though I think he knows Nathan now. He's been so good coming in every day to sit with him. It's doing him a power of good.'

Dan was clinging on to Anna's hands and staring into her face. His mouth worked. He was obviously trying to speak. At last, though the word was mumbled he said, 'Rosie.'

'No, I'm not Rosie,' Anna said gently. 'I'm Anna. I work at the hospital too.'

Dan was nodding, though whether it was a sign of understanding what she was saying or his condition, no one could say. 'Rosie,' he said again.

Listening, Ivy's eyes gleamed. So that was where Rosie Waterhouse was. What a nice juicy piece of gossip this was, as long as she swore everyone she told to secrecy. It wouldn't do for the master to get to know the girl's whereabouts. Fancy, Ivy thought, hugging the delicious secret to herself, Mrs Ramsey must have known all this time and never said a word, not even to her own husband. Things couldn't be very good between the two of them, especially with her staying away all that time. And now this.

Anna returned to Lincoln the following day.

'I'll come and see you as often as I can, if you let me know when you have a day off,' Nathan promised holding her hands tightly and kissing her gently.

'She's a nice lass,' Nell said. 'You could do a lot worse for yourself, Nathan.'

'I can hardly ask anyone to marry me, Mam, while I'm like this, now can I?'

'Give it a few more weeks, Nathan. Maybe Mr Pickering could find you some light work on the estate.'

'There's no such thing as "light work" on a farm, Mam.' Nathan laughed wryly. 'Mebbe I'd best think about taking up poaching.'

They smiled at each other, fondly remembering both Sam and his daughter. 'The villagers are missing them, you know,' Nell murmured. 'Times aren't easy now and they're going to get worse through the winter. But at least we seem to have a good man in Ralph Carter, the new gamekeeper. I don't think he's the sort to let anyone go hungry.'

'Time will tell on that score, Mam,' Nathan said, still sceptical. 'But not a word in front of Amos. I'm not sure where his loyalties lie.'

Nell eyed her son. Had he not guessed what Amos was doing now two or three nights a week? 'Well, not with the master,' she said. 'I can tell you that. But for me, he'd be in the workhouse.'

'Really?'

'Yes, really.'

Nathan sighed. 'Mr Ramsey's a hard man and no mistake. Are you still managing to meet the rent, Mam?'

'With what you give me from your army pay and with the washing I do for the manor and my little pension, I manage nicely. And before you say anything, I don't charge Amos. What he does around the place is payment enough. He does all sorts of things I can no longer manage.'

Nathan nodded. 'I know. I've seen him. By the way, I've had a letter. I've got to go to Lincoln in two weeks' time for a medical check. I think it's likely that they will invalid me out of the army. If they do, I can start looking around for something I could do.'

'Mebbe you could ask Ray's dad if he'd take you on to help out in his carpenter's workshop. I know he's been missing Ray badly. And poor Dan's not likely to return to work for him for a while yet.' She didn't add 'if ever', though it was in both their minds. Instead, Nell said, 'You were always clever at woodwork. I'm sure he'd give you a try.'

'That's a good suggestion, Mam. I'll think about that.'

Thirty-Two

Ivy Bates strutted down the village street on her way to the shop, carrying her shopping basket on her arm. She was the centre of attention. She had lost one son to the war and her other son was seriously wounded, unlikely ever to recover fully. While her heart ached for Joey, she couldn't help but enjoy being the object of sympathy.

'Oh, Ivy love,' the shopkeeper's wife, Mary Plant, greeted her and the two other customers touched her arm.

'What dreadful news,' Mary said. 'And on top of poor Dan too.'

Ivy wiped the tears from her eyes. 'You're all very kind. They were all very good to Dan in the hospital, you know, but I don't think there's a lot more they can do for him. That's why they've sent him home.'

'Is he showing any signs of improvement?'

'A little now and again. He actually spoke yesterday for the first time.'

'What did he say?'

'Rosie.'

'Rosie!' the other three women exclaimed at once and Mary added, 'Did he mean Rosie Waterhouse?'

'I don't know, but I expect so. It was when Nathan's young lady—'

'Has Nathan got a young lady, then?'

Ivy nodded. 'I think so. It's a young lass who was working at the Lincoln hospital when he was a patient there. She's not a proper nurse, but she helps the nurses. But when he saw her, my Dan said – as plain as anything – "Rosie".'

'Did he think she was Rosie?'

Ivy shook her head. 'Hard to say.'

'Do you think that's where Rosie is, then?' Mary Plant asked. 'Working at the hospital in Lincoln?'

'Well, it's as good a place as any to hide away, don't you think? But please' – Ivy put on her best pleading tone – 'please don't tell anyone I've told you this. If the master got to hear where she is . . .'

She didn't need to spell it out; they all knew exactly what Mr Ramsey would do if he found out where Rosie was.

'Of course we won't tell a soul,' they all promised, but by nightfall it was all around the village and being discussed in the pub.

Tucked in his usual corner in the bar, Lucas Brown overheard the gossip. He was not popular; the locals were wary of him and so he always sat alone with his solitary pint and listened, picking up titbits that might be of interest to the lord and master of the estate and its village.

'He's a spy for Ramsey,' the village men warned each other constantly.

But tonight, as the ale loosened their tongues, they

forgot about the head groom from the manor sitting quietly in the corner.

'Have you heard? My missus reckons young Rosie Waterhouse is working at the military hospital in Lincoln.'

'How's she heard that?'

'I don't rightly know, but it's all the talk among the women in the village.'

'Let's just hope *he* doesn't find out.'

'She had nowt to do with that bad business. I'd stake me life on it. Mind you, Sam were a different matter.'

'But Sam wouldn't have shot anyone deliberately. If it were him, it must have been a terrible accident.'

'Disappeared soon after, though, didn't he?'

'That's true. But Rosie didn't. She stayed here for a while.'

'Aye, with Nell Tranter.'

The guffaws were loud. 'Aye, well, she would, wouldn't she? Nell were Sam's bit on the side. We all knew that. We've known it for years.'

On and on the gossip went and Lucas Brown heard it all.

So, he thought, this girl they were talking about had to be the same one whom his master thought was an accessory to the murder of the gamekeeper. He was sure of it. If so, Lucas could certainly do himself no harm by informing William Ramsey what he'd overheard.

William was thoughtful, working out how he could use the new information. The local constabulary would be no help. Foster was useless and even his superiors in Louth wouldn't want to reopen the case. They would insist on there being new evidence before they would consider arresting Rosie. Then a small, but malicious smile curved his mouth. But there was one person whom he could perhaps still rely on. Years ago, at the time of Jim Tranter's death, there had been a police sergeant in Louth who had been 'persuaded' not to delve too deeply into the cause of the tragic accident. William had kept himself informed of the man's whereabouts and knew that he was now a high-ranking officer based in Lincoln. Perfect. William almost rubbed his hands in glee. It was time to seek out his old friend again.

'So, this is where you've been hiding.'

As Rosie walked through the hospital entrance hall, two figures stepped out from the shadows. She turned at the sound of his voice and her legs threatened to give way beneath her. Her hands began to tremble but she stood her ground, raised her chin and faced William Ramsey.

Behind him stood the threatening figure of a policeman.

'I haven't been hiding at all, Mr Ramsey,' she said, fighting to keep her voice calm. 'I have been helping to care for wounded soldiers.'

'So, the poacher has turned into a nurse, has she? How very altruistic.' He stepped closer to her, thrusting his face close to hers. 'So tell me, if you weren't trying to hide your identity, why did you change your name?'

Rosie did not have an answer and William knew it. He laughed cruelly and turned to the constable.

'This is the girl I was telling you about. I want you to arrest her on suspicion of being an accessory to the murder of Wilfred Darby on or about the second of August 1914 in Thornsby Woods.'

'I don't think there's any reason for an arrest to be made at this point, sir, if the young lady will agree to come to the station for questioning.'

'She's guilty, I tell you,' William spat, his voice rising. 'I want her arrested and thrown into gaol, where she belongs. In fact, I hope she hangs.'

'That would be for the court to decide, sir,' the constable said calmly. The young policeman didn't really understand what this was all about. He was merely obeying the orders of his superior officer.

'Well, that's what they *will* decide,' William spat. 'I guarantee it. I am personal friends with—'

The policeman held up his hand. 'That's not how the law works, sir.'

Oh doesn't it, young man? William thought. *We'll see about that.*

'Now, miss,' the constable was saying, 'if you would accompany me to the police station, perhaps we can get all this sorted out.'

'What is going on here, may I ask?' The matron's voice echoed through the hallway.

'He's here to arrest this girl,' William shouted. 'And you, madam, will not stand in his way.'

'I wouldn't dream of standing in the way of the law, but may I be permitted to know her crime?'

'Murder, madam,' William said. 'Or, to be precise, accessory to a murder. I am willing to accept that perhaps she did not actually fire the gun – her father was the one to do that – but she was there. I know she was there. He was a poacher and so was she.'

Connie glanced at Rosie, who remained stubbornly silent. 'I suppose you must go with the constable, Skelton.' There was infinite sorrow in the matron's tone.

'Skelton?' William laughed harshly. 'Is that what she calls herself? Her name's Waterhouse – Rosie Waterhouse. So, if she's not as guilty as sin, why would she change her name, eh? Tell me that.'

'If you would just come with me, miss . . .'

There was a black, horse-drawn vehicle waiting outside. Rosie climbed into it, feeling that eyes were watching her from every window of the hospital. She hadn't even been given a chance to change out of her uniform. She sat on the hard bench in the gloom as the van jolted and set off. At the police station she was put in a cell and the heavy door clanged shut.

And then, when there was no one to see, the tears came. 'Oh Byron,' she whispered. 'Where are you? Help me. Please, help me.'

'Matron, I'm sorry to ask again so soon after you kindly gave me a week off but I must go to Thornsby and tell Nathan and Mrs Tranter what has happened to Rosie.' Anna stood in front of the matron's desk. She was normally such a quiet little mouse, even though she had blossomed during the time she had worked at the hospital, but her friend being in trouble gave her strength and boldness. Rosie was Nathan's friend too.

Connie Archer was silent for a moment and then she nodded. 'Yes, I understand, but I don't think on this occasion we can ask for Mrs Ramsey's help. It wouldn't be fair on her since it is her husband who is trying to bring the charges against Rosie. Can you make your own way there?'

'I – I'll try.'

'Can you do the journey in two days, d'you think? I really can't spare you for longer than that, now we've lost Rosie.'

Anna nodded. 'Elsie has said she will do longer hours to help out.'

The girl set off early the following morning hitching lifts and reaching Thornsby in the late afternoon.

'Anna!' Nathan greeted her, folding his arms around her and kissing her. 'This is a lovely surprise. How did you wangle it?'

'It's wonderful to see you, Nathan,' Anna said shyly, 'but sadly my visit is serious. Rosie has been arrested.'

Nathan's face was bleak. 'Oh no!' he whispered. 'He caught up with her, then?'

'This man came to the hospital with a policeman and they took her away in a black van. I found out later it was Grace's husband, Mr Ramsey. But I don't know what it was all about.'

Nathan sighed as he took her hand and led her inside the cottage. 'Sit down while I fetch Mam. She's in the yard hanging out washing.'

Moments later, Nell came hurrying into the kitchen. 'Oh Anna, love. However can he have found out? Look, Nathan, you'd better tell Anna all about

327

it while I make her a drink. You poor dear, you look worn out and I bet you don't understand it all, do you?'

Anna shook her head so while Nell made a drink for them all, Nathan quietly explained the whole sorry story.

When he had finished speaking, Anna pressed trembling fingers against her lips.

'What is it? What's troubling you? I can see there's something,' Nathan prompted her gently.

'I'm just trying to think how it could have happened. How he found out. It must have been when you took me round to see Dan next door.'

Nathan was puzzled but he didn't interrupt her.

'He – he thought I was Rosie. Do you remember? You were there.'

Nathan nodded slowly. 'Yes, now you mention it, I do. I didn't think anything about it at the time because he didn't speak very clearly.'

'And was Ivy – Mrs Bates – there when he said it?' Nell butted in.

'I don't remember. I was looking at Dan all the time, holding his hands, and trying to get him to speak some more.'

Nathan sighed heavily. 'But I remember. Yes, she was there.' He glanced up at his mother and they exchanged a look that was full of fear.

'Ivy's been gossiping,' Nell whispered, 'and – somehow – it must have reached the master's ears.'

'How can we find out what is happening to her?'

'So – that man you came to see, Mrs Tranter,' Anna said. 'The one who died. His name was

Skelton, wasn't it, and he was Rosie's father? I'd heard rumours going among the nurses that that was who he was. So, why are they calling her Rosie Waterhouse now?'

'That was their real surname. That night – when he ran away – he volunteered and changed his name to Skelton. It was his wife's maiden name, I believe. It was a good job he did. If he'd have been caught, he'd have hanged for sure. There'd have been no mercy for him. He came back one night a few weeks later just to see Rosie, but I didn't see him. Rosie told me he – he wanted to come to see me but that he daren't because I live so close to the village.' There was a catch in her voice as she remembered Sam.

'I didn't know that, Mam.'

'You weren't here. You'd gone too by that time. But now, we've got to help Rosie. What do we need to do?'

'She'll never be able to have a defence counsellor. She couldn't afford one.'

'The villagers will help. Oh, they know Sam was probably guilty, but no one believes Rosie capable of murder. What they will remember, though, is how Sam and Rosie kept them fed through the harsh winters. That's what will count with them.'

Nathan glanced around him. 'What about Amos?' he asked softly. 'Where will his loyalties lie?'

'Not with old man Ramsey, that's for sure,' Nell said grimly. 'The person I'm most anxious about is Mrs Ramsey.'

'D'you mean Grace?' Anna asked. 'She's a lovely lady and – and – she is very fond of Rosie.'

Nell pondered aloud. 'She knew all about Rosie and yet . . . I wonder . . .'

'Mam, I know what you're thinking, but you can't put the poor woman in a difficult position. It's her *husband*.'

'I'm only asking her advice. I'm not expecting her to *do* anything.'

'I think she'd help you, Mrs Tranter, if she could,' Anna said quietly.

'Anna, what time do you have to be back tomorrow?'

'By night time, I suppose. I've got to start work again the day after tomorrow.'

'Will you come to the manor with me early tomorrow morning? We can use the excuse of taking the washing back. It'll have to be early though, or else Lucy will be on her way to fetch it. I'll get all the ironing done today and then—'

'I'll help you,' Anna said quickly.

'She's tired, Mam. You can see it in her face.'

'It's all right, Nathan.' Anna touched his cheek. 'I want to help your mam and I want to help Rosie.'

Thirty-Three

The same afternoon that Anna arrived at Nell's cottage, William entered the morning room with a piece of paper in his hand and a solemn expression on his face. 'My dear, I'm afraid I have bad news.'

Grace looked up from the lists she was making. There was to be a fundraising fete in the grounds of the manor in two weeks' time and there was still much to do. She held her breath, realizing that the piece of paper he held was a telegram.

'It's Byron,' he said, rather unnecessarily. He paused, making her wait. She stared at him, biting back the question.

'He's alive but he's been badly injured. He might lose his leg. He's in a field hospital in France at the moment but they are taking him to a hospital near the coast. I shall make preparations to go out there to be with him and, hopefully, bring him home as soon as he is fit enough to travel. I'll be leaving as soon as I can be ready. I want to make sure he has the best possible treatment. No doubt you will want to cancel your arrangements for the weekend after next.'

She stood up on legs that trembled slightly. 'No, I shan't cancel the fete. A great deal of work has already

331

gone into the preparations and the funds are to help injured soldiers just like Byron, but soldiers who have not the wealth behind them to give them the best possible care. I'm sure Byron would be the first to want me to continue with my plans.'

William's mouth was tight. He could no longer exert the control over his wife that he had once had. It made him angry, but he still had the power to hurt her. He was about to leave the room but he turned back to say, with a triumphant smile, 'Oh, and by the way, the girl is in Lincoln gaol awaiting trial as an accessory to murder.' There was no need for him to say her name; Grace knew exactly who he meant.

And then he left, slamming the door behind him while Grace sank back into her chair, holding her hand against her chest.

When Nell and Anna knocked on the kitchen door at the manor the following morning, Lucy, dressed in her hat and coat, opened it.

'Oh, Mrs Tranter. I was just on my way to your cottage, but you've beaten me to it. Come in. Let me take that bundle. Hello,' she added, spotting Anna. 'Who's this?'

'This is Anna. Nathan's young lady.'

Lucy's eyes widened. 'Oooh. I didn't know he'd got a young lady. How lovely. You're a very lucky girl, Anna, if you don't mind me saying so.'

The girl blushed, but smiled. She knew how lucky she was – she didn't need to be told – and even better was the fact that Nathan's mother liked her too.

As she handed the bundles of washing over to

Lucy, Nell said, 'I was wondering if it would be possible for us to have a quick word with the mistress?'

Lucy's face fell. 'Oh, I don't know about that. Madam had some bad news yesterday. Master Byron has been badly injured. He might lose his leg and he's still in France. The master left this morning before dawn. He's gone to be with him and to bring him home as soon as he's well enough to travel. It could be a while though.'

'I'm sorry to hear that – very sorry – but – but I think Mrs Ramsey would like to hear what we have to tell her.'

Lucy still looked doubtful but said, 'I'll ask Sarah. She'll know what to do for the best. Wait here.'

A few moments elapsed before Sarah came hurrying towards them. 'Anna, it's nice to see you – and you too, Mrs Tranter, but I don't think madam is up to seeing visitors.'

In a low voice, Nell said, 'This isn't a social call, Sarah. Somehow the master found out that Rosie was at the Lincoln hospital. He's had her arrested. She's in Lincoln gaol.'

Sarah covered her mouth with her hand. 'Oh no! Madam will be so upset. And coming on top of the news about Byron too. Oh dear. I don't know what I ought to do.'

'Just go and tell her we're here and *why* we're here. Let her decide.'

'Oh yes. Yes, of course. I'll do that.' The normally calm and collected Sarah was suddenly flustered. She hurried away.

Cook, who was just beginning her day and preparing a breakfast tray for her mistress, beckoned them further into the kitchen. 'Come away in, Mrs Tranter. I'll pour you a cup of tea while you wait.'

They had to wait several minutes and had drunk two cups of tea before Sarah returned. 'If you'll follow me, madam will see you in her bedroom.'

As they entered the room, Grace came towards them with her arms outstretched. They noticed how pale and drawn she was. 'My dears, I already know what you've come to tell me. My husband took great delight in telling me about Rosie just after he'd delivered the news about Byron. How can I help her?'

'But – but, madam, your son . . . ?'

'He will be well looked after. William will see to that. But I am distraught that it is my husband who is trying to wreak such revenge on Rosie. I am convinced she is entirely innocent, so, what can we do?'

'We don't know very much more than that she is in Lincoln prison. We don't know if she's been charged yet.'

'We must get a defence lawyer for her. I will write to Helene. She will help me, I know.'

'We think all the villagers would be willing to contribute to the cost—' Nell began but Grace waved her aside. 'Don't worry about that. I have money of my own. I will cover any costs.'

Nell couldn't believe what she was hearing. William Ramsey was the one who wanted Rosie prosecuted and his wife wanted to arrange and pay for the girl's defence. 'That would be very good of you, ma'am, especially in the circumstances.'

Grace nodded but said nothing. Deep inside her she knew it was guilt that was prompting her actions. She felt guilty because she had helped William to engineer an unsuitable marriage for their son to keep him apart from the girl he really loved and now that girl was in danger; a danger caused by her husband. If Byron had been here and in full health, she knew that he would fight for Rosie, so she must do it instead. And, too, she liked Rosie and didn't believe the girl bore any guilt for the murder of the gamekeeper.

Nell was undecided whether or not to tell Mrs Ramsey about the letter she had in her safekeeping, but something held her back. While, in the main, she trusted Mrs Ramsey, there was just that small seed of doubt that if anyone got to know about the letter before Rosie actually came to trial, it might be destroyed and all hope for the girl would be gone. So, for the moment, Nell remained silent.

Matters moved swiftly. With William conveniently out of the way, instead of writing to Helene, Grace travelled to Lincoln to see her friend, calling on her unannounced and breaking the social etiquette by which she had lived her life.

'My dear Helene,' she apologized at once as she entered the morning room in the elegant town house. 'Please forgive me, but this is a matter of life and death and I promise you I am not exaggerating.'

Helene rose at once and held out her hands to her friend. 'There is no need to apologize. Surely our long friendship outweighs such niceties. Sit down, my dear. I can see you're agitated. Is it Byron, and how can I help?'

Swiftly, Grace told Helene about Byron's injury first. 'But William is on his way to bring him home as soon as he can.' And then she explained about Rosie and asked Helene if she could recommend a good defence lawyer.

'My dear, what a difficult position you find yourself in. You are deliberately flouting your husband's wishes and William will not take kindly to that.'

Grace sighed deeply. 'No, he won't, but what else can I do? I cannot sit by and let the poor girl be imprisoned for life – or – or worse.'

'And you're sure she is entirely innocent.'

Grace bit her lip. 'I am sure she did not kill the gamekeeper. What I don't know, and perhaps none of us will ever know, is whether or not she was with her father the night it happened. But whatever *did* happen, Helene, it must have been a terrible accident. Sam Waterhouse would never have killed anyone deliberately. I am sure of that.'

Helene rose and paced the room for several minutes before coming to sit down beside Grace again. She took her hands. 'I think you should leave all this to me. I am a wealthy widow and not without a little influence in the city. I will arrange everything and you need take no part in it. Can you trust your friends – Mrs Tranter and her son, is it? – to say nothing to William?'

'Yes, I'm sure I can.'

'Does anyone else – apart from them – know that you're involving yourself in this?'

'Only Sarah and she is loyal to me. She will keep my secret.'

'Then go home and carry on with your arrangements for the fete. I hope to be able to attend, so I will see you there. Hopefully, I will have some news for you by then.'

'Oh Helene, I don't know how to thank you. You are indeed a true friend. Please come and stay with me on the Saturday night.'

The third Saturday in October – the day of the grand fete at the manor – dawned clear and bright. Nearly all of the women and children of the village trekked through the woods and the fields to the grounds of the manor. Several of the village men came too, anxious to help. Mrs Ramsey had assured them all that every penny of the money raised would go towards helping the soldiers and not into the government's coffers.

There were games for the children and stalls for the adults to visit and everyone contributed as much as they could afford. Thornsby village was a close-knit and caring community. They had already lost one of their boys to the war and Dan and Nathan had been seriously wounded. And now, today, they all heard of Byron's injury, and so they dug a little deeper into their pockets.

It had been a busy and tiring day, but as the villagers went home and the servants at the manor cleared up, Grace and Helene, who had arrived to stay the night, prepared for dinner. There were only the two of them, so once they had been served, they could talk freely.

When the door closed behind Baines, Helene said, 'I have instructed my solicitor, Mr Jones, to obtain the very best defence lawyer he can for Rosie. He is confident he can get Mr Patterson.'

'Oh my! Even I have heard of him.'

'He's reckoned to be the best that Lincolnshire has to offer. He's defended some very high-profile cases and has won most of them. There are only two I know of that he didn't win and' – she smiled – 'I think everyone knew the miscreants were guilty anyway, but, of course, under our laws, everyone deserves a defence.'

'I just hope he will believe Rosie.'

'Will you have a chance to see her before the trial?'

Grace shook her head. 'I doubt it. William will be home soon, hopefully bringing Byron.'

She didn't need to say any more; William must know nothing of what was being arranged for Rosie's defence.

Helene nodded. 'Then leave it with me. I will see to everything for you.'

The trial was set for two months' time.

'If the judge can fit us into his calendar, there's no need for a long delay,' Mr Patterson told Helene's solicitor. 'There is no evidence, no witnesses to call – only the girl herself.'

Thirty-Four

Locked away in the damp darkness of a cell in Lincoln prison, Rosie knew nothing of the efforts of her friends to help her. Nathan and Nell were beside themselves with worry about her but were powerless to help – at least at present. Nell still nursed her secret. Not even Nathan knew about the letter. No one here knew and, for the time being, that was the way she wanted it kept.

'We must trust in Mrs Ramsey,' was all she would say to Nathan when they were alone. They were careful not to say too much in front of Amos. Although they were both very fond of the old man – he had become one of the family – they were still not sure of his allegiance. But one evening over their meal, Amos himself brought up the subject.

'There's something I want to say to both of you. This business about Rosie Waterhouse has been weighing heavily on my mind.'

Nell and Nathan exchanged a glance, but said nothing.

'I knew what Sam Waterhouse was and what he did, but we had a sort of understanding. As long as he didn't poach the master's game birds . . .' Amos allowed himself a wry smile. 'Well, at least, not too many, I turned a blind eye. There were nights when I didn't go out – poachers' nights – when, if I'm honest, I knew he'd be out and about. But you see, I knew how he helped the villagers through hard times and he never charged a penny. As long as he had enough for him and young Rosie, he gave the rest away.'

Nell nodded. 'He did, Amos, you're right.'

'It was brave of you, Amos,' Nathan put in. 'If Mr Ramsey had found out, you'd have been sacked.'

'Aye, I've known all along what a cruel, vindictive man he is. Not like his poor father. He was a grand feller was Edward Ramsey. Little Titch – d'you remember him, Nell? – old man Ramsey never bothered him. Besides, these poachers are rat and mole catchers. And they keep the ditches running. They do all the mucky jobs that no one else wants. He reckoned they were doing more good than harm. Now, I'm hoping that Byron will be more like his grandfather when his turn comes. I just hope he comes back in one piece. Rumour has it that he might lose a leg.'

Nell stayed silent. She didn't want to give away the fact that she had been speaking to Grace recently. But word was getting around the village – especially since the fete on Saturday – about what had happened to Byron.

'Yes,' she said now to cover herself. 'There was talk about it on Saturday at the fete.'

'What I was leading up to, Nell, is that I'm all for helping young Rosie. She's been badly treated by the master.'

'As have you, Amos,' Nell said quietly. 'After all the years of service you've given him and his father before him, for Mr Ramsey to be ready to allow you to have to go into the workhouse – well, it's despicable.'

'He'd do the same to any of his tenants in the village, or his tenant farmers. Once our usefulness to him is over – or we can't pay the rent – he's done with us.'

'I don't think Master Byron will be like that, but it could be a few years before he takes over.'

'I'm not so sure,' Amos said. 'When Mr Ramsey was in a good mood – which wasn't often – but when he was, he would talk to me quite friendly, like. D'you remember he and his wife went on a round-the-world trip that had to be cut short because war was declared?'

'Oh yes, I do. Go on.'

'Well, a while before that' – he wrinkled his forehead trying to remember when events had occurred – 'in fact, it was just before the old bugger turned me out and brought Darby in. Anyway, that's by the by . . .'

Nell gritted her teeth. 'Get on with it, Amos,' she wanted to shout, but she let the old man ramble on at his own pace.

'He told me that he was leaving Byron in charge deliberately to see how he could cope with running the estate and, if all went well, and because Byron was married and had produced an heir, he was going to hand everything over to his son when he reached the age of twenty-five.'

'I doubt he'll do that now the lad's been injured, but we can hope.'

'I know one thing, but this is just between ourselves,' Nathan said. He glanced at Amos, prepared to trust him just a little more. 'If Byron was here, he'd help Rosie.'

But it seemed that Amos knew even more than they did. He laughed. 'Aye, they used to meet often when they were young. Nothing untoward, mark you,' he added swiftly, 'but the old man found out and put a stop to it. That was when he set about looking for a wife for Byron, but if you ask me, that's not worked out as he'd hoped. She spends more time at her parents' home than she does here. So,' he added, changing the subject back to the original topic, 'what d'you think is going to happen to Rosie, then?'

'I have no idea,' Nell said. 'I wish I could find out.'

'I'll see if I can learn owt in the pub. There's always gossip going on there.'

Again, Nell and Nathan exchanged a glance. They knew that all too well; most likely, that had been what had caused poor Rosie to be discovered.

When they were alone, Nell said, 'I'll go and see the mistress, Nathan. I think she might know something.'

Nell walked to the manor the following day. It was not a day to return the servants' washing, so really she had no excuse, but she couldn't afford to wait any longer. She entered by the back door again. Luckily, Sarah was in the kitchen and guessed the reason for another visit from Nell. Quietly, she said, 'I'll see if the mistress is free.'

Once in the morning room, Nell knew she could speak freely, even in front of Sarah.

'First, madam, is there any news of Byron?'

'There is and it's good news. Sadly, he's had to have his left leg amputated, but the operation has gone well. We hope he'll be fit enough to travel to be home for Christmas.'

'That is good news.' Nell smiled. 'I'm so glad.'

'It's kind of you to ask after him, Mrs Tranter, but I'm guessing that's not the only reason for your visit. You want to know if there's any news about Rosie.'

Nell nodded.

'As I'm sure you can appreciate this is a very delicate matter for me, but I have secured the help of a very dear friend of mine who has taken on the responsibility of obtaining a defence counsel for Rosie. She assured me she would do everything she could to find the very best and I think she has already done so because she has told me that the trial has been set for December. So now, we will just have to trust whoever she has appointed.'

Nell drew in her breath sharply. 'So soon? I thought this sort of thing usually took months.'

'Yes, it does, but in this case there is little evidence they can gather and obviously no witnesses, so there is no need to prolong the waiting time.'

Grace did not add that Helene had given her opinion that the solicitor thought the trial would not last long. 'It's an open-and-shut case,' he'd said but he would not be drawn into saying who he thought the victor would be.

'She'll be tried by jury.'

343

'Is that good or bad?' Nell asked.

'Sadly, I don't know, Mrs Tranter.'

'Are the public allowed to watch?'

'Oh yes.'

'Then Nathan and I will attend.'

'I'm afraid I won't be able to go, though I would love Rosie to see that I am giving her my support.'

'If I have the opportunity, I will make sure she knows how good you've been.'

'I just hope she's all right. Being in prison, even for only a few weeks, must be frightening for anyone and especially for a girl like Rosie so used to the outdoor life.'

Nell felt the tears prickle her eyes and her voice was unsteady as she said, 'I can't bear to think what she must be going through.'

The day before the trial was due to start, Nell and Nathan travelled to Lincoln and found cheap board and lodging. They intended to stay until the end of the trial, however long it took and however much it cost them.

When they entered the public gallery in the court, even Nell and Nathan were overawed by the huge room, the solemn-looking men in their black gowns and wigs, the bewildering solemnity of the proceedings and, most of all, they were daunted by the twelve men of the jury who would decide Rosie's fate.

'Whatever must she be feeling?' Nell muttered and then added, 'Which one is her defence counsel?'

'One of those two down there on either side, but I don't know which one.'

The proceedings began. If they hadn't been so anxious about Rosie, they would both have been intrigued by all the formalities. They glanced at the twelve men on the jury and were not encouraged by their solemn faces.

When Rosie appeared in the dock, they were shocked by her appearance. She was thin and pale, her pretty hair lank and dirty. She was a pitiful sight.

'Oh Nathan,' Nell whispered as she mopped her tears. She tried to catch Rosie's eye but the girl stood with her head bowed, not looking up at anyone.

The man, who was obviously the prosecution counsel, stood up and made his opening statement, setting out what he thought had been the events of that dreadful night when a man had lost his life at the hands of a poacher. He stated that the prosecution acknowledged that the girl in the dock had probably not actually fired the gun, but they believed she had been present that night and that she had aided and abetted the miscreant to escape justice.

'Samuel Waterhouse, a well-known poacher in the area, taught his daughter the tricks of his trade. It was undoubtedly he who shot the gamekeeper, but he has escaped justice by volunteering for the army.'

Then the defence counsel stood up to make his opening statement. He told the court that there was no proof that Rosie had even been in the woods that night. He even added that there was not even any proof that it had been Sam who had fired the deadly weapon.

'There were no witnesses to the event and we have no proof—'

At that moment, Nell stood up. 'Yes, you have. I have proof.'

There was a murmuring in the court and silence was called for. Nell left her seat, even though Nathan made a grab at her to make her sit down. She walked down to the front of the courtroom to stand beside the man whom she now knew to be the one defending Rosie. She opened her handbag and took out an envelope and handed it to him. 'This is Sam's confession, made when he was dying,' she whispered to the man. 'I wrote it all down for him and he signed it. I signed it too and we got the matron of the hospital to witness our signatures.'

The prosecution counsel leapt to his feet objecting at once to what was happening. However, the judge called for a short recess and asked both counsel to go to his rooms with him. The court was recessed for a short while.

Nell was asked to return to her seat but told that she must not leave the court. Rosie was escorted from the dock and disappeared.

'Mam, whatever are you doing?' Nathan hissed at her as she returned to her seat beside him.

'Helping to save Rosie, that's what,' she said firmly, but her knees were trembling.

'But – but I don't understand. What was it you gave the defence counsel? And what were you saying to him?'

'A letter.'

'What letter? Who's it from?'

'From Sam.'

'From Sam?'

'Nathan, stop repeating everything I say.'

'Just tell me, then.'

'Sam was brought into Lincoln hospital very badly wounded. Rosie sent word and I went to see him. He was dying, Nathan.' Tears sprang to her eyes as she remembered her dear friend. Whatever anyone else thought of him, he had been good to her and she had loved him. 'I wrote it all down for him – word for word – and he gave it to me to keep safe in case it should ever be needed to help Rosie. Well, it's needed now, don't you think?'

'What's in it?'

'It's his dying confession.'

'They're coming back . . .'

There was a stir in the courtroom as both counsel and the judge took their places again. Rosie was brought back into the dock.

The letter was admitted into evidence and Nell was asked to enter the witness box and take the oath. She was asked, quite gently, Nathan thought, by the defence counsel to explain how she had come by the letter. When she had repeated to the court what she had just told both the defence counsel and Nathan, he added, 'And do you know what is in the letter?'

'Yes, sir. I copied out every word just as he said it. Then we got the matron to witness both our signatures. She's willing to come and tell you herself, if you need her.'

The counsel smiled. 'I don't think that will be necessary, Mrs Tranter, but thank you. May I ask why you waited until now? Why did you not hand it over before?'

'Because I didn't know whom I could trust, sir. I didn't want it to get lost or to fall into the wrong hands.'

A murmur of laughter rippled round the courtroom.

'But you trust me?'

Nell looked straight into the eyes of the defence counsel. 'Yes, sir, I do.'

'Thank you, Mrs Tranter.' The man gave a little bow of acknowledgement at her compliment. 'At the moment, only the judge and my learned friend, the counsel for the prosecution, and I know the contents of the letter other than yourself, of course. Perhaps you would be kind enough to read it aloud for the benefit of the jury.'

The letter was handed to Nell and in a voice that shook a little she began to read aloud:

'I, Samuel Waterhouse, state that this is my dying declaration regarding the events of Sunday, 2 August 1914 on the Thornsby estate. I was out in the woods that night and had taken my gun with me. I rarely took a gun but that night I did. After I had been out for a short while, I heard a noise somewhere in front of me. I began to walk slowly backwards but as I did so, I fell over a fallen branch and the gun went off. I heard the sound of someone falling and went to look. I was horrified to see that I had shot the new gamekeeper, Mr Darby. I knew he was dead and that I would likely be hanged for his murder. I threw the gun into the lake at

Thornsby Manor. Then I went home and collected a few belongings, including anything to do with the gun. Cartridges and suchlike. I then walked to Skegness and threw everything off the end of the pier. I wish to state that Rosie was not with me when the accident happened. After that, I went to Lincoln and volunteered for the army, using my mother's surname. I visited Rosie once in the middle of the night. No one saw me but I wanted her to know what name I had used so that she could look out for it in the casualty lists. I told her that it was better to die fighting for my country than to dangle at the end of a hangman's rope. Eventually, I was sent abroad, wounded and brought home to England. I didn't see Rosie again until I was brought into the Lincoln hospital. I shall leave this letter in the trustworthy hands of my friend, Mrs Nell Tranter. I bitterly regret the events of that night.

I solemnly declare that no one else was involved in any way in the death of Wilfred Darby.

Samuel Waterhouse.'

Nell glanced up towards the defence counsel. 'It's also signed and dated by me and Miss Archer, the matron.'

When Nell had finished reading, she looked at Rosie. The girl was staring wide-eyed at her, but not a sound came from anyone in the courtroom until the judge asked the jury to retire and consider their verdict. Then the judge left the court and the jury were escorted to the jury room. The only advice the judge gave them was to say that they must decide if they believed the declaration of a dying man. 'If you do,' he instructed, 'then you should return the appropriate verdict of Not Guilty.'

They returned only twenty minutes later and gave a 'Not Guilty' verdict. Then everything seemed to happen very quickly. The judge told Rosie she was free to go and there was a buzz throughout the court.

'What do we do now?' Nell asked Nathan.

'We take Rosie home with us, Mam.'

And now it was Nathan who hurried as fast as he could down to the front of the courtroom to gather Rosie safely into his arms.

Thirty-Five

It took a month of Nell's and Nathan's tender care to restore Rosie to full health after her terrifying ordeal. She was with them through Christmas and into the New Year of 1917.

'D'you think they'll have me back at the hospital?' she asked, when she was feeling better.

'Why don't you write to the matron and ask her?'

'Yes, I will, but I'm a bit doubtful she'll want me.'

'She can only say "no", and you won't know if you don't ask.'

Outwardly, Rosie seemed fully recovered, but inside she still held a dark secret. A secret she would probably have to carry to her own grave. Her father's letter had saved her, but he had perjured himself. Luckily, she had not had to do so. When the defence counsel had questioned her in the prison, when he had agreed to defend her, she had said she knew nothing, but she had realized that if she'd had to stand up in court and swear on oath to tell the truth, she would have had to admit her part in the events of that night. And then . . .

She still shuddered at the thought of what might have happened. She realized she had had a very lucky escape.

*

The four of them spent a quiet Christmas together. They were all disappointed that Anna was unable to get leave to join them, but Matron had promised that she should have some leave early in the New Year if it proved possible.

We are still getting casualties as a result of the terrible battles on the Somme, even though it was supposed to have ended last month, Anna wrote to Nathan. *Matron just can't let anyone have leave at the moment. Please tell Rosie that as soon as she is well enough she must come back to us. We need her badly.*

But still Rosie clung to the safety of Nell's cottage. She rarely ventured out. Although she had been declared innocent by the court, she was still afraid of what William Ramsey might try to do to her.

Nathan and Amos came home from the pub on the night before New Year's Eve with two pieces of news.

'You know, Mam, he's quite a nice old boy,' Nathan had said when he realized how well Amos fitted into their home life. The former gamekeeper kept the garden neat and had developed a vegetable patch. He planned to grow pretty flowers for Nell in the summer. 'I'm pleased you saved him from going into the workhouse. He didn't deserve that.'

'No one does, Nathan,' Nell had replied tartly. 'And he's such a help about the place. I don't know how I ever managed without him after you volunteered. It was hard.'

'Yes, Mam. I know. I was a bit hasty. I'm lucky to have come back mostly in one piece.'

And tonight, Nathan had something else to tell his mother and Rosie.

'I've got two bits of news,' he said, with a wide grin, 'that I think you're both going to like.'

'The first one is that I've been talking to Johnnie Merryweather. He's just reached the age when he can go into a pub and order a drink legally.' Nathan laughed. 'He's been doing it for years, but now he doesn't have to dodge PC Foster anymore.'

'Rather like young Monty from the manor, eh?' Amos joined in the laugher.

'Johnnie's been working for Ray's dad in the joinery business as an apprentice, but now he's going to volunteer.'

'Oh no!' Nell was shocked. 'His poor mam. He's her only child and her husband died young. Johnnie was only eleven or so when that happened,' Nell said quietly and, with a swift glance at Amos, added, 'Sam kept the family fed for weeks.'

Amos nodded. 'Aye, I remember that time too. I heard about poor Merryweather and guessed what Sam would do. I was careful to stay in bed at night then.'

Rosie smiled, remembering the many times when Sam had said to her, 'I thought old Amos would have been on the prowl last night but he was nowhere to be seen.' Now she knew why. 'Go on,' she prompted Nathan.

'We got talking and he said he thought that perhaps I could take his place – at least until he comes back. Well, upshot of it is, Ray's dad has agreed to give me a trial.'

'You've nowt to lose,' Nell said. 'I think it's a great idea. And what's your other piece of news?'

Nathan glanced at Rosie as he said, 'Master Byron's home.'

'I do hope you're not thinking of going back to work at the Lincoln hospital,' William said. 'Your son needs you here now.'

Grace regarded him steadily. She had no intention of leaving home again; she was happily occupied now with her fundraising efforts, and yes, Byron did need her. But she decided to tease William just a little to puncture his pomposity.

'But surely Pearl and Bertie will come home now? She will care for Byron.'

William glared at her; he was getting angry now, the veins bulging on his temples.

'I forbid you to go. D'you hear me, Grace?'

She stood up, facing him with a calm smile. She knew she was pushing him a bit too far. 'Since you command me, William, I will stay here as a good and dutiful wife. After all, I did promise to obey you.'

He came towards her, his hands outstretched. 'Grace, dearest Grace, I don't want to quarrel with you. I want Pearl to bring Albert here. It's where the boy should be and when Byron is fully fit again—'

'He will never be fully fit, William. He's lost a leg.'

'I know, I know, but his mind is unimpaired.'

Grace wasn't so sure about that, but she said nothing.

'He will be able to run the estate and then you and I, my dear, can go travelling, like we did just before all this silly business started. The grand tour we planned was cut short, wasn't it?'

'I doubt Europe will be worth visiting for a while, even when it's all over. The land will be devastated.'

'Then we'll go somewhere else. There are plenty of places in the world that won't have been touched by the war. We could journey across America—'

'We'll see, William. We'll see how things work out. But first, you are quite right, we must get Pearl and little Bertie home.'

Pearl agreed with Grace's previous suggestion now that Byron was home for good. She would spend March to September at Thornsby Manor but would go home to her parents for the winter months. William was incensed. 'Her place is here with her husband all year round. I won't let Albert go for that long. What about his schooling?'

'She's planning to send him to a top-class boarding school – Eton, I think – when he's old enough and a good preparatory school before that.'

William struggled to answer. 'I suppose I can't fault her for that if she wants the best for the boy, so long as she's not doing it just to get him out of her way.'

'I don't think so, William. Besides, her own mother dotes on him. She wouldn't agree to it if that was the reason.'

'I have my suspicions as to what that young woman is up to. Would her mother know?'

'I think,' Grace said, smiling inwardly, 'that Bella Anderson is a lot shrewder than you think.'

William grunted. 'Let's hope so. Anyway, what does

Byron think about it? The boy being sent away to boarding school, I mean?'

'He hasn't said.'

'Then I think I should talk to him about it.'

'Will you leave that to me, William?'

Her husband hesitated and then agreed reluctantly. 'All right.'

Grace went to her son's sitting room on the first floor. She spent a lot of her time with him now, trying to coax him downstairs and even out into the garden. But Byron was reluctant to let anyone see him. The only people he allowed into his room were his parents – he had little choice where William was concerned – and Baines, who he allowed to help him wash and dress.

'Now, my darling,' she said as she entered the room and crossed to where he was sitting by the window, gazing listlessly out towards the lake and the wooded slope above it. 'We need to discuss my letter to Pearl asking her to bring Bertie home. You also need to decide whether or not you agree with her proposal to send him to a preparatory boarding school. I think she then hopes he will go to Eton or Harrow at the appropriate age.'

'I didn't go away at all.'

'No. We had excellent tutors for you here at home. Your father's main focus was on you learning how to run the estate.'

Byron merely grunted.

'So, what do you want for Bertie?'

For a moment, Byron's eyes softened. 'For him to be happy and to be able to choose for himself what he wants to do in his life.' He turned his gaze on his mother and she read in them the resentment he carried. 'And especially,' he added bitterly, 'for him to be able to marry the woman he loves who*ever* that might be.'

Grace sighed. 'I haven't told you what's been happening to Rosie, have I?'

Startled, Byron met her steady gaze. He hadn't realized that she knew, or at least had guessed, his feelings for Rosie.

'You – you know?'

Grace smiled sadly. 'Oh yes, I know. I just wish I'd known before it was too late – before you'd married Pearl. I feel so guilty because I was instrumental in bringing that about.'

'Don't,' Byron said more gently. 'It wasn't your fault. You were only trying to carry out your husband's – demands. It is I who should have stood up to him. I should have been strong enough and brave enough to go after what I wanted. But she was still only very young and the gulf between our circumstances was a chasm.' He sighed and then went on heavily, 'So tell me what it is I should know about Rosie.'

So Grace told him everything she knew about Rosie's arrest and her trial, ending, 'And now I have to confess something to you, but you must promise me that you will never tell your father.'

His voice was husky. 'Of course I won't.'

'I asked for Helene's help in finding a good defence lawyer for Rosie. I said I would pay – I have money of my own – but Helene insisted that she would see to it all. It was her own solicitor who found Mr Patterson.'

'So between you, you and Mrs Tranter – and Helene – you saved her from . . . Well, I hardly dare voice what might have happened to her.' He paused and then asked wistfully, 'Have you seen her? Do you know how she is?'

'Sarah takes the servants' washing to Nell every week and she knows I became very fond of Rosie when we worked in the hospital together. She brings me news. Rosie's staying with the Tranters at present, but I understand Nell is trying to persuade her to write to the matron to ask if she will take her back.'

'If only I could see her.'

'I know, my dear, but it would not be safe for her to come here. In fact, I think it will be much safer for her to go back to Lincoln. I don't think your father will ever give up the fight to have her convicted. If he can't manage that, then he will make trouble for her in some other way.' Her voice dropped to a whisper, even though there was no one else in the room to hear. 'If you love her, Byron, let her go.'

Byron nodded slowly, but the sorrow in his tone almost broke Grace's heart. 'Yes, I must.'

Thirty-Six

By February, Nell had persuaded Rosie to write to the matron and one morning, just after the postman had called, Rosie was holding a letter in her hand and smiling broadly. 'Guess what?'

'The matron has said you can go back.'

Rosie nodded and her eyes were shining. 'Yes, she has. I can hardly believe it.'

Nell shrugged. 'So she should. You shouldn't be penalized when you were found not guilty. When are you going?'

'Tomorrow.'

'That soon,' Nell murmured and her face fell. 'We shall miss you, Rosie.'

'And I'll miss you.' Rosie put her arms around Nell. 'You'll never know how grateful I am for all you've done for me and I don't mean just recently – though that as well. You've always been the mam I never had.'

'Oh go on with you.' Nell was embarrassed by the girl's show of emotion but she was touched nonetheless. She held her close for a moment. 'You know me an' your dad always wondered if you and Nathan would get together, but I can see that's not the way you feel about each other, is it?'

'No, it never has been and we both know that. But you like Anna, don't you?'

'Yes, I do. Very much. I think they'll be very happy together. Once this war's over and if Nathan can start to earn a living, I think he'll ask her to marry him.'

'Then no one will be happier for them both than me,' Rosie said. 'And now I must get my things together.'

Just before dawn the next morning, Rosie stood on the far side of the woods looking down at the lake and the manor house beyond it. If only she could see him for herself – just one more time – before she left. But it was impossible. The man she loved was in that house, but so was the man who hated her so much that he had tried to get her hanged for a crime she had not committed.

'One day, I'll come back, my love,' she said aloud, making a solemn vow. 'One day – I don't know how – but we'll be together.'

She turned, threaded her way back through the trees, picked up the bundle she'd left at the edge of the woods, then walked along the lane through the village to meet the early morning carrier's cart going to Lincoln.

'Welcome back, Waterhouse. I think it best if you go by your proper name now. Everyone here has been following the case and we're all relieved that you have been found not guilty. It is, after all, your legal name.'

'Thank you, Matron. And thank you for taking me back. I didn't know if you would.'

'I did have to run it by the board of governors of the hospital but they agreed unanimously that you should not be penalized. They were happy to go with the court's decision. You can start with a clean slate, Waterhouse. Now, there is one other thing. I wondered if you would like to train to be a *qualified* nurse.'

Rosie gaped at her, her eyes wide with surprise. 'Oh Matron, that would be wonderful. Can I really?'

'I've spoken to several of the ward sisters where you've been working as an assistant and we're all agreed that you have the makings of an excellent nurse.'

Rosie blushed. 'That's – that's very kind of them – of you all.'

'Kindness doesn't come into it.' Connie Archer smiled. 'We have to be scrupulously impartial in our decisions. I'll make all the necessary arrangements, order a uniform for you and you can start next Monday on Sister Carmichael's ward. It's the ward where Doctor Oldfield's special patients are nursed and I know you have a particular interest in them. Dr Oldfield is certainly winning his particular battle. There have been more articles in medical journals about shell shock. It's beginning to be officially recognized.'

Rosie couldn't believe how lucky she was. After the nightmare of her arrest, the weeks spent in gaol and the tension of the court proceedings, it felt as if she was suddenly in a wonderful dream. And best of all, she knew that Byron was safely home and out of the war. Though he was terribly injured, at least he would survive.

That night she wrote excitedly to Nell and Nathan, not forgetting to include Amos. She now regarded them all as her family. And soon it sounded as if her dear friend Anna would become part of that family too. Shyly, the young girl had confided in Rosie that Nathan had asked her to marry him as soon as he could provide a home for her.

'His mam has said we can live with her, but it's only a small cottage and besides' – she blushed prettily – 'we want a place of our own.'

'Why don't you write and ask Nathan to find out if he could have our old cottage? I won't be going back there and it's still empty.'

'I'll do that. Thanks, Rosie.'

Rosie grinned. 'I'd love to think of you both living there.'

'Byron, my dear,' Grace said entering his sitting room early one morning in the middle of March. 'I have some wonderful news for you . . .'

'Mother, have you seen the newspapers? There is dreadful unrest in Russia and the Tsar has abdicated.'

'Oh never mind all that. It has nothing to do with us.'

'I think it may have. They're our allies, after all. What we really need is for America to enter the war.' He laid his newspaper aside and glanced up at her. 'Anyway, what is this wonderful news?'

'Pearl and Bertie arrive today. They will be staying until the end of September.'

Now there was a flare of real interest in his eyes for the first time.

'Pearl and I have arranged between us that they should come here for the summer months and then go back to her parents' home for the winter.'

'I suppose it's better than nothing, which is what we have at present,' he said. 'But then he wouldn't be here for Christmas, would he?'

'No, but perhaps the Andersons would be kind enough to invite us to join them so that we could see him.'

Byron opened his mouth but Grace said quickly, 'We've no need to decide about that yet. Plenty of time. I think you might be feeling a lot better by then. You'll soon be able to have an artificial leg fitted, won't you?'

Listlessly, Byron said, 'I don't know. All I do know is that I'm not going to be wheeled about.'

'That won't be necessary. I've been looking into it and there have been huge advances in the making of artificial limbs, sadly hurried along by this war, I suppose. But surely your stump has healed well enough by now for you to have one fitted.'

Byron allowed himself a wry smile. 'You've got it all worked out, haven't you, Mother?'

'Indeed I have. I'm not going to let you languish in here for the rest of your life. You have a son to play with and teach things to . . .'

'But he's only going to be here for half the year, if that.'

'Then make the most of it while he is with us, my dear. We all must.' She leaned towards him. 'Get close to him, Byron, so that *he*'s the one asking to come to stay with us.'

363

Now he smiled widely. 'You're a crafty minx, Mother. I never knew you could be so devious.'

Grace laughed as she stood up. 'There's quite a lot you don't know about me, Byron, but now I must go and see that the rooms are ready for their arrival. We've opened one of the other bedrooms to make a playroom for him and taken all your toys from the attic. Lucy is busy cleaning old Dobbin as we speak.'

'Oh my,' Byron murmured. 'My old rocking horse.'

She stood looking down at him. 'Please think about allowing Baines to wheel you in the bath chair your father ordered for you. It won't be for ever, I promise you, but it would allow you to be with Bertie and to play with him. A little boy of three and a half would think it a great treat to ride in your chair with you. You'd be able to go out into the grounds and watch him. I shall be asking young Monty to play with him out of doors. The child must have some fresh air and exercise.'

'I'll think about it.'

'That's all I'm asking,' she said and then added playfully, 'For the moment.'

Pearl and Bertie settled in surprisingly well. It seemed as if the promise of being able to return to the place she still called home was enough inducement to keep them at Thornsby Manor for the summer months. The arrival of his son did Byron the world of good. He agreed to being wheeled about in the cumbersome bath chair by Baines or Monty, especially when, as Grace had predicted, a gleeful Bertie climbed in for a ride. Out in the grounds, Byron watched while Monty played cricket with Bertie or he was wheeled down to the edge of the lake in order to show the boy how to fish. He could cast a line from his chair and William soon insisted on buying his grandson a small fishing rod. They sat side by side on the bank of the lake for several hours, but Byron insisted that Monty should stay too.

'I can do nothing if he falls in the lake, Monty. I need you to stay with us.'

Although Lucas Brown grumbled constantly about his stable lad being missing for part of every day, there was nothing he could do. The orders came directly from William. Whatever Byron and Bertie wanted, they were to be indulged. And Monty, of course, was happy to oblige. It meant he too could sit by the lake for hours, even if it meant working late to look after the horses too.

'Would you like me to teach him to ride, Master Byron?' he asked one day. 'There are often some nice little ponies come up for sale in the cattle markets. I bet the master would get one for him.'

'That's a good idea, Monty. I'll speak to my father tonight.'

William would buy anything his grandson needed, if it kept the child happy and living there with them.

'Papa,' Bertie said one day, standing in front of his father who was sitting in his bath chair watching Monty teach the child the rudiments of cricket. 'What happened to your leg?'

Byron hesitated for a moment and then decided that for the inquisitive, intelligent child, young though he was, the truth was the best answer.

'It was very badly injured and the wound wasn't going to get better so the doctor had to cut it off.'

He waited, wondering if he had been too blunt, but Bertie seemed to accept the explanation. He was thoughtful as he looked down at the blanket on the bath chair that covered only one leg. He pointed at the empty space next to it. 'Can you get a wooden leg, Papa? Grandfather Anderson says you could. Then you could play cricket with me and Monty.'

'Perhaps I will, Bertie,' Byron said, smiling wryly to think that what his mother had not been able to manage, his son had done so in a few short words.

The boy grinned and ran off to find the ball that Monty had just batted into some bushes.

Even though the Ramseys were enjoying an almost idyllic summer, repercussions from the war were never very far away.

Although Byron's wish had come true and America had entered the war in April 1917, one of the most horrific battles began at the end of July. It was the third time a battle had been fought close to the Belgian town of Ypres but it was known by the name of a small township nearby, Passchendaele. Because of appalling summer weather, the soldiers, their horses and equipment were bogged down in mud and many lives were lost through drownings.

Nick Gill and Geoffrey Porter, two of the original six who had volunteered together soon after the declaration of war, were killed on the same day. The list for the village war memorial that would undoubtedly be erected on the village green after the war was growing ever longer. And then came the news that Johnnie Merryweather, who had so recently volunteered, had been killed too, leaving his widowed mother completely alone. On hearing the news, Nell hurried at once to Emily Merryweather's cottage which overlooked the village green.

'I don't want to go on living, Nell.' Emily was strangely dry-eyed. Nell suspected she had not wept at all. Her devastation was too deep for tears. 'No husband, no son, no prospect even of grandchildren now. What have I got left to live for?'

'Now, now, Emily, I don't want to hear that sort of talk. And before you say owt, yes, I know, I've been lucky. I've got my Nathan back, not exactly whole, but he's mending slowly.'

'What am I going to do, Nell? How am I going to live? Johnnie supported me. He'd started sending me a little bit each week. It wasn't much but it covered the rent. But that'll stop, won't it? And I don't earn enough in Jez Crowson's dairy to pay the rent and live as well.'

Nell frowned. 'Perhaps not, Emily, but you need to write to the Ministry of Pensions in London. I'll get the address for you. I've got it at home on a letter Nathan received.'

'I'm not much of a letter writer, Nell. I wasn't any good at school and me dad got me out working as soon as I was old enough.' She gave a wry smile even amidst all her sorrow. 'In fact, he sent me out before I should have gone. He lied about me age to my employers.'

'What did you do?' Nell asked. 'I can't remember knowing you before you married and came to live here.'

'I was a laundry maid at a big house in Alford.'

Nell's face brightened. 'There you are, then. That's your answer.'

Emily blinked and stared at her. 'What's my answer? I don't understand you, Nell.'

'You can help me with the washing I do for the manor. Since Rosie's gone, it's getting harder and harder. Nathan helped a bit but he's started working at Terry Chambers's place now. And besides, the men think it's beneath them, you know, to do women's work. I can't even get Amos to peg the washing on the line for me.'

Emily sighed heavily. 'It's good of you, Nell, and I 'preciate, it but you're a week too late.'

'Eh? How d'you mean?'

'Mr Pickering paid me a visit last week. I'd fallen behind with the rent even before I got the news about Johnnie. On the master's instructions, Pickering's given me notice to leave.'

'Never!'

'Pickering's Mr Ramsey's man through and through.'

Nell snorted. 'So's Lucas Brown. He sits in the corner of the pub and reports every snippet of gossip he hears straight back to old man Ramsey and Pickering's not much better.'

'I reckon the pair of them are in cahoots. Pair of bootlickers, that's what they are.'

Nell's eyes narrowed thoughtfully. 'Leave it with me, Emily. And no more talk of not wanting to go on living – and don't you dare start packing your belongings and heading for the workhouse. You're not going there, or my name's not Nell Tranter.'

'What are you going to do, Nell? Don't get yarsen in bother on my account.'

'I won't,' Nell said airily. 'Now let me get you summat to eat and drink before I go, because I bet you haven't eaten properly since you got the news about poor Johnnie, have you?'

Emily was obliged to agree that she had not. Plunged into abject despair, all she could think about was her own death, where there would be no more pain.

Thirty-Seven

Nell put on her sunhat and the coolest blouse she could find. Not that she possessed many, but the weather was so hot she would risk going out in just a blouse and skirt this afternoon. Perhaps it was not etiquette, but who cared on a day like this.

She walked up the slope and into the woods. Beneath the trees it was cooler but, emerging from the other side, the heat hit her forcibly again. It was still a fair way to the manor and she would have to walk right round the lake and cross the stream by the stepping stones. She shaded her eyes as she spotted three figures near the banks on the far side of the lake under a sunshade; two men and a boy. *That must be little Bertie*, she thought, a smile curving her mouth. She'd yet to meet him, but now might be the time. She set off towards them, skirting the cornfields that were almost ready for harvest. She crossed the stream and walked along the bank of the lake to where they were sitting, one of the men and the little boy holding fishing rods. She approached quietly, but Bertie's sharp hearing made him look up as she neared them. He must have said something, because the next moment Byron turned his head and saw her.

'Mrs Tranter, how nice to see you,' he said quietly. 'As you can see, my son and I are fishing.'

There was such a wealth of pride and love in his tone at the mention of his boy that Nell felt tears prickle the back of her throat. *If only . . .* she began to think, but then pushed the thought away.

Monty rose to his feet at once and offered her the stool he'd been sitting on.

'Oh please don't . . .' she began, but the young man only grinned. 'I can sit on the grass, Mrs Tranter. Please – take the stool.' He moved away to sit further along the bank, tactfully thinking that perhaps the conversation between Byron and Mrs Tranter might be private.

As she settled herself, Nell said, 'I was on my way to see your mother, Master Byron, but then I saw you here and thought I'd be cheeky and come to see this young man. We haven't met before.'

'Bertie, this is Mrs Tranter who lives in the village,' Byron said. 'Say "How do you do?".'

The boy laid aside his fishing rod carefully, stood up and held out his hand to Nell.

'How do you do, Mrs Tranter? I'm pleased to meet you.' And then he bowed courteously over her hand. He gave her a beaming smile and hurried back to pick up his fishing rod again.

'What a grand little lad he is, Master Byron. He must be nearly four now, isn't he? He looks very like you.'

Byron inclined his head at the compliment to his son, but said, 'How are you, Mrs Tranter? How is – everyone?'

'I'm fine, Master Byron, thank you. Amos has settled in very well . . .'

'Amos? What about Amos?'

'He's lodging with me. He had nowhere else to go when he left his cottage.'

Byron stared at her and, suddenly, his mouth tightened. 'Other than the workhouse, you mean?'

Nell nodded, but changed the subject quickly. 'And Nathan's doing very nicely. He's not quite fit enough to come back to the land, but he's working on trial with Mr Chambers, the carpenter. If he does well, there'll be a job for him there. Even when Ray comes back, Terry says there'll be enough work for the three of them, especially now that poor Johnnie Merryweather won't be returning.'

Out of the six from the village who had volunteered at the start of the war, three were back home with injuries that would keep them out of the war and two were dead. Only Ray Chambers remained on active service.

'And then,' Nell went on, 'we all hope Nathan'll be getting married.'

'Married?' His tone was sharp.

'Yes, he met a lovely little lass when he was in the Lincoln hospital. Anna. She's Rosie's friend.'

Nell couldn't fail to notice that he seemed to relax. She carried on with what she was telling him. 'And speaking of Rosie,' she said casually, 'the matron has set her on a course to qualify as a proper nurse. It's the best thing she could do.'

'So,' he said slowly, 'she won't be coming back to Thornsby?'

'No, Master Byron,' Nell said, adding gently, 'it'll be for the best.'

He didn't answer but Nell saw his bleak expression. 'Actually,' she said, 'I think if and when Nathan does marry, he's rather hoping he might be granted tenancy of the Waterhouses' cottage, if it was still available by then.'

'I don't think that would be a problem,' Byron murmured, but she could see that his mind was still elsewhere. 'Is that what you wanted to see my mother about?'

'No, Master Byron, Nathan isn't quite ready to be asking about that yet. He wants to be fit enough to get a full-time job and be able to keep them both.' She took a deep breath. 'I was on my way to see your mam about Emily Merryweather. Mr Pickering has given her notice to quit her cottage.'

Byron frowned. 'Why?'

'She's missed paying her rent for the last two months.'

'But – her son was killed recently. There won't have been time to sort out whether she's entitled to any pension yet, will there?'

'No, Master Byron. She is distraught and saying she doesn't want to go on living.'

Now Byron was angry. 'Leave it to me, Mrs Tranter. I will sort it out at once.' He turned to his son and his face softened. 'I'm sorry, Bertie, we have to go now.'

'But I want to catch a fish . . .' Bertie said.

'I'm sorry, but I have to do something important. We'll come back again this afternoon. We can leave all our fishing gear here.'

The little boy pulled his line from the water and laid his rod down on the bank. 'Monty,' he called, 'Papa needs you to push his chair.' He turned back to Nell. 'Goodbye, Mrs Tranter.'

'Goodbye, Master Bertie.' What a delightful little boy he was, she thought.

Back at the house, Byron sent Monty to look for Jack Pickering. It was an hour before the man arrived and entered the room Byron used as his own study.

'Pickering,' Byron said at once, coming straight to the point. 'What's this I hear about Mrs Merryweather being given notice to quit her cottage just because she's missed two months' rent?'

'It's always been your father's policy, Master Byron.'

'Were you not aware that she has just lost her only son – her only child – and, being already a widow, she has no means of support until any pension that might be due to her can be sorted out?'

The bailiff looked uncomfortable. 'I – er – had heard something about it, Master Byron, yes.'

'And don't you think you should have shown a little more compassion under those dreadful circumstances?'

Jack twirled his cap between agitated fingers before saying hesitantly, 'It was your father's instruction, sir.'

'In normal circumstances, yes, but these are not normal times.'

Jack grew red in the face as he blurted out, 'No, I mean that's what he told me to do now.'

Byron stared at the man, not wanting to believe what he was hearing. 'In that case, Pickering, you will go to the village right now, to Mrs Merryweather's cottage, and rescind your instruction. She will not be turned out of her cottage when she has just received such devastating news. And if I have anything to do with it, not at all.'

'But your father . . . ?'

'Leave my father to me,' Byron snapped.

Jack thought quickly, wondering how to save his own job and home. He too lived on the estate in a tied cottage in his capacity as bailiff. The young man in front of him, though wounded physically, was still in charge of his faculties. And one day – perhaps before too long – he would be the master of the Thornsby estate. 'I'll go at once, Master Byron,' he said meekly and left the room a lot quicker than he had entered it.

Byron opened his drawer and took out an amount of money from the cash box he kept there. Then he rang the bell for Baines, who came within minutes.

'Baines, I am sorry to trouble you – I don't know where Monty's disappeared to . . .'

'He's outside playing ball with Master Bertie. I think they're waiting for you to go back to the lake.'

'I will in a moment, Baines, but first, could you wheel me across the hall to my father's study? Give me a few minutes and then, if you would be so good as to tell Monty to fetch me, we will indeed return to the lake.'

Two minutes later he was facing his father across William's desk. He flung the money onto its leather surface. 'There's the rent that Mrs Merryweather owes you. Father, I am shocked that you could be so callous to the poor woman.'

William shrugged. 'Where's this money come from?

I expect the villagers have had a collection for her, have they? They'll soon tire of that.' When Byron did not answer, William went on, 'You can't afford to be soft in business, Byron, as you will find out when you take over the estate. If everyone who lost someone in the war is going to try to take advantage of the fact, the country will soon be in a sorry state.'

'The country is going to be in a sorry state, as you put it, anyway. By the time this is all over, we will have lost a whole generation of fine young men.' As Monty knocked on the door and entered the room, Byron added, 'From now on, Father, I shall be taking a much greater interest in running the estate. It's what you've always wanted me to do, isn't it?'

To that, William had no answer.

Pearl kept to her side of the bargain but when the end of September came, she and Bertie went back to Stamford.

The little boy wept openly and, for once, no one told him 'big boys don't cry', for they all felt the prickle of tears.

Bella Anderson had already written inviting them to stay with them at Christmas so that Byron was able to say to his little son, 'We'll see you when Father Christmas brings you lots of presents, won't we? We'll be there to see you open them all.'

And with that they all had to be content.

By the middle of November, the battle of Passchendaele was deemed to be at an end, but the losses on all sides of the conflict were catastrophic. Ray Chambers had miraculously survived it all and had come home on leave. He visited each of his comrades in turn.

'I'm glad you'll be working with us after the war,' he told Nathan. 'It'll be good to think I have something to come back to.'

'How's it going, do you think?' Nathan asked him. 'We only know what's in the newspapers.'

Ray pulled a face. 'It's pretty gruesome. In some ways Passchendaele was worse than the Somme and that was no picnic, but we'll win in the end. We've got to, Nathan.'

'D'you really think so?'

'I *know* so,' Ray laughed. 'We're not going to go through all this to end up giving up. Oh no. Now, will you come with me to see poor old Dan? Despite my bravado at the front, I'm a bit of a coward at seeing one of my mates in such a bad way. I went up to the manor this morning and it nearly broke me seeing Byron being wheeled about in a bath chair like an old man.'

'Of course. We'll go now.'

Ray stood in front of Dan, who looked up and gave him a wavering smile.

'Well, that's good,' Nathan said. 'I can tell he's recognized you.'

Ray squatted down in front of Dan, so that his gaze was level with the injured man's. 'Now then, old chap. How are you?'

Dan's shaking increased but he was still smiling as he said, quite clearly, 'Better, Ray. Good – to – see – you.'

377

Ivy, who was standing close by, said, 'Oh Ray, that's the most he's ever said all in one go. Isn't it, Nathan?'

Nathan nodded. He came in faithfully every day to sit and talk to Dan, so he hardly noticed the tiny improvements that were happening. But today was a milestone. For the next hour Ray and Nathan sat with Dan talking and attempting to include him as much as they could.

'Dr Oldfield from the Lincoln hospital still comes out to see you about once a month, doesn't he, Dan?' Nathan said and then turned to Ray. 'He's very optimistic. He's been making a study of Dan's case. I think there are a lot of articles in medical journals that are about Dan, though of course his name is never mentioned.'

'Why ever not? His picture ought to be on the front page of every newspaper in the land. Let people see for themselves what this stupid war is doing to our lads.'

'Mebbe you're right.'

As they left the Bates's cottage, Nathan said, 'Your visit's done him a power of good, Ray. Thanks for coming.'

'I won't be able to call again. I have to report back for duty tomorrow.'

'Will you – get sent out there again?'

'Oh, I expect so,' Ray said cheerfully. 'But I don't mind. We've got a war to win.'

The two friends stood together for a few moments.

'It's been good to see you, Nathan, and I'm so glad you and my dad are getting on so well. He's very pleased with your progress. Ses you'll make a fine carpenter and if – if I don't . . .'

'None of that, Ray, please. I can't wait for you to come back hale and hearty and for me to be working alongside you. So, just you mind you take good care of yourself.'

Ray gave a lopsided grin as he shook Nathan's hand warmly. 'I'll do my best. And will you please give my kind regards to Master Byron if you see him. I was so glad to hear they're getting him fitted up with an artificial leg. It'll help him to feel more normal.'

Nathan chuckled. 'He's more or less in charge of the estate now and folk are much better treated and happier under his benevolent hand.'

Ray laughed aloud. 'I bet the old man doesn't like that.'

Nathan grinned. 'He doesn't, but there's not much he can do about it.'

Ray's laughter died as he added, 'Dad was telling me all about poor Rosie and the court case. I'm so glad she got off. Where is she now?'

'Back working at the military hospital in Lincoln and doing well. She's training to be a proper nurse.'

'That's wonderful. Give her my warmest regards if you should see her, because – no offence – I don't want to see her myself, if you know what I mean.'

Nathan blinked and then realized what his friend meant. Ray did not want to encounter Rosie because it would mean that he had been admitted to the hospital as a casualty.

The following morning, Nathan and Ray's father

stood together on the village green to wave Ray off, neither knowing if they would ever see him again.

'He'll be back, Mr Chambers. I'm sure of it.'

'I wish I had your faith, Nathan. His mother couldn't even bear to come and see him go. She's that sure we've seen him for the last time.'

Thirty-Eight

Later that same month, there was great excitement at the manor; Byron was to get an artificial leg at last. It had taken him a long time to decide to have one fitted and he had Bertie to thank for encouraging him to do so. William had enlisted the help of the local doctors to secure the finest prothesis that had been invented.

'Even out of this catastrophic war,' Dr Wren said when he made one of his regular visits to check on Byron's progress, 'some good has come. New treatments, new medicines and there has also been vast strides in the manufacture of artificial limbs. A firm called the Desoutter Brothers set up in 1914 to manufacture artificial legs. One of the brothers had a flying accident and lost his leg. He became so frustrated with the cumbersome limb then available, that his brother set about inventing a lightweight one made out of metal. So, Master Byron, I will make enquiries for you. I am sure the stump has healed well enough now. We'll have you on your feet for Christmas.'

Byron had his artificial leg fitted at the end of November and though he suffered soreness from the chafing, he was determined to walk properly by the time he saw his son again. Grace, with her newfound knowledge of nursing, was able to help him keep the stump healthy.

The Andersons made the Ramseys very welcome in their home and the joy on Bertie's face when he saw his father standing and walking brought tears to the women's eyes. Even the menfolk had to clear their throats gruffly. Pearl was attentive to Byron and they seemed to find some mutual ground on which to proceed with their marriage. They were both determined to do the best for their little boy. Pearl promised to stick to the arrangement she had made with Grace and with that, everyone had to be content.

'It's not what I had hoped for,' Bella confided in Grace. 'I have done my best to persuade her to return to Thornsby permanently and just bring Bertie to see us now and again, but she is adamant. She has always been strong-willed. When she was younger, I'm not ashamed to admit I used all sorts of ploys to cajole her into doing what I wanted.' Bella sighed. 'But now, I no longer can. I'm sorry, Grace, but I'll do my best to make sure she sticks to the arrangement you have made with her. She and Bertie will spend the summer months with you and the winter months with us. And you are welcome here every Christmas.' She smiled. 'Bertie is so enjoying having us all together.'

'And you must visit us in the summer. You should see him playing outdoors in the fine weather and riding his pony.'

'We would both like that, Grace. Thank you.'

And so the two mothers came to an agreement that, if not quite what either of them wanted, at least satisfied everyone – apart from, of course, William.

The events of the war had shocked the whole world and even intruded into the secluded village of Thornsby. For years the inhabitants had lived their lives quietly, working hard at whatever employment they had, looking after their families and watching out for their neighbours and friends. The village was small enough for each person to know everyone else and to be a part of each other's lives. They shared joys – the weddings, the births and christenings – and they mourned together the loss of one of their number. Only occasional visits to nearby market towns brought them into contact with 'outsiders'. Now and then a young man would leave the village to seek a career elsewhere but mostly the youngsters found employment on the estate or with one of the tenant farmers. The only thing that had, until now, marred this idyllic way of life was that William Ramsey was a tyrannical lord and master without an ounce of sentiment or philanthropy. But even that had been overcome as, instead, his tenants looked out for one another. Over the last three and a half years, however, the world beyond had intruded with cruel suddenness. From waving off their boys as heroes and rejoicing with pride in the bravery of their sons, the villagers had come to understand the catastrophe of war. The village had been desecrated by the reality of a war that no one had asked for or wanted. They watched as their loved ones came home maimed for life or mourned for those who would never return at all. And, appalled, they witnessed the further heartlessness of William Ramsey when they heard of his plan to evict Emily Merryweather.

'But have you heard that Master Byron has paid her rent himself?' Amos told evening drinkers in the pub. He kept his voice low, for Lucas Brown was sitting in his usual corner. 'They were heard quarrelling in the master's study and Master Byron said that he would be taking a much more active part in the running of the estate from now on.'

'Praise be. Let's hope he does,' Terry muttered. 'How d'you get to know all this, Amos? You don't work for him anymore.'

Amos tapped the side of his nose. 'I still have my sources,' was all he would say. He glanced swiftly towards the head groom in the corner. 'But he wouldn't be best pleased if he knew just who that was.'

'Have you seen this, Nathan?' Terry Chambers jabbed his finger on the newspaper spread out on the bar when they met in the Thornsby Arms one evening just before Christmas.

'I haven't read it yet. Pint of bitter, please, Ted,' Nathan added, turning aside to order his drink first. Then he glanced down at the paper. 'What is it?'

'They're saying that this revolution in Russia could pull the Russians out of the war.'

'That'll not be good for us if that happens. Mind you, we have got America with us now.'

'There was dreadful hardship in Russia, you know, among the ordinary folk,' Terry said. 'And I suppose it didn't go down well with those who have nothing to see the Tsar and his family living in grand palaces. I expect that's why they were forced out. I read a while back that the whole family's in Siberia now.'

'Aye, well, there's been times when I'd like to send Mr William Ramsey to Siberia.'

Terry laughed. 'I know what you mean. But his lad's all right. Let's hope he takes over running the estate before long now that he's back home from the war.'

In the spring of 1918, hopes were rising that the war would soon be over. Although the arrival of the Americans had given fresh heart to the Allies, when Russia, embroiled in its own internal struggles, signed a peace treaty with Germany and its confederates in March, hopes were dashed with the departure of the vast nation.

'What'll happen now?' the men, gathered in the pub asked each other.

'Likely all the German troops who have been fighting the Russians will be turned on us now,' Terry Chambers said gloomily, thinking of his boy, who was still out there somewhere. He had no idea where Ray was now or even if he was still alive.

Britain and, perhaps, the whole world were appalled by the massacre of the Tsar and all his family by the Bolsheviks in July, but their focus was soon drawn back to the war. In August, in a final push on what became known as a 'black day' for Germany, the British and their allies went into action near Amiens and their enemy collapsed, though it was to be another three months before the war ended. There was, meanwhile, a new enemy lurking unseen that would become, over time, even more deadly than the German guns for it was indiscriminate in its choice of victim. The influenza-like disease was spreading across continents, and had arrived on Britain's shores in May.

'It's just flu,' those who contracted it said. By August, it had seemed to be over but, in October, the sickness had returned in a more virulent form and had spread throughout the country. Eventually it arrived in Lincolnshire.

The armistice was signed in November and the world could rejoice. The church bells rang throughout the land on Armistice Day. But just at this point, two of the wounded soldiers at the Lincoln hospital fell ill. At first, it was viewed as just an ordinary case of flu, but when three more patients caught it very quickly, Connie Archer shrewdly recognized this illness as something far worse. She ordered the isolation of the soldiers with the disease and asked for nurses to volunteer to care for them and, in so doing, keep themselves isolated from their colleagues and other members of staff. Rosie was one of the six nurses who volunteered to cut themselves off and she devoted herself to the care of the five wounded soldiers who were also ill. Between them, working twelve-hour shifts and keeping strictly away from the rest of the hospital, they halted the spread of the flu, although each of the nurses caught it and had to be cared for by their colleagues. Rosie was the last to succumb, and by the time she recovered, the war was over, but not the battle against this dreadful new disease.

As a celebration of the war being over at last, Pearl, her parents and Bertie had agreed to spend Christmas at the manor. When she'd first suggested the idea to Bella, Grace had been unsure whether the invitation would be accepted, but Bella was enchanted by the idea.

'I'm not sure if Pearl will agree, but Henry and I would love it. And I know Bertie would too. He misses Monty taking him out on his little pony – and his papa, of course,' she added, almost as an afterthought.

'You've entertained us at your home every year since Bertie's birth; it's high time we did our share. Christmas is a lot of work and especially when you have guests.'

'Oh, it's not that, Grace. I love entertaining and besides' – Bella smiled impishly – 'it's the servants who take the strain, not me. Do you know if William intends to revive the Boxing Day shoot? Henry would so enjoy that.'

'I think he hopes to. I'll talk to him. That's something Byron would enjoy too. In fact, it might be something he would organize. He's taking a much greater interest in running the estate now.'

*

Pearl fell ill the day following the Andersons' arrival at the manor for the festivities.

'Keep her isolated,' William demanded in panic. 'It could be this awful flu. We'll hire a nurse.'

But in this he was thwarted; no private nurse in the area was either free or willing to come to the manor to care for a patient with the disease which now appeared to be spreading even faster and was more deadly. People were dying every day.

'I'll contact the matron at the Lincoln hospital,' Grace said. 'Maybe she can help.'

'Take Monty and the carriage,' William urged. 'Get someone – anyone. I don't care who it is as long as Bertie doesn't catch it.'

So Grace travelled to Lincoln. Despite the seriousness of her errand, she was amused how William now pressed her to make the journey he had expressly forbidden her to do before now.

'Oh my dear Grace, how lovely to see you,' Connie said, when Grace was shown into her office. 'Please sit down.'

Peeling off her gloves, Grace said, 'The place seems very quiet. I thought it would be teeming with influenza patients.'

'We're starting to close down here. The building is to be returned to its rightful use next April. A school for boys. Most of our soldiers will go home, to other hospitals or to nursing homes. As for the influenza, there are signs that the numbers are still rising throughout the country, but in this area, those patients will now be dealt with by other hospitals. We had a few cases here but I isolated them and a band of dedicated nurses stayed with them. Sadly, they caught it too, Rosie among them.' Grace drew in a sharp breath, fearful she was going to hear dreadful news, but, swiftly, Connie continued. 'She recovered well – they all did – and are invaluable in helping at the moment. Rosie's a strong girl. She is becoming a fine nurse; I am arranging for her to transfer to another hospital when we close down here.'

'I'm delighted to hear she's doing so well, but I've come here on an urgent errand of mercy – though perhaps, after what you've just told me, you won't be in a position to help me.'

'You know I will if I possibly can,' Connie said gently.

'My daughter-in-law has the influenza and needs nursing care. No local nurse will come near us and we are so afraid it will spread through the household . . .'

'And you want to know if I can spare a nurse?'

'Exactly.'

Connie sighed. 'I want to help you . . .' She was thoughtful before adding slowly, 'Like I say, we are closing down here gradually, but of course other hospitals are struggling because of the influenza. The obvious choice is Rosie. She's had the disease and will have some immunity to it. And perhaps I could spare her for a week or so. She's certainly due some leave, although it will hardly be a rest for her, will it?' She paused and then met Grace's steady gaze. 'But will your husband countenance having Rosie in his house?'

Grace smiled wryly. 'I think he'd welcome the Devil himself if it protects his grandson.'

'Very well. I'll send for her and we can ask her together if she would be willing to come. I have to say, though, Grace, that the decision must be hers.'

'Of course.'

A few minutes later, Rosie entered the room, her face lighting up at once to see Grace. When they had greeted one another fondly, Grace said, 'Rosie, will you come to Thornsby Manor and nurse my daughter-in-law? I – I know it's a lot to ask of you, but she is very ill and we are so afraid the disease will spread through the whole household and – and especially to little Bertie.'

'What about – the master? He won't want me there.'

'If you were to protect the lives of his son and his grandson—'

'Byron? Has Byron got it?' There was terror in Rosie's eyes, plain for both women to see.

'No, no, he hasn't, but—'

'But he might catch it if his wife is not kept away from everyone else,' Rosie finished Grace's sentence.

'Yes, that's it exactly.'

'Of course I'll come. If Matron will release me . . . ?' Rosie turned towards Connie, who nodded willingly. 'Anna and Elsie will help cover your work, I'm sure.'

'Then if you can give me an hour,' Rosie said to Grace. 'I'll come back with you.'

Tears of relief flooded down Grace's face. 'Thank you, oh thank you, Rosie.'

As the girl hurried away, Connie said quietly, 'Just make sure that your husband doesn't have her arrested again when it's all over or, this time, he will have me to deal with.'

'Oh I will, Connie,' Grace said earnestly. 'I promise you I will.'

Thirty-Nine

Byron was sitting in his usual place by the window, with Bertie on his knee, reading a story to the boy. He glanced up as he heard the carriage drawing up outside the front door.

'That's Grandmama back home,' he said, smoothing back the boy's curly black hair. 'Just look out of the window to see if she has brought us a nurse to look after your mother.'

Bertie climbed onto the window seat.

'There's Grandmama getting out and – yes – there someone else. She's a very pretty lady with long red hair . . .'

Byron's heart skipped a beat. It couldn't be? Surely his mother hadn't brought Rosie here? And surely – with everything that had happened – Rosie hadn't agreed to come? He struggled up out of his chair but by the time he reached the window, the two women had come into the house. Then he heard voices on the landing and, yes, that was Rosie's voice. It had been so long since he had heard it, but he would have known it anywhere. He held his breath, but they did not come to his room.

Bertie clambered down from the window seat and would have run towards the door, but Byron was obliged to stop him. 'No, Bertie. You mustn't go. It's the nurse who has come to take care of your mother. You must stay here with me. I'm sure Grandmama will come in to see us in a few moments.'

But it was a long, agonizing hour before Grace entered his room. She sat down in front of Byron and took her grandson onto her knee.

'She's here. The nurse to care for Pearl. Byron, it's Rosie. She has had the disease herself and has recovered. She has also been caring for those sick with it in the hospital, including her own colleagues. There is no one better to care for Pearl. But you cannot see her. She must stay isolated with Pearl until the danger is past. You do understand that, don't you?' Reluctantly, Byron nodded and then whispered, 'What will Father say?'

'You leave your father to me,' Grace said firmly.

It was arranged that Rosie should sleep in a room which connected to her patient's and that their meals should be taken upstairs by the staff but left outside the bedroom door. No one else, apart from the visiting doctor, would come into contact with either Pearl or Rosie, especially not Bertie, who kept asking for his mother and also, now, if he could meet the 'pretty lady'.

The rest of the household tried to keep the little boy entertained, but he'd picked up on the tension among the adults and became fretful. On the fourth day after Rosie's arrival, Byron said, 'Mother, I'm sure Bertie is not well. His face is flushed and he feels hot to the touch. Is the doctor due today?'

'Yes. I'll get him to take a look at him.'

Later that afternoon on his routine visit to see Pearl, Dr Wren confirmed that Bertie too had the Spanish influenza.

For the next few nights, Rosie had little sleep. Pearl was starting to improve, but the little boy was extremely ill. And if Rosie and her patients were not sleeping, then neither was anyone else in the household; they were all so desperately worried.

'She will look after him, won't she?' William agonized. 'She won't take her spite against me out on a small boy, will she?'

'Oh William, of course she won't. Rosie is a lovely girl and she is a dedicated nurse. The matron at the hospital can't speak too highly of her.'

'But I – I . . .'

'I know exactly what you tried to do, William, and you should not have done it, but I'm sure Rosie wouldn't dream of taking her revenge on an innocent little boy.' And although she didn't voice it to her husband, privately Grace thought, *And neither would she harm a hair on the head of Byron's son.*

The days were long and filled with anxiety. Bella and Grace sat together in the morning room, or took walks in the gardens, wrapping up warmly against the wintry weather. They were a comfort to each other. Their menfolk – William and Henry – went out around the estate but were careful not to mix with anyone.

Only Byron did not leave the house. He stayed devotedly as near to his son as he was allowed to be.

And, of course there was always the chance he might catch sight of Rosie.

'You'll never guess what,' Ivy said triumphantly, as she entered Nell's cottage by the back door the day after Boxing Day. Ivy Bates would never quite regain her old joy of life, but she was coming closer to it. She still mourned the loss of Joey – and would do so for the rest of her life – but Dan was making definite signs of progress. With each day she could see improvement and now she had hope again.

'I don't expect I will,' Nell said, 'until you decide to tell me.'

Ivy nodded towards the two dead rabbits lying on Nell's scrubbed kitchen table, deliberately delaying sharing her news to tease Nell. 'I see Amos has been out and about again at night, has he? You'd never have thought it, would you, that he would become the local poacher?'

'There's a few families in this village wouldn't have had much of a Christmas dinner if it hadn't been for him, let me tell you.'

Ivy's face sobered and she said quietly, 'I know, Nell, and I'm one of them. He brought me a lovely big hare and a partridge that fed me and Dan for three days. So, how's Nathan?' she asked, putting off the moment even longer.

Nell smiled. 'Fine. He's getting on really well. Him and Anna are hoping to get married in the spring.

The only sad thing is that she'd like Rosie to be her bridesmaid, but I don't know if Rosie would want to come back here.'

'I shouldn't have thought that would be a problem, seein' as how she's here at the moment.'

Nell's head shot up and she stared at Ivy. 'What d'you mean She's here?'

'At the manor.'

'At the *manor*?' Nell repeated.

Enjoying the confusion and surprise she'd caused, Ivy smiled. 'That's what I said. She's at the manor nursing Byron's wife and their little boy. They've both got the flu. That's why yesterday's shoot was cancelled. The little lad's been very poorly, so I've heard, but he's on the mend now. Mrs Ramsey went to Lincoln herself to ask for help and it was Rosie what came back.'

Nell sat down suddenly on the nearest chair. 'Well, I never.'

'Aye, I thought that'd surprise you.'

'It certainly has, Ivy. Sit down and have a cuppa and tell me what else you know.'

Rosie nursed both mother and son devotedly and by the time the doctor was able to declare that Pearl was recovering well and that Bertie too was past the crisis, she was exhausted. When it was safe for other members of the household to take care of the patients, she took to her bed and slept the clock round. She awakened to find Grace standing by her bed with a tray in her hands.

Rosie struggled to sit up. 'You shouldn't be waiting on me, ma'am . . .'

'It's Grace,' she said with a smile. 'Have you forgotten so quickly?'

Rosie laughed. 'No, I haven't, but it doesn't seem right to call you that in your own home where you are once again the mistress.'

'Here,' Grace said, setting the tray down across Rosie's knees. 'You must eat and drink something now.'

'How are they?'

'Pearl is still in bed though she's obviously much better and Bertie, bless him, is fighting us to be let out of bed.'

'Children often recover remarkably quickly, though we had some very seriously poorly children in the hospital. They shouldn't have been there, really, it being a military hospital, but how can you turn away sick children if you've got the beds spare? We lost a few, I'm sad to say. That was devasting. All the nurses shed tears. Matron is always telling us we mustn't get involved with our patients, but you just can't help it sometimes, especially when they're so little and helpless. I'm just so thankful that Bertie is all right.'

'It's thanks to you that he is. We all know that. Now, eat your breakfast and get up whenever you feel like it.'

'If I'm no longer needed, then I will leave tomorrow . . .'

'I think we'd like you to stay another day or two, if you can, just to make sure that Bertie has really recovered. And besides, Byron wants to see you.'

Rosie looked up at her sharply and then glanced away, but in that moment, she had seen that Grace understood everything.

'I – don't know if that's a very good idea,' Rosie said haltingly.

'He's insisting. He'll never forgive me if I let you leave without seeing him.'

When she had eaten, Rosie washed and dressed and then went along to the nursery where Bertie was playing with his toys, still in his pyjamas.

'Now then, young man,' she said, smiling down at him. As he looked up at her with his dark brown eyes, he looked so like his father that Rosie's heart turned over. Bertie stood up and ran to her, throwing his arms around her legs and pressing his face against her. She stroked his hair as a lump came into her throat. How she wished . . . She pushed the thought away.

'I think you're well enough to get dressed today, don't you?'

'Can I see Papa? Am I better enough? Because I don't want to make him poorly.'

'I think it'll be fine for you to see him. Come, let's get you washed and dressed and then I must see your mother.'

Pearl was languishing in bed and in answer to Rosie's question, put her hand to her head. 'I feel so weak. I really can't get up today.'

'Do you think you could just get up out of bed and sit in a chair for a while in your dressing gown? The sooner you get up the sooner you will start to feel stronger.'

'Look, I'm grateful to you for nursing Bertie and me, but we're fine now. There's no need for you to stay any longer. I can make my own decisions about when I'm fit enough to get up and Bertie doesn't need you now either. There are plenty of people to take care of him.'

Rosie inclined her head. 'Very well. Then I'll be leaving tomorrow morning.'

'You can go this afternoon as far as I'm concerned.'

Rosie left the room without another word and went to find Grace.

'I think I should leave today. Mrs Ramsey junior has made it clear she and her son no longer need me so I think it's best if I leave at once.'

'But not before you've seen Byron. Please don't go before you've seen him.'

'Then can you find out for me if I can see him at eleven o'clock? I will have finished what I have to do by then and will be ready to leave once I've seen him.'

'I shall be sorry to see you go, Rosie. I wish we'd had more time to talk.'

Rosie smiled. 'So do I. I've missed our little chats.'

'Where will you go when you get back? Will you still be at the Fourth Northern?'

'For the time being, but I think Matron is arranging for me to transfer to the County Hospital soon.'

'That's wonderful. You know I wish you well, Rosie. And I can't thank you enough for what you've done here.'

'It's me who should be thanking you. Otherwise, I might still have been in gaol. Nell told me what you have done for me.'

Grace put her finger to her lips. 'Ssh. Not a word.'

'I wanted you to know how very grateful I am, that's all.'

Grace touched her hand. 'I know, I know,' she said softly.

Just after eleven o'clock, Grace took Rosie to Byron's room. He was sitting in his usual place in front of the window but his gaze was on the door as if he had been waiting for it to open. He stood up the moment she entered. A chair had been placed next to him for her. As they sat down together, he murmured. 'Rosie, oh Rosie.'

Quietly, Grace left the room.

For several moments, they just gazed at each other. They could both see their younger selves and yet there were changes wrought by what they had both been through.

'You've lost weight,' Rosie said softly at last. 'And your eyes don't twinkle with mischief like they used to.'

'You've still got all your lovely hair, but now it's tied up into a neat bun as befits a nurse. Your eyes hold a sadness too. I'm so very sorry for all that my father put you through. Oh Rosie, Rosie . . .' He took her hands. 'I have missed you so much all these years. You do know how very much I love you, don't you?'

'And I you,' she said huskily. 'But we could never have been together. We are from such different worlds, even now.'

'I just wish I had been strong enough to defy my father and carry you off on my white charger like the knights of old.'

Rosie giggled. 'I used to dream of something like that.' The years fell away and they were two youngsters again on the bank of the stream, poaching fish together.

'I must go,' she said at last, even though her hands were still resting warmly in his.

'No, stay another day . . .'

She shook her head sadly. 'No, I really can't.'

'Then – just one kiss.'

She stood up, bent over him and placed her lips gently against his for a long and loving moment. 'There,' she whispered, 'that's got to last us both a lifetime.'

'Rosie' – his voice broke – 'if ever there's a way we can be together, then we'll take it. I promise you.'

She had never had anything so hard to do in her life as to walk out of the room and away from Byron. She knew he was watching her go, but she did not dare look back. If she had, she would have run to him and never left.

Forty

Rosie went back to the nursery to say goodbye to Bertie but was startled to find William Ramsey watching over his grandson with doting eyes. She hesitated and made to turn away but William called to her, 'Rosie, please – come in.'

Her heart began to race as she stepped through the door. She stood in front of him, not knowing what to expect, while the thud, thud of the rocking horse sounded.

'Look, Rosie, I'm galloping,' Bertie shouted.

She smiled at him. 'So you are, but don't go too fast, will you?'

The little boy giggled as Rosie turned back to face William.

'My wife tells me that you have saved Bertie's life, and probably Pearl's too. I want to thank you from the bottom of my heart and to give you my solemn promise that I will never hound you again about – well, you know what about.'

Rosie remained silent; she still wasn't sure whether she could trust his promise and she wasn't going to tell him anything about that night. She had been found not guilty of any involvement and that's the way it was going to stay.

'Do – do you want to come back and live in your cottage?'

Rosie realized what a huge effort it was for him to offer this. 'No, thank you. I am making a life for myself in Lincoln as a nurse. I'm having proper training. The only time I will come back here is to visit Mrs Tranter and her son, Nathan. I believe he is planning to marry one of the nurses he met when he was in the Lincoln hospital. Perhaps – perhaps—' She paused, not sure if she dared to continue.

Surprisingly, William took the words from her. 'Perhaps they could have your cottage? Is that what you were going to say?'

She nodded.

'Then consider it done. Tell Nathan to come and see me when he's ready.'

'I'll just say goodbye to Bertie.'

She crossed the room to hug the little boy where he sat on his horse. He wound his arms around her neck. 'Don't go, Rosie. I want you to stay.'

'I can't, Master Bertie. There are other poorly little boys and girls I must look after.'

'I'll miss you.'

There was a catch in her throat as she said, 'And I'll miss you too.'

He was growing so like Byron, it broke her heart just to look at him. She released herself from his embrace and said firmly, 'Now, off you go. Ride over the hills and far away.'

'I will see you again, won't I?'

Rosie smiled. 'Perhaps – one day.'

With a swift 'Goodbye, sir,' to William, she hurried from the room.

She left the manor to stay at Nell's for a couple of nights. Grace had arranged for Monty to take her back to Lincoln after that.

'Oh it's good to see you, lass,' Nell greeted her, 'but you're looking very tired. You have a good rest while you're here and I'll feed you up a bit. How are things at the manor now?'

'Both Bertie and his mother are recovering well and luckily no one else has caught it. How's everyone in the village?'

'A few have had it but we've only had two deaths.'

'How's Nathan? I've a bit of good news for him.'

'You can tell us all after tea tonight unless, of course, it's private.'

'Heavens, no! I'll save it till then.'

As the four of them sat down that evening, Nell said, 'Rosie has some news for you, Nathan.'

Startled, he looked at her. Hurriedly, she said, 'It's all right. There's nothing wrong.' She smiled. 'It seems I am at last in Mr Ramsey's good books – at least for the moment – because I've nursed his grandson.'

'Is the little lad all right?'

'He's fine now though he was seriously ill for a couple of days. It was touch and go for a few hours.'

'The master will be grateful to you,' Nell said. 'He dotes on the boy from what Sarah tells me when she brings the washing. Nothing is too good for him. Oh, I still get all the gossip from the big house, don't you worry!'

'I'm surprised it's Sarah who fetches and carries. I thought that would be far beneath her, being Mrs Ramsey's lady's maid.'

'Oh, there are no airs and graces with Sarah. I think she likes a walk out and a good old gossip with me. I think she asked if she could do it. Anyway, go on, Rosie, lass. What is it you've got to tell Nathan?'

'Mr Ramsey asked if I was coming back here and did I want the cottage back.'

Nell's mouth dropped open. 'He asked you that? My word! Wonders never cease.'

'What did you tell him?' Nathan asked.

'I told him no, because I am training to be a qualified nurse. But I did tell him that you are planning to marry one of the nurses you'd met. I hardly dared to ask him outright but he said it for me. "Perhaps they could have your cottage? Is that what you were going to say?" So I said, yes, it was, and he said, "Then consider it done" and you're to go and see him when you're ready.'

'You have won him over and no mistake.'

Rosie pulled a face. 'Not sure I have completely, Nathan. I felt as if he was making the offer for me to come back here through gritted teeth and I'm sure he was relieved when I said no.'

'Well, thanks anyway, Rosie. Anna's coming to stay next week after she finishes at the hospital and I'm going to pop the question.'

Nell clapped her hands. 'That's wonderful. I'll have a daughter at last.' She glanced at Rosie. 'Well, *another* daughter. I've always looked on you as one of me own, as you well know.'

'So,' Rosie said, 'everything's going well with Mr Chambers, is it, Nathan?'

'Couldn't be better. And best of all, Ray has come home more or less unscathed. He's been lucky and he knows it.'

There had been great rejoicing on the day that Ray Chambers had come back. The whole village had turned out to welcome him and there had been heartfelt prayers said in the church for his safe return.

'So is there going to be enough work for all of you now he's back?'

'Oh yes. Now the war's over, the work's coming in at a steady pace. We're never idle, I'm pleased to say. His father's saying he'll retire when I've learned the trade properly and then Ray and me are planning to go into business together as equal partners.'

'So, we're all nicely settled, one way or another,' Rosie said, her mind shying away from thoughts of falling in love and marrying. Her heart belonged to Byron and if they couldn't be together, then she would focus on a career in nursing. 'I do hope,' she added, with a twinkle in her eyes, 'that Anna is going to ask me to be her bridesmaid.'

Nathan chuckled. 'I don't doubt it for a minute. That's if she says "yes", of course.'

'And I,' Rosie laughed, 'don't doubt *that* for a minute.'

'We're going home,' Pearl declared the following week. 'All of us. I'm not staying here another minute. We only intended to come for Christmas anyway. It's not the time of year when I should be here. Besides, it's not safe. Bertie and I both got ill being here.'

'You brought the sickness with you. None of us had it,' William snapped. 'And this is your home. You're a wife and mother, Pearl, and it's time you realized your place is here with your husband and your son now that Byron is back home. You need to pick up the reins from Grace and do your duty as the mistress of the manor. Byron is taking over the management of the estate from me. He's well enough now and then Grace and I intend to travel.'

Pearl shrugged. What he was saying was of no consequence to her. 'I have no intention of taking over as mistress of the manor. You have quite enough servants to help you do that. I am going home and I don't intend to come back.'

William turned white and held on to a chair for support. 'But – but Bertie . . . ?'

Pearl was thoughtful for a moment, working things out in her head. She had to be careful. She knew what a vindictive man William Ramsey could be. If she crossed him too much, he was likely to deny Bertie his rightful inheritance. Byron could divorce her, marry again and have other children.

'I don't want to come back here, but I am prepared to allow Bertie to live with you, if you will provide a tutor for him until he goes to boarding school, which he will as soon as he is old enough. After that he can spend the school holidays with you.'

'But – but you won't see him?'

She shrugged again. 'I'm not the maternal type. He's a nice little boy and I love him, but I'm not good with small children. He'd be better here with you. I want to lead my own life.'

'I bet you do,' William said harshly.

'What's that supposed to mean?'

'Exactly what I say.'

They glared at each other until William added quietly but with menace in his tone, 'We're not stupid, Pearl. None of us. We've guessed you've built another life for yourself. I have no doubt you've taken a lover.' Pearl looked away, no longer willing to meet his gaze. 'Ah, I thought as much. Well, there will be no divorce. Not in this family.'

She met his gaze once more, her mouth tight. 'In that, you and my father seem to be in agreement.'

'Won't your parents miss Bertie?'

'I'm sure they will, but they'll do what I want.'

'My word, you're a spoiled girl if ever there was one. I wish I had seen it before I'd agreed to Byron marrying you.'

Her head shot up again. 'You didn't *agree* to the marriage, you forced it upon us both. You and my ambitious mother. Well, now you know how arranged marriages work out. Sometimes, not for the best. Perhaps – if nothing else – this war has done a lot to help women.' She turned away. 'I'll be leaving tomorrow. I may visit from time to time just so that my son doesn't forget me entirely.'

And with that parting shot, she left the room leaving a stunned William staring at the closed door.

Forty-One

Byron would not have admitted it to a soul, not even to his mother who was his closest confidant, but all he felt when Pearl left was relief; relief that she had gone and that she had chosen to leave Bertie with him. He loved the little boy devotedly and his son was the reason he was striving to recover and lead as normal a life as possible. He did feel some sympathy for his in-laws; he knew they loved Bertie too and he agreed with his mother that they should be invited to the manor often if they cared to come.

And there was another reason driving him forward to get better and better each day: Rosie. He wanted to seek her out and tell her what had happened in his life. He couldn't offer marriage to her, but – well, he told himself, the decision would be up to her.

As the winter turned into spring, Byron worked to become fit and strong again. He could ride his horse and drive the carriage or the pony and trap too. He toured the estate and took on more and more responsibility. He visited every house in the village and made himself known personally to his tenants and workers. He was no longer the handsome, out-of-reach, young master. He knew each of them by name, knew their circumstances and made sure he offered help where it was needed. And he always found time to play with Bertie and to teach him all about the estate that would one day be his.

William did not agree with everything that Byron was doing – he thought the boy soft – but then he reminded himself that if this was what it took to keep both his son and grandson with him, then it was a small price to pay.

Grace was perhaps the happiest she had ever been in her life since the early days of her marriage after her son had been born. Now, she had him back safe, and, even if not altogether sound, at least he was alive. And she had her grandson too. She only wished her son was happy in his marriage, but she could see that it was not to be. If only – she would dream sometimes – if only Rosie could come back. But that would cause a scandal and William might forget the promise he had made to the girl. Grace sighed. Life would never be perfect, but she would make the best – no, the most – of what she had.

Rosie did return to the village briefly for the wedding in the little church of Nathan and Anna. Byron knew she was there, less than a mile away, but he dared not seek her out. He knew he would not be able to hold back. After the service in the church and the wedding breakfast in the Thornsby Arms, Nathan and Anna moved into the cottage that had once been the home of Sam and Rosie. With his newfound skills as a carpenter and joiner, Nathan soon did any repairs needed and Anna, thrilled to have her own little home for the first time in her life, listened and learned from her mother-in-law, who had already become to her the mother she had never had.

Rosie left the village with a mixture of emotions; she was happy to see her dearest friends settled into her old home. Nell too was happy with her lot. She had her boy safely back and Amos was still her companion. And Dan was now improving in leaps and bounds. He had, to everyone's delight, been able to stand beside Nathan in the church as his best man. The whole village had turned out on the day to toast Nathan and his pretty bride.

'It's a happier day than the last wedding we witnessed in that church,' Ivy said to Nell.'

Nell did not answer her friend. She knew Ivy was referring to Byron's marriage.

'If ever a groom looked as if he was heading for the guillotine,' Ivy chattered on, 'it was Byron Ramsey on his wedding day. I've heard she's left him now. Gone back to live with her parents, but the little lad's still here.'

'I wouldn't know, Ivy,' Nell murmured and was thankful that her gossiping neighbour knew nothing about the love that Rosie and Byron had for each other. Nell prayed she would never find out. For if she did, the tidal wave of scandal surging through the village would be impossible to stop.

Byron knocked on the door of the morning room and entered when his mother invited him to 'Come in'.

'Mother,' he said as she patted the seat on the sofa beside her. 'I need to have a very serious talk with you.'

Grace sighed. 'Yes, that doesn't surprise me.'

Byron raised his eyebrows. 'It doesn't?'

'No. I've rather been expecting it since Pearl left, presumably for good this time.'

Byron nodded slowly. 'I realize you've guessed my feelings for Rosie.'

'And hers for you,' Grace said simply, 'so I think I've guessed what you've come to talk to me about.'

'Pearl has a lover in Stamford. That's why she wanted to go back to her home.'

'Did she tell you that?'

Byron shook his head. 'No, but I've found out that it's true.'

'Do her parents know?'

Byron smiled wryly. 'I suspect her mother will guess. She's a shrewd woman.'

'I rather like Bella,' Grace murmured. 'I do hope she will still visit now and again. We get on well and she always did her best to curb Pearl's' – she paused, searching for the right word – 'selfishness.'

'She's a very spoiled young woman. I shall endeavour to see that Bertie is *not* spoiled.'

Grace smiled. 'He's such an adorable little boy, it's hard not to indulge him, but we'll do our best.' There was silence between them until Grace said, 'What do you intend to do? Ask Rosie to become your mistress?'

Byron shook his head. 'No, I love and respect her too much to do that.'

'So, you're going to try to divorce Pearl on the grounds of her adultery? I don't think either your father or Mr Anderson will be happy about that.'

'I don't expect either will agree to divorce at all,'

Byron said grimly. 'But I intend to go and talk seriously to Pearl. If she's in love with someone else and they want to marry, then – then maybe we can work something out that will suit us both.'

But Byron was thwarted in his good intentions. Pearl would not agree to a divorce that would leave her as a shamed woman. 'I'm quite happy as I am, thank you. Yes, I admit I have a lover, but, as he is also married, there is little to be gained by us divorcing, Byron.' She eyed him perceptively and said softly, 'I take it there is someone you wish to marry.'

There was no point in lying; it was time for honesty between them.

'Yes, there is.'

'Will she not agree to become your mistress?'

'I – I haven't asked her.'

'Then you should. If she truly loves you, you might have a pleasant surprise.'

One fine morning in May, without telling his family where he was going, Byron harnessed the pony and trap and drove to Lincoln and to the hospital where he guessed Rosie was now working.

He was very circumspect in his approach; he didn't want to cause trouble for her and he guessed that the rules and regulations for nurses were very strict. He made enquiries at the entrance and was told that Rosie was on duty until two o'clock and wouldn't be able to see him until then.

'I can take a note to her, if that would help, so she knows you're waiting for her,' the receptionist offered helpfully.

'That's very kind of you. Just tell her Byron is here to see her. I'll come back at two o'clock.'

He drove down into the city and found a hotel where he could leave the pony and trap and have some lunch. He drew up outside the hospital again just before two o'clock and, watching the door, waited for her to appear. At ten minutes past the hour, he saw her emerge and stand for a moment looking about her, until she saw him. She looked smart and efficient in her nurse's uniform and he knew a moment's misgiving at the thought of what he was going to ask her; all that he was going to ask her to give up for him.

She climbed up to sit beside him. 'What is it, Byron? I hope nothing's wrong. Has someone come down with the influenza?'

He took up the reins and the trap moved off. 'No,' he said, above the noise of the horse's hooves and the wheels rattling on the road. 'There's nothing wrong. Well, not in the way you mean.'

She frowned, mystified, but it wasn't until he had driven a short distance from the outskirts of the city that he pulled the horse to a halt in a quiet country lane and turned to face her.

'Pearl has gone back to live with her parents,' he said, coming straight to the point. 'She won't be coming back to live at the manor again.'

Rosie pulled in a deep breath and stared at him. 'And Bertie?'

'He's with us and he's staying with us.' He paused and then added bluntly, 'She has a lover, but she won't agree to a divorce.'

414

Rosie's mouth dropped open. 'You've asked her?'

'Yes, I have. As the law stands at present, I can divorce her on the grounds of *her* adultery, but she can't divorce me. But – I – I can't do that to her. I can't see her disgraced in the eyes of the society she lives in. The fact is, we should never have married at all. We were pushed into it by our parents and she's as much a victim of it as I am. Now, if the law were to change – and there are rumours that it might in a year or two's time – I could give her grounds for divorcing me. She would be the innocent party then. So, what I'm asking, Rosie, is, will you wait for me?'

Rosie was silent for some time before saying slowly, 'I want to carry on with my nursing, Byron. I grew up a poacher's daughter, living just on the wrong side of the law and then worse still, a murderer's daughter, accused of aiding and abetting my father in his crime. But I have been given a chance to make something of myself.'

Byron's face was bleak. 'I'm sorry, I shouldn't have asked you such a thing. Forgive me.'

Now, she grasped his hand. 'There's nothing to forgive. I love you too, Byron, more than I can find the words to tell you and, yes, we will be together but not in Thornsby. I can't come back to the village, Byron. You know that, but if you can find a little cottage somewhere out here' – she flung out her arm to encompass the flat land around them – 'where no one will know us, no one will find us, we can be together on my days off.'

'You – you'd become my mistress? Is that what you're saying?'

Rosie chuckled. 'Well, yes, I suppose I am.'

He raised her hand to his lips and murmured, 'I'll never desert you, Rosie. I'll take care of you always. I love you and I always will. I can't bear to think of spending the rest of my life without you. And one day, I promise, I'll get a divorce and take you to live in Thornsby Manor where you should be.' He paused and then looking deep into her sparkling eyes before asking, 'Do you mean it? Do you really mean it?'

'Yes, I do. This war, and everything that has happened to me, has shown me that you have to snatch happiness wherever you can find it. All those fine young men we've lost never had a chance to love and be loved. How many young women are today regretting that they never gave themselves to their sweethearts? How many are going to be old maids because, now, there aren't enough young men to go around? I don't want to be one of them, Byron.'

'But we'll be living in sin,' he murmured. 'You'll become the object of gossip and—'

Rosie threw back her head and laughed aloud. 'And don't you think I've been that all my life?' Then she became serious again. 'It can't be a sin to love and be loved as we do, and if it is' – her smile broadened – 'then it's only one more to add to my ever-growing list. Now, stop worrying, Byron Ramsey, and kiss me.'

Epilogue

Byron kept his promise to Rosie. The world was a very different place after the Great War. Women, many of them, who would be spinsters for life, carved out careers for themselves. They fought for independence in all areas of their lives, none more so than in marriage. In 1923 new laws were passed concerning divorce. The Matrimonial Causes Act 1923 made it possible for a woman to petition for divorce on the grounds of her husband's adultery. Pearl now wished to marry again. Her lover was also freed under the same new laws so Byron happily provided Pearl with the grounds to divorce him.

Byron and Rosie were married in Lincoln in 1925 but kept their marriage secret for two years. Rosie even carried on nursing at the County Hospital until the sudden death of William Ramsey in 1927, when Byron took her to live in Thornsby Manor. Grace now had everything she had ever wanted and, at only fifty-eight, was still young enough to enjoy her new life to the full. She had her son, her grandson and now the girl she had grown to love too. As for Bertie, he adored his stepmother and would grow into a handsome, caring young man, just like his father.

The villagers rejoiced in the news of Byron's marriage to Rosie, though, as Nell had predicted, the initial gossip spread like wildfire through the neighbourhood. But, in time, the inhabitants of Thornsby flourished under Byron's stewardship of the estate. There was no longer the threat of the workhouse when any of his tenants faced hard times; he cared for them all. Ironically, there was no longer any need for a local poacher. The villagers were housed and fed through the bleakest of winters.

And now and again on quiet summer evenings, Byron and Rosie would take a walk arm in arm down to the stream and watch for the trout under the stones. Rosie would glance up to the woods at the top of the slope and remember the dark nights she had trespassed on land that now belonged to her husband. Then her glance would roam skywards and a smile would curve her mouth.

Are you watching, Dad? she would say silently to the stars. *I told you that one day I would be mistress of Thornsby Manor.* And somewhere through the darkness, she was sure she could hear his deep chuckle.

Wartime Friends

By Margaret Dickinson

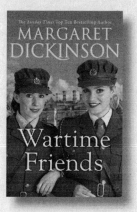

*Courage, love, friendship and
hidden secrets among a family at war.*

It is 1940 in coastal Lincolnshire and the storm clouds of
war are gathering over Britain. Two brave young women
discover the value of true friendship, as they deal with
troubles of their own while the lives of those they love
are put at risk.

Carolyn Holmes is keen to do what she can for the
war effort. Raised on the family farm, she battles with
her mother, Lilian, to further her education – although
nothing is too good for her brother, Tom. Phyllis Carter,
a bitter widow from the Great War, lives close by with her
son, Peter, who works on the farm. When Peter decides to
volunteer, a distraught Phyllis blames Carolyn, who leaves
to join the ATS. There she meets Beryl Morley, who will
become a lifelong friend.

Carolyn and Beryl are posted to Beaumanor Hall in
Leicestershire as 'listeners', the most difficult of signals intelli-
gence gathering. As the war unfolds and their work becomes
even more vital, Carolyn and Beryl's friendship deepens,
and in the dangerous times that follow, they support each
other through some of the darkest days they will ever know.